The Architect Of Law

Ordering Information: For quantity sales details and orders by U.S.
trade bookstores and wholesalers, please contact Novabook Publishing
at info@novabook.us or 323-871-0889.

First published in the United States by Novabook Publishing 2013.
10 9 8 7 6 5 4 3 2 1

NOVABOOK

Novabook Publishing
Los Angeles
www.novabook.us

ISBN 978-0-9894896-4-5

THE ARCHITECT OF LAW

A Novel by

Michael Jeffery Blair

Law is wholly indifferent to
the internal phenomena of conscience.

– Oliver Wendell Holmes – 1881

CONTENTS

*There are many Brazilian and Portuguese terms used throughout
the story, most of which are defined in the text. A glossary has
been provided so that any unfamiliar words can be clarified.*

BOOK I

BRUSHSTROKES IN THE MIST

BRUSHSTROKES IN THE MIST

I

A phantom drummer somewhere up the street pounded out hot *batuques* that ricocheted off walls and cascaded down in a mesmerizing brew. A dancing woman lured with her rolling hips silhouetted by flare from the lights–beads of perspiration dancing on her breasts. He looked right through her. Tarisco was full of nervous energy, he had places to go. Tonight he waited impatiently for money. The weight of the old .45 caliber Taurus automatic in the holster he had specially made that he stuck under his belt inside his trousers beneath his coat dragged at him. It was a tool he had become accustomed to, but tonight it irritated him. The saints were restless.

Sudden beauty. The sky erupted crimson, aflame for as far as anyone could see. The great movement of day becoming night took place across a landscape filled with hushed and breathless whispers. The Mato Grosso was subdued by its humid kiss. Bahia surrendered. Amazonas rejoiced a thousand miles from the sea raging with life in verdant groves and in flying and running things that have managed to elude the touch of man for all these years. They alone were truly wild.

The firmament shifted despite those who remained convinced that everything was as it had always been since the beginning, those who found peace in the thought that the universe ran a constant river through each night until morning one day very much like the next. There was only the slightest rustling as the world migrated from light to dark like a distant movement by some unknown presence; full skirts, perhaps, brushing through a doorway unseen, a linen jacket against a silk vest, muted voices that carelessly stirred up fears in the dark and then left them behind for the sleepless to wrestle with. Or perhaps it was the stalking jaguar who cannot get used to asphalt streets under which lay toiling vines and roots ready to burst out and reclaim what was rightly theirs. The specter of things wanted but never achieved lived in these regions between sunlight and shade and those pursued by dreams felt lucky if they made it past the vigilant gaze of nature because above all it was the feeling of being watched that permeated the land.

The teeming earth rolled out endless before the approaching eventide that slowly captured a shoreline of nearly four thousand miles. All along that coast leapt porpoises gleaming high in the salt wind to see the last rays of the sun as it disappeared and then sliced back into the glassine sea without a splash or a sound of any kind. It was their secret ritual. Some said it was preparation for their twilight journey onto land where they assumed the form of blossoming, brown skinned women and caught up hearts just as fishermen of the tuna trawlers trapped and pulled fishes down into the brine tangled in twisted nets where the air gives out. The Macumba priests reassured everyone that the fish was not malicious, just its way of dancing with the saints, speaking with the *Orixás*. Even men who disbelieved the rural tales sought out the sounding porpoises as light grew thin and the boundary between land and ocean became obscured by mists. They always happened to be looking out to sea at nightfall, but if asked would casually indicate an oil tanker that had caught their eye in the fading distances heading for New Orleans or Galveston. For some men it was the sense of danger that drew them and if they could bear the paradox of the rosary and the Candomble rituals, the Virgin Mary and the *Orixá Imanjá* living inside them then they might seek out the sea-women for their power. All things help in this life.

Recent evidence suggests that men inhabited Brazil long before any creature stood on two legs in North America. This was a fact the white man, particularly the Spanish and Portuguese of earlier centuries, had great difficulty embracing for it suggested a spontaneous and coincidental evolution, perhaps even an immaculate one, that flew squarely in the face of their own deeply harbored religious beliefs. Spirits prevailed here, wild and fine and restless. It was simply a different relationship between humans and the natural world and quite possibly the inevitable result of the overwhelming spiritual endowment that infused this submissive and fertile land with life of such grandeur that anything less than the miraculous became common place. Some men were awed and had the wisdom to know they were in the presence of God. Others saw the profit potential. Therein lies the difference.

On the edge of a vast, merciless desert in sub-Saharan Africa other men in other times were lured by visions too. They built cities as monuments to their ownership of nature, as testament to the unflagging rush of humanity across the playing fields of spirits without regard to the laws that governed them. The unspoken laws. The cities were golden with epithets etched into the granite walls for we of the future to understand how the structures came to be and what they represented. Then the sands came. Sometimes within a year they reclaimed their territory, inch by inch, foot by foot until the deserted streets lay fallow washed by the grains that piled up high against the sides of the monuments. Now they are cities of dunes.

As nightfall saturated the land with deep indigo all the creatures found their places. Those that were hunted scurried through the jungles of Amazonas or across the boundless grasslands of the Mato Grosso in terror paying little attention to the rubber plantations that had rotted in the humid air and been crushed eight decades ago by the anxious growth of a hundred varieties of plants and trees that had only waited patiently for the men to pass. Even the magnificent houses of the *fazendas*, the estates, witnessed their own end strangled by vines as thick as a man's waist, buckled by roots too vivacious to be kept underground, infested by crawling things more numerous than all the people of the earth. The hunters had yellow eyes. They were full of life. They danced on the million leaves, touched down across a hundred thousand branches and spoke fluently to all their kind in the language of animals that humans had thankfully forgotten. Life was in motion intertwined with the endless landscape and it kept all things changing

3

in constant evolution. In other places men had become complacent, they had decimated all the predators, tamed the rivers until now they trickled through cement corridors no bigger than a doorway, cowered in air conditioned shelters pretending that nature was under control and would never rise again to challenge their lordship. But it only waits for them to pass, for them to fulfill their moment in evolution and move on into memory. Nature waited and watched. Above all was the feeling of being watched. In the cities and jungles of Brazil there were eyes everywhere.

Tarisco Sivuca leaned up against a plastered over brick wall that was so moist with humidity it was in danger of collapse at any time. He glanced sideways down the narrow glistening street and saw children in a ragged group at the end practicing their samba steps silhouetted by a street lamp. He had been there. The sounds of their voices chimed with recognition. His pale linen suit was a mass of wrinkles that had become pressed into it by sweat within an hour of putting it on. Underneath he wore a sparkling white sleeveless undershirt, nearly new, that contrasted with his nut-brown skin in the low light under which he stood. A sheen of perspiration was on his face.

His blue eyes could not be explained. Tarisco defied description. He thought of himself as *indio prêto*, a black Indian, but was most likely to be referred to as *escuro*–black with Caucasian features and especially so because of his eye color. None of it meant anything to him because as the saying went, "a poor white is black, but a wealthy black is white." He was finding success where many had failed so it was said of him now that he "used to be black".

He was completely at home in the slums of Rio called *favelas*, especially Rocinha where he had spent his elusive childhood with 200,000 others. Fleeting memories were all that remained of his youth and only images of climbing the hill above sheet metal and cardboard houses where he and his friends had the finest view in Rio De Janero hinted that he was ever young at all. From on high they could look down on the Corcovado and imagine themselves luxuriating on Copacabana beach, or Ipanema or even on the Avenida Rio Branco where colonial buildings still hovered as ghosts filled with the echoes of black slaves

4

and the Portuguese. Gleaming automobiles paraded past. The hand of the night caressed his cheek languidly as he heard the sounds of the *favelados* that wafted down the hillside into the street where he stood waiting. He had watched the tin and paper become cinder block and red brick as the inhabitants slowly gained title to the land where they had lived since 1896 and marveled as city services began to appear just as he escaped. He always returned though, because there is no escaping where the heart is.

The bitter repression of a rural rebellion in the *Nordeste* eight years after the emancipation of the slaves in 1880 spawned the *favelas* of Rio. The army swollen with bluster and bravado, its ranks bolstered with blacks and mulattos, many former slaves, reigned terror in the *Guerra da Canudos* against its own people. It was an insidious test of loyalties, of slave against slave. When the bloodletting was exhausted soldiers returned to the civilized towns finding again, as soldiers often do descending like seed pods dispursed by far blowing winds, that there was no place for them in peace. They wandered from central Bahia to the capital to demand their pensions and when they were not forthcoming, camped near the army headquarters. On a nearby hillside grew the *favela* bush, which bore a cooking spice native to their *Nordeste* homes, and the camp became known as the *Morro da Favela*. They never left. Their spirits linger still. The soldiers passed from memory, but the *favelados* were born of desperation. Cariocan blacks and other ex-slaves appeared and blended in to the city of the dispossessed where industrial scrap, oil drums and anything that was useful fashioned shelters. Whether they imagined them temporary or not became lost in time, but as Tarisco stood in the humid warmth of the night there were over four hundred neighborhoods like Rocinha with names such as Hurry-up-hill, Sky Gardens and Hill of Hope. *Favelados* numbered over one million as migrants from all over Brazil created shadow worlds of their rural life with all the social intricacies and their religion–Macumba. To the *Marajá*, the bureaucratic fat cats, they were cheap hands and dancing feet. To themselves they were desperate, inexorably caught up in the struggle to survive.

He knew his roots, but held it within himself even as he grew older and the knowledge no longer had any importance and never told anyone. It was a matter of honor. This quality he had learned in the streets when he was too young to remember, (but every instance breathed with him), and therefore the incident always held some unreality that bordered on the transcendental. Tarisco was around six years old when he received his confirmation. At that time age had little meaning and things were measured in terms of will to survive or not, which he and the other free children he ran with all seemed to know instinctively.

They had stolen a piece of fruit from a seller's stall on the boulevard. It was not that they were hungry, though that was more often the case, but that they had to constantly test the envelope so when push came to shove they would know exactly where they stood. It was a common occurrence for the shopkeepers and vendors who were plagued by homeless children with nothing to do other than scratch out a survival and nowhere to go other than the streets. Brazil was home to six million such children that it enclosed within its cocoon of wildness edged by out of control urban centers on the brink. They were *pivetes*, "little farts", perhaps because it justified their abuse by making nothing of them. Tarisco was not so fast and struggle as he would his little legs just could not generate much speed. The grocer, who was standing nearby, calmly pulled out a short length of wooden doweling he kept at hand for just such occasions and swatted him across the back of the skull with a loud, hollow crack that caused passers-by to momentarily look up in realization somebody else was on earth. Tarisco tumbled over next to the cardboard boxes that stank of rotten papaya crushed near their bottoms and settled there unconscious with blood flowing down the back of his small head. After the first shock of the sound no one paid any further attention to him and he lay there as if refuse.

All the other children, who were older than he and more experienced in the etiquette of the streets, huddled across a small plaza and anxiously peered at their fallen comrade from around the corner and through the legs of people walking by indifferently.

"Ayee...He's got blood on him!" One exclaimed.

"Shut up!" Cried the oldest in controlled fury.

Another quietly and somberly began praying to the Macumba spirits. "Eleg...ba...open the door for Ogún..."

"Shut up!"

"He's dead," came the whisper.

"The Orixás help those that help themselves."

"He's dead!"

"Shut up! He'd not dead!"

Their faces were of hardened adults cloned on scared and bruised young bodies and their mouths hung open in dismay showing brown and cracked teeth. The grocer, who had a bald spot on the back of his head, was not a large man, but none the less a man who had reached maturity and had acquired a comfortable layer of fat around his middle by the good fortune of his work that placed him in the proximity of food all the time. A formidable enemy. And so it was the great shock when he was suddenly overwhelmed by the *pivetes,* who in their frenzy brought him crashing down into the elaborate displays of mangos, onions, cassava, tomatoes, cherries, peppers, apricots, tangelos and eggplant that worked in their favor. Everything flew high into the air like a tossed salad as he wiggled against mashed fruit and struggled with the *little farts* two on each arm and each leg while the oldest, the strongest held him from behind around the neck. The others busy lifting up Tarisco and shunted him from the scene above their heads as if he were being evacuated from a field of battle.

The one boy remaining, the strongest one who held his forearm against the vendor's windpipe so that both knew he, as small as he was, could crush it with one final push, bent close to the man's ear and seethed. "Remember me!"

His fury was the spice that the mulatto boy dipped into when he needed extraordinary virtuosity. He did not believe in the Orixás or the saints of the church because he could not hold them in his hand and no matter how many times the Father had tried to explain the concept of faith to him, he could rely only on himself. In his right hand was a piece of broken bottle that he always kept in his pocket. He had found it at the beach one day. It was pale green and had three sides, two of which were sanded dull by years of ocean sand washing against it, but one side was still sharp with a vicious point. The scintillating sparkle from the sand had revealed it to him and that was the only faith he knew. The mulatto boy brought it up against the man's cheek.

"Remember me." He said as he cut a three-inch gash into the grocer's flesh, and then ran off across the plaza as fast as he could.

"That *pivete* cut me!" The grocer yelled from out of the rubble of his meticulous displays clutching his cheek and screaming after him in disbelief. "You little son of a bitch!"

Beneath the hill of the Rocinha Favela he felt whole perhaps as in no other place on Earth. He was not a *pivete* any longer. The image in his mind was that of a tempestuous misfit who had trapped himself in a complex chrysalis seemingly impossible to escape from, yet because of that would be many times more beautiful emerged. It wasn't as if he'd arrived, he wasn't there yet, but undeniably he was on his way. It was something so tangible he could touch it and for the first time in his life he was buoyed by hope. Soon, if everything went well, he would be a *Bicherio*, a big boss, one of the chosen who ran the *Jogo De Bicho*, the fanatically popular numbers racket based on animals that ran rampant out of Rio and across all Brazil. He already had a network of runners, *aviõezinhos*, "little airplanes"... pivetes who would do anything for him because he had been confirmed and was one of them no matter how hard he tried to distance himself from them. He also sponsored a Samba school, a fact that added much to his prestige in the neighborhood and it was the one link he had to the legitimate world that lay outside the favela for when Carnival exploded there were television cameras everywhere and everyone knew which samba school was his. He was riding high on the back of life, except for one thing. Valdemiro Veloso.

Tarisco stood on the corner because of Veloso, he breathed because of Veloso and all of his profit and his position in life were because of Veloso. He financed a samba school, but Veloso owned whole favelas running in sewer pipes, water and electricity when the city would not. He was cursed with the luck that had brought him this far, but it was his own ambition that would create the crowning achievement of his life. Then he would have nothing to do with drugs again. That was Veloso's domain and he had never wanted entry, yet in the favela it was his only ladder and he would rather have been dead than worked hand to mouth his whole life and at the end be as poor as at the beginning. He, too, had been somebody's *aviõezinho*. It was always the great conflict between the rich and the impoverished that fought inside him, he longed for the space and time that money bought while at once appalled by it's unjustness. The whole thing was epitomized by the sole ownership of the vast majority of wealth and resources in Brazil by a very small minority, mostly white, he even now after so many years could hardly bring himself to say it. Brazil was a white country, but he "used to be black", so it didn't matter. It was popular opinion that everyone had the opportunity to make good, that in the market economy all men could be kings, but he knew there was not enough to go around.

Although he gloated silently within himself when he considered his foresight in organizing the pivetes into a network of runners, for he could accomplish many times what any other Veloso operation was able to do. It gave him time, almost like being wealthy, in which he could talk to the spirits and sort out the more important things of life.

Tarisco was more apprehensive than usual as he waited impatiently for the moneybag because he had seen a bad omen on entering the favela. A vulture perched high up on the hill that seemed to be waiting too and he would have gone to the Mother of Saints to be rid of it, but did not have time. Veloso would meet him later. There was not a great sum involved, but it was significant and especially so in a favela. He had always trusted the pivetes who worked for him implicitly and consequently never had one of them steal from him–and they were paid well. Tonight he was apprehensive; the usual ease with which he carried himself through the streets of Rio was missing. The man nervously fingered the cool, blue steel of the gun stuck awkwardly in his trousers beneath the wrinkled coat.

Without turning he knew the boy was there because nobody could approach that he did not perceive and so he continued to watch the samba dancers in silhouette as if he were alone.

"They're dead," came a small, breathless voice.

Tarisco replied stoically, "Who's dead?"

"Nogento, Marcelo and Gambazinho."

"What do you mean?"

The ragged little boy who was roughly eleven years old and had bare feet with a dirty face and grubby fingers looked wooden. "Shot dead."

Remembering, as the ice flowed through him numbing all feeling to a point where even the *batuques* could not penetrate. "Tell me what happened?" he asked in an even voice so as not to alarm the boy.

"Candelária..."

"The church?"

"Yes."

"What were you doing there?"

The moment began to catch up with the boy and his breathing became rapid. "Marcelo wanted to stop, a friend owed him money... they slept there, about fifty *pivetes*."

"What happened?"

"Two cars drove up. Some men...eight, nine maybe...they jumped out and shot. Just shot. They shot Gambazinho and many others."

"Marcelo, what of Marcelo?"

"He ran. They shot him too."

"How do you know they're dead?"

"Blood." As if a well had been tapped tears sprang like rivers out of the solitary eyes, without any show of emotion, leaving furrows of soil down the boy's cheeks, but he did not change the stoic expression. He cried as if it was beyond him, as if the tears welled up and came from a primeval source too far detached from the present for him to touch yet still he burned with compassion for the injustices suffered upon the weak. "There's too much blood."

"Who were they?"

"I don't know"

"Police?"

"Black hoods. "

Suddenly he grabbed the boy's arm. "The bag? Where's the bag?" Then they ran, both of them, the man and the boy. Off in the distance the vulture had vanished.

The sounds of their footsteps beat off the hollow streets. He remembered. He would never be far enough away from the favelas. Veloso himself looked at him in that erudite patronizing way that left him with a deep understanding that he would never be allowed into the silent circle of *fazendeiros*, property owners, even though he was becoming a man of substance. The color of his skin and his Indian grandmother were too close, not enough generations in between. He remembered the girls who would not go out with him because they were looking for a man with lighter skin so that even if they could not, their children could begin the long slow climb of the social ladder. But more than that it was the stigma of the dust that could not be vanquished in the minds of the powers of the world. It had clung to him from childhood as a permanent tattoo from the years of running barefoot like the boy who ran before him now and despite his fervor to succeed and his emulation of the ruling class he still wore it like a badge. When it came right down to it there was a philosophy at stake, a relationship to the world that was vital to who he was and who he would always be. There were things that could not be erased from the heart.

Up on the hill of the favela of Tavares Baixo the old ruined building lorded over the pivetes who would shrink in abject terror at the mention of Parque Guinle while its image burned in their memories indelible forever. He remembered. Dragged off in the darkness and tortured with electric prods. They left no mark so even if there was someone to report it to no one would believe him. But it took him five days to remember his name, and seven days before he could navigate the streets of Rio again from memory. The men had black hoods too. He ran faster through the alleys.

Thin, scampering children filled the streets the week after the Association of Hoteliers won an injunction against the city to act in removing the homeless minors from tourist zones. Then came another terror. The *mendingança*, the van of the anti-truant brigade of the *Funabem*, the facilities of the "National Foundation for the Well being of Minors." It would swoop down and gather up as many as it could hold and rush them off to the state institution where they would be beaten into correction as if pain and punishment could give them parents or change their skin color or improve their economic condition. He remembered. The van itself was an instrument of terror calling to mind the tale of *Papai Figo* who is said to collect up children in the night and sell their organs for transplants in the morning. He remembered the children who were no longer children, simply eyesores, nuisances and ran faster until he felt his heart would burst.

In the streetlights he saw them. At once he thought they must be bundles of delicate flowers laid at the church's door in memory or in thanks and the sweet smell of gardenias permeated his nostrils with their saccharin odor that was replaced, as he drew closer, by the odor of blood. He had never realized how similarly they smelled before now as he looked down upon the crumpled bodies of children shot where they slept near the steps of this famous place.

"Here!" the boy called to him in a trembling whisper that he heard all across the courtyard.

Standing over the body of Marcelo *his* aviõezinho, *his* little airplane, he felt shame that he had sent him on the errand that ended this way. "He ran." Blood had spilled out of the wound in his head and made a maroon stain on the ground beside him. He prayed to Oyá, the Mother of Nine who guarded the gates of the cemetery hoping for the strength to ferry him through the night.

Suddenly there was a sound.

"There!" The boy quickly pointed to the corner of the building where in the peripheral shadow of the yellow light a figure just slipped out of sight.

Again he ran. He ran as if a coiled spring had been waiting all his life to unleash its fury and gave him the loft and elevation of a dancer as he easily glided over hedges and benches and bounced across car hoods in pursuit of the fleeing phantom of death. "Oshosi!" He cried aloud as he ran at full speed. "Oshosi!!" He said again, and continued to call upon the Orixá praying that he would respond even though he, by necessity had to bypass Elegguá and open the gate himself to the spirit world. He needed the warriors. He needed the wind of their breath.

By the time he caught up with the scrambling man he was chanting *Oshosi* over and over in a breathless flurry without realizing he was doing so. Tarisco grabbed the collar and pulled as hard as he could digging his heels in and lurching back at the same time. The man flipped over backwards completely the stroke was so violent and landed on the asphalt face down with tremendous thud and a grunt of air being expelled from his overworked lungs. Tarisco jumped on his back and wrapped his arm around the man's throat and yanked back just to the point before his windpipe would be crushed.

"Why are you running?" He muttered into the man's ear.

"Why are you chasing me?" Stuttered the man breathlessly feigning a weakness that Tarisco did not buy because he could feel the well muscled frame lying beneath him.

"What is this bag around your neck."

"Mine. It is mine."

"It looks just like the one I lost."

"No...no. I don't think so."

Tarisco shoved one hand into the deep pocket of the bag that still was strung over the man's shoulder. Inside he felt something hard, cold and heavy. It was wrapped in cloth. He pulled it out and while still holding the man by the throat looked at it in the dim light. It was a gun. He stood up quickly, unwrapping the weapon from the cloth and then pointed it at the man.

"Get up!" He said.

Rising the man turned hunkered over in a bear like manner revealing to Tarisco the burly strength of his arms and back. He was a thick stocky white man with a two day growth of beard.

"What's this?" He held up the gun still pointed at the man.

"I am a policeman."

Tarisco held up the cloth the gun had been wrapped in to the faint light the street lamp gave and unfurled it revealing the two eye holes in the black hood. His low, grim voice seethed from between clenched teeth. "What's this?!"

The man became angry. "Who are you anyway?!"

The shot rang out with the clean finality of a surgeon's first cut and echoed for a brief moment off the surrounding buildings and then it fell silent again except for the sound of the city that always murmured in the background, day or night.

"I am a *pivete!*"

BRUSHSTROKES IN THE MIST

II

A rustle of silk pierced the harbor night. The gnashing of rusty gears was overshadowed as was the squealing hoist and the drone of a compressor in the distance. A smooth white hand flashed through the darkness. The smell of wild roses lingered momentarily and was gone. Her cheekbones had the patina of polished blonde ebony and her eyes were dark cauldrons of swirling, interstellar medium. "What are we doing?" she asked in a wistful, searching voice. "It's cold."

The harbor slept yet murmurs from the bay made it an uneasy nocturne. It was never at rest. Amber lights from the tanker's quay trailed out into the infinite and raised shimmering mirages on the water over which the dispossessed believe they can walk, beneath which the huge leviathan glides oblivious and all knowing, sublime and primeval. The planks of the wharf were old. Forgotten were the hands of the makers whose callused lives long since had faded from memory and the wood, gathered from the northern mountain forests two generations ago, lay alternately bleached and sodden from sun and mist, fogs and waves unspoken. The grain was etched deep by the weather and could be felt even with soled feet in the night going about their silent business. Huge ropes cascaded down rusting hulls onto pilings where pelicans roosted keeping secure the precious cargo–sailors deep in holds a long way from home–by some ships they were coiled neatly, carefully, by

15

others they were strewn in haphazard sprawl by belligerent and surly men anxious to be encircled by the sea once more.

Tugs lumbered across the silky deep as they weighed out a living and strained against heavy, penumbral vessels lying half seen and mysterious up against the hush of night. Ships sailed without regard to politics, sounds of them groaning on the water could be heard if they could not be seen and it has always been that way and always will be as long as there are men who cannot settle down in one place for very long.

The car door slammed with the solid sound of precision engineering. "Smell that!" The man breathed in a great draught. "Isn't it great? ...can you smell it?"

"Yes..." she replied dismayed huddling in her coat, pulling it close to the sweep of her neck with both hands, feeling the silky garments underneath slide smoothly across her bare skin, "...it smells like the zoo, or sewage treatment."

"It's the ocean," he said flashing a look at the woman's face from the corner of his eye furling his eyebrows adding, "...no imagination?"

The long, pointed heel of her shoe got stuck in a crack. The tall, thin blonde woman nearly toppled over, swaying for a few precarious moments like a crystal wine glass teetering on a shelf during an earth tremor, but freeing it regained her composure and with graceful, practiced steps and continued to glide through the mist not allowing anything, particularly of the natural world, to impinge on her if she could help it. She tasted salt in the air, the musk of sea life and pollution that always occurred on the fringe where civilization met the wild ocean.

"Can't imagine why we're here," she said raising her wrist to her nose hoping the perfume would give her respite from the real.

The first movement of the night came with the great horns that warned against an approaching shore, or of shoals and reefs and hidden barges. Whispering timbers replied, swaying with the pitch and roll of the bluegreen water, rubbing up against massive hulls that loomed in the darkness, unseen, ever present, known only by the moaning wharves. Voices were muted by damp sea air that was thick, (salty and sweet and leaving its taste), making the dour words uttered by a sailor out of Baladiyat 'Adan and the shouts off a distant fantail by another from Primorsko, (who used to fish the Black Sea for sturgeon), become indistinguishable echoes. Brushstrokes in the mist. Machinery whined in the distances and would to all hours. Freighters came and men were eager to unload and be on their way again. Many longings filled the harbor.

Eyes followed the man and woman. Callused hands clasped each other in an effort to get warm and someone watched from the shadows. Peering out from beneath an overhang hidden by darkness. A presence bathed in ultramarine tracked their every movement. It imagined, dreamed, conjured, pictured, wondered about the lithe figure of the woman moving beneath the flowing garments that sailed with the wind and marveled at the flashes of ebony white skin, which shocked the darkness, and speculated at what the man might be carrying into the wharves this late hour.

Laughter pealed in the cool air. It echoed slightly and then vanished. Fog wisps curled through the damp lights outside Alesandro's Grill in the harbor's heart where the maze of narrow roads eventually led everyone. The air surrounding the cafe was tinged with aromas of fried fish and the peculiar odor that cooking oil had when it was recycled day after day in the deep vats through which squid, shrimp and other creatures of the velvet ocean passed before ending up on somebody's plate. Longshoremen, stevedores, warehousemen, teamsters, pilots, freight handlers and all manner of sailors had been eating at Alesandro's for nearly half a century and little had changed except that now it was owned by a Korean and not the fat Portuguese man whose wife would show up at three each afternoon and drink herself silly in the same booth day after day until closing time. When stinking with alcohol Alesandro was pleased to tell people he had been in a movie once and indeed had gotten drunk with a famous director who had come to the docks to film a story about the waterfront. Outside the cafe windows appeared steamy and streaked with salt and corrosion while the tin roof was oxidized blue. The small building sat in the middle of an asphalt lot that had been built up around it for one reason; the Portuguese man had been stubborn and refused to sell even though he had received offers far in excess of what the property was worth as the developer who envisioned the parking lot could not imagine the panorama broken by a rundown diner. Though truth was that it was not run down and looked today very much as it always had, the Portuguese had simply decided that no matter how much money he was offered it was not worth the value of his life, which revolved around the cafe rituals and its patrons. The asphalt lot doubled as short term storage for Japanese automobiles, which seemed to flow into the country as spawning salmon in a never ending stream, and a brief resting place for outward bound cargo containers and parking. Tonight it was empty but for one low, sleek car that sat like a diamond in a black man's ear.

Randall DesVergers felt eddies of wind push against him biting his cheeks and slicing through his Italian wool jacket and cashmere over-coat causing him to shiver. He loved the feeling. *If only the wind could wash a man clean*, the wisp of a thought passed over him quickly like a shadow from a cloud he would rather not deal with. A gull cried off in the distance as he watched Monica enjoying the way her body moved and was finally satisfied he was doing the right thing, satisfied with the sleek automobile that had brought them there, and the thin soled, finely crafted Italian shoes through which he could feel every loose pebble on the asphalt, and the exquisite blonde woman.

"I've always loved the harbor ..." he uttered as he straightened up getting a crimp out of his back that had developed from sitting in the soft, orthopedic car seat for the last forty minutes. Then he slipped on some pigskin gloves he had bought exclusively for driving, though he had only worn them twice because the weather was so warm in Los Angeles. As a result they were spotless, subtly tanned and so porous they could not be used for anything else as they would pick up dirt and oil. He simply liked the idea of the gloves. "It makes me feel close to people," he said with a quiet, nasal voice that implied a deep moral significance, "besides, I'm hungry. You know these cafes always have the best food."

"God!" She exclaimed. "Looks like a dive to me!" Yellow light streamed out the muddy windows as if in perpetual welcome. She could see mysterious blurred movements inside.

A foghorn unleashed its deep baritone from the mouth of the harbor and ship's bells could just barely be heard further off. She could easily have drifted off into the tapestry of the somber dark joining the interweaving light and shadow, the promises in the bay having no allure to hold her, no grounding responsibilities and only the question of who she really was remained unanswered. It was enough, (she told herself), the silky fabrics next to her skin that caressed sensuously with every fluid motion of her body and the ability to charm. Men were instinctive.

Out across the wharves were ghostly silhouettes of ships in the fog lit glow. Some with cranes and piping on their decks, others deep in the water with four layers of cargo containers looming high above, but most sat as through a scrim in a play, lifeless and motionless thrust up against the quay in careful abandon to rest from the years of voyages and forget the terrible incidents of their past completely.

"I could live on a boat like that," Rand said pointing across the channel to a cruise liner painted white, "I could live on it easily."

"I think it's a ship."

"What's that?" He responded absently filled with the dance of the harbor.

"A ship not a boat. It has to do with si…"

He turned and kissed her on the mouth quickly and impulsively tasting her sweetness. It was warm and wet and her breath was honeyed. "You are hungry." she said bitingly running the back of her hand across her lips and looking at him with hurt, sulking eyes implying that there was something he should know. "Chili and jalapiños…?" she teased looking at him sourly feeling pleasure when he obediently smiled.

"…beer to wash it down? C'mon, you'll like it." Rand slipped his arm comfortably around her feeling the warm area at the small of her back and sensed the strength of her muscles as he pulled close wishing to possess and feeling no resistance. They recklessly pushed through the front door of Alesandro's.

Some of the menu was still in Portuguese, and though most was in English the second half was entirely Korean. "I always feel like they're hiding something when I see this," Monica whispered hoarsely shaking her head in disgust and leaning back in the red vinyl booth holding the menu delicately in her left hand while the right hung poised in the air, propped up on an elbow, as if fearing to make too much contact with the environment, "...like they really only cook well for their own."

"Think so?" Rand absently raised his eyes from the menu he had been studying.

The floor of the restaurant was a checkerboard of dingy black and white tile that was brittle, cracked and worn smooth by generations of harbor dwellers with shiny patches of concrete showing through burnished by shuffling feet. The seats of the booths were a reddish vinyl with a leather texture pressed into it, mostly worn away by arms, backs and legs so all that remained was a smooth blur. A strong smell of cooking oil and an odor of cleaning solvent were in the air.

When a dour Korean woman appeared Monica ordered fried clams. "It's safe," she said, "at least I know what it is." Rand pointed to an item on the Korean side of the menu that took up four lines. "OK smart guy, what did you order?" Monica chided after the waitress had gone.

"Don't know..." he glibly replied.

"Don't know?"

"...looked good."

"Maybeee...you'll be sorry."

"That's impossible..."

"...could burn the roof of your mouth off."

He smiled unconcerned, "...that's the way I like it best."

" ...and full of unidentifiable sea creatures and those little maroon tentacles that you find at the bottom of Italian salads ?"

He leaned over the table and patted her hand. "Then you'll eat it."

Monica laughed. Her teeth showed like pearls. "Loopholes! "

"You don't expect me to eat tentacles?"

She leaned across the table and looked him in the eye. "Where do lawyers learn about loopholes?"

There was a deceiving strength to her face that had drawn him at once making him want her the way he wanted a beautiful automobile, or a fine Italian suit, or any of the other things he rapaciously collected and once obtained, forgot. Intelligent breeding met his eyes whenever he looked at her and raw sexual abandon on the brink. There was something entirely erotic about her, something unexplainable. Monica was about as near to physical perfection as Rand had ever personally been close to. A genetic masterpiece. When she walked, the symmetry with which her body moved formed a sensuous tableau with the environment whether she willed it or not. He memorized her moves and contours from the instant they first met so he could envision her in his sleep, getting to know who she was before they even knew each other he had put an imagined person in her place—like a mask. From then on any deviation from his idea of who-she-was-supposed-to-be was a flaw to his eyes in the standard by which she was judged. She had strong Nordic features, chiseled, European, and a flair, a poise, a posture, which caused Rand to endow her with mystic, feminine qualities she may or may not have actually possessed.

"Tell me again about your father."

"What...?" she smiled, amused, and tried to look out the window at the blurred images of ships. "...you mean that he slept with a gun or that he slept on the couch.?"

"You're making it up aren't you?"

"No. Of course I'm not making it up. He was afraid. Haven't you ever been afraid?"

"Not often," he lied thinking of nights, many nights when he had lain awake unwilling to fully face his own existence. The little things. If he would impress someone or make a bad show of himself and forever miss an opportunity; or if he actually had the character to stand up for a belief, any belief, when pressured as he never had been; or if he would survive at all and not simply fall victim to some purely human ailment like heart failure. "Why do you think he was afraid?"

"He was a crook." She crossed her legs under the table letting one shoe drop off and rested her bare foot against Rand's calf. Her gaze fell across him as a beacon of light clearing all other thoughts except

21

those of her, knowing perfectly well she had created the desired effect. "He worked in the defense industry. Must have got to him after all those years. Sold bombers I think..." nudging with her foot under the table to emphasize each point. "...attack bombers," she pronounced surgically, "...got to be an expert at it too. He always wanted to be in domestic sales...you know...? Military...captive market...? God! Don't you lawyers know anything? He got perks all right, so he kept with it..." she shook her head and smiled pursing her lips slightly and looking sideways without turning her head. "You see, domestic sales were easy, you just answered the phone and took the order...but he had to sell surplus on the international market. Jeeze...! Can you imagine what that would be like? Governments turning over like crazy...and with the wars...I don't think he ever had a clear idea of who he was dealing with, just names and numbers. Always some nondescript looking man from the state department at the door to discuss business with him."

"The gun...what about the gun?"

"As I said, he got to be an expert at it..." She looked out the window.

"I see. That explains a lot. Would you like to elaborate on this subject or should we discuss the Zen of inferred meanings or the art of elliptical sentences?"

"What I mean is he got good, very good at selling on the international market. I must have been about seven or eight..."

"You were never seven..."

"...we started having money, lots of money. First the car, and clothes, we all got clothes, then the houses, about one every two years always larger and in a better area...and anything else we wanted. Guess we were rich. They must have moved so much because they got bored."

"Sounds pretty good to me." The waitress brought two beers and set them down with a loud clatter on the table. Ice hung on the glasses. "So, when did he start sleeping on the couch?"

"Later, when I was seventeen or eighteen. He started getting real nervous all the time, couldn't sit still, just walk in and out of rooms and hardly ever sat down for more than two minutes. Hired a bodyguard..." she looked up at the ceiling and smiled holding her beer with two hands. "One day he brought this strange man in and said, 'This is Bud, he's from college, he'll be with staying with us for a while'." Monica laughed hard. "This guy was a no-neck. Just a lump on his shoulders and hair on his back and arms and he wore these old T-shirts that had Marine Corps insignia on them."

Rand drank his beer. "Maybe they were football buddies."

"He did it for us," she continued in dead earnest. "The gun was never hidden. Sometimes he'd leave it under the pillow on the couch all day...he got very absent minded...just a criminal, god knows what he had to do to sell those planes or who was after him or why, but he wasn't an honest man. He couldn't even sleep."

The waitress returned juggling all the plates of food on one arm and deftly shoveled them onto the table with a great racket filling up every inch of available space with small saucers of condiments and empty side dishes as if for bread or rolls of which there were none. The woman rushed through the serving with such fury that she gave the impression the place was teeming with customers and her orders were backed up at the kitchen window ten deep where the drawn, sardonic face of a heavy Korean man appeared now and then as if he were checking on sleeping children. There were only two other people in the whole place.

"She might be practicing for the lunch hour," Rand observed quietly. "You must have liked having money."

"I liked having whatever I wanted," she looked up at him with a quick jerk of the head to throw the blonde hair from her face, "I liked getting an impulse and being able to realize it without any trouble at all, reaching out and bringing back a full hand...I was a mercenary kid and I wanted everything I could get. Wouldn't you?"

"Sometimes I think that's why were here." Rand rejoined holding up his $14,825 Vacheron Constantin wristwatch to the light then settled back in the worn vinyl seat sipping his beer feeling the complete rush of the harbor flow through him in a transcendental exchange of his rootless life for its permanence and character. He really didn't know if he believed that or not. "I used to go down to the docks where the fishing fleet was moored," he told her with illuminated eyes, "and watch them go out on windy days. It made me feel..." and though he searched

23

for words he couldn't describe the way it made him feel because he didn't have a good enough grasp of it himself. But it was a strong, heady feeling that he somehow always connected to the sea and that he never felt anywhere else. Most of his life was spent inside rooms, offices and hallways where he dealt with the ideas of men, their thoughts and beliefs and what others had written about their actions and so he was inclined to fanciful imaginings that helped him cope with the confinement. He had subscribed to *Shotgun Hunter* magazine for a time even though he had never been hunting and did not own a shotgun, or even a pistol for that fact. "I treasure the sea. It gives me hope."

Soon the table became littered with empty beer bottles and the leftovers of their Korean-Portuguese feast. The waitress paid no attention to them and worked furiously cleaning dishes, floors, counters and all manner of serving utensil. Rand watched her hands. They were nimble and brown, the knuckles were large and the skin, though pulled tight, was dry with lines drawn across it, (one for each day of her life), and she attacked her surroundings with her fingers touching everything, wanting to possess the tactile knowledge of it and fully know its nature. He was fascinated and repulsed by the woman. When she came with the check he gave her a twenty dollar tip, which she didn't even look at tucking it immediately into the folds of her apron and loading her sinewy right arm with most of the dishes before they could even rise from the table. They wandered past two old men at the door who were speaking some Slavic language that he could not recognize and as the scent of wild roses settled upon them with Monica's passing the one nearest the door nearly swooned loosing his train of thought entirely and turned to watch her white ankle disappear into the night rubbing the gray stubble on his chin with remembering hands.

Down to the water's edge where the dock rose up over the black swirling brine dropping its concrete pillars into the sea bottom to hold fast the berth of ships and the platform for cargo handlers and men. How many impoverished souls had worked these piers burdened by dreams no one knew. Few found their way off the docks. Their lives became the planks on which Rand and the white ebony woman walked, their intention alone drew the ships in from all across the world shining

24

out like beacons in the ether, drawing like to like, misfit to misfit, where the language of the dispossessed was spoken.

"Think I'll buy a new car," Rand pronounced into the breath of the harbor. "This German one I've been driving for nearly eight months now…its got these rattles…can't get rid of them." Monica looked at him without expression, no wrinkles, keeping perfect symmetry. "It's Japanese. I wouldn't have believed I'd own a Japanese car…but you should see the wood dash and the color of the leather is just…" he motioned with both hands impassioned and clawing the air for the right adjective as he was at a loss to describe the ecstasy of his feelings, and finally let the thought go being unable to do it justice with words alone.

Slipping her hand through his arm she pressed against him. "I think you should get it… if you want it."

It made him feel secure knowing that someone else felt the same way he did and he thrust his hands into the deep pockets of his cashmere overcoat and hunched his shoulders to bring the collar close to his neck and keep the chill away. "A lot's hanging on a deal I'm involved in," he explained confidentially, "very risky…could see some real profit though, real profit." Rand liked to talk about money. The whole ambiance of the subject was weighty and significant and by its nature important. It implied that one was either an *insider* or an *outsider*, depending on his intimacy with the nomenclature. "…but with the capital gains tax going up," he continued shaking his head pensively, "…this damn deficit mentality–I'm hoping to defer the additional income realized from this deal directly into a liquid retained earnings account from last year that doesn't show on the books, which will rollover into a mutual funds account avoiding taxes, which in turn will pay for the car as a business asset." He glanced at her with hooded eyes, "Is that smart?"

"Can you get away with it?"

"I'm a lawyer." Rand kicked at a huge rope fastened around a rusted iron stay that was as big as a horse's head. The rope, wet with tears from the sea, hung out over the end of the wharf bowing into a graceful arc under its own ponderous weight then soaring up into the mists nestling against the steel plates of a Norwegian freighter whose bulk it helped to keep from drifting out into the open ocean. It was a hemp rope, made from fibers grown in the Anatolian hill country of Turkey where it was shipped by barge down river to Mersin and then loaded aboard a Cypriot steamer bound for Lisbon. From there the cargo found its way into the European grain exchange along with the products of a hundred other countries speaking a thousand languages. It finally ended up on Lake Superior, having been purchased and sold again many times while en route by traders out of Chicago. Some was bought by a small company in Maine whose sole business was the manufacture of rope and had been since 1703 when it supplied local fishing boats and whalers who shipped out at winter's end from New England harbors. There men still wove the giant coils by hand drawing them out on long tables in narrow wooden buildings that stretched a city block with the strength of their arms and the tenacity of their fingers. It was a dying business. But they were holding on till the end with their meager subsidies too proud to give it up even though every year they fell further behind. Rand kicked it again with particular malice.

"There's so much money traveling through the company accounts not even the IRS can tell where it all comes from." Satisfied that it was a good idea, "It's de rigueur, everybody does it, and besides…" he thought of the leather upholstered seats, the smell of a new car's interior and the ten glossy coats of hand rubbed lacquer, "I want it."

A sudden gust of wind caught them and sent their coat tails flying up like a scarecrow's tattered arms. Monica buried her face in Rand's shoulder holding tight "Jesus its cold!" she said.

He pulled her closer feeling her breast against him and walked into the night languishing in the growing awareness that he was on the edge. There was a thrill to it, an indescribable sensation that would disappear entirely if he ever gave in all the way and crossed the line. Danger lurked just out of sight. Animals perceive the same thing when they are on the hunt and seek out the weak who stray too close to the edge fearing, (if not desiring), to sacrifice their lives. Flirting with eternity gave certain rewards. The chance of disaster only made it sweeter, and with every step further down into the maze of docks and ships Rand's perceptions heightened. He tuned into the night amidst the dilapidated warehouses and other buildings, the purpose of which were completely lost in time, and pushed on flaunting risk. Monica trembled, (cold she thought), her eyes darting around to the shadowed corners.

"It's all laziness, you see," he spoke quietly with a nervous edge to his voice, "really, a complete lack of discipline. Anyone can make money, you just have to really want it and be willing to do whatever it takes. There's always opportunity, there always has been...fact is you don't even have to work very hard." His voice trailed off behind into the sea fog turned murky by the yellow lights.

The alcohol impaired her judgment just enough so that all she felt under the dim lights was a profound loneliness like an echo running up beside her from somewhere in the city that was overflowing with human life. Yet she was aloof from it all, certain that its fingers could never touch her or follow into her sanctuaries. The refuge of a man's arms was one, a hollow shelter that had sought her out early in life and she had used it when necessary. Men wanted Monica, perhaps not in spirit, she thought, but the flesh. It made little difference because the act itself had no consequence one way or the other and was just a part of the fabric no better or worse than any other part.

"Why don't they get jobs? There's so many street people around my apartment I can hardly get to my car...they're always setting the alarm off."

"It's a problem."

"I can do without it," she rejoined and a ray of yellow light sparkled off the cluster of diamonds hanging from her ear, "it's hard to enjoy life with some misfortunate shoved in your face."

Rand smiled, "...I get it from some damn civil liberties lawyer beating the drum for an underdog...who just happens to be suing for millions of dollars to fund his retirement. People are natural opportunists, don't you think?" He slipped his arm under her coat and around her waist, kissed her cheek lightly and felt her move in the soft place between her ribs and the top op her hip. "Maybe it's true, the meek shall inherit the earth...through litigation and welfare."

Tattered rags were wrapped around ankles, but the shoes were still good and sturdy. The cloth only a precaution against the night weather, as he had learned in the Marines, (from a former lifetime it seemed).

And the coat was still water resistant. Glad there was strength in his arms from the last time he had worked with the longshoremen over two months ago unloading cargo, but the money had long since run out and he had become so accustomed to hunger it was hardly noticeable. Hallucinations occasionally, seeing blue flashes of light, but he fought it off disgusted at any sign of weakness. "Semper Fi'!," he muttered to himself. The union card still floated in his pocket. Though he had not paid dues for more than two years he found that by flashing it while covering the date with his thumb he could get work, on occasion, when it was available and they were paying scale or below. He knew the really good jobs went to the Mexicans, especially the young ones. He followed the silhouette the couple made against the backdrop of iron hulls and listened carefully, (scarcely breathing), for their words, hoping for a clue, (some insight), and an edge. Each step they took, he took two, and then fell silent, watching.

"You feel warm to me."

"It's all this walking."

"When I get my god dammed new car..." He mused with a smile on his face tight from the beer. Their heels clicked against concrete and the sound came back off the walls of warehouses and other buildings in between wind noises. Rand felt comfortable, relaxed and... comfortable. Even in the chill of night. It was something he had worked at for many years and now he was approaching that state where successful men end up...complacency. But with each step he unconsciously longed for sensation, something that would remind him he was alive and spur him into the future like a roman candle. It was all wrong, the whole premise and fabric of his life yet its resolution evaded him and so he continued as he was supposed to. As a result he flirted with danger in the same way that he flirted with life, never really committing to it but skirting the periphery and taking all its resources while giving little back. The scales were unbalanced and though he was not cognizant of what it was, he knew something about it was immoral. It made him worry and go without sleep, made him desire uncommitted sexual liaisons, money and possessions. It also caused him to seek out danger, (as if he was searching for the festering wound that he might heal it), and walk the edge between degradation and wholeness without ever touching either world, but viewing each as a witness to other mens' natures. He was full but not sated; there was always room to have more. He pulled Monica tight and walked over to the metal railing where he stopped

A kiss was never again as sweet as that first one, never as tender as in the mind and never as innocent as one wished it to be. She threw one arm across his shoulder, straight, elbow down sticking out like an awkward flagpole and languidly held him with the other while he groped for the railing, pushing her back. They stood at the fringe of a pale light that hung high against a pole and sent out a dank, circular glow that drew its outline on the ground. It threw them half into the shadow of the wharves and half into the light. His hand found her breast and she gave no resistance, but let it happen as a spectator interested from a distance while he kissed her neck and searched for the elusive feeling that alcohol helped hide the remnants of. She, with only one whimper, "Rand, someone might see..." surrendered to a brief interlude knowing that she was paying wages, drawing him by the leash, but most of all she had been seduced by the risk of the place that he had drawn her into. What if someone was watching? It lured and repulsed her. He ran his hand up the inside of her thigh until it stopped on her sex and she arched against him slightly feigning attempts at pushing him away. A sigh escape her lips and she raised her left leg just enough to wrap her ankle around his. Sensation slowly began to cloud her more responsible faculties.

Eyes flickered with a dim light that had never glowed brightly, but gave that illusion, following her hand. The shock of white ebony peeking beyond the rich fur, probing deftly, hesitantly, searching for the core as if by mindless instinct then suddenly grasping it making him suck in his breath even while he kissed her. A shuffling was lost in the muffled night air. A movement vanished in the fog. A ghost like presence missed.

"Hey buddy..." came the wheezing, rasping, sudden voice.

Hands racing, eyes looking frantically, garments pulled tight, withdrawing, close together, rapid, fleeting movement...but above all were the heartbeats drumming out all sounds in the ears with their excited tattoos.

"Jesus!!" Rand jumped startled out of his wits. "What the hell do you want?! He shouted at the tattered man, who loomed close and because of the light seemed larger than he actually was. "Who the hell are you?!" He demanded while Monica tried to cower behind him though he moved so quickly she was left exposed, vulnerable and so stood silently, as if dead, her flushed cheeks suddenly white, her eyes riveted.

"Ya got any money?" the man said gruffly, though it was almost inaudible, "I'm hungry…"

Pushing close Monica spoke in a low, deep voice as if the man was not there. "I think he wants your money." Her face frozen and without expression.

"What do you want?!" Rand kept yelling.

"…hungry…" The man just growled, menacingly, looking sideways, and down and shuffling forward.

Turning to Monica, "What's he saying?"

"He wants your money….!" She said angrily with an even voice, her eyes fixed on the ragged man in the army jacket with the unkempt beard and rags wrapped around his ankles. "He's just like the one that sets off my alarm."

Rand was suddenly angry. "Oh for Christ sakes! You want a handout, here in the dark! You almost gave me a heart attack!"

The man took two steps toward them suddenly encouraged, his hands concealed in the pockets of his coat. He thought he might even get two or three dollars off this guy, he really looked set. Five would be great, he could almost taste that hamburger with the grilled onions just the way he liked it. It was late and he knew he had no pretense to give, his pride had long ago dissolved. "…c'mon buddy, I'm a Marine."

Monica whispered hoarsely, "He's got a gun!"

"What…?" As the man moved slowly closer looking at them from under thick, oily, furled brows Rand glanced quickly at Monica for confirmation. She nodded. His heart raced so hard in his chest it ached. There were no thoughts, as if he were suddenly naked, as if his possessions had been already been taken and he lie pauperized and exposed. He could not control himself and began to shake aware of how it must look. "Jesus it's cold." A slight image of a turquoise blue glassine sea began to pervade him. The yellow sun bathed it in warmth and light. A slight breeze carried scents of saffron. He began to feel sleepy and overcome and longed to be there, in the mental image, anywhere else.

Monica's voice drifted into his consciousness. "Give him your car keys." She said disgusted and afraid as she pawed him, trying in some way to get inside and hide.

"My what?"

"Your keys," she whispered in his ear so the stranger wouldn't hear, "if he has your car he'll leave us alone."

Rand frowned. But then he thought *why not?* The insurance would cover it, and he wanted that new Japanese model... "I might be able to suggest an amicable settlement here," he raised his index finger to make the point, "that is if you're willing to settle." He looked at Monica.

The man stopped and wiped his mouth with the back of his hand squinting up his eyes philosophically at this new turn of events. "Sure I'll settle." He said hoarsely, willing to take almost anything at this time of night. He knew he wasn't reaching these people, but had a feeling if he played his cards right he might get that five, perhaps more... if he was lucky that is. Then this humiliation would let up for a while, a day or so...could get something hot to eat and find a warm place to sleep out of the dammed sea mist. Tomorrow he would find work, he was sure of it. "I feel lucky." He said, however, the one thing he knew he couldn't have he just took with furtive glances, he breathed her in when the breeze brought her scent to him. He was intoxicated by her presence. "Sure." He said with hooded eyes.

"I've got a car over there that's worth eighty-six thousand dollars." The bearded man looked over his shoulder into the mist seeing only the street lamps reflected back, but he pushed his hands deeper into the pockets causing Rand to be more certain than ever he had a gun. He held out his keys. "It's yours... just leave us alone. We don't want any trouble, no violence..."

A moment of silence passed while the vagrant observed the couple before him for the first time. It was in the eyes, he thought looking at Rand's complacent face. (Was this the price of breeding? Like a Persian cat so refined it could no longer breathe properly?) It was the essence that reached him, not the words, or the fear or the low level to which his life had dwindled. The man's car? *"fer Chrisakes!"*, he exclaimed to himself–really to the heart of the matter here. What else was there, the car, credit cards, for a while he could emulate and no one would be wiser. And the woman? "Why not?" He burst out, absently, from the maelstrom howling in his head. (Did this man know he was on the edge, tipping into the whirlpool?) God, anything for a drink, "Man...I don't want your car..." he groped to articulate the subtle feelings he was experiencing just at that moment. He thought back to when he was a Dutchman traveling to England to be the King, he thought of centuries unfolding, of huge migrations and extinctions, of loves and families and ten thousand shouting soldiers embracing in wild collision as they violently tore at one another, the devil's blood in their eyes. "I'm just hungry..." he replied, "cantcha' help me? I used to be a Marine."

"Give him the keys!" Monica prodded, and seizing them from Rand threw them jangling to the ground before the ruffled stranger who seemed to loom in front of them in the dank shadows of the wharves.

The stranger regarded them coldly and then finally exhorted without hunger or need or second thoughts of any kind, "My disgust!" The three of them stood befuddled, each waiting for the other. "My disgust," he said at last and turned from them disappearing into the mist.

After his shuffling footsteps were out of earshot, a long silence ensued. "Can you beat that?" Rand pondered, slightly disappointed that he could not now get the insurance company to finance his new car and that he would have to wait a while longer before he could afford it. He saw Monica was trembling and took her hand, it was ice cold.

"I thought he would kill us," she whispered trembling.

In the car Rand suddenly embraced Monica and kissed her on the mouth. He was aroused by the encounter with the man and wanted something more now that he'd had a taste. It was a long, deep kiss.

He imagined he had flirted with danger and felt immediately virile and wild. She kissed him back with equal strength sensing the impulse that was out of control, and in some protracted manner took credit for inciting him to such passion. Men were instinctive, she thought as she slipped her hand over the top or his trousers and felt his flesh and hair. He jumped because her touch was ice cold. Rough hands swept across her secret parts, under her thin dress, inside her stockinged thighs and to her core as she watched a freighter being loaded through the rapidly fogging windows with lazy eyes. She gasped slightly despite herself as he removed her undergarment. Buttons loosened on the dress, clasps were undone and two small white breasts were exposed to the night. The feeling pervaded both that the bearded man was still watching. And who knows who else? It heightened the euphoria. The mix of danger and alcohol brought Rand to a reckless edge.

Monica anxiously desired to feel the heat of his flesh against her by a primal nature she had never understood that seemed to violate every convention people had tried to pound into her since birth. Despite it all she wished to ingest him by some mysterious method and hold him captive at the peak of ecstasy until his breath was gone and he had expired from unfulfilled longing. At the same time she felt compromised and seduced as an ancient moral code ceaselessly pulled at her no matter how she might wish to be.

He didn't say a word, never talking during sex, but mindlessly pulled her close stifling a brief cry of protest. She looked up and with frightened eyes succumbed not to him, but to her own state of mind knowing that she always desired pleasure and that she had never possessed the moral stamina required to temper physical sensation with emotional reason and so always felt violated, brutalized, even though she demanded with her body what she denied with her intellect. It was that way now, she savored the way he smelled, luxuriated in the familiar feeling of the opposite sex and knew that's what men liked. They needed to have attention lavished on them, to be coddled like they were injured children and caressed and kissed and held. Monica simply liked the way he felt, and would have gotten her satisfaction from just that if he had let her, but this was payment due, and she fell into the routine like a fisherman's whore and limply let him have his way being cold, uncomfortable and somewhat drunk from the Chinese beer.

The cold fog swirled around them both. The captured essence of scents and heartbeats, voices and murmured cries, of tangled slippery limbs, their breath and dance, the desire and the unconscious animal passion all mingled with the thick sea air and was swept into the harbor's womb where fishes and hidden ocean creatures live out their lives as they had for all of man's history.

BRUSHSTROKES IN THE MIST

III

Brown hands trembled holding the fine white bone china cups. They were so delicate, like the tiny, brightly colored, *pájaro* figures his mother used to make from red clay and suspend with thread from the ceiling. Not like a machete, nor the wood handles or any of the tools he was familiar with. It was a hard thing to control, so small, insignificant and fragile. With great skill and spiritual restraint he mustered just the amount of poise needed and with a straight back poured the dark steaming *café* into each of the cups until it was exactly a quarter of an inch from the top, never more or less. It was a game he had devised to prove to himself he was still *macho* and this was just a passing phase in his life, something he had to endure, (a penance for unknown sins), and satisfying himself that even if it was for some *borracho gringo*, it would never spill onto the saucer before it reached the table. The coffee was named *Guatemala Antigua*, and though from regions close to *Cerro Tres Cruces, Chiapas* where he was born and spent most of his life, he had never heard of it until he came to Los Angeles.

Three men and a woman sat at the table. He hovered hesitantly in the distance and then approached them from across the room drawn to the rich fabrics of their suits, the burnished leathers of the shoes that undoubtedly cost many times his weekly salary, the glittering timepieces on their wrists that took his breath away when one of them would slide into view from behind a crisp, white cuff. He was enveloped by the heady scent of wealth, the intoxicating magnetism of money, which, unlike anything else on earth, seemed to him as elusive as immortality. Yet here it was, before him, unashamed.

His hair was slicked back and he had not worn his wide brimmed straw hat on the way to the restaurant before dawn this morning because he wanted it to remain perfect all day. His frayed black slacks were ironed until the seams were shiny and he wore a tight fitting white shirt with a starched collar turned slightly yellow on the inside. The black vest belonged to the restaurant and he was required to leave it at the end of each day to be laundered or for somebody else to wear. Everything was just right, the coffee was still hot when he glided the cups down with studied grace and placed them in front of *los ricos gringos*, even though they may be *borrachos*, without a sound or a breath of air out of place and with such perfect elegance he thought for sure he would be noticed, thanked warmly and perhaps even congratulated on his thoroughness and expertise. That was not to be.

It could have been an open door, sunlight spilling haphazardly into a room touching someone's arm slightly; a wisp of air across the roof hardly raising the leaves that had fallen there the night before; a child's silent gaze where eyes become frozen on an image of an angel in the mind; the passing of one day to the next; a heart breaking; a fleeting thought of mortality; words unspoken...the three people continued as if nothing, nothing had occurred. He cut through them like an apparition and consequently was certain himself that he did not exist, and thought, as he retreated across the restaurant floor, that it was true, the old religion of the *Yaqui brujo*. Brown men did live in a separate world and the white men had just not learned *seeing* yet.

"We've brought some information with us, preliminary..." Veronique Anotil touched the cup to her lips painted dark red and hesitantly sipped the coffee leaving crimson marks around its rim. She exuded an aura of impatience. Pulling some overstuffed files out of a briefcase she looked at Rand. "We don't want you to do anything yet, not yet..." she paused, "we have confidence, but we just want to give you a taste of the complete proposal so you can begin to get a feel for what we believe is the tremendous impact our system will have on global communications."

She carelessly shuffled through the papers "...corporate restructuring, taxes, copyright litigation, contracts, SEC clearances and so on. It' all there...most of it's on disk." The stack was placed in front of Ash, but she spoke to Rand. "We think it's the most exciting thing that's ever happened."

Rand watched the sculpted symmetry of her face in admiration. "I always felt uncommitted until I became a partner." He confided in his most disarming manner having practiced it until phrases rolled off his tongue like pearls dropping into mineral oil. "I understand."

"If you did, you never let on." A tall, elegant, angular man interjected and then added lifting his cup, "I hate to think of all those perks going to waste."

Ashford Van Riper was the founder of VanRiper, Hazeltine & Brock and the fatherly image he portrayed was a carefully crafted portrait that towered above the feeble attempts of mortal men at humility. Having become wealthy in his mid twenties by pioneering product liability cases he was a tremendously cultured man who like to drink ouzo and carried a small caliber pistol around with him wherever he went. Hazeltine, however, was an ambulance chaser on a grand scale and had built his career on class action disaster litigation. Fortunately at the time they became partners the fields were just being developed so the unquenchable thirst for money met headlong with the proliferation of lucrative cases. Ash built a huge mountain top mansion in a section of National Forest land he managed to buy through one of his friends. His wife refused to live so remotely, consequently he spent half the week there and the other half in town at the office. It was simply called the Ranch. Every month he had a group of lawyers and other chums over for a chili barbecue where they would all dress up like cowboys and drink expensive whiskey, smoke contraband Havana cigars that Ash bought in Canada at fifteen hundred dollars a box and ride the surrounding hills on his stable of thoroughbred horses. The third partner Brock, on the other hand, was a quiet man. He possessed a dry, acerbic sense of humor that only his closest associates appreciated and had enraptured Van Riper and Hazeltine with his vision of the future. According to Brock the world was facing a period of consolidation and mergers. *It's inevitable,* he was fond of saying, *because there are neither enough jobs or resources to go around.* His expertise was corporate law. His gospel was embodied in the brass and wood plaque he had mounted on his desk... "Sue the bastards!"

Veronique rolled her eyes up from the steaming liquid regarding Rand anxiously without expression, but smiled politely still sipping her coffee piercing his attempted naiveté.

Gordon Dahlquest, eyed him suspiciously with his thick eyebrows set in a natural furl. He was thinking of the Adirondacks and the old lodge he used to visit every summer as a child, how the cool mornings rose up out of the ground as an indistinct mist taking form as the light arrived. His gaze made Rand uneasy, but what he perceived as a certain peace in the man, a wholesomeness that was missing in his own experience was in fact an apathy that had evolved incrementally over the years from too many compromises, too many failed hopes and a suppressed yet desperate urge to escape at all costs.

Gordon Dahlquest shifted in his seat. "I understand you won't be doing most of the work," he paused then quietly added, as if an afterthought, *"yourself."*

"That's right." Rand replied brightly.

Clearly the smell of cedar intruded in the old man's thoughts, crisp morning air, loon cries...and he pondered the answer that came to him as if from a distance taking the time that old men do having earned the right. "What's your line then?"

"We specialize in all phases of corporate law. Particularly mergers and acquisitions." Ash answered for him becoming nervous as he did whenever his sixth sense told him the deal was slipping. "Most of your work will be done by our task force composed of corporate specialist teams."

"Shouldn't we be talking to them?'

"No. We do everything in account groups. The partners usually act as group heads and supervise strategically selected crews of lawyers and other experts to fit each client's needs. Collectively we call them *The Team,* and you have one expressly assigned to your company."

"But," Gordon said directly to Rand, " you, personally, you don't actually do the work?"

"Not actually."

"Then what *do* you do?"

The moment when his uneasiness turned to dislike was difficult to discern, but it had without doubt been passed. He was willing from the start to forgive the man for who he might be, if the ruddy face and red nose, the stocky frame that gave him trouble sitting down in the straight backed chair and the frowning demeanor was anything to judge by. His carelessly abandoned gray hair looked as though it might have been a sandy blonde in his youth but now was thick and stricken with cowlicks and wisps that went the wrong way no matter how he may have tried to groom it. He was a sun burnt Midwesterner. Prairie wind still lived in those clear blue eyes that peered out from under the furled brows in piercing beacons. *Hands that built America*, Rand thought sarcastically, but trembled slightly as his gaze fell to the two massive paws resting on the table, dry and weathered with age spots yet still strong enough. Rope pullers, wagon tillers, log handlers ..."You're a tough man Gordon. I do what it takes in the interest of my clients." He said calmly.

"Anything?"

"Almost," he looked across at Ash who had been watching them intently still holding the files, "short of murder."

Ashford Van Riper smiled in the confident way a man does when he knows that he has enough money, that he will always have enough money and the affairs at hand are inconsequential to survival and are being undertaken just out of love for the task. "Unless we must. We don't like to lose Mr. Dahlquest."

"I'm glad to hear that Ash," he pursed up his lower lip and squinted nodding slightly, "glad indeed." The scents of Cedar, clear White Pine and rich, moist earth rose up inside him riding on the back of a cool wind. Images of wild mornings, forest glades half hidden in haze, shafts of sunlight filtering down from the paths of geese and Gray Herons tumbled by. Mallard ducks called out and he heard them. He remembered all the voices that cried through the woodlands as he walked trying to name each one by its true name like he had been taught as a boy. Pine needles springing under his feet. Here now, so far away in time from that early history the old man could not even get a hint of his own true name that was so apparent for so long. It evaded him. Sometimes he would perceive an instant that was vividly clear yet so out of balance with his life that it jarred every moral sense he possessed and demanded change. To what he did not know, and as he grew older and his options ran thin it became even more obscure. So he endured, pressed on, survived. Some say, (he remembered), that was all there was, just to continue was the purpose of life. But then what of the deeper feelings he knew existed, (he remembered), he wished for them many times in his life. Many bleak times. It was a blind remark. Though on the chance it may be true he held out for the meaning hoping that when he retired and had the time to reflect and pursue such things that he will not have forgotten.

"You see Mr. DesVergers those of us who don't play the market back in New York are essentially simple people," he ran the tips of his massive fingers across the pure, white linen tablecloth bringing them to rest on the heavy silver spoon that shone brightly even though scratched from years of use, "and despite myself I'm still wondering why we had to come to Los Angeles for a law firm."

"Are we still being examined?" It wasn't that he needed the business, Ash thought, it was the principle. He could have sent someone else, someone in a lower echelon to deal with this meeting, but he didn't and so answered for Rand. "We have a very impressive record." He replied, (though he could not smile) and wanted to leave it at that. Pure, simple, austere, yet he felt like he had to say more, to justify why he was there and what he was doing with his life, and that made him furious. "Would you like some fresh coffee?"

"So I'm told. Veronique sold me, she had to convince me, though trust me I personally read each word of your capabilities presentation."

"Ours is a complex and vitally important project for your firm to handle..." Veronique spoke, "...it involves a lot of money."

"For example?" Rand asked.

"A considerable amount..." The old man interjected. "Perhaps I will have some fresh coffee." Rand signaled for the waiter.

"From the start it will take total commitment." Veronique continued, "Total. You will not be allowed to back out in the middle of things, there's too much at stake." She outlined a capital funding plan that was ambitious enough to convert most all of the subsidiary companies of each partner to liquid assets without alerting any unions or the Securities and Exchange Commission beforehand. Or any of the nine thousand employees that stood to lose their livelihood as a result of the incipient act of God otherwise known as corporate downsizing. Each major point was emphasized by placing her index finger firmly on the table directly in front of them and pressing it so hard that white spots appeared under her fingernail. "It requires an out of town agency," she said confidentially tapping the finger, "because the world is changing, it's changing more rapidly than anyone would ever believe and we intend to be there when it arrives."

Rand watched the woman as she spoke, nodding occasionally to assure her he was hanging on every word, but did not want to follow too closely because the details were never as important as their sum. He perceived himself as a creative thinker preferring to absorb information in his own way until he attained a complete conceptual understanding. Then anything was possible. The bane of his life was people who were obsessed with the minutiae while, in his opinion, missing the big picture. It was flying with closed eyes.

"We've both read your initial briefs..." Rand deferred to Ashford who nodded acquiescence from under hooded eyes, "and fully understand the scope of your plans."

A strong woman. Resilient. Her voice was husky. Her eyes a rich brown. Her skin was lush with the pure, milk fed glow of a farm girl; her thick, wavy brown hair sprouting abundantly like alfalfa or the wheat that Rand remembered seeing when he was a child rushing off to the horizon a yellow blaze in all directions as the hand of the wind rolled over it. A sea of grass. There was a wholesome look to her that did not suit the spirit that raged inside and the only evidence something was askew was the fact that her clothes were ill fitting. A symptom. It wasn't from the anomalies of the body that had blessed some with one arm slightly shorter than the other or a shoulder that rose higher, or a hip that was not quite right... she was imbued with a near perfect symmetry and an animal like grace she was not even aware of. *Carelessness*, Rand thought, *she doesn't pay attention.*

Three weeks ago Ashford had abruptly pulled him into his private office and sat him down on the red leather couch that was draped with a Navajo weaving from the 1880s. The entire room was paneled in rose wood and every inch burnished to a liquid patina by hand. One wall was glass and framed a panoramic vista of lush, green, rolling hills at the edge where the city eclipsed the exclusive residential sections. One wall was law books. The remainder of the room was cluttered with artifacts reflecting his love of the West. Anasazi pot shards, Hohokem and Mogollan baskets. There were Brightly colored Germantown rugs from Navajoland and rare Chief's blankets that were worth over a hundred thousand dollars each and which he had out bid a museum in order to possess. An enormous, round oak table filled the center of the space. It sat on a huge central post supported by four extended legs each with the paw of a lion carved into it clasping a brass ball. Ash was excited, grinning and agitated at the same time and could not stand still. Rand listened while he nervously paced.

"Care for a cigar?" He inquired with an anxious distraction.

"No." Rand replied, "I don't..."

"You must." Ash insisted shoving a long, black gnarled stick into his face. "It's a genuine Cuban Maduro, a Cohiba. Very rare. Vintage. Mild and sweet, yet with a bite and just the right amount of spice." He struck the flame of the lighter while Rand awkwardly puffed to get it lit. "Fidel Castro smoked this brand, before he quit."

The thick and humid smoke filled his mouth and he was careful not to inhale. It was rich and nut like and made him dizzy. "Great," he said weakly, "really...pretty good."

"I'm..." Ash puffed up his chest and wagged his head back and forth a couple times searching for the right words, "extremely excited at this moment." He lit his own cigar.

"Yes," Rand replied sitting back on the couch in his shirtsleeves, suspenders and the Italian silk neck tie he had just bought, "I can see that."

"We've got some new business...and it's very exciting."

"What is it...?"

"I say that because it isn't just some new business, it's the new business and we are poised, just now, to ride it into the new economy, the new century!"

"Congratulations..."

"Having said that," his face suddenly worried, "it is a gamble, but..."

"OK. Alright. I'm dying. Tell me what it is."

The man turned to Rand bursting with energy yet living with the seed of an idea so new to him that he was unable to clarify it enough in his own mind to put it into words. "You see it's not the money. I don't give a goddamn for money. It's something else."

"Alright, what?" Rand said anxious for the point.

He raised his index finger before his face and silently counted out several tense beats. "Success is coincidence." He said. "It just happens in the same way that bad things happen to good people. The only reason is coincidence. The right place, the right time, all that."

"Ash! I'm working pretty hard you know, I mean to hear this. Are you telling me that it doesn't matter?"

"It matters. But everybody's working hard. Real success is what I'm talking about. Power. Why do some get it and some don't even though they're equal? Not everyone can win. It just comes without warning, steals into your life and seduces you before there's any time to understand it or fully encompass its magic." Ash paused holding his breath and pointed at him. "It comes on quiet footsteps."

"Look, this must be *some* business and now you've really got me interested! Come on, tell me!"

"Once you've had it you can't continue without it...living loses its juice. I've been on a roll most of my life but these past few years the world's passed me. I admit it, it's all in the hands of a different generation...and I don't recognize them."

"I understand." Rand listened and tried to follow the elliptical conversation suddenly realizing that it was some sort of confession, a clearing of the soul he was witnessing.

"I'm back on the cutting edge." Ash said brashly.

"The new business?"

"That's right," he turned to the window puffing on his cigar absently sending up plumes of white smoke and making the tip glow red. "We are going to play an integral part in the transformation of the world as we know it. And I, for one, feel that this last act before I retire will be what I am remembered for. It's a visionary undertaking."

"You'll never retire, but now you've got me excited and I don't have the slightest idea what you're talking about."

"The Interactive Satellite Consortium." The gray haired man stated with a profound finality.

"Didn't I read something about that in the Times...?" Rand frowned trying to recall. "What the hell was it now..."

It's still merger and acquisitions." He asserted betraying some private inner joke he was urgently trying to share. "Basic. In all the complexity of all the universe it still comes down to basics. The fucking world didn't pass me by!" He snarled belligerently. "They just use different words, semantics...all fucking semantics."

"Wasn't that the forming of the new communications conglomerate?"

"Yes." Ashford answered unexpectedly all business. "It's very confidential and as you become more involved you'll see why. I want you to head the team, with myself of course...but you, it's an exciting project."

"Tell me more." Rand said thrilling at the prospect of huge amounts of money.

Ash explained that for years the television and Internet industries had been grappling with the physical limitations of transmitting

44

high-end video communications both ways. "Even optical line has too small a bandwidth for all the information to flow with the immediacy for true interactivity to be commercially viable. They can send video down the line, but can't send the same amount of data up. So real personal interaction has been impossible." Now, something had changed. A small high technology company in Bangor Maine had made a breakthrough in compression technology. It was based on a chaos theory that was espoused by a radical, young quantum physicist who, in turn, had developed a new theoretical mathematics rooted in ones and zeros as traditional math, but also based on a variable that was a third type of element. It was not a theoretical variable as in algebra, but a new particle in the quantum universe. He first demonstrated it by calculating a series of pre-determined curves where the bends in the lines were not interpolations extracted from the fixed points between straight lines as in traditional mathematics, but actual curved and fluctuating points in space. It proved out as if a layer in the universe had been peeled back and the inner workings exposed.

"This is all highly confidential," Ash confided to Rand in a slightly sinister manner, " I've signed a personal bond."

"You mean we've already accepted the business?"

"Not two hours ago." He went on to explain that by using this entirely new premise for relational mathematics the problem of compression ratios for transmitting high capacity video and sound both down and uploading was solved. But the exciting part was what followed. A new wavelength was discovered to exist coincidentally with the new particle. There was almost zero resistance in the real world and the degree that it slowed or lost energy was negligible.

"That is really fantastic! But, what the hell does it mean to a person like me for instance?"

"It means that cable, even optical, as the world knows it, is essentially obsolete. And this new technology will take its place. It will change the world. The ISC, Interactive Satellite Consortium, plans a massive global blanketing utilizing low orbit satellites to broadcast this digital signal to all parts of the planet. You see don't you, in a stroke the old world is gone and the new one is here. Television signals along with computer networks and voice and video phone all will transmit with the same technology. No wires. They have the patents on it, a partnership with a national cable network, a regional phone company, a satellite division of an aerospace giant and the small high technology firm in Bangor Maine."

"How do we fit in?" Rand asked.

"We have been retained to, in a word, make it work. There are massive obstacles, legal issues involving the monopoly it will create, the liquidation of subsidiary holdings, and financing. It will cost billions and very quickly too. The older man gloated with the fifty dollar cigar clenched between his teeth feeling the strength of purpose flowing through him. "I'm back!"

The restaurant had been chosen as a neutral ground. Less intimidating than the cavernous conference room at Van Riper, Hazeltine & Brock and more intimate than the temporary corporate offices of ISC.

"Speaking for myself," Rand continued, "it's a pretty aggressive program."

"The real problems may come from anti-trust actions," Veronique brusquely added, "as soon as the government gets wind of it."

Gordon smiled. "We don't intend to go public until the first units are up."

"You mean you're not going to file with the FCC?" Rand asked.

"Of course not," she paused a moment, hesitantly looking at Ashford, then at Gordon. "This is client privileged...?"

"Certainly." Ash bluntly replied casting a cold eye at Rand.

"...not until everything is in place." Veronique continued. "This is revolutionary technology. We can't give anything away." Astonished that the question had come up. "You must know billions are at stake." Then, before Rand could respond she smiled seductively, showing emotion for the first time, "We have complete faith in you despite any misgivings that may have been expressed."

"It's plain enough the communications market is changing rapidly and we're on the edge of it." The older man watched Rand's eyes become bright and clear, and felt sad. There wasn't a moment of hesitation to his greed he thought, and though his own equaled it, perhaps surpassed it, the two faces before him were a reflection of himself he did not like. In a year he would be able to retire to his lodge in the Adirondacks, as he had wanted to do for most of his time in the business world. He would be rich beyond all expectation. "It will mean sacrificing the subsidiaries and substantial job loss, but in the main a new industry will be created that will more than make up for it. That's where we will get political support." At some undefined moment during his life that was passed without the slightest pause he had concluded that the myth of money being the root of social evils had its origin with the rich in a effort to minimize the competition and that he had been deluded through his prime earning years. So he pursued money now as if possessed even though it defied his own perception of what was right and what was wrong. All that was left was a log house in the mountains filled with simple treasures he had not had the opportunity to enjoy yet even though his time on earth was almost over.

Rand shook the thin white hand of the woman who gripped him firmly and aggressively and the thick pudgy hand of the old man who lingered for no reason and left a ten dollar tip on the table, which was recovered by brown hands, invisible hands…"*Borracho gringos!*"

BRUSHSTROKES IN THE MIST

IV

The moment when he had decided to kill the man was obscured by ephemeral flights of genius. The thought simply appeared. It was perhaps one of the few human qualities left in what otherwise was a shell encompassing a virtual personality. A persona beautified by evolution and deified by every smooth faced, clear eyed young lion that ever thrilled to the sensation of electronic technology. He had been told he was a genius since he was old enough to remember, and finally began to believe it.

His was a quantum universe, a place of desolation where the qualities that distinguished a living being from a theoretical ghost had been replaced by invented ideas. Chimeras. Somewhere in time the false eventually displaced the true. For a while he lost all bearing completely and drifted bedazzled yet confused awed by the power of science, absolutely baffled at where to direct it. Then slowly he began to replace his once existing values and eventually rebuilt a relationship to the world realizing that life was completely under his control. The mind could be programmed just like any computer. Even his. And so it happened that the question of human life came up to be compared against the multitude of other datums he had amassed, which had proven themselves out making a material world more malleable, functional and had provided him with great financial rewards. The conclusion that life was just one variable in a universal cauldron to which he had found the key and had resulted in such wonders as digital television, tablet computers and robotic production lines that made people unnecessary and spared them the drudgery of work would not, he knew, be a popular sentiment. He kept it to himself. A human life was an expendable component no more or less important than any other component in any given situation. Function was everything. If it worked, it was true. Engineering, he decided, was the fundamental philosophy and chided himself for not having the insight before.

The simplicity of weeding out the unworkable provided him with a God-like transcendence over the mundane goings on of living that polished off his universal disdain for the mob and served to enhance his reputation as a young, eccentric genius riding on the edge of the new millennium. Homo novis, new man, inhabitant of the twenty-first century. All that had come before was obsolete. Derian Baxter decreed it so.

Under the hot lights his inner fumings became more restive. He found himself thrust into a situation where he had to communicate with obviously inferior beings and could not retreat into his own thoughts. A microphone swooped down from the dark reaches of the ceiling and hovered above him out of camera. The mainstream beckoned.

"Bax...do you mind if I call you Bax?" The blonde newswoman's effervescence bubbled up contagiously. She was not pretty but possessed of a near perfect symmetry; even her teeth were a mirror image from one side of her smile to the other.

"All my friends call me Bax." He confided. "I only make lawyers call me by my full name." To his surprise the studio audience laughed. His publicist had set up the interview, his psychiatrist had advised him to place himself into public situations in order to get a grip. He had told Derian he was detached from reality, at which point the man was fired and sued for malpractice.

"Bax, it's no secret that your picture has been on the cover of probably every business magazine at least once this last year. Isn't that right? You've been touted as the genius," making double quotation signs in the air with her pink, wiggling fingers, "behind the season's most successful blockbuster computer game, *Pax Nemisis*...and head of what has been described as an upstart technology company viewed by your own industry as a threat to the entrenched powers-that-be. What do you say to that?"

"We don't really pay much attention." He replied clenching his teeth into a smile. "It's a very close community. Everyone in the business is committed to the promise of technology and are supportive and as excited by others' discoveries as if they were their own. It spurs us all on." He smiled impassively. "The fact is we just came up with some proprietary technology as a result of our experience with the military, which explains the hyper-realism achieved, and as you know we worked with an industry giant Lenor Croft and Croft Systems in the development and marketing of *Pax Nemisis*." Bax started to feel a fullness of self.

"She is one of the wealthiest people in the world. And a woman. Tell me, did that intimidate you?"

A heat flush raced across him and he began to sweat causing little water blisters to form beneath the heavy pancake makeup. "No Sarah, not at all." The turmoil that was constantly boiling around him came instantly alive.

"What was it like working with her?" The newswoman asked with agitated electricity suddenly in her eyes. "Personally I mean, up close. She is certainly amazing, didn't you find her so?"

"Well, of course Sarah, but we really..."

"Come on, there must be something you can tell us about your experience with her?"

The fury that followed could not be explained in mere language, but was masterfully controlled the way his former psychiatrist had taught him so that he would be able to fit in. The idea that he was always in somebody's shadow infuriated him. Over the years he had watched colleagues become millionaires, and a few become billionaires while he languished wasting brilliant and innovative technology on the military for the sake of a steady income. It was lawyers, all lawyers he decided. They held the world by the balls. *Pax Nemisis* was the first real money he'd tasted, and now he couldn't do without it. Before the mediocre had surpassed him by some existential quirk of fate that he attributed to the dull nature of the mob, but now he was ascending to the prominence he deserved. So, biting his tongue to maintain an even keel he cordially related some brief anecdotes of working with Croft, a hellish she-bitch if he'd ever met one, and then began telling lies about his company, LYNX, as well. Bax wasn't about to reveal anything essential. Some things were better unknown. PR had little to do with the truth.

LYNX, a small privately owned high-tech firm, had been one of the fastest rising industry stars of the decade. Founded by Derian Baxter and two other brilliant engineers who had spent their entire academic careers specializing in digital broadcasting and computer imagery. When the military had approached them offering handsome financing they jumped at it without fully understanding what was to be required of them. However, what the government wanted was encrypted, high resolution earth imaging systems that would effectively increase their viewing of satellite earth images from its ten meter resolution, about close enough to view a whole city from space, to substantially smaller than a one meter resolution, which would give details of an area less than a city block. Since its inception government contracts had sustained it and for ten years the men were able to research and produce startling results without having to deal with the pressures of commercial marketing and sales or even compromising much. All that changed with the volatile political environment spurned to stringent economizing by a deep recession. Government cut backs hit them immediately and the satellite business was the first to go.

With the imminent collapse of the company and all their amassed research of the past decade in jeopardy the company's principals hit the streets like door-to-door salesmen trying to discover a market they could create and sell a product in that would put their expertise to use. All avenues seemed closed. There were simply no markets available. Just when things were at their bleakest point and even the building had been put on the market, Gordon Dahlquest entered the picture.

He was a phone company veteran and had been instrumental in piloting the drive for all digital communications resulting in the re-cabling of worldwide systems to accommodate optical technology. Recently he had been working on mergers of cable and telecommunications companies hoping for an industry boom. After the first cable-phone company interactive television project failed in its test market, he redirected his efforts as a result of what he had learned during the experience. The technical problem that could not be overcome, even with the new broadband optical cables, was the fact that the pipe was still too small for audio, video plus computer and communications services to go down all at once and allow for any sort of user communication or interaction coming back up the line. Satellite technology didn't have this problem, theoretically. It had possibilities that intrigued him, but the insurmountable limitation of ever being able to compress so much information to easily transmit while encrypting it to prohibit unauthorized access and further to allow user communications and interaction made it only science fiction.

Then he discovered LYNX. The small, distressed company was desperately seeking SEC approval to go public in an effort to fund their troubled forays into the commercial market. He called Derian Baxter on a Saturday night, and by mid afternoon Sunday the man had flown to New York and they met. The meeting left Dahlquest reeling with euphoria at the possibilities. Monday morning he flew to Bangor, Maine for a demonstration of the High Resolution Imagery technology, which they provided by a still maintained connection to the military satellites the government had lost interest in. By that afternoon a new idea had taken shape, Gordon Dahlquest was about to become an entrepreneur. The leap from where they were with the image compression and resolution enhancement to fully interactive video was conceivable; it was because of new technology as revolutionary as the first telephone had been. By Monday evening his lawyers had drafted preliminary contracts and at midnight they were signed.

Veronique was approached by Gordon at an industry forum on digital broadcasting and she recognized fate instantly. The advanced nature of the new technology and the fact that it would reach every corner of the planet making it universally and easily accessible brought her on board. The triad formed a pact of secrecy. No nonessential person would be privileged to this enterprise until they approached the Federal Communications Commission for license. All three parties signed mutually payable bonds, and contracted to the terms.

Money had come and Lynx had been resurrected, but the funding had not moved along as fast as had been promised in the beginning when the three principals had eagerly, avariciously signed away their complete rights to the technology. Derian Baxter had bills he could not pay despite lucrative royalties from his game *Pax Nemisis*.

The limousine absorbed him at the studio entrance the moment the broadcast was complete. He welcomed the respite from the real as the lone occupant of a cavernous rear seat. In the subdued quiet he began to regain his private thoughts and poured himself a short single malt from a cut crystal decanter sitting in the small rosewood bar. It was a taste he'd acquired with the first influx of real money. He was worried someone else knew, someone outside the pact. It would of course diversify the wealth he expected for himself and that he could not allow. He considered filing suit and cashing in for the millions he could get for breach of contract, but opted for the probable billions when the deal went through with ISC.

The lawyer had to die. It was obvious. It seemed predestined; as he had known all along someone would have to die for this much money. The thought just appeared. He would remove the unworkable. Simple. "I want complete, detailed surveillance maintained on that lawyer, the one from Van Riper, Hazeltine & Brock." He spoke measurably into the satellite phone, "I don't think we can trust him. You know the one. His name is Randall DesVergers."

It was a rare, brisk few days at the end of March. Life was thundering forth under fingers of cirrus clouds raked by cold, blustering gusts that swept the chasms of the city and the wastes of the great Mojave Desert in one long low pass over the earth. The native chaparral spread tough skinned and motionless across the hills inured to sun and wind. Its intoxicating scent ranged far from its rooted home.

Geraniums spoke of crimsons, peach and fuchsia. Daylilies, tulips and bearded irises made their annual appearance beneath the dogwood, oak, ficus, poplar and flowering trees whose names nobody knew or could easily remember. None of them were aboriginal and like most inhabitants of Los Angeles had been transplanted in hope.

The Team sat quietly. They marveled at the panoramic view out the floor to ceiling windows of the office that stretched from across the Hollywood Hills and the Santa Monica mountains to the Pacific Ocean, where on an exceptionally clear day one could imagine seeing the Channel Islands shimmering off Santa Barbara. They assembled within moments coffee sloshing from their cups, clipboards, notepads, loud suspenders, white shirts, short skirts, neckties and herringbone worsted jackets. It was a representation of some of the finest law schools in the country. Intellectual thoroughbreds. Rand had not looked up as they entered but sat engrossed in a file that rested in his lap. He always wore his coat at the office, even on the hottest days when the air conditioning strained to keep the artificial environment in delicate balance between the heat beating down on the glass walls of the hi-rise and the needs of hundreds of people inside to never, under any circumstance, perspire while working. The cost was enormous. He tossed the file on the desk when the small assembled group had become still and it was so quiet he heard the sound of a brief spring shower pattering on the window.

"Very interesting..." he said raising a cocked index finger to his lips resting the crook of his thumb on his chin, "very interesting." Visions of the dark haired woman invaded every effort he made at concentration and the whole time he had been gazing at the file was filled with reveries about the rendezvous he had managed to arrange with her under the guise of friendly legal advice. She had been the complete object of his thoughts for weeks. He had breathed in her scent and became entranced, compelled to have her out of some dark, enturbulated desire that swirled around him and made it difficult to sleep. His intention was to avoid pressure and give an excuse for her husband. He didn't feel good about it, but would do it anyway. The arrogant toss of the brief on the desk was self assured enough, though he knew something was terribly wrong in his life. His confidence was eroding. Files had begun to stack up on his desk. Messages clogged his voice mail and the electronic box on the office's computer network ceased to accept new ones as it had achieved its maximal limit according to some anonymous virtual god who had programmed it that way on a whim. He came in late, which no one noticed because of the fact he had always come and gone on his own schedule and it was assumed he had worked the night before. Besides, he was a partner responsible for so much income that as long as it came in there was little interest what his personal timetable was, but in fact he had fallen to habit.

Out the window he had searched the green hills for mansions of the very rich that lie nestled among the trees. He could see their roofs; gabled, red tiled, flat, shingled, and imagined what lives might be in the balance beneath them. It gave him immense pleasure on the thirty-third floor of his glass tower to be able to peer into the back yards of the elite.

"We need to identify the fundamental issue here." He spoke suddenly focusing in. The project, he explained, was difficult because of the existing business climate and the fact of a liberal administration, which some said gave the courts a more populist view, "...but as we all know," he added acerbically, "the law is a system untainted by the desires of men. Therefore, we must prepare an agenda that parallels related precedent cases and so...I've compiled an overview of the ICS project to bring you all up to speed."

Books lined one entire wall floor to ceiling for nearly thirty feet. They were overwhelmingly the focal point of the room. Bindings, some old and others contemporary, glared down in dark leather, cloth, embossed, gold leaf and stamped designs. The rich Italian furniture, whose dramatic and sweeping lines sated the aesthetic senses with a sublime pleasure, was only an accent. They reflected an earlier incarnation of Randall DesVergers. A time when things were more clearly seen. The effect of the wall of books was that it muted the resonance of voices so people tended to speak either more loudly than usual or, feeling the air rarefied as in a library, more softly.

In dim memory Rand had pursued an illusive ideal that he imagined to be the one fundamental and terrible element upon which all justice could be based. It was the same beckoning whisper that other legal thinkers had chased until their breath ran out. They strove to develop a government of laws and not of men, one that would hover above the weary, bickering people and dole out impartial judgments based on axiomatic law and not interpretation. Human beings, after all, had proven throughout history they could not be trusted with the rendering of natural law as it applied to actual life since the basis of legalism was commonly agreed to be the *Law of Nature and it's Author.* What man could presume to be God? Especially so in this great experiment in a free society whose avowed purpose was to escape now and forever the plague of tyranny. It was to have been autonomous to the whims of vested interest, this Law, and contain an air of inevitability about legal decisions.

A tattered volume of Aristotle's *Politics,* which he had bought used in a college bookstore while in his first year of law school, stood next to revolutionary writings of the British Chief Justice Lord Mansfield on conceptions of general jurisprudence as an embodiment of law dating from the 1760s and nearly a century before the real codification movement began. A first edition of Blackstone's *Commentaries* with its daring scientific approach to the law of property before legal contracts were recognized by the courts resided quietly close by having had its time. He had amassed every 19th century legal text in existence, supplemented by the hundreds of handwritten precedent books circulated by legal writers after the Revolutionary War in an effort to more precisely define American law as opposed to British law. Professor Adam Smith's *Wealth Of Nations* bellied up to Joseph Story's *Book of Pleadings* of 1805 in which he postulated a split between private and public law opinions. Kent's *Commentaries* sat with Nathan Dane's *Abridgment* from 1823, which not only insisted upon a separation between law and politics, but between law and morality as well in a futile effort to render sanity to the decision making process. Francis Hillard's *The Law of Torts* of 1859 leaned against a series of fat volumes by Oliver Wendall Holmes Jr., the masterpiece of which was *The Common Law,* 1870, written when he was still a young man.

It was while reading this book that something quite out of his control happened to Rand, something he thereafter attributed to the terrible chimera he had been hunting whose face he imagined leered at him from out of those pages at that instant and caused him to alter his perception of the law and therefore his purpose in life. Until that point he had conceived of Law as paternalistic, protective of rights and above all an expression of the moral sense of the community. There was a passage in that book, though it had been long overshadowed in Rand's memory, which at the time he read it had a profound and lasting effect of him. *"...the law only works within the sphere of the senses. The external phenomena, the manifest acts and omissions. It is wholly indifferent to the internal phenomena of conscience."* The change began. At first he simply could not think with the concept, and then became morose, demoralized and rarely left his rooms except for classes, and then sometimes he would skip telling himself he was ill, or not well rested and could not concentrate anyway. He found that there were omissions in his memory after study and had to work twice as hard as before to retain and make sense of information. Finally though, the new mindset began to take hold. He gradually perceived the Law as merely an instrument of individual desires, simply a reflection of current economic and social powers. It settled in. He became comfortable with the understanding. Perhaps, he mused, it had been a misconception from the start, blind adolescent idealism that thankfully had been corrected.

From that moment on Randall DesVergers felt abandoned by God.

To separate law from morality and conscience had been inconceivable to Rand and so when the alien concept washed over him it corroded his veneer of idealism until it reached the raw essence. The basic urge. Survival. It took him the remainder of his legal education to come to grips with it. He saw things differently in the end and so managed to blend seamlessly when he had been hired by Van Riper, Hazeltine & Brock, who had each learned the same lesson a generation earlier.

An ash blonde woman with long lustrous hair sat directly across from Rand's desk and fidgeted nervously. She drummed the lean, perfectly, manicured fingers of her right hand upon the taupe wool interleave of the couch's arm at the end she had appropriated for her exclusive use during the meeting. There were pens and notebooks and a purse between her own person and that of the young, muscular, sweating man named Mace who occupied the other end. The perfect harmony of her face was alarming, her features sculpted with mathematical perfection as if all the measurements for beauty had been averaged out to create the ideal yet having omitted the one ephemeral quality that gave a person warmth. Cynthia was cold. Her demeanor was like polished marble. Alabaster. Her skin was impossibly smooth, free of any observable blemishes and cream white contrasting with her rubine lipstick, which matched the color of her nails. The nearly turquoise eyes shot racing glances out across the room in fleeting bursts never landing in one place for very long. "Lyle," she erupted unable to keep her energy contained, "How does it feel to be a living extension of tradition this morning?" She said while she straightened the jacket of her mocha white silk suit under which she enticingly wore nothing at all, and tugged annoyingly at the hem of her skirt.

The pale man in a chair to the right with short dark hair swept back off his forehead continued reading the ISC outline and making rapid notations in his tablet. "Personally," he rejoined immediately, "I feel like a legend."

In one of two chairs against the glass Bill Ruskin sat. He had lost nearly all the hair on the top of his head and as a symbol of his rebellion against the toll of the body he wore what remained cropped perilously close to the scalp that he kept very tan. "So, what are we talking about?" He exclaimed loudly scanning the document he had been given.

"Power, Bill." Mace replied from the couch next to Cynthia and held up the papers in his fist letting them imagine that he was flexing his well developed arm under the gray suit. "It was inevitable...social Darwinism."

"...oh Christ." Cynthia muttered under her breath and held her face between thumb and forefingers as she attempted to concentrate on the documents. "You learn that at the gym?" The young man just smiled and clenched his teeth.

"Ashford feels very strongly about this project," Rand offered. "In fact, he thinks its the firm's link into the next century."

"What happened to this one?" interjected Morgan wearily from the corner chair where the glass wall met bookshelves. He spoke quietly from behind thick, black rimmed glasses, hushed and studious. "I can't even catch up with my own thoughts…next century?"

"Here's the deal," continued Rand, "in a nutshell here it is, ISC is poised to render the cable television industry obsolete within a year of full financing. Obsolete."

"That's hard to believe," said Lyle, "after all, it's not necessarily the quality of product that determines share, it's who saturates the market first. Cable's here…" he shrugged.

"Rand's right." Naomi replied. She sat alone at the right hand side of the desk. Isolated by an air of inevitability that imbued her immediate space and made her seem stoic or terribly brave depending on who perceived it and what their state of mind was at the moment. She had taken control of that particular chair and no one else presumed to sit there even if she came late because Naomi had officially assumed responsibility for answering phones during gatherings and took minutes out of habit distributing conference reports to everyone the day following a meeting. "When I represented the National Association of Broadcasters it was pretty clear, even then, what direction the technology was taking. High definition TV was just the first phase…everything went digital and every station in America's invested in new equipment…but this," she held up the prospectus, "it's geometric progression…they just leapt years ahead of any competition. Nothing stays the same and the fact is that the industry was pressured by other economic forces to expand or relinquish some of their free public resources. We're singularly helping to form ISC's constitution and secure their initial funding." She shook her head, "It's the beginning of an industry with our firm on the ground floor." Then, after a pause, she added, "Nothing stays the same."

"So," Cynthia commented her fingers kneading the air absently next to her lips still watching Naomi, who she admired secretly for the wholesome richness that was missing in her own make up, "what about that new car Randall? The silver one or the blue one?" Everyone laughed in tight little exhalations that relieved the pressure while still preserving the tension that was so essential to their profession. It lie coiled up inside, a nurtured presence that prevented any one of them from relaxing too completely in fear they may never again attain the edge, for that was what kept them alive.

"I haven't made up my mind."

"You're going to do it aren't you?"

"Well..." He replied equivocally.

Rand swiveled in his chair to look out the window behind him. The automobile had been an obsession among his many obsessions for months. From the moment he had seen its pearlescent finish gleaming under the showroom lights he had desired it in the way he wanted a woman; a determined, dogged relentless way that always overcame him in the end regardless of its rightness or wrongness. It was the act that was important. Without it he could not exist. In its essence was his only brush with a true sense of being alive. There was a thrill and a danger to it, like touching belladonna to one's lips to see what the effects might be. The automobile was extravagant, if ninety-six thousand dollars for transportation could be called excessive. It was far more than he had ever thought he should spend and could easily remember shunting the price of a car off into the realm of the unimportant, the material and transitory having set a limit on what he felt was equitable in the world. Somewhere along the line a weakness had crept in and began to work on his life and desire had replaced prudence in many areas.

"...teal is actually my favorite color."

"This is great." Mace said studiously his attention fixed on the paperwork in hand. "Very exciting." The man was sweating as if he had just puffed up some stairs. It was a purifying sheen that made his short but thick sandy hair stand up and glisten and was the result of an unholy adherence to the cult of the body which had occupied all his spare time since he was a young child. It was from this primal instinct that his strong sense of justice grew. He believed deeply in the "invisible hand" of a self regulating market. The natural and impartial economic laws that evolved out of the desperate struggle to survive and which must, by their essence, remain free from the intervention of any political influence.

"Teal...?" Lyle puzzled.

Rand slowly washed his gaze across the desk at the comment focusing in on the young man with a mildly amused glint in his eye yet feeling unsettled. "I'm...still just thinking...haven't decided."

"Government accountants will have a field day with this." With her darting eyes trailing the contours of Mace's body, which was athletically draped across the opposite end of the couch from her, Cynthia absorbed the sensation of its closeness and could smell the musky faint odor of locker rooms he carried around with him letting it reach a nerve and convey the titillation to the ends of her fingers. She felt disdain for him yet wondered at the great biological force he possessed that impressed itself upon her whether she wanted it or not. The curse. She resisted it and it caused her to become antagonistic, and to desire it against her will. "I can name at least two dozen potential tax and fee structures that would hobble the operation even before it went to the FCC."

"Exactly!" Rand exclaimed. "Which is why I want you to address those concerns, Cynthia?"

"Think jobs...new industries, state contracts with tax incentive zones..."

"Appears...correct me if I'm misreading, were in business here to eliminate jobs. From first glance, lots of them." Morgan didn't seem to belong in the group. He was slightly rumpled, his clothing was not as stylish and was thrown together in a perfunctory way covering all the basic points; light weight gabardine English cut suit with a three harness weave, a two-button double breasted jacket with slightly peaked lapels, double pleated slacks, the ubiquitous white shirt and a striped tie. He had never learned to tie a Windsor knot and so it always hung a little loose at the collar in a bulky, equilateral triangle.

"Redistribute the wealth...why not?" Mace injected as if he was waiting for the comment.

"I just don't think it's proper logic as a strategy."

"Point taken." Rand said dryly. "ISC hasn't really provided statistics, but they implied the industrial base required to support the satellite system would absorb most of the displaced..."

"It's not really our business is it?" Lyle added impatient with ideological details. "We're simply instruments."

"We're talkin' a few jobs, "Bill Russel butted in, "some reeducation...job training, no big deal these days." Inadvertently in his mind he pictured the sprawling, shaded ranch house he owned outright just north of the city that included fifteen acres of grassland dotted by oaks, clumps of chaparral and a spring fed pond. He thought warmly of his wife, Clara, who plodded around barefoot spending much of her time near the swimming pool with his two children, aged four and six, or exercising one of their two horses. During warm summer days he loved to go out and sit in the shade of the massive cluster of Blue Palo Verde and Mesquite by the pond, which he had stocked with Texas bullfrogs, because it reminded him of where he had grown up and come of age near Houston. It was a closed community and that always gave him a sense of security. No one could drive down Bill Russel's road without passing through the guarded gates. He was proud of that. "What the hell. It's progress...things always work out."

"Yea, like in the farm industry..." Morgan uttered covertly half under his breath.

"What's that?"

"Nothing...nothing."

"Part of FCC concerns with High Definition TV, then digital, was the ability of the television industry to cope with the rapid change. Economically." Naomi said. "The stations had to lobby as a group to keep from being forced to buy into the new technology before they could afford it. The solution was a sort of an ecological approach to the new era, a gradient curve."

"We're not informing the FCC." Cynthia replied blandly reading the papers.

"Nor the Securities and Exchange Commission..."

"Until we're ready." Rand intervened. "This is a one shot deal. Competition, according to the ISC, would drive up the costs so high it would delay implementation for maybe...twenty years. Our job is to develop a corporate coup, unanticipated and complete."

They all looked to each other. "I'm game." Said Cynthia.

"They will postulate a date at which point the planned actions will go into effect and each division must be perfectly realized with any opposition anticipated and allowed for."

"It pivots on complete financing," Morgan leafed quickly through the brief, "looks like anyway."

"That's it. We landed this account not only because of our experience, but...'

"We've got something they want." Lyle interjected acerbically tossing down the papers.

Bright young lawyers, Rand thought, were a pain in the ass sometimes. "Yes..."

"Let me guess..." Lyle continued undaunted, "in a word, Veloso."

Only Cynthia appreciated his insidious humor. "You're so cunning."

A sullenness suddenly hung over the room. Each person was restless. Veloso. They all knew the name. The enigmatic South American billionaire who had retained the firm to channel his investments wisely, as it had been stated two years ago in the memorandum when the firm had acquired the client. He had not wanted money managers, or investment bankers because he had emphasized, when he retained Van Riper, Hazeltine & Brock, the importance of moral decisions concerning the investment of his money, which was conservatively estimated to be around eighteen billion. Valdemiro Veloso explained passionately and with humility that coming from Brazil, a poor country, he was tremendously burdened by his wealth and this sense of responsibility must be followed by the investment of his capital where its use would be unimpeachable and could provide not only adequate returns, but pride in the need it was filling. Valdemiro Veloso was in tune with the needs of men. Of course, nobody except Ashford Van Riper knew all the details and only a few of the firm had actually met with the import export magnate as he never came to the United States and would periodically summon one or more of the staff to Rio for a conference about his accounts. There were, however, rumors.

The rule of law, he vividly recalled the old man wheezing through his teeth, *has not come from logic, but from experience. It is the social theology that allows men to live with men in a free society. Without it, we are lost. It is a reflection of the American Society. Whatever greatness we may obtain is because of it.* On cold winter days he would crowd into the stuffy, over heated lecture room with a hundred other eager listeners rapacious for this new religion of the law being meted out in measured units by Arnold Blaustein a professor of legal history. He was a man who by all rights should have passed long before then, but had held out for a better contract. He was of an earlier century and embodied values and notions of life that had come, been consumed by the voracity of events that surround us and had moved silently on as a tide race yet lingered still in his reality. Professor Blaustein's watery eyes narrowed when he spoke and he became possessed of a spirit that in others had been wicked away somewhere over Europe and somewhere over Asia at the same instant sometime during the Second World War. He spoke and his words were drunk in like cool water.

If one looked for a reason to define his value it lie in the fact that the man remained unmoved as the world had reeled under the fist of tyranny. For the third time since the fall of democracy in Germany during the 1880s had the four horsemen been resurrected in boiling rage this time determined on the final cataclysm. Then, when it was over, and silent eyes were closed never again to grasp the light of day and the tears of the fallen ran in the Rhine and the Danube and the Seine and the Themes until they mingled and were washed beyond by the oceans mighty benevolence saying go away now and sin no more... he was unmoved. For the unknown casualty was in the place where the heart and the mind collide to form the ideas which are then transferred father to son in the great oral tradition down the ages across the spans of endless generations and into the unknown. Men questioned. They introspected and examined. They raked the principles until they were raw, until they bled, they suffered unto themselves the responsibilities forsaken by others. They assumed the evil as a puzzle of logic. The one overwhelming issue that occupied the intellectual community was how it could have happened? Was it the lack of values or the enforcement of values that gave rise to totalitarianism? Was it essential in the nature of the arts and sciences as they had been taught? If so, how could they be changed? In the end by reason of questioning their own certainties the final casualty of the conflict was brought down. Values changed. Wisdom was lost. Yet Arnold Blaustein was unmoved for he possessed a stable datum upon which he rested such certainty he could not separate it from himself. He became an evangelist for *The Rule of Law.*

His suits were always of the old style woolen cloth that was much thicker than modern weaves and so hung differently, giving him a straighter more formal look. He was never seen without a shirt and tie and a vest, except on exceptionally cold days when he would wear a sleeveless sweater instead buttoned all the way up, under his coat. While the assembled students would be sweating in the forced steam heated room where the temperature was acerbated by the congregation of bodies, the professor would never exhibit the slightest look of discomfort and one could imagine the earlier generations stiffly going about their business in high, starched collars and heavy suiting during the hot, humid days of summer undeterred from their duty as men.

From those lectures there was the one thing that Randall knew absolutely. As a man one had certain inalienable duties. A personal responsibility. Failing in that someone else inevitably had to pick it up. The law had arisen out of the conflict of forsaken responsibilities. It was only many years later, after his disillusionment was nearly complete, as one by one the precepts he had learned as truths had been shattered that this understanding slipped his mind altogether. Only in dim memory did its echoes haunt him as a ghost of hope that lives in every man no matter how far he has traveled. Sitting with the young lawyers he remembered Arnold Blaustein.

The sea held its breath. Whispers accompanied the movements of the tides. Pelicans angled in for their silent landings whistling over the waves near the shore in formation clearing the crests and hollows by mere inches gliding on the magic by which they were able to fly for miles without moving their wings. Out on the borderline was a haze that concealed the dawn as yet not fully realized and water to sky changed from a muted, cerulean blue, where it was still occupied by the evensong, to a pale gray-green blue to a translucent bird's egg blue in one seamless stroke. There were no waves and the swell was so gentle as to be imperceptible to all but the eidolons of the deep who were old and had the skills for knowing such things that men somewhere had lost faith in. Seagulls cried. Salt air hung heavily. Far off in the ocean's center perhaps lay an essence that would make even the most disenfranchised person whole and was the reason some were drawn here. The waters cover the earth as living plasma in which not one drop is devoid of life and all creatures in it move to the same rhythm and the same law, to survive. Human beings are not that simple.

Rand spent the night on his boat Sojourner immersed in phantasms so complete that he had to struggle through them as if swimming in honey to awake. They were all encompassing and remained with him long after he rose and it was only with the help of three strong cups of coffee that he was able to break their spell at all. He had been driven to the sea. Something was wrong in his life and after the meeting in his office he had come straight to the boat for refuge.

In the quiet of the sea night it had almost come. In the clammy dampness where the stars rode restless across the sky. Resolution was almost realized. The massive weight that had been smothering him began to lift, silently and...it was almost there, so close its hot breath laid upon him. Epiphany. Understanding. Redemption. But it vanished then without a sign. No signal to go by. No clue. Into the mists, the muggy depths. No map was left to follow and he was as lost as before, maybe more so knowing that he had glimpsed the egress, but could not retrace the steps that brought him there. He emerged on deck into the perfect stillness and huddled under his jacket to keep warm. A humid pall hovered over the harbor and he breathed its breath tasting the mix of living things on land and those of the sea that made the air viscous and salty and set his gaze out over the wan, ochre haze of Los Angeles where the creatures of day were just coming to life while those of night had yet to fade away. He sensed the power and the thunder simmering in the sleeping metropolis its muted roar beginning to rise to the crescendo it reached each day by mid afternoon. It was the cusp of morning, the time in between, an interval which could not be called either night or day and for this reason he loved it and treasured the moments he found himself alone in it.

Los Angeles spread for a over a hundred miles in all directions, a raging torrent of ambition that long ago suffocated any hint of the wild as it surged forward a relentless tsunami swamping everything and everyone in its path. There was no flavor to it anymore. It had become all flavors heightened to their peak, taken to their extreme heat and forced over the edge until all that remained was a sensation so blinding that nothing of any distinction could be discerned. Borderlines were crossed. Race became devoured.

The art deco masterpiece of the Griffith Observatory resplendent in its occidental fluted stucco and oxidized brass fittings lorded down from the hills. It was a bastion of cultural idealism meant to inspire the teeming masses in the city below to recreate a golden age. It loomed over Western Avenue where once men of European ancestry struggled in the heat to create a boulevard of commerce that mirrored those in Cincinnati or Chicago or Detroit lined with furniture manufacturers, printing plants and retail stores. Later it had become a cauldron of races where all aspirations melted away into the limits of what was possible. Now within a ten mile stretch only a few words of English dotted the Hispanic landscape of carcenerias and discount stores; blending seamlessly into the Thai community where expatriates had settled in; which in turn faded into Koreatown where the gaudy, cloistered buildings hovered over the street with imposing oriental facades through the windows of which, on the second floors, groups of intent Korean business men could bee seen in mysterious meetings all wearing white shirts, black slacks and dark neck ties.

A thousand smells filled the air. Chili and oil, garlic and oil, ginger and oil...and the exhaust of diesel buses ferrying desperate, carless hoards to and from unknown destinations. The songs of languages resounding. Eighty or ninety different languages, a blur, a racing panoply of sights and sounds that baffled the most articulate and perceptive observer and drove those of weak moral character into a funk realizing the hopelessness of it all, the absolute nihilism of trying to survive against such overwhelming odds. In Los Angeles the world had outgrown itself, had become a parfait of cultures all sleeping and living on top of each other, existing and mingling with one another, each individual man hard put just to keep his own identity let alone any sense of cultural identity. Men slept with other men's dreams without complaint because it was better than where they had come from.

Randall DesVergers thought of none of these things. He looked out to the west, out over the great Pacific sea, the one direction that Los Angeles had not usurped in its uncontrolled fury except for a few off shore oil rigs to the north, which had only in recent years occasioned environmental alarm, and the scattering of a few tiny islands. Out there was the hint that something fundamental was missing, something so precious that he dared not ever speak about it to anybody for fear that even one slight transgression might cause it to vanish entirely. And he never did speak about it, but came to the ocean a pilgrim searching its fathoms for a reason to believe.

He bought the Sojourner the year he was made a partner at Van Riper, Hazeltine & Brock. She was a fifty-two foot sloop built in Hong Kong replicating a famous yacht of the 1930's designed by the renowned Danish craftsman Ejnar Ulrikson. Its fittings were modern as was its state-of-the-art satellite navigation system and computer operated radio, rigging and auto pilot, but its sleek, black hull was of another era. Most important it was a wooden boat with a solid teak deck and masts made from single trees felled in the Malaysian jungle. Everyone tried to dissuade him from buying a wooden boat, they were nothing but trouble he was informed, once a year in dry dock, scraping of hulls, caulking and recaulking...and in fact none were manufactured in the States anymore except custom work because the modern materials were so superior. However, it was undeniable that there was something about the feel of a natural substance beneath that drew a bond between man and the roiling sea that could not be ignored and every serious sailor secretly wished for the long, low wooden craft he saw occasionally glide by under the hand of some wealthy personage who had either restored the vessel or had purchased it as a symbol of protest against the loss of all things fine to technology. Rand flew to Hong Kong and spent a three week vacation visiting the boat yards in and around the peninsula and its islands. He had to have one.

The night he arrived an overloaded ferry on its evening run to Kowloon had been rammed by a Javanese freighter in Victoria Harbor and was slowly sinking after its huge aft doors sprung open and began dropping automobiles and people into the sea. The lights of rescue craft flared high into the night sky and were clearly visible from the plane as it made its approach to Hong Kong International, but it was Rand's first visit to the Orient and so the activity passed him by. Other thoughts occupied him and the sight was only one part of the panoply served up to his senses of which each element had equal importance. In the airport bar he stopped briefly to revive himself with a gin and tonic before moving on to the crush of the baggage claim area, where he assumed the wait would be interminable. The television monitors were overflowing with human misery. Images flitted across the screens bathed in alternate red and white lights of sopping wet people being fished from the harbor in their business suits, of bobbing cars soon to disappear beneath the waves, and more than a few corpses mostly drowned from the shock rather than from the injury. When he finally reached his room on the twenty-seventh floor and closed the door it was well after three AM. He undressed and walked to the window where, after turning off all but one small light by his bed, he flung open the curtains and stood stark naked spellbound by the glittering landscape absorbing as much of the city and its famous harbor as he could. The emergency vessels could be seen far below jockeying around the mostly submerged ferry as they desperately scoured the surface for signs of life in the inky waters shimmering with reflections, but Rand did not notice them. He imagined the wealth rolling beneath him in undulating golden waves spawned by the Tai Pans of the last century who ascended to the gates of heaven by the grace of nearly free labor and iron clad trading cartels, which were inviolable, enforced on mainland China by British gun boat diplomacy. The feel of riches and gin coursed through him as he relished the thought of his search for the perfect sailing boat for which he was prepared to pay cash on the spot.

In the harbor's heart, as sleep softly embraced Rand, others slept with the fishes. The gateman who rode the ferry day after day performing the same chores until they were rote, senseless machinations that required no further human thought or reasoning and so made invalid the immortal being who acquiesced to the drudgery in order to feed and house a family; the engineer who received his training in England twenty years before and had a wife and six children who would miss him dearly; the acerbic British captain who had been drinking and went below the waves blaming the manufacturer of the vessel for failing to make doors that would withstand a minor collision and remain secure. All slept now with unfulfilled wishes.

For the next six days he traveled with an Englishman to every reputable yacht dealer in the area. The smell of the China sea followed them and got in his clothes and stayed with him so that he had to shower before it would leave. The ocean was different here than his native West Coast. More complex, more alive as if the people and the water were of one source and their life's breath mingled indiscriminately until it was impossible to separate one from the other. On the seventh day as they walked along a dock in a boat yard he saw three brightly striped water snakes just on the surface by the edge under the oil slick water. He knelt and watched them. They seemed to follow his movements and as he raised his hand they swam to its shadow. He reached down and splashed into the water and they came racing up at him. "I wouldn't do that if I were you old boy." Came the droll sound of the Englishman's voice. "Poison, kill you in ten minutes you know." He recoiled from the water as if the small snakes would leap out and attach themselves to his forearm never to be pried loose again and fell backwards.

It was then that he saw it. Beneath the rough wood scaffolding of a boat in dry dock he glimpsed the flare of its profile and winced as the sun glinted off its gloss finish. She sat in the water as if coiled, in motion, unable to be still. The red bottom was topped by a white line that separated it from her gleaming, hand rubbed black hull. The stern was long and tapered and sat lofted out over the water giving the whole boat a rakish slant, fluid and restless. At the same time he heard the silence and so from that day confessed that he was destined to own the boat and truly believed that fate, if not God, had led him to it.

"Am I early?"

The moment shattered. Rand, startled, glanced up at Gordon Dahlquest, forced a smile. "You kidding? ...been waiting."

"Well," the older man grunted uncomfortably as he tried to swing his small flight bag onto the deck while he awkwardly lowered himself, "I'm up at dawn...don't sleep much in hotels."

"Veronique...?"

She was frowning and walking fast. "I just hope you've got coffee?" The voice drifted wearily down the dock. A mass of wavy brown hair was pulled back off her face. "Is the sun up yet?" She athletically swung her legs up over the rope and settled down on a cushion at the stern behind dark glasses.

In the distance a lone sliding seat scull noiselessly glided by leaving barely a ripple in the water as the rower expertly feathered the ten foot graphite shell oars. Rand emerged from the galley where caterers had just left all the food for the day and poured a cup of coffee handing it to Veronique. "Nectar de los Dios."

"Gods huh?" She clasped the cup and inhaled the aroma. "It better be at this hour."

"Gordon was telling me he didn't sleep much."

She scowled at him. "We sleep separately."

"Of course..."

She was wearing skin tight white pants that appeared as if they were at least a size too small, but somehow were very flattering. They suited her, left nothing to imagination... and a teal parka over a stretched halter top of muted fuchsia.

"Rand!"

He looked up and waved.

"We've been here for twenty minutes. Ashford's on long distance. Business!"

"No hurry!" He called back. "Naomi, my assistant."

Veronique sat quietly, coffee warming her hands ostensibly trying to understand why they had arisen so early, but in reality looking forward to getting the measure of the men who would make ISC work, if they passed her inspection. She was wind tossed, disturbed, Rand thought as he removed the covers from the sails and stowed them, there was something dangerous about her that appealed to him. Gordon Dahlquest, on the other hand, looked as though he had not slept at all. His face was contorted up into a concentrated mask that revealed the turmoils playing out in his mind. He had come wearing heavy, crepe rubber soled moccasins and a loose, plaid flannel shirt with the sleeves rolled up under which was a dark crew necked jersey. The boat would make them comfortable he knew. That was its magic.

"Gordon." Ashford Van Riper stepped boldly across the cushioned seat and firmly grasped the older man's hand in a ritual of men that had been lost somewhere in the transmigration from one generation to the next.

The woman that followed looked out of place. "I'm Naomi Arrabito." Her mother was a Cuban black who refused to learn to speak English even though she lived in the United States for thirty-three years. She, however, was mysteriously inspired and bright enough to receive a scholarship from New York University Law School, and then another scholarship to Stanford. "Hello." she said,

The wind caught the sails with one enormous crack of the canvas making the boat heel over and slice the waves sending shot sprays over the bow. The Sojourner had majestically emerged from behind the breakwater when Rand cut the engines. Suddenly there was silence. The release from the land was a euphoric feeling that they shared. Rand had always been able to imagine what it must have been like from the eyes of ancient mariners who braved the ocean's endless plains in search of an ephemeral destination while haunted by terrible misgivings that they lied to their crews about. It was an act of faith he could not match in his own life, though he understood it and harbored his own desperate urge to escape. Complacency festered in him. On the sea was the only place life sparkled for brief moments. Life, as he knew it should be ragged and wild, restive and unrestrained.

Naomi slipped her shoes off and gingerly climbed up over the cold, teak deck to the bow where she sat facing the wind curling her brown legs underneath holding on to the brass fittings of the hatch cover. Her face was of a child that had not yet matured and developed the lines and creases that go into the complete statement of a person's character. She was short and firm, her breasts were full, hips wide, legs sinewy and strong and she gave the impression of being born for the sole purpose of bearing and raising children. Her large, brown eyes looked straight ahead. Long, curly black hair was swept off her forehead and salt spray began to settle there as diamonds glinting in first light. Her mother had been proud to confess she was a Catholic though in practice she was a follower of Santeria, a blending of Catholicism and the West African spiritualism of the Yorba people. While growing up they had gone to the priests with confessions of past sins and to the Mother of Saints with hopes for the future. In a corner of their apartment an altar to the Orixás shared space with Jesus on the cross. The gods of Europe and of Africa converged in Naomi.

The boat cut a path across the Santa Monica bay heading up the coast in the soft, fresh wind towards the Channel Islands leaving a straight white wake. Long stretches of silence ensued where the only sounds were those of the wind in the sails and the chop of the water against the hull. Miles slipped by as racing swells rolled under them. The sun rose higher and it became one of those clear breezy days where sea and sky collide to form a universe apart from that of land giving to some a feeling of freedom while to others a sense of being lost. High above spirits saw the tiny sailboat inch its way across the vast, shimmering sea.

Rand was tense behind the wheel, a large, dull gray titanium alloy affair over a third of which disappeared below deck in a groove. The sun bore down on his shoulders. He wore a thin-shell peacock anorak over his T-shirt, khaki shorts and dark aviator glasses. "Waking up?" He glanced recklessly toward Veronique as the sensation of the vessel surging through the waves played in counterpoint to the perfect pressure on the wheel keeping the sails precisely to the wind.

"I am."

"You can't see it yet," Rand pointed off in the direction to which the boat was heading, "an island..."

Gordon interjected. "Anacapa?"

"Yes...you know it?"

"I was there once, Santa Cruz too."

"Gordon tells me that he sailed up the coast from San Diego to Eureka." Ashford added to ingratiate himself and seem more human in an effort to overcome the impression of being patronized he knew others felt around him. "Jesus Christ I wish I'd have done that!"

"Don't think so. It was cold and wet...we were young, that's all."

Veronique sat on the edge of the cushion filled with disdain, elbows on her knees her back straight and her gaze unwavering. "Gordon prefers mountains." She said tersely fingering the empty white coffee mug contemplating whether a fourth cup would send her over the edge or whether it would counteract the nerve racking calm that accompanied leisure sailing. Veronique did not relax easily. Business life and personal life were inseparable. But then there was the rush, the feeling of power which was an elixir to any of the innumerable dull moments of existence, from which she fled in abject revulsion. A conflux of highs and lows had given her a life on the edge, a fleeting romance with the near future where everything was just out of reach. She had been absorbed by television's culture from the moment she chanced a job in marketing with a cable network. She was a natural. In her first decade she crossed the line from the secular to the clerical to the profane until she could not think other than in the context of programming, market share and total mass worldwide viewership. It was only widespread illiteracy and a pervasive sense of moral atrophy that prevented the mob from understanding television's full impact. To her it was obvious. The governing of man had outgrown politics and was now the responsibility of the media, and it was the battle for viewership that had displaced the vote.

Her evangelism had not gone unrewarded. She was included in the private afternoon talks of the Chairman intended to be creative discussions and it was with trepidation and feelings of inadequacy that Veronique joined the old boys club. From the first meeting her disillusionment began. The men spoke the broad language of power, which at first passed her by completely, but the meaning soon began to take hold. She discovered the values she had always believed in were as fluid as the barrier of disbelief between performer and audience and could disappear with only one gesture or phrase or word. They were created or taken away at will by the voice of the media. Here were the concepts of daily life being debated in terms of interest, ratings and share and cost per second. At one point she found herself with no personal thoughts at all, completely devoid of concept as if she had been erased and was absolutely invalid. But eventually her place in the world would be resurrected with more complete concepts that she liked to think of as a higher evolution. She had been reborn. These men and their counterparts were shaping the future. It was with that realization that she finally began to conceptualize the new world.

Veronique had been blessed with a complete vision of the global order. "The event horizon," she liked to say, "has already been crossed." The point past which Veronique believed the world culture had gone by reason of its burgeoning population. "No longer will men be able to create enough economy to support themselves!" She would argue. "Representative government and market economies are obsolete. It's too late," she lamented with a toss of her hand, "developing countries came to the table too late." Her purpose had given new focus to events. It was all clear now. The new model would be interactive television, the only medium ubiquitous enough for a democracy. The world was already wired, and addicted to entertainment she just needed to give people the ability to talk back, technologically impossibly until now. ISC had come along at just the right time.

Naomi had watched Rand all morning from the bow where she sat letting the effects of the preceding week peel away from her in layers of volatile emotion until by midday she took her first clear breath and began to realize that she was surrounded by wind and crystalline water. He was helpless, she thought. In the galley she fumbled with the poached salmon and dijon dill sauce, cold asparagus, brie cheese canapés with stone ground water crackers and Greek olives, vegetarian rolled crepes in moo shoo sauce and fresh baguettes. She brought out long stemmed, fluted glasses and set them on the mahogany table. The chilled white, a Pouilly-Fumé of the Loire Valley from de Ladoucette vintage 1988, and a red Rioja of Spain from Marqués de Cáceres vintage 1982. She opened one of each to let them breathe.

The water had given everyone an appetite. They ate ravenously. "Well then," Rand boomed raising his glass, "here's to Naomi without whose help none of us could get along." Rand drank his entire glass and then bent down and innocently kissed her cheek. She smelled of wet hay, of sweet animals, of fresh air and open spaces.

Naomi rose, went to the galley then emerged with two more bottles, a red and a white one in each hand. "It's about time I got my due. More wine?"

She didn't want Rand to kiss her and hoped that her reaction was hidden. The last thing she wanted was to go over the edge with her boss, to be discovered...she'd dreamt of him night after night at times for months on end occasionally waking with damp sheets clinging to her perspiring skin, one leg thrown across a pillow and a breast exposed to a streak of moonlight that had invaded her bedroom imagining his flesh against hers. Up until now her desire had been sublimated by the simpler urge to take care of him, which she did compulsively at the office and on moments such as this. But his touch was intolerable.

It was how Naomi was. Had always been. It was the devil she had always fought. Cursed by the Orixás. Her mother was the one who had revealed it, the secret of how some women were hot to the touch and could not resist no matter how they might try and that it was an overwhelming passion apart from who they were so that they could neither help nor fight even with the assistance of the Orixás, who favored them exactly for their easy virtue. When small it confused her and not until her thirtieth year did she realize she did not have control of her feelings. Women like her were conduits for the saints and perhaps the lack of control was the reason they were so preferred by men. She was like that. She fell complete and immediate. No middle ground. She held out in hope of fulfillment with abstinence living alone and did not see men often. Perhaps, in earlier centuries if her fertility had been allowed the cycle would have come full circle and she would have been completed by a large family of sons and daughters. Naomi was also a terribly good lawyer; bright, articulate and possessed with an appreciation of moral common sense that was missing entirely in most of the profession. This only made matters worse. She understood how easily she could descend and so withheld herself, an act that made her appear fragile and delicate. When she returned to the bow she lay face down on a broad white towel, the bright yellow of her bathing suit contrasting with the deep, copper brown of her luxurious skin. She dreamed of dolphins and of Orcas with six foot dorsal fins cutting through still water.

"This is it." Rand exclaimed with broad hand gestures to the surrounding water. What else is there?"

"You're trying to tell us something?" Veronique smiled anxiously.

"There's nowhere else I'd rather be right now. Isn't this...damned incredible?"

"I suppose..." She replied with disinterest. "Fine boat."

"Isn't she?"

Sipping the Spanish Rioja Veronique threw one hand up behind her head to lift her hair off her neck in the heat of the direct sun feeling stifled, impatient and frustrated with the banality of leisure for leisure's sake. "I don't think protectionism ever really worked for very long," she burst out suddenly as if mid-conversation removing her jacket and stuffing it behind her as a cushion. "Television, for instance, had to go global, communications became too immediate so it became a matter of who could provide the best product in any market. Foreign distribution is a major part of the business."

Rand watched her move. He had developed the ability to appear as if he was listening intently while on another train of thought entirely and so his eyes traced the contour of her breasts cradled snugly in the halter top and traveled down to the bare midriff making him suddenly realize that she was not only pretty, in a disheveled way, but embodied a disquieting sexuality. A slight befuddled frown crossed his face as he couldn't understand how he could have missed that before and though he didn't know what she was talking about immediately became more interested.

"What about the Japanese?" Rand spoke with effort. "That's protectionism."

"Yes." Veronique replied. "That was political. Congress was scared; they wanted to give the impression of creating jobs..." she accidentally brushed her hand across his bare leg, "they're just fighting obsolescence.""

"Right," he was startled by her touch, "we almost lost it there." Finishing his wine with one swallow.

"What's that?" Veronique asked.

"...to the Japanese. Christ, the steel industry, automobiles, home electronics..."

"Digital television." Naomi interjected.

"I'm not following..."

"The race for High Definition Television." Veronique replied to Rand, her voice suddenly husky, sensual, quieter and more personal as she looked directly at him without moving her head and felt an energy coil up in her stomach aching to be released. "The Japanese had already developed it and had it in production from the early eighties, but congress wouldn't allow them to set the standard in the U.S. because they were afraid they'd lose another industry to them." She touched his arm and smiled, "It was a good system too, clearly better than anything from the States for at least ten years."

"Really?" Said Rand confusion settling in.

"That's right." She chirped.

Rand frowned and poured himself a third glass of Rioja beginning to feel high. Earlier things seemed as if they were clearing up, he'd even considered leaving the firm despite the fact that he would then never acquire that new car he had wanted so desperately. Somehow in the night the needs vanished and the simplicity of living well made everything he was doing inconsequential. It had almost come then and in its aftermath he had resolved to live differently, to be good and perhaps that would atone for lost years. He spread his arms dramatically across the deck, "I give you the sea, a beautiful day and a ride on my yacht with lunch to boot!"

"Ah yes," Veronique got to her feet, "these thing we know are without price, but we're talking about affairs that matter. Money talk." Sitting down close enough for him to feel her breath. "If congress hadn't initiated the race then the approximately seven hundred and fifty million dollars in research wouldn't have been spent by major electronics firms and our interactive digital satellite technology would never have happened. That makes me just wild. I love money, don't you? It excites me."

"Yes...I..." Her hand rested on his thigh and was warm. It moved lightly across his flesh making him wonder if she was inching it purposely up under the hem of his khaki shorts or was an innocent gesture. He didn't move.

Gordon Dahlquest and Ashford had gone below and were sitting at the mahogany table getting drunk from the hundred dollar bottles of wine, which they were finishing one after another. Loud manly voices boomed up on deck. From somewhere Cuban cigars had materialized so that smoke wafted out of the open door and was whipped away by the wind. Naomi slept on the bow.

"This is my dream from last night." Veronique's leg touched his. Do you want to hear it?"

"Yes."

"My dream went like this. I walked into a hotel restaurant and sat at the bar. It was late and I was...I wanted someone, someone anonymous. A man, a man sitting across the room. A gray suit on. I watched him. After my third drink I went over and sat down. I placed my hand on his leg, like I'm doing now," she moved her fingers against him and squeezed gently, "the fabric of his suit was cool yet I could feel the warmth underneath even in my dream and I looked in his eyes for a reaction. He was shocked of course, like you are, but when he started to speak I just put my finger to his lips. I didn't want him to speak. I took his hand and led him into an elevator in the lobby. Maybe I was surprised that he followed without comment, but he did. I pushed a button, a random button. The car stopped on a floor. He was blushing and confused and I suppose that made me more determined. I was violating him. I again led him by the hand down the hall. I tried each door until one opened, and then brought the man inside." Her hand had slid to the top of his inner thigh and Veronique's one finger touched Rand intimately and he grew tense. "There were three men and a woman in the room sitting at a table smoking cigarettes. We walked past them. They were shocked of course, I mean we had just walked into their hotel room unannounced. I paid no attention to them and took off all the strange man's clothes and made him stand before the window naked. To see him. To absorb his nakedness. He was embarrassed; the people in the room fell silent. By the time I had removed my dress he was completely aroused. We had sex inside that room. I would not let him speak. Not once. Then I woke up. Why do you think I did that?"

"Why are you telling me this?" Rand sat in a lost silence completely enveloped in swirling leaves. He could not reach nor could he withdraw. The altruism of the morning was overwhelmed with a carnal frustration and he knew then that he could never escape. The world was the way it was, no amount of philosophizing could alter its basic make up.

"Have you ever had sex with a complete stranger?" She suddenly withdrew her hand all business and whispered in his ear. "I fellated a man in a public park once, I didn't even know his name. It was tremendously exciting. Money is like that. Exciting. It will change your life. I want you to work for me, work hard on this ISC deal. There's more money in it than you've ever seen."

He though for a moment and it was exciting. He could feel the excitement and forgot about her hand on his thigh and the eroticism of her story.

"Can you stop the boat?" She asked breathlessly.

"What do you mean?"

"Can you?"

"Of course, but why?"

Veronique rose smiling and removed her shoes. She climbed to the top of the cabin and stood above him facing the wind holding onto the lanyard. Rand admired her and confirmed to himself that she was indeed lovely. She faced him. Peeled off her halter top tossing it to the deck exposing her small, round breasts. Her eyes locked on his until he had to blink. The white trousers were stripped down her long smooth white legs and he glimpsed the lithe nude form unabashed against the bright blue sky primal and pale with dark hair covering her sex. On the ball of her foot she wheeled and sprang high into the air as if a dolphin

80

of Naomi's dream lofting out over the water, arms outstretched, flying for a brief instant, soaring in an effort to escape the bonds of earth and return to the ether from where we all have come.

He could make out the two figures sitting aft, but not their faces. Three miles away a long, open cockpit cigar boat idled in the water its dual motors rumbling a deep, throaty growl. Exhaust bubbled up from behind the name scrawled across its aft in a furious, scratchy font. *Scorpion II* was painted with a cantilevered stripe of metallic Tahitian orange dissecting its navy blue hull like flames. A huge flying bridge soared at the same angle as the stripes back above the open seating area with one small satellite dish and two long antennas pointed at the sky. The pilot's seat was occupied by a pale young man with dark oily hair and goatee. One hand tried to keep the boat facing leeward while the other frantically entered numbers into a portable satellite navigation system that lay adjacent him on the short, black dashboard. The size of a small briefcase its buttons, keys, dials and numbers were backlit with amber red that contrasted with its rich gray finish, but could not be seen in the bright, afternoon sun. Every few minutes he would raise the small, olive colored electronically stabilized binoculars that he had hanging around his neck to his eyes and again pinpoint the location of the Sojourner.

After a moment he raised a cellular phone to his ear and spoke loudly into it feeling he had to shout to make up for the distance. "Have you got it?" He demanded.

Nearly three thousand miles away in Bangor Maine three other young men hovered hesitantly around a grouping of monitors haphazardly assembled on tables and network racks filled with cables, wires and switchboxes. In the center was a large, sixty-five inch, HD flat screen monitor across which still images appeared, lingered for a moment or two, and then were redrawn from the top down with an updated picture similar to the one before yet showing the change of position of objects in space. The color was somewhat grainy and pixilated because much of it was computer interpolated because high altitude imagery had the disadvantage of peering through the earth's atmosphere, which acted as a diffusion filter effectively blocking certain wavelengths of light.

"Yes...yes we do." Came the reply of the man nearest the viewing area into his telephone handset.

Triangulation. The coordinates from the long cigar boat, those of the satellite that orbited the pole and their own location in Bangor Maine allowed them to get an accurate fix on the Sojourner. On the high definition screen over compensation gave the waters of Santa Monica bay a turquoise color contrasting with too much red on the teak deck where Naomi lay in a blur of bright yellow. Figures could be seen moving. The boat nearly filled the entire screen. In the dark room Derian Baxter and the other two young men were thinking the same thought at once. Listening in had to be the next step.

BRUSHSTROKES IN THE MIST

V

A man of social standing traditionally has been expected to avoid work, except when necessary. It was not regarded as a meritorious activity. So Andrade Veloso had decided not to enter the University as his father had always planned for him. Though it pained him deeply to go against Valdemiro's wishes, there it was. His father's heart would necessarily be broken. He imagined the drawn, somber face and melancholy eyes that would reproach him much more effectively than rage would when he broke the news after dinner at the *fazenda* to the south near Ipanema where his father's imperial residence was land locked between twenty story high-security condominiums. They still had a view to the ocean though, and beyond to the Sargasso Sea in between the rains. He stood the risk of being disinherited in which case he would be forced to work. That was a situation he could not allow to happen as it would undermine his entire strategy of existence, which had been carefully worked out during his twenty years on this earth with the spiritual guidance of Father Javier Abraho the Jesuit from across the new four billion dollar bridge at the mouth of the bay of Guanabara in the town of Niteroi. Christ the Redeemer himself, whose arms are lifted in benediction of the disparate millions, was raised to his pinnacle on the Corcovado in 1931 by local church donations elicited by the Jesuits so who was he to doubt their wisdom, and indeed not the priest Javier Abraho whom his own father introduced as a kind of surrogate when in the early years he was absent for many months at a time developing his import export business. With these thoughts in mind the plan took form.

Reason drove him. Faith was something he could never get his hands around. Father Abraho knew this about him yet for some reason seemed to respect him all the more for it as he vainly tried to teach him the Catechism, which Andrade would memorize finding some applicable sense to each lesson, but never really grasping the fundamental concepts of the Catholic Faith.

When he was seven years old he saw a manitou at the mouth of the Paríaba River not far from his home in Ipanema while on a short trip with his father. Whenever he told of his sighting he was told that it was probably a porpoise or a seal of the variety that are found hundreds of miles up the Amazon that still have vestiges of their four legs. He had, up until then, spent very little time in school and ran with some of the local children who had not yet formed their socioracial predispositions, so was included in the mix of mestiços and mulattos, (orphans of the street), and whites, such as himself, who had escaped from their formal homes to their adopted ones on the boulevard. They had begun calling him *branco do Bahia* (white from Bahia, a region traditionally of dark skin where African cultural patterns distinguished it from other parts of the country), after it was enforced in the especially rude way that children sometimes have that his mother, whom he had never known, was *indio prêto,* a black Indian, and that was why he was the color of coffee with cream and had dark amber eyes. He did not fight for race but because he missed not having a mother even though many of his street friends had neither parent. Following the incident he was left with an aftertaste that remained and a mystery hung over his mother that his father kept from him. It wasn't until years later when he reached adolescence and began to have some experience with girls that he finally found peace with the thought that many women had been known to call themselves mestiços when they really weren't because of men's alleged preferences for women of color as sexual companions. Then he thought of his father whispering to his mother humidly...*minha nêgra,* my little negro, and everything seemed as it should be.

It was the children who also told him about the Orixá Imanjá who lured sailors to their deaths and he began to realize that it was she he had encountered instead of the manitou, who were known to have nudged unconscious sailors to safety–a fact that had been testified to recently in the Church of the Holy Eucharist as having happened exactly that way by three shark fishermen who had clung to debris for 55 hours after their boat sank beneath them before being discovered mysteriously washed up on a beach oblivious to the world but otherwise in good health. It was said by the local business men that they had made it up because the owner of the boat, who had lent them the use of it for a portion of the catch, believed the men had taken his boat to Rio and sold it. But in God's house the man could not deny the miracle. From that moment on Andrade could not sleep one night through without waking in terror that Imanjá was calling him in his sleep and that if he returned to the land of night he would never awake. This was an unknown fact for many months because he did not cry out or in any way reveal the state he was in and it was only discovered by accident when his father happened to look in on him and find him sitting straight up in bed covered with a sheen of perspiration.

The next day his father bundled him off in the car to the Church of the Sacred Heart in Niteroi where the Jesuit priest Father Javier Abraho ran a school. It was warm and pouring rain dark as night in the mid afternoon as they all sat down in the priest's office behind the lobby of the rectory. "My son," his father said solemnly with an adult voice that was devoid of any form of patronization, "this is Father Abraho."

"How do you do." The priest said kindly.

"Father," he began, "the boy is confused." He paused and looked at his son with the oddest most forlorn expression that Andrade had ever seen. "I regret that I have not been the example I was taught is right in the holy church and that things which may come naturally to you with little sacrifice are completely beyond my reach because I am…" Andrade always imagined that his father meant to say weak at that point, but his father was strong, machismo, and would never admit to being weak so took a moment to formulate his concept and choose carefully the next word so that he would not be misunderstood, "inclined to sin by my nature. I have not evangelized my son nor have I educated him in the faith. This I confess in front of you both."

Father Abraho having found the wisdom somewhere perceived the difficulty with which Valdemiro Veloso was having prostrating himself before the faith and simply acknowledged him. "I understand, Miro." He concluded that he was a good man because he had donated heavily for many years and knew that behind such charity was a deep burning for salvation inspired by what hidden turmoils he could only imagine.

He looked at his son and then at the priest. "He does not sleep and is afraid of the Orixás," and then leaned forward stiffly and confidentially as if to impart an air of intimacy to his confession, "which I think he was told of by the *pivetes* who I have forced upon him as his only company because I have to be away from home so much in my business. I do not want him to end up with a bullet in the head paid for by some disgruntled shop owner who is annoyed at his merchandise being pilfered, nor do I want him to be without a proper education...in the old way. Do you get my meaning?"

"You are doing the right thing." Father Abraho said.

"I give him to you."

"I accept him."

"Make a man of him."

From then on whenever his father was away on business he would stay at the Sacred Heart School and even when he was living at home went on a daily basis. Sunday he began attending mass though his father would not accompany him and so sent along the maid, a dark, leggy mestiço with a penchant for bright red orange and indigo whose loose manner and sashaying walk did more for church attendance than all the encyclicals of the past hundred years.

Father Javier Abraho began the task of initiating him into the mysteries of the faith. When Andrade asked him why they were mysteries he was told because they were not easily understood, they were of unseen cause. This made perfect sense to him and so he decided from the start that the man was honest and gave credence to what he said. He spent eleven years at the school and with the priest and often the old Jesuit would try to engage him in a philosophical debate challenged by his lack of grasp of the Catholic discipline. He would bait him with the sacraments, defying his logic and daring him to define life, what he knew of it, in linear terms. In truth, he could not. So, it was in those intellectual crapshoots that he finally came to formulate his own path, his own ideas and design on life. He finally confessed to Father Abraho that he could never live the life of Christ and be truly enjoined by the sacraments to the benefits of the Church and its apostolic wisdom even though he had learned the arts of an altar boy and had carried the Eucharist and helped administer the holy act. "I have a strategy now!" he said enthusiastically. "I have a…perspective on existence, a spiritual plan." And the old priest at last counted the boy as a convert.

Andrade supposed he could have had any car he chose as he had never been denied anything he really wanted, but was satisfied with the one he had been given on his seventeenth birthday even though it was the one his father had driven for more than ten years. He was not an avaricious person, though he truly loved automobiles and each spring would cancel his life for a week to attend the Grand Prix de Brazil in Rio, all the time trials and festivities, which commonly escalated into a brief Carnival fever before they were through. Caetano Silva, the famous Formula One world champion, was a native of Rio De Janero and drew crowds wherever he went. Andrade prided himself on having learned many driving techniques from watching him. The silver 1955 gull-wing Mercedes, whose red leather upholstery was still supple and free from any major cracks, clung to the road west leaving the city along the coast burrowing through a tunnel under the *favela* Rocinha. In his rear view mirror he could see the shacks that hung over the tunnel exit above the commuters escaping to their beachfront homes up the coast. He knew Tarisco had come from Rochina, but it didn't matter.

Brazil was an essence inexpressible. A restless and humid kiss that left one awake night after night in heated longings for that which he could not touch. Its life too abundant to be contained. Its spirit too inextinguishable. So, it spilled out in a multitude of rivers, always muddy from the renewal, and poured from towering nimbus clouds where faces of Tupinambá warriors could be seen and whose fury was spent in the daily deluges that endlessly recycled the blood of the land. Water. It was everywhere. Foliage that burst with it in lush and luxuriant explosions of every shade of green imaginable. It stretched from the coastal ranges of Serra do Mar, running north from Santa Catarina a thousand miles to Rio de Janero and further as Serra do Orgãos towards Espiritu Santo, to the eastern frontiers swept with infinite grasses. They undulated with rhythm. The waters shimmered with it. People lived by it, were contained and set free by it and were ruled by its ritual being free like the air, bowing to no class or color distinction where the astonishing palette of racial hues became as meaningless as the color of dirt. The wealthy and the dispossessed, *branco*, (white), and *prêto*, (black), alike were its concubines. The *batuques* were rhythms of the soul spontaneously erupting from the primal will to live and sounded out as heartbeats of the collective body of life, which endowed the land and all who graced its countrysides.

Tarisco wished to be known by the son of his employer Valdemiro Veloso as a *pistolão*, a benefactor to those less fortunate, though in truth he was in the umbra of Andrade owing all his success in life to the grace of his father. This was a fact he chose at times to set aside feeling that a man could never truly have integrity while he was completely in the debt of another. It was in these brief intervals of freedom that he had secured his reputation in certain *favela* neighborhoods as a *pistolão* and command the respect of those whose need was beyond speaking yet whose vivacity and attack on life never faltered. It was out of esteem for them that he had taken some of his money and financed one local sewer system, and ran electrical wiring into certain neighborhoods so that now over even the flimsiest of shacks the spider like television antennas could be seen. Despite all his good works he could never escape what he perceived as a taint caused by his dependence on the good will of a *fazendario*, a man of too much property, in his journey out of the slums. He was still more at home among the *descamisados*, people without shirts, than the bourgeois he emulated with his linen suits and saw himself living in the shadows between two worlds. He could never decide whether this meant he was a small being lacking the breadth of spirit to amount to something or if he had missed his calling as a priest.

He had arisen before dawn, before light had reached the vast interior of Brazil causing the cool night air to leap up as wind and swirl in one brief moment of exalted celebration, stirring the myriad of trees, the living things that lie in wait for daylight by the billions upon billions and had done so since eons before man had appeared on their verdant playing field. Tarisco was a part of the whole; he fulfilled his synergistic duty because good or evil in the natural world is determined only by its relation to all other things. When the sun filled the streets between the cafes and the beachfront condominiums where he lived he had been up for two hours already. He had tasted bitter coffee and composed himself into who he thought he was for the day ahead.

By the time he'd entered the warehouse he was strong, ready for life. It was perhaps for this reason that the pulse made by the *batucada,* that was already beating out rhythms of the samba, possessed him so completely. He felt enlivened by the fusillade of vitality slowly filling the old building as people showed their faces from behind doors and windows peering inside to see if anyone had arrived before them and if so, who. Music echoed from the rough wood rafters making him tap his feet and swivel his hips as he went for more coffee. Tarisco rented the huge warehouse on alternating Saturdays when it became jammed to overflowing with mulatto dancers, fat women costumers, singers, guitarists and percussion musicians of the *batucadas.* Members of the *sociedad,* the local social club, all came together in order to practice for Carnival and work out the bugs in their glorious costumes. It was the crowning achievement of his ascendancy from the *favela* and he saw it as a bridge from his begrudged commitment to Veloso to his desire of becoming a *bicherio* on his own wherein he would find his salvation. This was his blood's desire.

A lone dancer in a red taffeta dress with a full skirt shuffled across the floor to the ubiquitous beat. Her young black skin shone with innocent purity against the crimson. The sound of her feet could be heard and she hoarsely whispered the words to a song without singing it out loud. Others loitered, talking to one another, laughing and clapping hands on backs, shoulders, thighs and picking up Styrofoam coffee cups. Giggling girls ran down the dirt hillside wearing their finest costumes whose colors caught the sun bringing out their most vibrant hues and burst through the door. Little storms. Their eyes were puffy with sleep yet bright and even through the deep color of their skin the flush of youth could be seen. Voices chimed in the air. Tarisco's determination was embodied in the *escola de samba,* the samba school, which he financed one hundred percent–though with his lifestyle at the beach it taxed him to the limit. The necessity it had engendered propelled him into the numbers racket, the *Jogo de Bicho,* where he hoped to earn not only his fortune but his own self reliance and respect. It was important to him that Andrade see him in his element. That is why he had arranged the meeting in the warehouse on one of the alternating Saturdays in the midst of the whirl and color and tempestuousness.

"Oi! Tarisco!" One after another the salutations flooded upon him, hands clasped tightly gripping, strength to strength, *de homen para homen,* man to man. The benefactor, the *pistolão.* He sat comfortably in an old chair where he presided over each rehearsal with his legs crossed carefully so as not to cause too many new wrinkles in the linen suit, his hair slicked back a black sheen rich against the deep color of his face. The whites of his eyes were brilliant. Young women watched him from their forming groups around the room, he was a catch, though they'd never let him know...he'd escaped the *favela* and ignited a possibility of hope in each of them. Eyes played their silent dance. Never touching.

Tarisco loved everything about his alternating Saturdays. The sounds of which he had been born to, even the smells that came on gradually as the people filled the room and the sun rose and the dance grew more fevered. Palm oil, perfume and hair pomade. Perspiration and lingering odors of all types of humans; sweet ones, strong ones, gaunt and agile ones. A bouquet of the living.

It started with a low hum barely distinguishable from the traffic noises of the streets and rose as if a soul in transmigration gaining strength and power as it left the body soaring at last on the wings of expectation...as if the rhythm never really ceased but only ebbed and flowed and remained always tattooed in the memory of the cariocans, those of Rio de Janero, regardless of class. The high croaking *batuques* and the infectious shake of the marimba-like gourds that wafted through the open windows as musicians arrived from down the hillsides and off the street playing as they walked in time with their breathing. Shorts and bare feet converged in small groups throughout the old warehouse all playing the same rhythm until the foundation of the building itself reverberated with the samba. The dancers were shining in silky, ruffled, sheer, reflective, metallic, gossamer splendor. Fifty shades of brown skin contrasted with the fuchsias, blue violets, tangerines and lime greens. Everyone was smiling. Life was good.

The two men shook hands amidst the scramble of dancers. Andrade, in his freshly starched white shirt with the open collar sat beside Tarisco in his chair of importance flanked by a table with coffee and rolls along the wall in the middle of the room each layer of dancers revolving around him at the center. It was Tarisco's school, everyone knew that, and he took extreme pride in the fact.

"Como vai?" Andrade inquired distracted by all the costumed, undulating young women unable to take his eyes off them for long.

"Oi." Replied Tarisco knowing it was Andrade who was the interloper. He was in his element.

"I'm dazzled!" The young Veloso said as three young girls whose skin was the color of toffee sailed by in the throb of the dance nearly nude wearing only silver, spangled g-strings and brief coverings of their breasts under the long flowing robes of iridescent silver feathers and tall head dresses strewn with glittering glass diamonds. They took mincing, rhythmic steps in their high, stiletto heels.

"They meet every other Saturday," Tarisco said humbly as if none of it were his doing, "and practice."

"Perhaps," he began trying not to seem obvious, "after the first place of Carnival two years ago, I have never seen finer dancers." Andrade knew that it was bad manners but wished to acknowledge Tarisco's charity without appearing *ele não tem edução,* (one who has no education), and embarrassing both of them. The man had always been like an older brother to him, like kin who knew the pitfalls. It was he, after all, who had come to ask the favor.

Tarisco smiled and after a moment replied, "You really think so?" He sat looking very satisfied across the moving room.

"Yes, I do!"

"It's good to hear you say that!" He shouted above the din. "You never know until it's judged especially since we practice in such a secluded environment..." leaning close and speaking loudly over the music into Andrade's ear, "we are always indoors, so nobody will steal the songs."

Nodding in agreement, "It pays."

"Don't I know," Tarisco replied smugly for his reputation of competence precluded all of his activities and was the one outstanding characteristic about him.

Brown thighs of the cariocan ladies made shoulders shimmy and shake letting the beat flood over them in waves of subconscious plea-sure. "They are all like little birds floating on the *batugues*." Andrade watched while he tried to focus on the real purpose of his visit. Both of them knew why he had come but neither mentioned it. A favor, a deadly favor that Miro Veloso may not like and in Tarisco's humble opinion, if he was any judge of men which he surely was having come from the belly of men...would not take kindly to.

"Yes," more iridescent silver feathers swept by, "little flightless birds." He wondered how long the small talk would go on before the son of Veloso came to the point.

"Tarisco," he began in earnest, "I've known you for a long time."

"That's right. Since you were small."

"My father is man of strong and fixed opinions."

That was something Tarisco need not be reminded of. "He is a very powerful man to say the least."

"Did you know that he was involved in the *irmandades?*

The incongruity of Valdemiro Veloso's involvement in the Roman Catholic lay societies of brotherhoods distracted him from the girl's efforts to get his attention. "No." He said.

"He has always been a major donor to the Church of the Sacred Heart in Niteroi."

"I didn't know..."

"...since before I was born." The samba rhythm intensified. It was seeking a point where it was a self perpetuating natural phenomenon and all the dancers could not stop, even if they willed it, for the Orixás would have been awakened and have taken over and entered the world, the same world in which Andrade and Tarisco spoke amid the swirl of spirits. "He has always been convinced of his rightness and even when he is wrong refuses to admit it...he is a man and in his mind there is nothing above a man except God. I sometimes feel he is simply paying off the Almighty with his donations so he can act without moral questions. He must be right. His life depends on it."

Tarisco looked at the young man who in turn was staring straight ahead speaking quite, calmly and intimately as if to a friend and he had the impression that the son was ignorant of the father. "A man is who he is." A man who to him possessed the allegiance of life and death from his employees, who were more like *parentela,* an extended family of kin, than paid colleagues. Perhaps because Miro had no wife and only one son. "Surely you were taught the chastity and self mastery of charity at the Sacred Heart School."

"We had discussions."

"You know your catechism?"

"I have my beliefs."

"Well," sighed Tarisco suddenly feeling very old around the man-boy who was still clear skinned, strong armed and straight backed and had not yet the stoop of disappointment that visits a man without his consent when he first realizes he has failed compared with his ideals and has not the time left to recoup his losses, "life is relentless. Though it may seem very long to you now, it is not nearly long enough you will find."

"I am a realist."

"Then you should understand compassion."

"I want something of my own, Tarisco, without having to give in to him. Also," he added with a subdues hostility, "I've met a girl."

"A girl?"

"Yes."

"Yes?"

"I cannot go away to the university now as my Father always planned for me because it was never what I wanted. He is obsessed with it even to the point of having paid for six years tuition in advance!"

Tarisco shuddered. "*Patrão* usually gets what he wants."

"You thought about what I asked you?"

"I have."

"What about it?"

"Who is this...girl?"

"She is from the *sertão*."

"Christ! Some barefoot *mestiço*?"

"Maybe...maybe I want to grow coffee, raise pigs...maybe just race cars in the Grand Prix."

"Do you think you have to be stupid to do that?"

Andrade insisted. "What about it?"

Two weeks ago Tarisco had been sitting in a bar where a singer was baring his soul and he too had met a woman. She was sweet and dark and had the smell of burnt sugar the way all things in Rio de Janero had from the combination of sugar derived alcohol and gasoline that powered many of the cars and lingers in the air when it is still like the odor around a cotton candy concession. He remembered the exact moment because he had just slipped his hand under the woman's dress along the top of her silky nylon stockings and her heat was burning his hand when Andrade appeared at the table with a huge grin pasted on his face. The embarrassed woman stood up quickly, straightened her skirt and then left without a word, much to Tarisco's frustration.

From some untapped deposit of insanity in the rich *fazenderio's* son the scheme had been devised without the benefit of strong drink, or drugs, withheld sexual favors or any of the other substances that traditionally compelled desperate acts. "I want to transfer some goods." He had said solemnly meaning simply that he wanted to oversee a shipment of cocaine from the Colombian region through Brazil into the most lucrative and richest market on the planet, the United States.

"Does your father know you're here?" Tarisco calmly asked without raising his eyes from the table upon which he absently and nervously tapped the index finger of his left hand, a table which had rings etched in its wood surface testament to the generations of glasses that had stood there and drops of whiskey that had spilled when the woman had jumped up and so hurriedly left leaving Tarisco to watch her swaying hips through the tight fitting skirt thinking of what might have been.

"This doesn't concern my father."

"He is my *Patrão*."

"He is my blood."

Tarisco did not know at the time exactly how much Andrade knew about Valdemiro Veloso, his father who was respectfully called Miro by close associates, and his import export business. So, he guarded his response. "It's not that simple." He told him hoping to discourage even their discussion and that the boy would forget it and never mention it again and go to the university to wind up as a doctor or an accountant or a dentist someplace and leave him the hell alone. But the point was pressed and he, out of deference to his employer, his *pistolão* listened quietly.

The little shit wanted money. Tarisco could hardly believe his ears but then realized that greed infects everyone regardless of their financial status. He had always managed to find justification for his acts by reason of his desperate climb out of the *favela* having spent most of his life without anything, hope least of all. He had been hungry so many times that he ceased to be hungry. It was a shock hearing it from the boy who had everything he ever wanted and had lived all his life in the house of the imperial era surrounded by opulence and security and shade palms and jacaranda trees that filtered the tropical light through white wooden shutters. They too had muffled the sounds of the streets where voices were kept quiet by the military who considered any form of dissent a threat to economic stability. Andrade explained that maybe he wished to buy a ranch and that his father would never allow him to retreat to the *sertão* where wild peccaries run in herds and form battle lines in defense of predators; where tapirs, anteaters and the hundred and fifty pound rodent capybaras range; where the rat-like pacas grow to be the size of small dogs. Maybe he wanted to finance a Formula-1 racing team, hire the famous Caetano Silva and be the desire of every hot woman in Rio just like he was. Maybe it was his business. He just wanted his own money. Valdemiro Veloso believed in a form of manifest destiny, that a strong culture predestined some to lead the urban crusade otherwise civilization would go feral. His son disagreed violently. It was the essence of Brazil that flowed through him as a legacy from his ancestors who were white European and black African and brown Indian. A true scion could not deny himself or suffer self abnegation. He was convinced that his destiny lie with the land. "Without it," he said, "we are nothing."

Tarisco knew that he had never fully loved as a man, a fact that he attributed to having loved too completely as a boy. In the days of sun and wind on the hill when rains spilled down every afternoon and ran in deep muddy trenches from their scenic heights into the wealthy neighborhoods below where concrete drainage ditches funneled the runoff into a causeway, which in turn swept it out into the bay of Guanabara. The Sargasso sea, he imagined, was enriched by some of his back yard. It had not occurred to him that there was any life other than that he had been born to, and in fact it mattered little for when he was young the *Orixás* embraced him with such completeness that he barely touched the earth. He remembered the feel of the warm dirt packed hard as cement from the cycle of rain and sun beneath his feet as he padded from house to house with his friends, (little voices shrill with the joy of existence), across the neighborhoods where he eventually knew everybody and the old as well as the young all formed a woven sky fabric where he imagined people like stars, close yet separate, a part of the world yet untouchable. Afternoons he would steal into a garden and peel off the ears of a fresh piece of corn and eat it down to the cob. A friend introduced him to sweet peas, which he recalled plucking from the vines and cracking the shell letting the small, round balls roll into his hand. They popped with sweetness in his mouth. He dropped a cassava once from his shoulder while carrying it at the end of a line of older boys who had stolen it from a market down in the city. It cracked wide open and though he was humiliated and ridiculed for being such a klutz, it tasted good just the same. At night he remembered as if a dream floating up into the moonlight where the whole neighborhood was bathed in a silver glow tinted with an iridescent phosphorus and he could travel from house to house visiting this way without a body still feeling the same emotions and having the same thoughts as he did in the day. He loved a girl named Petra eight years his senior who would tell them ghost stories and from day to day never once thought of the future until it happened.

He lived with a woman who was not his mother, and she told him this frankly and plainly without hesitation and in the same breath instructed him to call her *cunhada*, sister-in-law, since she was without a man and by letting people think that she had been married and was perhaps a widow, or without a husband by some other natural act of God she decided it would help her chances. This was a small concession to be able to live with someone who would take care of him so Tarisco propagated the charade and after a while even began to believe it himself conjuring up memories of his own mother, whom he had never even known, and the nebulous face of a man that was somehow associated with being his father.

The woman had appropriated a corrugated tin, cardboard and wood remnants shack that was remarkably sound and free from leaks during the rains. Each day Tarisco managed to salvage a piece of some useful material for the house whether it was a cooking utensil like the iron frying pan he found once so covered in baked on creosote and grease that it was as if enameled. He brought tiles for the roof, radishes, chilies and tomatoes pilfered from gardens and occasionally a chicken or some other piece of meat. She was a marvelous cook and could make anything delicious through the magic delivered to her from her spice rack, which hung prominently above the oil drum cooking stove. There were dozens of small jars and tin containers, none of them labeled, that only she knew what they were. All her life since a girl she had been collecting them and whenever she would travel they accompanied her in a special suitcase that she kept for that reason. It was a supreme joy to Tarisco who had never had the luxury of formal meals as far back as he could remember except for stints locked up in the concrete building of the National Foundation for the Well Being of Minors. After a few years he forgot she was not his mother.

His foraging trips took him all over the city and often he would be gone all day and only return home after the sun had set. *Cunhada* was always cooking and as he approached his house he always knew it and could have easily found it with his eyes closed because of the aromas of food. On that one particular day it was not yet dark but the twilight had advanced into the waning moments of light where the sky bathed the landscape with an impossibly soft incandescence the source and the nature of which defied the men of science to explain. It was the hour he knew in which the spirits crossed over and the gates to the *Orixás* were opened for those seeking guidance and the silver blue phosphorus glow settled on the neighborhood to light the way for his dream like rounds. He remembered carrying a heavy iron pot on his back with a long handle. Inside were two fat yellowtail snapper he had swiped from a market stall when the fishmonger wasn't looking. But as he rounded the corner where he customarily reached the bottom of the dirt trail that led through the shacks to his own he found heavy equipment parked. Caterpillar tractors with huge maws scraped and rusty, mud caked on the metal tread and baked on splattered up the sides. It smelled like grease and diesel oil. There were enormous piles of debris everywhere and two mounds nearly twenty feet high where he could plainly see the remains of doors, window sashes, whole walls some covered with gaily festooned wallpaper, broken chairs and glass shards. It was all broken and mashed and mixed with dirt and mud…it was as if the hand of God had reached down in an overpowering moment of rage and clawed the vestiges of men away leaving only scared and tattered earth where the collapse of homes had been obscured by the tread marks of the caterpillar tractors of the city. Down on the highway were hundreds of people. Small piles of belongings stood beside them indistinguishably washed in the dim light of evensong. The sounds of keening women could be heard indistinctly wailing up the hillside where it made the hair on the workmen's spine stand up and the crying of small children asking, in their way, for dinner. *Who gets the bones?* He wondered and he ambled down to the group looking for the woman and hoping she had salvaged her suitcase of spices so that they could cook the Yellowtail.

The battle had been raging for more than a century. The city had brought in bulldozers and forcefully evicted several neighborhoods of *favelados,* cheap hands and dancing feet now huddled by the highway as night fell with no place to go embraced only by the encroaching darkness. Tarisco could not forget, he would not allow himself to. From that moment, which was indelibly etched in his memory he had not loved. Instead he had devoted every instant to raising himself out of the slums without regard to the method. He became resourceful to a point of fault, self reliant and fastidious, ruthless... he latter quality is what brought him rapid advancement as a *little airplane* for the neighborhood drug and numbers dealers of his vanished youth. It was those same qualities that brought him to the attention of Valdemiro Veloso fifteen years ago and he had been in Miro's employ ever since. It had been a relationship that allowed him to escape the constricting grip of poverty. But never again did he see the twilight in quite the same way, nor did he see or even remember, except in rare moments of extreme introspection, the silver blue phosphorus glow upon the hillside in the night when he could go visiting as a spirit without the encumbrance of a body. The Orixás had failed him and so he seized his opportunities without regard to the values he had been born with.

For two weeks Tarisco had struggled with the question. The balance of all things in his life, which he had so delicately shorn up haphazardly patching compromises and humiliation with an overwhelming and blind urge to survive. Now he reasoned he must be getting old and life had lost some of its sweetness. Its promise had vanished. He knew he had never really loved as a man and considered it a great flaw for he nurtured and perceived in others that deep well of spirit of which they could share. He had not a portion of it though he vaguely remembered the hope of such things. Perhaps Andrade Veloso was looking for hope and it was not greed which drove him to ask for such a deadly favor, perhaps he was driven by the same spirit that buoyed Tarisco out of poverty and into the light.

The wild, uncontrolled dash of the samba arrived. It caromed off the walls and ceiling and through the windows into the sky, and up over the hills into the cinder block houses where millions of feet awaited the signal so they can leap and whirl and dance in breath and step. Heartbeat to heartbeat. Tarisco was suddenly troubled. He watched the lead dancer. A beautiful mulatto with a jewel in her navel, almost naked underneath her cape of streaming gold, undulating and writhing to the music along with two hundred others. She was performing lewd and delicate pelvic thrusts displaying unabashed sexuality, making the light play on her abdomen where her muscles rippled invitingly. He watched her prepare for the penance and fasting of Lent and the four brief days preceding Ash Wednesday when the bacchanal was unleashed in the streets and masked young girls ran uncovered and strange men ran their hands over them, rubbing up against them in the crush and the madness and the heat before abstinence. Tarisco could imagine losing it all, but even that could not explain why he agreed to set up a shipment for Andrade Veloso. Perhaps he did it for the brown *mestiço* girl waiting in the *sertão* and for the great expectations that he had never been allowed to look forward to with any confidence of fulfillment and for the one thing that he had no hope of finding in his own life.

BRUSHSTROKES IN THE MIST

VI

Somewhere in the night a man stood with his back pressed flat against a brick wall in a warm spring rain. Despite the rain he was sweating, and there were beads of his sweat mingling with the drops from the clouds. The wet brought out the deeper reddish hues of the old terra cotta against pale mortar, some chipped and some still as smooth as the day they had been laid over a hundred and fifty years ago. Rich oxide red contrasted with the partially sandblasted pale pea green paint left over from a structure that used to stand against the barrier where the man now stood. Perspiration made the hair on his neck lie flat. High above, faded from decades of weather, lording over the city stylish deco lettering proclaimed Escandinha's, an upscale garage that had once existed on that spot and had offered all day parking. The man's cheeks were rough and brown and hollow beneath protruding bones and above the angular jaw the muscle just adjacent the ear flexed tight as he ground his rear teeth together and drew his lips into a thin taut line. Red, blue and yellow lights from the street glistened off the side of his forehead under the curled black mass of wet hair, which held drops of moisture that sparkled like tiny round prisms each reflecting the whole skyline of the city in its heart. He wore a brilliant flowered necktie and a cream colored suit that had the smell linen gets when wet, an animal smell, an odor of musk and hay and earth all rolled together. The rain pelted him and made tiny pattering sounds as it hit his clothing

101

running down the long sleeve and over the tortoise shell button, across the starched white cuff now puckered with the moisture and continuing on down his little dark finger where it gathered at a large, gold ring into which a fire opal was set, falling then to the toe of his flat, moccasin style loafer of green ostrich skin. His face was poised in fear, eyes mere slits their whites flickering against his dark skin as he looked as far as he could to the right without moving his head. His breathing was even yet deep, and in his stomach lie curled a red buck deer ready to leap up and vanish in an instant.

The blinding white light flashed through the city's canyons from a massive fork of lightening that stretched across the sky for ten miles. It paled the neon and the phosphorus glow of street lamps, and nullified the headlights of rushing cars. Deep, black shadows came and went with a whisper across the landscape. By the time the thunder cracked the heavens, shaking the immigrant babies in their beds, the man was halfway down the alley bounding through puddles and sending up sheets of water over trashcans and vacant doorways. In a moment, he was gone, leaving no witness save the quiet walls that held him.

Breathless and angry he huddled in a phone booth frantically fumbling with his last coins when the shadow fell across him. A car pulled up suddenly and screeched to a halt in the rain slick street. Three shots rang out. The glass didn't even shatter, but small holes were left through which beads of moisture came from the weather outside. The man lie crumpled on the floor half hidden by the base of the booth. One green ostrich skin shoe protruded outside.

Castor Gustavo Monassa had been a policeman in Rio's *Zona Norte* for ten years before he was made a commissioner. Once a simple man from the coastal town of Salvador in the state of Bahia content to live shoulder to shoulder with people of his own kind from the region where he had been born, he was now an important figure in local conservative politics. As a child he inherited a house from his father, who died when he was very young in a tragic argument at the docks that ended when the man he confronted cracked his skull open with a fishing gaff. His mother was forced to hold suzerainty over him and the property until he was of age for his own good, as she told him. The house was two stories and solidly built of plastered over adobe brick and though the layers of pastel paint were chipped and peeling in huge swatches, the front facing the street he always kept fresh because of his sense of civic duty. The window sashes and door jams were mahogany hard wood with brass fixtures from the Portuguese who had built it in the late eighteen hundreds. It was constructed on a narrow lot so that it was deeper than it was wide and was wedged in between two other buildings, which made it appear as if they shared walls. They did not however, and as a consequence the walls to his neighbors were double thick and not once during the whole time when he had lived there growing up did he hear a sound come through them. It was only when he was a grown man and spent restless nights of his own in the heat of summer unable to sleep that he heard the Spanish lady next door, who was a known flamenco dancer at a local bar by profession, and a widow like his mother had been, only once did he hear her. Sounds of lovemaking drifted over him in warm rushes. He tried not to listen, but it was hot, all the windows were open and he could not sleep himself a young man on his own experiencing the frustrations of being shy around women, which he attributed to his square, stocky physique and his plain, broad face with fleshy cheeks. It got to him. Finally he placed his ear up against the cool, smooth plaster that felt like chalk against his swarthy skin and listened. He could hear the bed creaking every few moments, and then it stopped. He thought he faintly heard the Spanish dancer say to the mysterious lover, the identity of whom he imagined to be a dark Latin man, "It wasn't like my husband."

Being an owner of property and the son of his father Luis, who many remembered even though he had died years before, because he was a good and honest man who ran fishing boats out of the harbor and provided employment, gave Castor Gustavo Monassa a certain aura of respectability. He was attributed with a knowledge he in fact did not possess. As time went by his neighbors began coming to him and asking personal advice as if he had been educated, as if he had gone to the University. It was for this reason that he became a policeman. Castor decided that his wisdom and his strength would make the perfect combination of intelligence and force and that would take him far.

During all the years he was a constable in the town of Salvador he had not gathered one bad report on his record. People admired him because he was friendly, of the people and spoke the same language and could drink heavily with his friends and never appear intoxicated in any way. Because he was a *tabaréus*, uneducated peasant, and a dark skinned *Nordestino* who had made good. But most of all he was admired for his sense of humility and propriety. This was why the change in him was such a shock to the community.

In nineteen sixty-four everything changed. There had never been a strike in Salvador and when in the late 50s they occurred frequently accompanied by riots over the high cost of living the residents read about them in the newspapers and saw them on the Tele-Globo news from São Paulo and Rio De Janero. When Jânio Quandros took office as President in January 1961 inflation was the highest in the history of Brazil. He expressed admiration for the Soviet Union and Fidel Castro and pledged protection against foreign exploiters. The budget deficit and foreign debt had increased rapidly prior to his election, the printing of paper money had exploded and huge sums had been spent on the visionary development and construction of the new city Brasilia, architect Oscar Neimeyer's futuristic vision, on the plains in the state of Goiás six hundred miles northwest of Rio which was to open up the Central-West region to economic growth. Though it was to come to fruition eventually, it had not as yet happened. The man resigned in disgrace when his foreign policy was attacked and left the country. His Vice President, Goulart, who had just returned from a visit to Peking where he praised Mao Tse-tung and his revolution, assumed the reigns even though the chiefs of staff of the armed forces, most of the state governors and leading newspapers opposed him. In March of sixty-four the new President reacted to military opposition by appealing to men in the ranks to rise against their officers. When sailors and marines mutinied in Rio De Janero and were subsequently pardoned the army's revolt against the President brought the government under military control and Goulart narrowly escaped to Uruguay and twenty-one years of military rule began.

The martial rulers presupposed that the people were the enemy of the state and so formed the doctrine of national security enforced by the special Military Police and therein lay the roots of the death squads.

Castor Gustavo Monassa knew his calling had come and he went to Rio where he became a policeman of the special branch in the *Zona Norte*. He left very suddenly even before his house had been sold and so he left it in the hands of the local mayor to manage for him with the thought in the back of his mind that if things didn't work out he would always have a place to retreat to. A refuge. The people of Salvador, whom he had known for all those years, were shocked and saw his enlistment in the Military Police as a betrayal to the people, especially the poor workers, the *descamisados*, and it was commonly said of him that he had acquired the *Olho Grande*, the Big Eye, a euphemism among the men of the town indicating a person overcome by greed.

It was during this period that he developed his political philosophy. Social order was bringing about real economic gains and by 1971 Brazil enjoyed the highest rate of economic growth in its history, and one of the highest in the world. This fact Castor related directly to the control of *Marginals*; those outside the working community that included vagrants, criminals, drug pushers, street children, homeless people and any suspicious character or immigrant from a rural area who had no business to attend to. By the time he attained Commissioner he boasted about the execution of over two hundred and twenty *Marginals*. In Rio De Janero the assassination of a man can be bought for two hundred and fifty dollars, but for a child of the streets it only costs seventy. No one had ever officially linked him to the death squads, composed of ex-military policemen, security guards and hired killers, but he made no secret of his feelings stating that the death squads were fulfilling a "necessary job" and seeking election as a state deputy in order to repre-sent this view. In the meantime, he had been given summary powers to deal with drugs in Brazil and was the Director of the Anti-Narcotics unit of Brazil's Federal Police. To him the man in the phone booth was just a *pivete* fully grown, a marginal whose life impinged upon the economic success of a poor country and he had dealt with him in passing without much thought for tonight he had a truly important meeting to attend.

Kirkland Bosch, U.S. Assistant Secretary of State for International Narcotics Matters, was feeling contentious. He sat rigid in a straight backed chair in the four-star hotel in downtown Rio. The air conditioning was turned up to its coldest point and roared out of the ceiling vents because since he had arrived in the country that afternoon he had been in one meeting after another and had not been able to remove his coat once–owing to the excessive formality of the Brazilians who required a coat and tie to be worn in their largest movie theaters up until 1974 and would not allow some postal delivery personnel to enter the more fashionable high rise apartments because bermuda shorts were part of their uniform–and he was hot. Very hot. A native of New Hampshire he was not accustomed to the tropical climate and it got under his skin and irritated him. In his mind he had imagined a country where the women dressed in *saídas*, short wraps of toweling he had seen in photographs, but it wasn't so.

"It's time."

"Shit." He muttered under his breath and then immediately caught himself and was sorry he had done it. Language was a very important tool and he never allowed himself to swear in public and certainly not in a diplomatic function. This was different, he rationalized, because the only people within ear shot were secret service personnel. No one else had accompanied him to Brazil, not his secretary, his assistant, or any other State Department personnel. Nobody. He clandestinely glared up from under his brow anyway to ensure that no one had heard him. There were two cars that slipped through the streets that night, both late model limousines that looked like they belonged to business men, nothing out of the ordinary to draw attention and no way for the casual observer to know they were equipped with bullet proof glass and were double reinforced with alloy steel plates in the doors and roof and beneath the floor board to protect them from land mines. Even Kirkland Bosch was unaware of the circumstances of his envelope only thankful that the air conditioning worked well.

All he saw was rain. He was unaware that he was a man caught in the vast breathing landscape whose grandeur and expanse he could never fathom not being of the same essence as those who rise up out of the ground mist and come to maturity within this tropical landscape. Flare from lights caromed off the automobile's dark polished fenders camouflaging its lines as they passed restaurants filled with humanity where he imagined sizzling platters of *camarões bahiana*, highly seasoned shrimp prepared with tomato: *bife de panela*, thin sliced beef grilled over and open fire with onions: *vatupá*, coconut and peppers thickened with flour, pounded and cooked with shrimp and chicken and served under a sauce of highly spiced palm oil. Perhaps turtle meat, succulent and rich as in dozens of Amazonian lowland dishes served always with *manioc*, the staff of life in the Northeast as he recalled from the Foreign Area studies he undertook at the American University in Washington. He had already sampled *cachaça*, a crude but powerful light rum. Despite the air conditioning he tasted the piquant, humid atmosphere with the flavor of moss; leaves that lie in compost at the foot of massive, old growth trees; decaying wood fallen in a stream ripe with fungal and mushroom growth. It crept across his skin until even in the sterile automobile he had to rub his arm to make sure nothing was crawling on it. Though the windows, he knew, were tinted, there was the all pervasive feeling of being watched. He remembered that in the summer of 1964 a U.S. warship had come to the bay off Rio De Janero and made its presence felt in the event the revolution turned in the direction of Communism. It had been a strong issue in the preceding three civil administrations because the recurrence of Fidel Castro's Cuba would not be tolerated in this hemisphere. Veering down the Copacabana he could see the glimmering footprints of lights reflected when small waves broke and the brief ruffle of phosphorous glowing dull white as if a mirage. Things were simpler in the 1960's. The world was drawn up in two colors. Black and white.

The incessant rain that had been with him ever since he arrived finally let up. He sat in the wooden launch flanked by three morose secret service men-who no longer had the demeanor of thugs that had been clipped and scrubbed and dressed up in suits and ties to hide their social origins. Now they looked more like ex-college jocks, big boned, athletic and clear skinned who were more at home in tennis shoes than wing tip oxfords like the silent young officers recently graduated from the Military Academy of Black Needles at Campinas that they actually were. There they were schooled in the doctrine of national security and then assigned to the anti-narcotics unit of the Federal Police whether they wanted it or not. No one spoke. All that he could hear was the muted growl of the marine motor as it belched its exhaust up from the brine and the occasional lap of water as they glided across the glassine harbor. Odors of the Sargasso Sea wafted coolly by.

On the face of the deep he could see reflected stars peering through expanses of clear, black sky as fleece-edged clouds receded, their tips lit up like white-fire from a full moon hidden. Kirkland Bosch was not accustomed to the ritual of the rains–the endless cycle, which he lived outside of. He perceived only that it was different here in the tropics and that in some way he rode in the womb of the earth having traveled from its head and through its heart. The seat cushions were still moist from where they were hastily wiped down just before his arrival, and the wood smelled dank, of sea life and silent harvests of kelp and barnacles, anemones and scurrying tidepool creatures fleeing from approaching shadows. The stillness was overwhelming and pressed upon his senses until they roared and tumbled with the cacophony of the language of nature, which he had forgotten if indeed he had ever known it at all. No longer did he taste the charcoal-industrial soot that covered nearly everything in Washington D.C. and numbed the senses to such a degree that all perceptions came down to explanations of their intellectual qualities in books or brief exclamations between the bursts of taxi cab exhaust or the blast of carbon monoxide and black smoke pouring out the stacks of the municipal buses. The quiet forced his nerves to scream as they lingered close to the surface in anticipation of the real, from which they had been separated since birth as everything in the modern industrial world became a metaphor for the act of living.

A flying fish broke the water and soared across their bow directly in Kirkland's line of sight. His heart raced and his eyes froze wide startled out of his wits by this simple act. Up ahead he could see the motor yacht. It was long and high against the murky horizon. Tiny wafts of coolness pummeled his cheeks as if unseen dolphins blew against him. The cabin was clear with yellow light glowing from behind drawn curtain out the high windows of the wooden framed aft section. Her hull was white and reflected moonlight in the rippled sea. As they came alongside he stood before the boats had touched anxious to escape the sensual vulnerability that grew uncontrolled in him as the abyss of Rio De Janero seduced and beckoned him like a silkie.

He was glad for the drink, which he held comfortably in his right hand resting on the shoulder of the over stuffed arm chair covered in a deep chartreuse wool pile with a pattern of swirling rhododendron leaves. On the foreword bulkhead two pictures hung of broad magnolia blossoms done in a Mexican style surrounded by pale cream matting and black lacquer frames. The remaining three walls of the aft lounge were wooden half-windows allowing both the top or the bottom to slide open. They were all closed. On the lee side, toward the shore, white curtains were drawn yet against the other wall they were left tied back to the open ocean. The entire compartment, floor, walls, ceiling, was made of richly varnished mahogany. His host had not arrived and thankfully he had time to compose his thoughts and prepare to hold court from the heaviest, most imposing chair in the cabin. A formally dressed steward stood at the door in a starched, white waist coat and black trousers. One secret service man distanced himself and was sitting at the far end in a cane-backed chair, the others had embarked on a sweep of the vessel with the young Brazilian officers to whom they showed great disdain.

The diesel engine reported his arrival. Kirkland heard it in the distance as he sipped his iced *cachaça* and had peered out from behind the curtained window where he saw the launch motoring toward them. The ivory moon had been revealed by drawn clouds and shimmered across the water outlining the silhouette of the small boat as it steadily forged ahead. On its bow was the shape of a massive figure standing stoutly with one leg up on the gunwale. It was the first time he laid eyes on Castor Gustavo Monassa.

"How do you do." He pronounced in English with the thick-voweled Portuguese accent efforting at the elocution offering his huge paw. Castor had grown larger with age, though he still retained the swarthy complexion that for the rest of his life labeled him as a *Nordestino*. He proudly wore it taking great joy in the racial diversity of Brazil.

He still had the broad face of the young man from Salvador though his cheeks had become somewhat sallow and were not as fleshy as they were. His belly had extended and added to the already tremendous girth and to Kirkland's surprise he was dressed impeccably in an American style navy blue serge suit with a crisp, white starched shirt and a red knit tie. He had expected the man to arrive in uniform, hopefully not the full dress type of his imagination that seemed to be a cliché of banana republics. Kirkland reminded himself he was dealing with the sixth largest nation on earth.

"Kirkland Bosch." They shook hands firmly, strongly both leaning forward with their weight on the front foot. Just then the secret service men swept through the corner of the room with electronic scanners in their hands carefully taking readings. The Brazilian policeman glanced at them and shrugged questioningly. "Security," Kirkland replied, "I can't go anywhere without them."

"Of course," the big man said still holding on with his right hand and cupping the American's shoulder with his left steering him back to the chair he had risen out of. "Sorry I was delayed, a small matter...do you care for a drink?"

"No. I have one," he replied seating himself and watching the steward at the bar pour three shots of vodka followed by a generous shaking of Tabasco into a tall, iced Bloody Mary with a long celery stalk, which he then delivered to the Director on a silver tray. The man grasped it in the process of sitting down in the chair adjacent Kirkland's without even looking as if he had expected it to be there much in the way a trapeze artist relies on his partner to be in exactly the right place at the precise moment when he will be expected to grasp arms tightly by the wrists and narrowly avoid a terrible death.

"Well then. I am glad to finally meet you," he said taking a long drink of the Bloody Mary. "I can't tell you how much I've been looking forward to this."

"Myself as well." He lied.

For the next hour they sat facing each other engaged in a dialogue. Kirkland was amazed at how much of the Anti-Narcotics Unit's resources were tied up in local enforcement often mired down in the efforts to apprehend small time bosses who operated out of the *favelas* of Rio and similar neighborhoods in São Paulo and other industrial cities. Especially preceding and during Carnival when the demand for marijuana and cocaine was unprecedented. Just three nights ago a surveillance helicopter had crashed while involved in a sting operation in the neighborhood of Juramento as a cordon of police tightened around one of Rio's oldest known suppliers. He explained the neighborhood is "unimproved", meaning the shacks had no glass in their windows, no electricity or water except what can be tapped from the municipal supply and no sewers or drainage so with the rains came the torrents of mud and sewage that clog the gutters. The hill is honeycombed, like most similar *favelas*, with narrow lanes, alleys and passages through corridors the haphazard jumble of refuse and buildings make. The inhabitants know them all and their memories, like the hills where they reside, are riddled with entrances and escape routes so no one can pin them down for very long. It was rumored that children flew kites to warn of approaching police having formed, with their parents, a cadre of support for the pushers who, unlike city officials, garnered their loyalty by distributing clothing and medicine, even footing hospital bills and on occasion funding utility construction projects. "They do not rely on the police," he emphasized, "but on criminals who give them protection." It was a kite sucked into the engine that brought down the chopper. The pilot and three of his best agents died, the neighborhood rejoiced and the newspapers took swipes at the Anti-Narcotics unit for harassment claiming it was only a hellhole after the police arrived.

"What can I do?" He exclaimed, "What can I do? We cannot approach from below because whole communities are involved."

"I understand." Said Kirkland sympathetically, when in actual fact he didn't. Since the first day he entered law school twenty-seven years ago it had been impressed upon him that his role was to facilitate relations between contentious viewpoints in the hope that a rational agreement could be worked out and people would then get on with the business of living. "Let's approach it from a different angle..." He said as the looming figure of Castor Monassa glowered over him from the adjacent chair still fuming over the loss of his helicopter and four good men who he had hand trained.

Once again he explained the tired theory of cutting the source of supply and failing that the supply routes as he attempted, through the energy of his personal magnetism, to make it appear fresh and appealing and not the same political rhetoric that had been bandied back and forth between nations for a decade. He tried to present it without justifying the rural producers of drugs in their raw state. Since there was no economy to supplant it with he understood it was a sensitive issue in countries striving simply to feed their people and prevent malnutrition. Instead he concentrated on the organized, criminal elements that administered the refining and export business making it one of the top three industries in the world.

"At this juncture," he announced firmly yet hesitantly, "I'm willing to make a concrete offer for a concession on your part that will help us gain a foothold using the force of intellect instead of the force of arms because as I'm sure you're aware, there's always more of them than there are of us."

Kirkland Bosch had said exactly the right thing. Castor had always known it, and dared not speak it for fear his machismo would be called into question or his superiors would assume that he did not have the courage it took to confront and handle the marginals, even though he had proved his mettle in that arena with blood. There were more of them! They didn't have to be paid from the public repository, were not subject to the constitution, which to his dismay was one of the most sweeping and liberal in the modern world, and finally the rewards were simply more suited as an incentive for initiative. Boldness was rewarded. A policeman had a small pension to look forward to if he was lucky, if not a bullet. Five years of work in the illegal drug trade and a man was set up for life. In the Colombian highlands much of the coca and cannabis was grown by landless peasants whose *pistolão* would buy as much as they could grow and protect them as well. Is not life the prime mover? Who can argue with money? It is more important than the other things that motivate men, for in the end all that really matters is if one can continue to live.

He slammed his hand down hard flat across the arm of the chair and sat forward aggressively. "You are precisely right!" He raised a clenched fist between them and gripped and shook it to emphasize his resolve. Then he paused, having learned the art of bargaining in Salvador where everyone was a salesman and said, "Fortunately, my country has just grossed 1.8 billion dollars selling mobile telephone rights to North American companies...what can you offer us?" He sat back waiting.

For the first time since he had arrived he did not feel too hot and was even comfortable in his tropical weight charcoal gray suit. With his elbow on the arm of the chair he casually swung his hand over to pick up his drink once more and swirled the melting ice cubes around in the glass. Now he was in his element. "We think it's time for international legal cooperation. Clearly force of arms holds no solution and we would not presume to violate yours, or any other Latin nation's sovereignty. Although, as you know, it's been discussed..."

"This is a legislative problem, not for me to decide." He dismissed the comment with a wave of his hand.

"...the judiciary and prosecutors of your country are the ones that take the heat, am I correct?"

"We are not Columbia."

"You are the silk road...a major conduit and you know it."

Castor rose and lumbered over to the bar where, to the mollification of the steward who was standing just out of ear shot, began mixing another Bloody Mary on his own. "There is traffic in illegal substances certainly, but Brazil is a huge country..." he turned to face the man, "did you know the central-west is still largely a frontier region? How long has it been since there was a frontier in the United States?"

"We intend to cut the flow from Brazil into the United States completely. The first thing I can offer you is American jurisprudence. It is the strongest in the world. The envy of every nation. We want to initiate international legal cooperation and as a first gesture we will assume the risk and the costs of prosecution." He smiled smugly and firmly as if in finality he had set things right once and for all.

Castor stood for a moment at the bar and looked down at Kirkland Bosch who was reclining confidently in the chartreuse chair with his legs crossed. He had the smooth white skin of the Europeans that formed part of his own ancestry yet lacked the true understanding of the Indians because the *norte americanos* had settled their continent with bigotry and hate from the old world intact. In Brazil nature was too strong, too omnipresent, it overpowered man-created falsehoods and made small any man who tried to violate natural law. "You know of course we still trade with Cuba?" He said reaching over and opening a large humidor made with a beautiful rich brown finely textured Imbuya wood, Brazilian walnut, and lined with Spanish cedar. I have some truly fine *Habanas*, would you like one?"

"No. Thank you."

"Suit yourself." He lifted a corona from the box and, after carefully closing the lid and clipping the end of it, lit the cigar keeping the flame to it until it glowed red-orange. Peering out from a blue haze with a look of sublime pleasure on his face he spoke of a rooster that lived in Salvador, the small town where he was born. The bird was feral, he imagined, because it was larger than other roosters, bold enough to attack medium sized dogs and no one had ever been able to catch it. " It's amazing to me..." He said puffing on the cigar and again taking his seat across from Kirkland Bosch, " the resourcefulness of animals. They're opportunists, they never ever miss. The rooster", he went on with unfailing enthusiasm in his own recounting, paying no attention at all as to whether Kirkland showed interest or not and amused at drawing out the apprehension, "had been seen in the town for many years and in this place, the town where I was born, grew up and learned my profession as a policeman, where many people often did not have a full plate, had grown fat and his feathers sleek and oily. His wings had grown out fully from the days when he was a barnyard resident and so he could manage short flights, thus," he thundered raising his index finger through the pall of smoke that was developing around him, "his remarkable evasive tactics."

"One day a boy was trying to grab the bird, as boys will do especially in a rural community such as Salvador, did I tell you I was born there...? But the old rooster just played with him, having more years than the boy and knowing well the boy-tricks from his wide experience among humans. Each time he got close the wings would spread and he would kick up the dust half jumping, half flying out of reach. But the boy kept at it knowing that he was a human and far superior to the fowl like those he had eaten many times. He did it just for the pleasure of seeing a rooster fly laughing every time. Pretty soon some older boys began to chase the bird too, and not long after that a group of workers came by and they, too, chased the chicken. There were even bets, farmers are very serious about their animals, and a rooster was *their* animal, not one to be off alone like any wild thing. It went against their grain I think and so money changed hands. Now, let me tell you that Salvador, especially at that time, was a poor community and for a hard workingman to lay cash money on the line was serious. All afternoon the men chased the bird, taking little breaks now and then for a drink and generally were having a grand time. More men came in from the surrounding farms as time wore on, and when they did more would try to catch him and more money changed hands. It was a hot day and a man likes to have a cold *cerveja* after he's worked, you know? So as the sun began to disappear and the blood had been worked up with chasing the animal and making the bets a little fight started, then a big fight, and that was the end of chasing the bird. But there was not one person in the whole town who could get used to a rooster who could fly, do you see? It was almost as if it were against nature." He paused and took a deep drag on the *Habana* cigar squinting his eyes and letting them glaze over, "We do too much harm to the natural world, don't you think? Too much control, too much tampering."

It was quiet in the cabin, and though it was cool from the night air off the water, Kirkland was sweating again unsure of the moral of the story.

After a moment, Castor continued. "He also was a finely colored bird, red the hue of iron ore streaked on the rocks, and bright, shiny green and black feathers with a white pattern. Beautiful! Never lost his confidence, he was an extremely proud rooster and with one look you would know he will never go back to the barnyard and stoop to the station from where he had escaped. But the mystery of his livelihood was finally solved. I had seen the animal in the back of a feed store early one morning pecking at discarded feedbags in the dim hour just as the sun was awakening before anyone was around. I was his only witness."

"But you know," Castor continued with particular intent, "there is a very small airstrip by this little town and all around it is tall grass. Each winter the grass is cut back, but in the spring it comes again and by late summer is long and yellow once more. As I was leaving my home town to come to Rio, where I had just taken a position in the special police unit, we were just lifting off and I'll be damned if that rooster didn't fly up in front of the plane and get sucked into the engine." He took a moment, his steady coal black eyes staring with morbid amazement. Kirkland could smell the stale tobacco on his breath from across the room, and the slight hint of alcohol mixed with perspiration that the fine clothing of the man could not disguise. "Well, of course we had to land because that engine would no longer work. I think he was trying to stop me, don't you? I was the only one who knew, the only one...it's amazing to me the resourcefulness of animals. They are so small and stupid, and we are so big and smart."

"We will provide direct funding for the Anti-Narcotics Unit of the Federal Police. You may never see any of that 1.8 billion because it won't even cover the deficit and Brazil has one of the largest foreign debts of all developing nations." Kirkland conceded finally getting the drift of the story.

"Go on..."

"We will set up military hardware contracts for your unit."

"Alright then. We do see eye-to-eye. What can we do for you my friend?"

"I want to arrange a kidnapping."

Castor Gustavo Monassa sat back in his chair and brought his hands together interlocking their fingers and raised them up under his chin as if he were praying while his cigar simmered. A concern crossed his face like a storm. "You mean an extradition?"

"A kidnapping."

"This sounds like a small thing to do. What in Brazil we would call a *jeito,* meaning a way of getting around the system that is not strictly legal."

"Yes! A *jeito* then, a *jeito* so that we can bring targeted individuals to the United States where they will be publicly tried for drug trafficking and other such criminal charges that are warranted. We will set a precedent, no one will escape the law."

"Even though they are citizens of Brazil you want me to deliver them to you?"

"Of course I wouldn't ask you to do that. You are running for office aren't you?"

"Yes. As a State Deputy."

"No. We will arrange everything, you don't need to know the details...however, we must have your help. Am I making myself clear?"

"Very clear."

"I am going to give you an envelope. When I leave please open it and everything will be fully explained." And with that he passed a small, plain white envelope across to the man.

Later that night as Castor was in the bedroom of his home, a fine home that he had been able to buy many years ago before the dictatorship had ended where he had lived alone all these years never having the pleasure of a family and still retaining his shyness around women, although at his age it made little difference. His mother had passed several years earlier, but she had lived well into her nineties and so he always looked forward to a long life coming from good stock. Castor was saddened that his father had not lived to see him succeed and rise up in society from his humble beginning in the town of Salvador where his mother, the *mestiço* daughter of a landless farmer, fell in love with his father, an itinerant fisherman and where he had grown up next door to a flamenco dancer who was a widow like his mother.

Reaching down he picked up the plain white envelope and tore it open. When he unfolded the single sheet of paper inside there was only one word on it. Veloso.

BOOK II

BETWEEN THE LABYRINTH AND THE SKY

Between the Labyrinth and the Sky

VII

Suddenly cirrus clouds were tinted crimson against the dark blue heavens and then quickly vanished. Night approached. The sea raced before the wind. Waves spoke in soundless, muted greens their surface alive with bristling white water feathering off into the infinite telling tales of the ocean's history. It was the cool breath of the East that swept across it's watery plain in a hunger, a rapaciousness swelling with each mile, becoming voracious until at last it boiled up among the breakers and the rocks and loam on the western shore where it exploded in wild collision. Plumes of salt spray shot out of the crags sounding fury. Sea foam lingered in eddies. Tiny creatures scurried into their shelters. Mist swirled high and mysterious into the air and then dissipated, vanishing as it had appeared. It was the dance of earth, a song from the great mother, where all things worked in unison out on the edge of the plain of men. He was witness to it all from the moment his automobile sped over the hill and became a part of the panorama.

In the distances, far past the horizon line in the dim light they were there. Millions of eyes looking back. Dark men roaming the Pacific rim tied to the shore by their roots, eternal strivings inherited from their fathers, something over which they had no control, no choice. Cries of desperation could be heard as their voices whipped on the rush of wind that ferried them as if from the womb across the wide ocean where they rode until reaching shore and caromed up the cliffs. The homeless who huddled under shelters on cold nights were haunted by the sound and sent back their spirit messengers in consolation because that was all that they could do. To him, in the sleek automobile, it was of no consequence. Not even the wind's passing could be heard inside. Music filled his ears and he adjusted the volume higher to be completely numbed by the sound. The crescendo of nature he had passed through, the desperate journey of day into night where all things change following the ritual had failed to move him. He had barely noticed driven by other impulses and rejoiced more to the feel of speed, the whine of the engine and the caress of burnished leather seats.

The car parted the darkness with effortless fury as it roared on its mission. Headlamps pierced the shadows and drew hard edges along the cliffs with flaming yellow beams in the mist as he traveled north up the coast highway past clusters of small businesses. Here lights glittering, shining. Here closed doors, darkness and desolation. He was lulled into a feeling of power by the machine, a transcendental experience in which each fine component, the sound system, the automatic cruise control, the electrically adjusted seat positions all monitored by a subtle yet glorious array of amber lights tastefully splashed across the dashboard seemed to be vying to substitute for all of his self determined functions. No pleasure was left to chance, no need unfulfilled. A wave of drowsiness swept over him with little soft fingers leaving his eyes heavy and his sight indistinct. The complete lack of exertion that it took to travel at high speed over rough asphalt with crumbling sandstone cliffs on one side and sheer inches from the road edge on the other lulled him. One tiny error would send the pearlescent, teal colored bullet tumbling like a lacquered comet into the crags with a terrible show of sparks and fire, storming the night with a high pitched screech of tires screaming off the soft shoulder into the air for a brief moment, then the collision of reinforced sheet metal crumpling like cellophane under the full impact against the granite rocks below. Rocks along the shore, where quiet waves gently soothed the mussels clinging to their bellies. These dangerous thoughts never occurred to him as he gloated over his new car and how good life was. How complete.

High above the jetstream first lights began to appear. Venus, dim on the horizon, then the jewels Vega and Aldebaran, and finally a faint and eerie Polaris that marked the appearance of what constellations were still visible in the murky, industrial sky. Ursa Major, Lyra, Cassiopeia and a few others made halfhearted appearances, the rest obscured by clouds as he sped by far below, but were not missed by him who had never seen them in real life. There in the electronic glow of the house that lie sprawled resplendently along the coast off the highway where the lights of man had overtaken those more primal to our nature was Rand to finally feel at ease. From the moment he drove up to the great front door and released his machine to a valet his confidence grew. Without this human interference he felt lost like one blade of grass, one star, one grain of sand...to him the structure glittered incandescently and breathed and gave life.

Inside voices rose to a roar between the sips of wine and hors d'oeuvres of foie gras, raw oysters in their shells with a brush of lemon and a sprinkling of black pepper, truffled pate, roquefort-stuffed shrimps, crab and artichoke canapés, camembert, brie, a variety of breads and crackers, and fondue bruxelloise. He glided across carpets that cushioned his feet and breathed in the aroma of food, cigarette smoke, perfumes and the scents of humans all blended in one devastating symphony. Looming out over the tideland the house soared up the cliff from the ocean a monument, casting lights and shadows upon the water. The facing wall was tinted glass and hugging its western front was a deck straining above the sheer drop for the winds to whistle over when they came. To the left were wooden stairs winding down the steep embankment to the beach below where another, smaller house rested. Earlier in the evening people moved up and down the steps in congregations and many more lingered on the deck until the chill of night forced all to take refuge in the huge central living room where a massive river stone fireplace embraced a fire flickering shadows. Rand absorbed the atmosphere the way a flower sustains life from light. The grand house was his for the moment. He rejoiced in the way the doors fit, moving from room to room talking mindlessly, gliding through the sea of bodies with great buoyancy elated at his wit, delighted in his quick rejoinders, opening and closing glass and french and dutch doors, double ones, single ones, narrow carved ones with antique hardware and broad solid wood ones like houses used to have at the turn of the 19th century when home still had meaning. He marveled at their craftsmanship, even the common ones, as if they were museum pieces. The ceilings were a crazed jumble of matchstick beams tossed in the air and then frozen by a sorcerer's hand giving each room a feeling of danger as if they would come crashing down. It was a permanent sketch. The abstraction of the architecture bedazzled him. The entire house seemed built of levitated materials that defied the laws of the physical world and then the whole perched like an albatross on the cliff out over the ocean and it gave him a feeling of elation. One thing he was sure of, he would have a house like this one day, after all the fine automobile awaiting him outside had started with a wish.

"Your eyes are sparkling tonight...!" A husky woman's voice overtook Rand. A hand caught his arm causing the wine to spill out of his glass in tiny golden droplets, which floated to the floor and were instantly absorbed by the Turkish Kalim on which he stood. A middle aged woman, thin with flesh drawn tightly across her cheekbones from too many cosmetic surgeries stood facing him with a smile.

"Are they ?"

"...oh yes," she brushed his lips slightly with a kiss. "Nice to see you Rand."

Rand smiled. "And... you Marianne." Inhaling the scent of flowers, alcohol and the heady woman scent watching how the silk skirt slid sensuously across her buttocks as she walked away. She was a woman who never married, but seemed comfortable with it, at ease. Perhaps the appointment to the judiciary could conceivably supplant desire.

"Good things ..." said a heavy man in his early sixties whose hair was coarse, gray and flowing over his ears. He was eating shrimp from a glass plate and there was butter glistening on his fingers and his chin. A huge belly hung over his trousers. "Good things come with age I meant to say, but my mouth was too pig full."

"Gavin!" he frowned, "How the hell...? I haven't seen you since... when was that?"

"Oh yes, oh God..." he sputtered between gulps of shrimp, "*that was a horrible night!*" Pausing to suck the butter off his fingers and give them a cursory wipe on a cocktail napkin before grasping Rand's hand with a smothering grip.

"Yes...depends I suppose."

"Yes ...yes ..." he held on for a long time smiling and looking smug as if some unspoken joke was passing between them. It escaped Rand altogether. "You know I've been meaning to call you." Still holding the hand.

Suddenly apprehensive Rand withdrew though tried to keep up the camaraderie. "Well," he said, "here I am. What about?"

"Business, I ..." he paused and introspected.

"Oh...that."

"Fact is I've taken on a criminal case, drug case to be specific, and uh...you know, spent most of the last ten years primarily focused on financial matters...now the climate is...Christ there's so much competition and the cases are available..." he wheezed as he talked the air forcing itself up through his large frame and no matter how friendly and good natured he tried to be there was a sullen tone to his voice. "One of my former clients, seems there had been some laundering..."

Rand was genuinely surprised, "You want advice from me?" condescending without meaning to be.

Gavin conceded begrudgingly. "Suppose I do." Images flashed of an even younger Rand DesVergers who used to sit in the polished cordovan leather chair in his office and agonize over the most remedial cases. He wondered how the man had managed to succeed so brilliantly when he, well, one who had a truly sound understanding of constitutional law... "Yes, it is a..." he paused, " but I understand you've had a bit of experience with these cases, and I thought perhaps you could bring me up to date a bit."

He glowed with a self satisfaction that he hoped wouldn't show. "Sure. Any time, any time. Just call me."

"Thanks."

The moment was an uneasy one and after a silence Rand finally asked. "Did you see the game Saturday?"

"Uh...no."

"What a fucked performance!" He clapped the older man on the shoulder relieved to have an excuse for talking. "Those sons of bitches really let me down this year! They were undefeated. I lost five hundred bucks, can you believe that?"

"I never bet."

"Too bad Gavin." he stood there consolingly and quietly with his hand on the big man's shoulder trying to maintain some sense of levity, "too bad." He watched his old friend fumble with a shrimp. The man had not been doing well the last few years, too many bright young lawyers who would work at any price. He wasn't doing well at all. " I'm going to try some of those shrimp you've been stuffing in your mouth...call me now," he spoke, retreating, "Call me, I'll be glad to help."

The older man forced a smile, "You bet pal," but spoke glumly, "thanks." He lifted a shrimp as a toast.

He didn't like to give advice for free, especially about drug cases, it touched a nerve. His eye caught a fleeting image. At first he just watched absently wondering why Gavin had specifically asked about drugs, and if someone had put him up to it, or if he knew more than he was saying...he watched not knowing why he watched with riveted attention thinking other thoughts of other things but still...she seemed to be looking directly at him in the reflection forming a perfect vignette among the clusters of leaves and tiny lights...but when he turned and found her in the crowd he realized that she had been looking through him as if he were invisible. The dark haired woman. Maybe she really just needed legal advice, he'd never thought of that. She didn't seem to remember him.

"I love lingerie!" The young woman on the couch between the two men intoned punctuated with a squeeze to the thigh of the man on her right, and by a drop in her eyelids and a forced sultry smile. "I have a wonderful collection...but never anyone to wear them for..."

An older woman in a black suit scowled, took out a cigarette and pounded it on the table to pack the tobacco in the old style, before they put filters on everything. A couple of men chuckled. Rand sat comfortably in the empty chair feeling very relaxed from the wine and more at ease since the whiskey. "I was drawn by the intellectual nature of this conversation."

"We were just being given a verbal tour of Paulene's underwear," the woman in black offered passively blue smoke curling from her mouth and nose in defiance of anyone who might object.

A man raised his glass losing some of its contents in the process. "Here's to candid conversation."

"Warren," Rand turned to the man on whose thigh Paulene's hand rested, "what do you think? "

The man considered for a moment rubbing his finger and thumb on the bridge of his nose as he always did causing his gray eyebrows to rise in worried little arches and his mouth to purse and turn down at the corners emphasizing the blueness of his lips. Smelling the burning cigarette at the table made him want one, desperately want one, long for one with a craving only an addict could comprehend, but since his bypass surgery he had been able to quit, and though he didn't really believe they were unhealthy, he hadn't had one since. Clearing his throat and raising his head up to stroke his chin he proclaimed in a gravel like whispery voice, "I think there'll be war."

"Paulene, will there be war?" Rand asked bluntly.

"Never happen," she replied without hesitation.

"How you can be so sure of yourself?" The woman across the table cut with an icy remark not even looking at her as if to say *how can you be sure of anything at your age?*

Paulene skillfully placed her glass on the table looking calm and certain. It was something she'd learned from having spent years as a receptionist before she worked her way up to being an executive secretary and then, after night school, a paralegal "I just am."

"That's nice Pauline, but it's unavoidable at this point. To think otherwise is simply naive."

"I don't know about that. Where's your faith?" a younger man with shiny black hair responded. "No one's out for blood."

Rand spoke, "Not the blood…it's money."

The woman in the black suit nodded her head in silent agreement and looked away across the room having had this conversation before. "It's money!"

A man across the table hooked one thumb under the lapel of his jacket and slid his hand down to where it was neatly buttoned enjoying the feel of the material. "Money's not it...power. I hate to think what would happen if we didn't have some kind of say so in managing the flow of oil–and of governments."

"Well," said Paulene emphatically, "Glad you two aren't in charge." The fire burned high and crackled fiercely sending hot air rushing up the chimney.

"You don't really know what war is?" The woman in black had listened to the conversation trying not to get involved. But a memory had been resurrected. One that she had not called for and he came now in his white linen suit, always crumpled at the elbows and knees. These young men had some of the same qualities about them, but only some. They lacked a certain desperateness, perhaps the most memorable thing about him. There were many with that characteristic then, it was a product of civil disorder, of the times. He was too young, she recalled now, to grasp the significance of his actions but had the physical energy to accomplish them unlike the old ones who were already defeated. She could remember his smell as if it were only a few days ago. It wasn't until long after that she knew what he was doing, and later still that love had gone. She looked around the table again, she would never have loved one of these men–they lacked desperation.

Her hair was close cropped and graying, the face was strong, determined though still feminine and faintly Rand thought he perceived a look of someone who had lost something irretrievable. "I think I understand what war is. In this case it's a matter of looking after our democratic interests, and the action would be justified...if we didn't prolong it like Afghanistan and Iraq."

"Whose interests? What would be the first thing you'd do with the rumor of war?"

One man replied, "I'd call my broker!" Acting as if he would laugh, looking to the others for reassurance, finding none, and at last giving it up.

The woman smiled, "Exactly so."

"It's only natural", Rand interjected, "to look after your investments."

"Not everybody has investments."

He set his glass down. "Oh come on! I didn't know you were a democrat."

There was stiff laughter at the table everyone thinking that with that the party mood would resume, but Rand felt annoyed. There was no reason behind this feeling, it clouded his vision and made him frown. "A man has a right to take a profit, and to look after its source. That's the free market."

The woman was calm and gentle, and completely without malice. "Let me ask you," she paused and watched him for a moment, "do you believe in justice?"

"You don't become a lawyer without some faith in the constitution," he replied stiffly and sat back taking a quick drink.

Paulene was uncomfortable and uncrossed her legs, then crossed them again. The conversation had suddenly become intense and to her dismay no one at the table was paying any attention to her anymore.

"But do you believe in justice?"

Looking hard at her he quietly replied, "Of course I do."

The woman nodded. "Then let me ask you this, do you think a man tests himself?" she asked with sincerity and then continued without pausing for an answer. "I think a man lives his life and does those things that align with his view of the world and what he wants from it. I think that he puts himself in circumstances where he'll find out what he's made of." Their eyes met and embraced beyond the veil of reason. "Don't you think we're all tested like that?" She paused.

He was mystified at what impulse could have possibly inspired this conversation, but at the same time was disturbed by it and felt accused. "Well that's an interesting idea, I can't say I've never heard it before...I'm more concerned with...the present...that is myself...just living..." he struggled to articulate a particular attitude, "living well is its own reward...I don't think I test myself. I think survival is the test, just making it. Some people can do it well and some can't, but I'm not going to give it up just because there are those who are unable to have it, or don't want it. Justice has a price, and I think that price is being able to cut it. I like my life, I like having money, being around my friends," gesturing to the others at the table eliciting semi-intoxicated mumbles of good natured approval, "and I like houses like this one." Feeling more confident now and letting the alcohol take effect, "I will say if there has to be a war to protect the economy then so be it. I'm not looking back."

"I missed the war," Warren said in dead earnest pointing to his chest, "heart murmur."

"You wouldn't believe the case I've got this time." The man with shiny black hair spoke loudly from too many drinks. There was smoothness to his voice, a cultured sound. His fingers were very slender and long and he had a habit of placing them together without letting the palms touch when he talked. A very expensive suit was draped around him like a Botticelli painting, a gold, flat watch with roman numerals on its dial graced his left wrist and he wore woven Italian shoes with the laces looped through the holes so that they showed only in straight lines never crossing or touching. In his pocket was a thousand dollars in a tight, little money clip that he liked to caress and hold when he was speaking with his clients so that he would not forget his roots. "This kid can hardly speak English...he's one tough guy..." he went on, wondering to himself what his father would think now, being here among some of the most successful lawyers in the city, his friends, *his kind* as the old man used to say, though he was a public defender and all the others in private practice...a way to justify the wealth he'd been born into. The old man saw it differently and decided his son was not very bright. He was smart though, but confused, and standing in the squalor of the "fleeting masses", as he called them, whose time on earth was so fragile being balanced by their angry passions, addictions and penchant for trouble, which seemed to come easily to those who could not earn a decent living. He raged in the center of a life he detested but continued to uphold as a gesture of feigned nobility. "... charged with murder. A truck crashed through a neighborhood grocery window, you see, and the owner, a middle aged Arab man, was found underneath it. Dead. The man had called the police two days earlier because of drug dealings in front of his store and some Latinos were arrested. The kid's part of a gang."

"Interesting," said Warren in his most sardonic manner.

A bit agitated, Rand welcomed the distraction. "Well, is he guilty?"

The other man sat back and put his hand in his trouser pocket getting comfortable and holding his thousand dollar money clip. He explained that the boy was arrested in his home and a considerable amount of crack cocaine was found hidden in a box in his closet under some magazines, and that his finger prints were found in the truck, on top of which there is a witness who is fairly certain she could identify him as the one seen running from the crash. "He says it's mistaken identity." The man smiled, "his only alibi is that he was asleep at the time."

Rand grinned. "You can beat it, there's always a technicality in these cases."

"I'm not so sure he should beat it." The woman in the black suit said quietly.

"Why not," Rand replied still looking at the public defender, "it's your duty, he's your client. That's what they pay you for isn't it?"

"Yes," said the man fumbling with the money clip wishing his arms were feathered wings and all he had to do was raise them to the fury which bore down on him and mount the wind so it would ferry him, cradle him aloft as he hung suspended over the dark sea, the waters torn by a million wind-fingers, the sanctuary of solitary mariners, the womb of fishes, the naked back of irreclaimable spirits stretching from man-shore to siren's lair. Here he imagined he would find his requiem for he had long ago passed from life and had yet to be acknowledged. The law of Abraham haunted his every evening, and he thought now about the young tough boy who had killed a man for having done his civic duty, and he, who had chosen to defend those without means so that all men might reach some level of equity before the books, was once again burdened by the proof of innocence. How many crimes could one man withhold before his usefulness dissipated even if they were not his own? Committed on a path to disaster he was yet too proud to admit he was wrong, and had no idea who he really was amidst the moral chaos. "The truck was owned by a friend, he'd been in it before, and his home was searched without a warrant, and he's got a clean record believe it or not."

"See," Rand asserted, "I told you." He was pleased, and went on to explain the real issue. How it wasn't the fact of drugs but the relationships of people to the world of drugs that needed an arbitrator. "...otherwise, it's just a witch hunt. These people need someone to be their voice and place their actions in proper perspective so there will be no violation of constitutional rights, and often procedural errors can be uncovered, iniquities that if left standing can place a person's civil liberties in jeopardy." Here was the real challenge, he continued, feeling more at ease and losing the jagged edge now that he could speak about something of weight and be understood by his peers.

Soon enough the conversation turned to cars, his new pearlescent teal vehicle sitting outside, the stock market and the cost of real estate on the West Side reaching those common denominators that everybody could agree on and that made them all, in the end, such good company for each other. Outside the wind pummeled the glass and whipped the chimney smoke away never to be seen again.

An inebriated Randall DesVergers managed to corner the woman who so bewitched him with her reflection earlier. The dark haired one. His obsession. Her eyes were shadowy and she had the moist, smooth brown skin of a Eurasian with black perfect hair shining and wild. Long fingers caressed the air as she spoke with delicate abandon, and lips the color of ripe fuchsias that danced deliciously over her white teeth. She struck poses, timid, then bold, then vulnerable like a mannequin in a shop window. The woman was young and perfect and married to an older man for what reason he could only guess, but Rand could not hear her words and only played his eyes over her body as he secretly wished she was not married and even despite this drawback tried to reconfirm a rendezvous where he might further posses her.

Two figures stood close. Out of the mainstream of lights and conversation where her husband was. "I thought you'd forgotten."

"You did?" She fidgeted and could not keep still looking around, sipping at her drink holding her arms in tight to her sides accenting her perfectly poised shoulders and uncommonly straight posture. Her thin dress hung by two narrow threads that lay across her brown skin like pencil lines, she seemed to float in it separate and unattached as if a fresh primeval life form swimming naked in its nourishing plasma anxious for escape.

Randall inhaled her essence. It washed over him like the scent of a fresh cut mango. "You looked as if you didn't recognize me."

"I did?"

Anxious. "It's just...I'm looking forward to...Sunday." Trying to read her as she moved with incessant waves and ripples and refused to meet his gaze.

"I can't make that." She said tersely not letting her eyes fall on him once.

Confusion struck. "I guess I'm glad I ran into you." Rand frowned. He attempted to look at the ground, but instead found himself looking at her legs just below the hem of her dress, the skin of her knees and thighs as she shifted her weight, and imagined never being able to possess her. He could not explain the attraction that seemed to pull him from his solar plexus to hers completely against his will without any transcendental thoughts whatsoever. All he knew was that it obscured his judgment.

"Yes." She said.

He raced. "Can we reschedule?" Looking sideways quickly.

"No. My husband..." She began, and then stopped with some tiny little inner frustration that ruffled her poise for a fleeting instant. "I'll be out of town."

"My luck."

With a slight exasperated sigh she glided past him, leaned for a moment up against the door frame and looked directly at him with large, dark eyes that were extraordinarily white against her skin and breathed so that her breasts rose and fell brazenly beneath the layer of modesty.

"Teake..." he began to place his hand on the wall and incline over her, but she floated around the edge of the doorway and vanished with a flare of her loose, gauzy dress. Two steps into the hall where she stood he followed. Suddenly, Teake grasped him firmly around the back of the neck with one hand and pulled him violently to her. She kissed him with an open mouth raising one knee. Her tongue invading. Her breath mingling. Rand could taste the waxy soap like flavor of her lipstick, the alcohol, and the basic sweetness of her that was, like her smell, imbued with ambrosia like quality that he desired obsessively without limit. With her left hand she grasped his crotch harshly and gripped tightly causing him to wince. Her hand moved in a slow, tiny, circular motion, but did not release the pressure that was close to pain.

Rough strokes across her right breast. The hard nipple caressed his palm through the thin, silken fabric. His hand ran down the side of her lean body in one long rapid stroke until he felt the warm flesh of her leg. Teake breathed into him hotly as he ran his hand up over her buttocks, lifting the edge of her dress, praying no one would walk around the corner and especially not her husband who was an appellate court judge. A finger placed under the single strap of her thong panties. It made her press her mouth harder against him. Emboldened his hand rested upon her wet sex, but he did not move or caress her, just inserted one finger and kept absolutely still letting the heat sear him to her as if he had placed his hand in a boiling kettle.

Teake sucked his breath away, arched her back and looked at him eight inches from his face, but made no move to retreat. The muscles flexed in her right arm as she applied more pressure to his genitals while her eyes flared and he concentrated on the pain to keep from getting a full erection. She glared at him. Her lips drew back slightly from her teeth, lipstick smeared recklessly around her mouth. "We're going to Aspen this weekend. "she whispered hoarsely with a rush of honeyed air through her teeth and squeezed him once more. "Why don't you come?"

BETWEEN THE LABYRINTH AND THE SKY

VIII

Life was full of distances. Randall DesVergers was certain of that one fact because all his travels loomed up over him and layered, one upon the other, forming a linear history of places and events that defined who he was. They gave him refuge and solace from the harshness inherent in living that he had difficulty facing. Distance gave him the opportunity to be anonymous. He could be enigmatic and elusive sweeping through other's lives as a silent shadow leaving them to wonder at the event of his passing figuring on who he might be by adding up the quality of his characteristics deftly revealed as clues and evidence. He knew there was life below him, but all he could see was the sky. It had burned brightly, a fire along the horizon, since he lifted off from Los Angeles in the small, chartered jet in which there were only four other passengers, who had left their own traces, the mystery of which for others to ponder.

Marmots and pure white ermines bounded through freshly powdered snow a lifetime below the aircraft. In the fading embers the sun rolled off over Asia where teeming billions toiled and worried in the struggle having waited throughout the long night for the flaming yellow star to once again appear and give them a reason. Wind whistled in the hollows. Streams lie frozen. Spirits listened. The night visitors made ready for their rounds.

Rand had taken a limousine to the airport. He had finagled an invitation to the "Smoker," an event lavishly sponsored once a year by the cowboy lawyers who ran in Ashford Van Riper's circle. "Too rich for the blood," Ashford had replied when Rand asked why he wasn't attending this year, though he had not missed one from the start of the tradition and always returned laden with thousands of dollars in illegal Cubans destined for his home's built-in wall-sized humidor rumored to be one of the best stocked in the city. The event took on heroic proportions boasting reclusive celebrities, ex-presidents, former astronauts, literary lions, tattooed and earringed multimillionaire sports figures, network anchormen and old money ranchers turned real estate barons deftly maneuvering to position themselves among the elite for the legendary weekend where deals materialized out of the haunts of power. Fortunately, the unused invitation was easily transferred to him with one brief telephone call from the senior partner. "Are you planning to run for office?" Ashton jibed with the phone to his ear, "most of the supreme court usually shows up."

He did not smoke cigars except when forced to on such occasions as in Ashton's office. Rand did not understand bonding. He had always liked women far more than men and if given a choice would rather have been in their company and only when this was not possible did he gravitate toward the assemblage of males that always seemed to be congregating somewhere. He thought bonding was overrated and shunted it off to the same category as "quality time" and other end-of-the-century banalities that had been forced on him by the socially liberal of his generation whom he had little in common with; and who had bequeathed a legacy of soldiers trained to kill who could sleep with one another, as long as no one asked, but would be imprisoned for patting a woman on the butt.

His fingers curled around a short glass of smoked whiskey and he swirled the ice cubes in it every few minutes as he alternately sipped and looked out the small, oval window at the vanishing landscape rolling up beneath them into the night. It took him at least an hour in flight before he could feel that he had left Los Angels and at the boundary between the labyrinth and the sky he soared momentarily out of his body in a burst of freedom that he, without reason, felt that men were born to. The cold haunting of the Rocky Mountains enfolded him as the plane raced past the limits of cities leaving their glittering neon in its wake. Sleep found Rand and with it came peace for he did not dream and lingered between two worlds waiting for an unknown resolution.

The shudder was fierce. It sounded as if heavy link chains were being wildly thrashed against the sides of the bulkheads and the skin of the jet was rippling away from its alloy ribs. Rand woke into a torrential scream of noise floating in mid air ten inches above his seat suspended on the loose straps of his safety belt and tried to yell, but no sound escaped or if it did was lost in the banshee wail of the wind rush. His whiskey glass slowly drifted past his face, the golden liquid languidly sloshing up one side as it levitated weightless, the remnants of ice cubes still in place. The whole aircraft shook violently and he gasped sucking in all his breath at once and looked out the window to his right to make sure the wing had not torn free and then to the left. *Christ*, he thought, *I'm going to die!* One man he could see, several seats ahead of him, was struggling on the ceiling having failed to keep his belt fastened and all over the cabin magazines, newspapers and other personal belongings tossed about helter skelter. Outside was total blackness. The painted crimson line that had followed them for so long had finally been extinguished and so Rand could not tell if they were heading straight down or...*how long*, he wondered, *how long would it be before they hit*? Did he have time to remember all the things that he had always wished he could accomplish in this life? Would there be precious seconds to dredge up and relish the moments that he had been immeasurably happy to have been alive, where the life was bursting vibrantly forth in him and with such immutable boldness that he shone like northern lights; Could he recount all the transgressions he had so recklessly committed without thought and find God at this final instant to deliver him? Would there be one last sweet breath where every moment of his life was at his calling, remembered all at once in a grand sweep as if all the experience he had ever gained would be sung out in one long low note in a voice over the reaches and the vast plains and off into the wastes of all the oceans of the world?

Even then he did not pray, never having believed in God and so at this final moment maintained his resolve that life, however spiritual, was in control of its own destiny for good or evil. Though he wished, longed for the power of the air to reach out in its infinite mercy and with its hands lift them up from their descent; the crazy, headlong dive which none of them had ever wished for and must only have come about of ignorance, of foolishness, of pride…if only it wasn't this way…it was the closest he ever came to prayer. Then, at precisely that moment Randall DesVergers would have been willing to give over his life into the hands of providence, into the bosom of Abraham if only he could live for one more day, only one more day. It was then he felt it. So subtle was its presence he would never be able to describe it later, but without question there was an effort to lift the aircraft from it path of disaster. He felt the wild, frenetic, desperate struggle, could almost see through the eyes and wretched his head around to peer helplessly at the wings wanting to see something that would give him hope. That would demand hope. Yet still the battle raged in frenzied helplessness and he closed his eyes to concentrate on it as if to endow it with all of his life energy, all of his intellect, all of his emotion. And then with one massive, turbulent shake the plane wretched itself from the gaping maw of catastrophe and began to level off. He crashed back down into his seat with a thud despite the thick padding and the glass of whiskey tumbled to the floor spilling its contents all over him in the process. The man in the front of the cabin fell heavily off the ceiling and grunted loudly as the back of the seat caught him just below the kidney and dumped him harshly into the isle. An older blonde woman, a gash on her head and blood flowing into her eyes, grabbed at his shirt to keep him from bouncing around. Just then Rand glimpsed lights out of the corner of his eye and instinctively turned just in time to see the glimmer of runway beacons. Within an instant they touched down in a perfect landing where all three wheels met the tarmac at exactly the same time and not one person on the plane could tell when precisely that was they landed so smoothly.

Later, when Rand was leaving the plane and the pilot stood near the door breathlessly explaining in a trembling yet firm voice about wind shear and fluctuating pressure zones affecting lift and vertical stability he had grasped the man's hand with both of his and just stood there before him, both men struck speechless as the dynamics of their lives intermingled and the power swelled around them in swirling, rushing eddies.

Hotel Jerome had been built in 1892 by the silver barons of Aspen Colorado. It stood now at the apex of luxury having been restored to its original splendor by conspiratorial entrepreneurs and furnished with authentic antiques of the period. Rand rented a luxury four wheel drive vehicle at the airport and cautiously drove over the packed snow of the road to the hotel with the heater blasting against the cold. He was still shivering from the acquaintance he had nearly made with death and was surprised that he never heard its footsteps. On the periphery lingered the thought of how fragile life was and with what ease it could be snatched away.

It was the last week in March and the Rockies were experiencing a series of spring snowstorms that had dumped the heaviest pack of powder anyone could easily remember. The town was overflowing tourists. The privileged from all over the world had come to ski, to dine on gourmet cuisine, to peruse the haute élégant and simply be in the company of their own rarefied kind for no where else could they be understood so well and pandered to with such grace. Rand inched his way down the icy thoroughfares gripping the wheel needlessly his eyes bothered by the flare of lights from oncoming cars, feeling disoriented from the flight and finding it difficult to breathe in the altitude. He felt the overwhelming stillness that rushed down the freshly powdered fifteen thousand foot slopes and filled the valley with a lament of nature so poignant and beguiling that even the rich were enraptured. There was something decidedly inhuman and wild about it. Snow fell lightly dancing with little flurries in front of the windscreen. The headlights' glare stood out in yellow beams cut through the air. Rand did feel light however, buoyant almost and remarkably strong as if his blood raced through his veins and muscles were flexed in anticipation of something unknown. A breezy, reckless sensation flowed over him, which he ascribed to the lack of oxygen.

"Yer hand's shakin' buddy."

"Yes," Rand replied retrieving a whiskey and water from the man behind the bar and turning to face the room full of people. He stood straight in an old fashioned, formal manner and hoped the drink would loosen him up as he was still tied up in cases from the office that he desperately wished he could set aside for the weekend. It was a dimly lit room. The light was a subtle ochre that bathed people's faces in a painterly manner reminding him of the Vermeers he'd seen. Each line and angle was accentuated until the masks became characterizations of the person behind it. The bistro was elegantly designed as it would have been in nineteenth century Europe with a low ceiling compartmented into sections by finely finished woodworked beams, a chandelier wrought in filigreed leaves that radiated down as if filled with candles and walls of dark mocha with a broad, ivory molding. Through the white lace curtains, across the tables– each of which supported a large, silver candelabra in its center–he glimpsed the snow falling lightly in the street. In the back of the restaurant rose an antique, carved marble fireplace that reached from the floor to the ceiling and out of its mouth roared a hardwood fire that resonated crackles and pops with bursts of light when reservoirs of sap were consumed. Aromas of food perme- ated everything while the whole place was suspended on voices like the refrains of a violin; hushed, boisterous, whispered, coy, sardonic, searching, sad overwhelmed ones that mirrored human beings every- where regardless of their social standing.

A touch on his shoulder. "You were on the plane, weren't you?" A masculine, melodic rolling voice curled over him. "Of course. Awww Jesus, what a ride!"

Rand turned. Standing next to him at the bar was the man he had seen tumbling in the isle, as the jet broke free of the wind sheer. "Obviously you weren't hurt," he said like a lawyer pointing out the fact before a claim can be made to the contrary.

"Disappointed?" He cracked lightly being tipsy and slurring his vowels, which were delivered in a practiced elocution that revealed theatrical training somewhere in his past. "Naw, I was mad not hurt..." and he added emphatically, "but I have talked to my attorney already!"

"Good for you. We need the money." Rand said in an effort to mask a slight feeling of shame, as one engaged in some grand fraud to which he subscribed with the tacit consent of those around him yet still bearing its fault.

"Hey," he lurched over and patted Rand on the shoulder, "come... lemme buy you a drink." He raised the whiskey glass between them and smiled haplessly in hopes it would discourage any further discussion, but instead it brought an invitation to join the man and his friends at their table. He followed the stranger through the maze of chatting diners and was awkwardly introduced to another couple of men and a woman, all of whom looked too sophisticated for real life. The men were excessively tanned and the woman, in her late thirties, too, had an aggressive, unnaturally healthy glow. "You eaten here before?" She asked, "The menu's great." Red Mediterranean mullets with pistou sauce; salmon scallops with sorrel á la Troisgros; partridge with red cabbage; pheasant stuffed with fresh goose liver á la Souvarov; hot river trout mousse with crayfish sauce followed by a medley of deserts that ranged from oranges soufflés to pears with Beaujolais. The man insisted upon ordering wine for everyone contentiously portraying himself as a connoisseur subsequently having three bottles of Château Margaux 1926 on the table throughout the meal, which Rand happened to notice from the wine list cost $250 a bottle and so drank it copiously in the mood of the windfall. By the end of the meal he had nearly forgotten about his near brush with disaster.

It was a fitful, intoxicated sleep. Shadows circled and ran their fingers across him leaving trails of fire that burned and made him restless. She was there, the dark haired woman though now in the turbulence that the alcohol brought about she became temporary and waif like at once looming in damp and dense repose beckoning with her skirts drawn back over her toffee brown thighs, blouse thrown open and then vanishing as he moved to her. He woke, and again slept just as suddenly throughout the night. Rand rose early. The spiritual storm of the night left him wounded. He remembered nothing of his dreams.

The air was pure, crisp, still and cold enough to hurt his lungs when he breathed. These altitudes were not natural to men. Golden sunlight was just beginning to tip the high peaks, painting them in bronze-ochers and yellow-oranges above the pale, blue-violet shadows of the crags. It crossed snowy meadows hitting the aspen's sinewy boughs and turning them white against the sky. The sky shone an incandescent blue as the valley slowly came alive. Yellow lights still glowed out windows and smoke had just begun to curl up from chimneys twisting into the oblivion of the winds. It was enough for Rand to know that he was confused, that the tumult of life's distances had alienated him from things that mattered, things he only had faint reminiscences of from when he was young that now went the way of the chimney smoke and breezes. So he walked. He walked all the way through the town with its few hardy souls up at dawn readying their establishments for the day's business and the die-hard skiers heading out to be the first ones on the slopes. A lone skater strode across the municipal ice rink in shadows with her hands clasped behind her back leaning into her stride parting the wind with her grace. A large Irish Setter stood watching from one end its breath visible in little bursts of steam. Deciduous tree branches were barren scribbles against the blue, frosted and shining alternately with ice and snow, great icicles hung undisturbed from the night before and massive trunks lie half hidden in the drifts of snow. Everything was white. The landscape radiated in an aesthetic dance so beautiful that words failed, were too far below, were inadequate. *Some things must be experienced*, Rand mused over the land, *some things are best unspoken*. The snowplow had only reached one side of the street and it left the night's wonder piled in a white hedge three feet high beside the road. He touched the earth and he was glad.

An hour later he returned to the center of town with his trouser legs wet from traipsing through knee deep snow drifts and sat busily eating a plate of ham and eggs with salsa in a crowded, bustling cafe. *To the living,* he thought, while he perused a Denver newspaper whose front page story was a grim tale of a young policeman engaged to be married who had been shot execution style by a gang member during a petty hold up just because he was a cop. "To the living," he mumbled and swallowed dark, bitter coffee whose stale aroma he even enjoyed and for a flitting, brief almost indistinguishable instant Rand had a clear concept of his purpose, of what he should be doing in life though it passed quickly. The day had warmed up from the night and a wall of sunlight peered over the ridge finally making its way down the mountain into the valley. But what really brought him to consciousness was the noise of people; the guffaws and laughter; the silly, saccharine whining; the wails of a small child testing out his vocal chords and the smells of them all mixed with after shave, soap, perfume, mouthwash and bacon. Here was where he belonged in the belly of humanity, on the run of it where the tapestry of people made up the landscape and their voices were the music and their movements were the ebb and flow and all of life congregated in their ideas that were envisioned in glass and steel and concrete. When he walked out into the street again he was almost giddy.

The first thing he bought that day was a scarf and he did it without thinking. It was, he confided to the salesman in the store, the most useless thing to own in Los Angeles, yet he purchased it anyway as if he were destined to be someone else and could not bring himself to give up the icons. From there he proceeded to hit every shop in town, methodically, as they opened their doors aimlessly rummaging through the shelves and racks. He bought a black and white sweater imported from Italy with a heavy, roll down cowl neck for three hundred and ninety-five dollars; a ski parka for seven hundred and fifty; two more sweaters; a pair of alpine hiking boots even though he hadn't hiked since college, but imagined he might start; a four hundred and fifty dollar pair of polarized sunglasses that tinted dark when light hit them and paled in its absence; a digital sports watch that had an altimeter and heart rate monitor and finally a complete set of skis, boots, bindings and poles that were, the sales person assured him, state-of-the-art, computer designed, driven by technology and tested by the extreme ski team who were out to make extreme skiing an official Olympic sport for the next winter games. The set up cost him thirty two hundred dollars.

Wind whistled by in gusts as he stood alone on the ridge of the mountain having caught a tow rope from the lift drop off point that whisked him away from the crowd. Fleecy, white clouds traveled above him closer than they could ever be down below, in the domains of men. Rand smelled snow, the astringent coolness of it and pine that came with the rushes of air. Below him on one side was a high mountain meadow– ringed by stately, guarding evergreens laden with heaps of white powder from the night before and stands of aspen looking as if they'd been planted in rows– that gently curved down into a bowl where skiers floated gracefully in slow, precious arcs. On the other side was the valley. Tiny dots of color raced headlong down the precipice from the lift end barreling through waist high drifts with huge rooster tails pluming up in white showers as they crisscrossed the slope. The town lie sheltered. Sunlight tipped its outskirts. He could see cars traveling slowly on the streets, ice glistening on the rooftops, but heard nothing as if it were a miniature in a bell jar filled with liquid and tumbling flakes. When he was a child he had found things in nature to supplant the relationships he imagined were supposed to exist in a family. He ran to the forests always where the bosom of eternity held him close to its mossy heart.

He was born during the great shift of generations when the world was transforming itself from the tragic climax of mistaken and ill founded ideologies that had, for the second time in the century, swept away the future. He arrived in a place of confusion and tumult where the fabric of daily life that had been woven through succeeding centuries was under scrutiny and men's ideas were subject to confinement and attack. Radical swings in both directions defined the conflict of minds in the intellectual community of the early sixties and eventually would cause the wall to crumble, but for the most part a frightened conservatism gripped the people of the mainstream. His father, having missed the war by reason of physical disability, was a proud soldier of the reconstruction driven mercilessly to succeed by his sense of failure at not sacrificing his life for victory as so many others had done. He adopted the promotion of business, industry and all the engineering and mechanical developments that mushroomed as a byproduct of the concentrated war effort as his divine cause and became a marketing man for large corporations. To his father there was nothing else. The earth and all its resources were simply there to fuel his contribution to the old and nearly forgotten doctrine of manifest destiny. In running from the past, people had retreated to it. This was the world in which Rand found himself and it impressed upon him a way of living that was always to overrule his own inclinations as if he were bound in an iron cast and would guide his moral choices along the well defined paths that those before him had laid out just for this purpose; to provide a course to a successful life. The trouble was that the definition of success had changed over time and in truth the whole of the relationships between men and the environment, between themselves, between groups and corporations and special interests and governments and churches had undergone a debilitating catharsis leaving in its wake furrows of ethical principles, moral codes, tenets, ideologies, theories and maxims that all had equal importance and equal validity. Everything began to equal everything as vestiges of the empire of human knowledge dissolved like steam. Truth was up for grabs. Living in the world had come down to common denominators. Technological principles. Life itself was just part of the whole, no longer the prime mover. Rand had no need to look for excuses because they were provided for him and he had only to buy into the mainstream where the violence of life, the raw struggle was hidden by the ease with which words flowed from the mouths of vested interests and the cries of the victims.

They lived in a gray, two story shingled house with a brick foundation in the township adjacent to Grosse Point, Michigan. There were sumacs, oak and elm trees in the yard that threw cool shade over the grass during the humid summers and elderberries grew wild up over the back fence. His father had taken a job in the marketing department of the Ford Motor Company and even though his place of work was too far away to comfortably travel, he commuted every day by train just so he could reside in the neighborhood near the wealthy and their mansions and where the security of old money lay.

Rand remembered his father most clearly from when he was small as he appeared in the doorway near bedtime having just come home from the office; his uniform dark suit and mandatory white shirt and neck tie stooped over holding a hat in his hand with the light streaming in from behind so that he appeared only in silhouette and Rand could not make out his features. It was a mystery to him whether his father was happy or disillusioned or harbored some wound that made him continually sad. "Goodnight son." He would say, simply and tersely and then close the door. When Rand awoke in the morning he was gone again. His mother, who was a shy, fragile woman, would spend hours talking to him and made an effort to explain her husband, whom she loved and clung to as a harbor in her desperate search for dry land. "He loves you," she would tell him, "it's just his way...he doesn't mean it. Dad's just looking after all of us." And in her eyes he remembered seeing seagulls flying, soaring in the blue, watery expanses of her and to him it always brought to mind the fact that she was only passing, transitory, a sojourner not having found in this life what she had been after. He was only ten when she died. The doctors had said it was from "natural causes", probably a heart attack, but his father knew exactly why and consequently would not allow an autopsy. "She was weak," he told his son not long after her passing without a hint of what emotion he might be feeling, "no matter what anyone will tell you in this life, strength is the only thing that will pull you through. People only really respect you if you're unwavering. Never give up son. Never."

Rand's childhood had been extremely lonely, but despite this he was friendly and loved being around people finding it easy to talk to strangers, not at all the way his mother had been. He missed her terribly for a while, he missed their talks and the searching expanse of her eyes and the warm smell of her. Of his playmates and other children in the neighborhood he only became close with one. A deaf girl. She was bright, beautiful and articulate in the way that a hearing person could never be. They were inseparable. It was from her that he learned the language of the forest as a result of their long hikes that were completely silent and devoid of the kid banter that usually reduced the finer things to adolescent banalities. She taught him the names of all the trees stopping at each unique species and writing out its genus with her finger in the moist soil and moss by its trunk, in Latin and English, and then would write out its true name, the name that only the protector of the forests knew and if spoken by any other person would fall away with no sound from their lips no matter how hard they tried. This name she wrote in Gaelic, a language her father, who had been a professor at the University in Ann Arbor for many years and now taught at the local high school, had taught her. Rand never learned to say these names because she could not speak well and so there was no way for him to hear exactly how they sounded. He preferred to think that it was by reason of their nature though that he could not speak them, for no matter how hard he tried no sound would come out.

They ran through the snow and ice skated together on the rink in the vacant lot next door, which they flooded with the garden hose when the weather got cold enough and would play hockey, one against the other even letting kids from the neighborhood join in and sometimes setting up formal teams with all the positions filled just like the Red Wings from Detroit and battle it out into the dark or until a disagreement broke out that could not be resolved causing everyone to disperse and go home to supper. They stole away and spent afternoons sliding down the huge grassy slopes, that were covered with snow, on long sleds across the river from the insane asylum, though it was called a mental hospital by then, but still had the look of a nineteenth century prison with its soot covered red brick and small bleak windows that were covered with iron bars. They imagined they saw faces peering at them from behind the confines and Rand swore he could hear a scream now and then.

In the summer they ran barefoot everywhere because it made them feel as if they were violating some moral principle that held society together and by doing so were exerting their independence. They swam together constantly in a huge pond that lie deep in the leafy forest, fed by an underground spring and surrounded by nettles, poison oak and maple trees and sometimes they swam in the nude coming to the place on impulse, being close friends and thinking nothing about it even though Rand was nearly sixteen and she the same.

The summers were unbearably hot. In August through September the temperatures ranged from the mid-eighties to the low nineties, which wasn't so untenable except for the humidity, which hovered between ninety-five and ninety-nine throughout the last part of the season. By eight thirty in the morning a sheen of perspiration had appeared and no matter how freshly clothing was from the start, by noon it was a rumpled mess giving everyone a rural, homespun look and making them talk more intimately to each other than they would had done normally. On one particular day, August twenty-second, which Rand always remembered for the two events that occurred which altered his life irreversibly, they had been in the forest and she had been busily writing out the Gaelic names for a new grove of trees they had just discovered when they decided they were so hot a swim was the best thing that they could possibly do. Silently they walked through the forest with heat radiating from its usually cool floor, which was covered with detritus and broad fallen oak and elm leaves, partially rotted branches and green leafy growing things of every description that pushed up through the floor in bright profusion. Rand heard their feet plodding along and could smell the humid, musty odors released by the heat and moisture into the air and the sweetness of animals that had passed and now lie unseen, but he knew they were there. The pond was half in shadow and shimmered steamily, languidly nestled in the crook of the forest. As soon as they arrived they both peeled off their moist clothing with difficulty and dove into the clear water. It was warm like a bath from the constant heat that stayed throughout the night and made them both feel as if they were swimming in some primordial brine teeming with single celled creatures, insects and salamander like crawling things that spent their lives half in the water and half out caught midway in the transgression of evolution. It made their bodies shiver with life and endowed them with a burst of energy which spent itself through the hours in splashing, diving and racing around the pond chasing each other like two sea otters after a full meal of abalone and crabs. For that sudden moment they were one with nature as if its dynamic enfolded them and exchanged life energy with them breathing in and breathing out. They both knew without reason it would be the last time.

Rand lay on his side with his head propped up on his elbow panting, laughing and smiling, his eyes sparkling still wet from the swim. She lie on her back breathless, blue eyes wide, laughing with abandon, exhausted from the exercise water streaming off of her. Beautiful, Rand thought, like a forest creature she lay in front of him with the smooth, flawless skin of the very young that would never again be so wholesome, never so innocent, drops of water running over her arms, across her abdomen and down her thighs and from her hair. On impulse he reached over and touched the nipple of her breast, lightly, then rested his hand full upon her. She continued to laugh and did not take it as anything out of the ordinary laying her hand across his and pressing him closer she turned her head to face him with the joyful, beaming face that he had known for nearly six years now, the face that was so familiar and so precious to him. The skin of her breast was impossibly smooth and he though no wonder women kept them covered they were so sensitive, so vulnerable. And it was warm, far warmer than the day, which had grown intensely hot and humid, yet her flesh burned through it. The thump of her heart could be felt, pulsating and moving inside and he could feel the blood coursing through her veins and rushing to all parts of her body. Nothing would ever be so perfect as she was right now. She reached up and pulled his face down close to hers with her hand behind his neck and then pressed her lips to his in the gentlest, quietest touch he could ever have imagined and would ever know and they stayed their like that for the longest time both understanding that it could never again be like this for either of them and that like a flower its beauty was a fleeting instant before the race of time.

That evening the police came to the door. Rand was still euphoric from the idyllic afternoon and heard them talking with his father in the foyer, but could not make out what they were saying. The voices drifted up the stairs in indistinguishable man-tones filled with the weight and importance men gave to their own affairs and although he strained to understand what was going on, he could not. Outside there was a squad car, a Ford, and Rand was surprised that its red light wasn't shining. It made him feel the visit was unofficial, probably the neighbor's dog again since it was always causing trouble and had chased the milkman through his truck one morning biting off one of his gloves and tearing a hole in the poor man's pants. But it wasn't unofficial and presently his father came up to his room and stuck his head in the door. His face was white. He had the somber look of a man heading off to war knowing he would never come back, never see his family or taste the comforts that living with a woman could bring again, but stoically bore his duty to the grave.

"I'm going out now," he said, "I don't think I'll be back tonight."

"What's going on?"

"It's nothing, just some business. Unfinished business. I have to go."

"What are the police doing here?"

"Just business. Here," he handed Rand a white business card, "call this number after a while and ask to talk to Alexander, Alexander Nachman. Tell him who you are. He'll know what to do." Then he walked over and shook Rand's hand. "Remember, never give up."

He watched from the upstairs window as his father was handcuffed and placed in the rear seat of the police car and felt a cold numbness overtake him slowly blotting out the memory of all that had happened today. After an hour he called the number.

"Hello." He said.

"Nachman residence." Came the voice of a young girl.

"May I speak to..." he fumbled with the card having forgotten the name already, "Alexander Nachman"

"Hold on." Then in a moment a man's voice came on the line, it was friendly and human sounding with a New England accent not at all like the men he was used to hearing. "Yes? Alexander Nachman here."

"It's Rand DesVergers, my father..."

"Yes, yes..."

Rand stuttered, confused and driven, "He gave me your card..."

"Yes, yes...I've been expecting your call."

"It says here you're a lawyer."

"That's right."

There was an uncomfortable moment. "Are you a friend of my fathers?"

"In a way, he's an old associate of mine."

"Why were the police here tonight? Where did they take my father?"

"We need to talk about that..." he said reassuringly trying to keep everything calm.

"Why do we need a lawyer?"

"I'd like to come over..."

"What's going on anyway"

I'm going to get in my car," he spoke slowly, deliberately, " and come over, is that alright?"

"First tell me..."

"Alright. What do you want to know?"

"Was my father arrested?"

"Yes."

"Why? He hasn't done anything!"

"That's why I'm here. You see..."

Why was he arrested?!"

Alexander Nachman replied tersely in an effort to shunt off the demand, praying he wouldn't have to answer on the telephone to a kid miles away. "Just some business?"

"Why won't you tell me?"

"I think it's better in person?"

" I want to know why?"

There was a long silence on the other end and then a sigh of resignation. "Murder." Said the man's voice. "Now can I come and get you?"

"What do you mean murder? Who?

My father never murdered anyone? Who?"

Another sigh traveled down the line as if to say *you deserve what you get.* "Your mother."

"What? I don't believe it!"

"They've arrested him for the murder of you mother?"

"She wasn't murdered, she died of a heart attack! I don't believe it!"

"Randall?" There was absolute silence and then he asked again, quietly but firmly, "Randall?"

After a moment. "Yes?"

"I'm coming. Stay right there."

The trial was scandalous for the primary reason that he had lived in the community adjacent to Grosse Point where the rich had their mansions and old money lie and where anything that happened was news. The newspapers, particularly the Detroit Free Press, were relentless in their dogged pursuit of inside knowledge because the man had worked at Ford, a dynamic and major economic force in the community that by reason of its impact on the daily lives of thousands of workers commanded respect, and at the same time was renowned for its legions of politically conservative, sober business men few of whom had enough individual personality to be distinguished from one another and were famous for their back stabbing to advance up the corporate ladder. Headlines hearkened back to the era of Randolph Hearst. *Murder in Grosse Point Love Nest; Ford Executive Kills Wife In Love Triangle; Secret Sex Orgies End In Murder.* It seems that Rand's quiet and conservative father had been having an affair for several years with the wife of a senior Ford executive whose Grosse Point mansion was only a few miles away from their own house. He had spend many of those late nights at the office in sexual liaison with his paramour when her husband was called out of town, as he often was, and it was most likely in one of those passionate embraces that the plan was hatched. It may have arisen out of the frustration his father must have felt at knowing he was at the limits of his ability and though he could push harder and work longer hours it was unlikely he would advance in his career any further for the simple reason that he just wasn't able enough and no amount of gloss over of the issue could hide the fact. Perhaps if he had chosen another discipline than marketing, the performance of which was immediately measurable in sales and repeat purchases and ultimately reflected in the bottom line and viability of any given model automobile, perhaps if he had been in human resources, or accounting, or engineering where the R&D was nothing but a country club...but as it was he could only show a certain level of results no matter what he did and so would always be regulated to the lower echelons of management. There was nowhere to go.

Until he met Sarah the bored, alcoholic wife of the senior VP for Sales worldwide. She was East Coast, many generations in the money and aside from her husband's fortune was endowed with a large inheritance. There was one stipulation in her Puritanesque family's hold over her trust, that she could never divorce. Fate brought them together on the expansive lawn of the imposing, brick castle that had been designed by a famous architect in the nineteen thirties after an English manner house. Fate and desire. Sarah, having had too much to drink as usual pulled Rand's father away from the crowd that lingered just outside the door on the patio, but stayed mostly inside around the food and wine and complementary bar. It was late fall and though unusually warm for that time of year was closer to winter than summer. She danced in the darkness while the lights from the party streamed off into the sky and then she kissed him, without reason and with no intent just out of the fuming intoxication that drove her to irresponsible acts. He kissed her back for no reason other than the fact that his wife, whom he loved and respected, was too weak to provide the kind of fulfillment he had always desired and consequently the sexual fury pent up inside him, not helped by the fact that he was a quiet and withdrawn man, tended to overpower his good sense. Sarah, however, had kissed a great many men and was widely known to be promiscuous right under her husband's nose and it was thought with his tacit consent, most of their friends allowing for it because of the fact that in Grosse Point it was well known that the rich are not like everybody, they're different. So it was that with a kiss the woman was inspired to perform an awkward striptease right on the grass, out in the acreage that ran down to the lake that was referred to as their back yard, in full sight of the partygoers under yellow bug lights on the patio. She stripped right down to her bare skin except for her red, high heeled shoes and silk stockings, which were pulled down around her ankles.

"What doooya think of that now mister?" She demanded with her hands on her hips brazenly facing him from the shadows hoping like hell that she had shocked the poor quiet man. "Didn't think I would didja?"

His brows furled and his thoughts fumed from behind dark eyes. She was in her early forties and not a beautiful woman, but her body was firm and well proportioned and fit due to the daily tennis matches she had played for the past ten years. He grabbed her wrist like a vise and pulled her roughly toward him.

"Hey!" She objected, "That's enough." But he paid no attention and kissed her roughly on the mouth. She pushed away again. "Don't, fun's over...I was just..." He kissed her again and fondled her body with his big hands running their roughness over her breasts and between her legs causing her to squirm. This time she pushed away violently and wiped her mouth with the back of her hand stumbling in the grass, her high heels kept sinking into the moist earth. "You better leave me alone." She cried quietly yet coyly looking over at him aroused by the power she had unleashed, taunting him naked and vulnerable and searching in vain through drunken eyes for her clothing that she had so recklessly tossed off. She fell to the grass. He was on her in an instant lifting her up, rolling her over and forcing her legs open with his knees and then took her from behind fully clothed with only his trouser zipper undone and she completely naked except for her shoes in the cool night with the faint yellow light from the patio drifting up to them. Their breath vaporized in the night air.

From that moment on Sarah demanded more of the same from him. Their secret liaisons began to occur in more and more bizarre locations; the boat house, the gazebo; the dock; the garage. And ultimately the plan was decided upon by the two of them neither one fingering the other as the mastermind. Rand's father was to dispose of his wife, divorce was frowned upon in the company as well, and then after a year of so, when there would be no suspicion whatsoever they would kill her husband. She would have her full inheritance and him as well, he would have a shot at the big time in the company by marrying her, and if not the fortune would ease the pain of failure. All this came out at the trial. And in the newspapers. Rand couldn't believe it at first and sat watching the proceedings day after day as if it were a bad play, one in which the disbelief could not be suspended by reason of a plot that was too incredible, too improbable. Indeed, that was what they both had hoped would save them, the fact that it was too out of character for both, but one dogged policeman had followed up the rumors of Sarah's promiscuity and from there the case had been built. It was so overwhelmingly conclusive that when it finally came to trial there was little Alexander Nachman could do other than to try for a pea bargain, which got Rand's father life instead of execution by lethal injection.

At the request of his father, Alexander Nachman took over the guardianship of Rand and brought him in to the family with his wife and young daughter and became the executor of the estate put in trust. One beneficial thing happened as a result of the tragedy, and that occurred in the courtroom where Rand sat having nothing else to do other than to follow the lawyers with their arguments and try to make sense out of the complex procedures and layered rules. Many times there were statements objected to and evidence denied that seemed to defy common sense and when, late in the evening, he would ask Alexander the reply was simply, "It's the rule of law." That was the first time he had ever heard the phrase, which would end up as a haunting refrain overseeing everything he would go on to do in his life. He began to look into the imposing, simulated leather, gilt edged law books that were in the dark oak shelves of the downstairs library. After a while the lawyer, noticing a natural interest, directed him, gave him study assignments and then began to question him as to what he'd read, later question him as to what he thought about it and later still asked him to reason out a situation using the principles of law he had learned. It came naturally to Rand, as naturally as sin came to his father as if in some past life that now lie buried in the sordid incidents and painful losses of history he had known it all before and only required hints and nudges to call it all to mind again. By the time he had graduated high school he had learned as much from the library as a first year law student. He had found his calling; or rather it had found him, sought him out in the mysterious way of providence and forced itself upon him. All the other subjects followed suit as his purpose was so utterly consuming that all the disciplines of knowledge fell into place crystallized by the one key element. The rule of law. He understood it completely from the beginning and it clarified all of human relations and political undertakings for within the law he felt was the codification of the complete cyclopedia of human wisdom. Alexander Nachman assumed the role of mentor, and over the years sacrificed much that Rand could receive the best legal education available and ultimately attend Harvard Law School where he graduated among the top of his class.

BETWEEN THE LABYRINTH AND THE SKY

IX

Rand exploded from the ridge of the mountain throwing up plumes of tiny, white crystals that caught a fleeting rainbow in the sun. He raced ferociously down the deeply powdered face praying he hadn't made a mistake. He had not even tested the new equipment. Somehow the cost of it gave him confidence. His legs bent and twisted and turned as he angled down the slopes throwing all the weight into the final moment of the curves, gaining speed and push from the gravity drawing him down at an ever increasing rate. The frigid air roared and burned his ears. Far below he could see the village through the trees as if from an airplane. Just as the feeling of hitting his stride descended upon him and he was truly soaring, he imagined, in a state mirroring perfection two extreme skiers crisscrossed in front of him, arching from each side, traveling at least twice as fast as he and executing turns he had never dreamed of humbling him again. Their grace threw him and he caught an edge nearly tumbling, but was able to regain control at the last moment. It made him confident. He spread his arms out widely on the turns as if to glide, as if to emulate the red tailed hawk he saw in the distance.

The exhilaration left him breathless. Every muscle strained past its limit to maintain command and his legs began to ache from their lack of exercise. Rand descended into the valley with little jerking turns that caught him in the gut with a jolt at each apex and colossal sweeping arcs where he encompassed acres at a time devouring the distances between earth and sky. He gulped the air, demanding more oxygen than was available in the altitude yet each swallow filled him with a satisfying reaffirmation that he was truly alive even at the edge of the world where men did not really belong. Barreling through shoots in the trees narrow enough to allow only one at a time he shot out into the open powder of the meadow. The gentle rung at the bottom gradually leveled off and he sped over the rutted surface that made his teeth chatter and slowly drifted into a long, sliding, curving arc of a stop sending up sheets of snow with great theatrical flourish feeling like all eyes were upon him.

The mob was elegant. They mingled jubilantly across the expanse of the living room faced on the north side by a wall of glass two stories high. Near twilight the crescent moon could be glimpsed. The doors were cracked open letting in fresh air because, despite the cold outside, it was warm from the milling bodies and the huge river stone fireplace at the end of the room that belched out flames from an over fed oak fire. Knits and flannels of every description filled the huge room; colors coordinated revealing the charade, unmasking the rural, homespun, countrified, gentry for the opulent, manipulative, gaudy, urbane consumers that they actually were. Famous faces could be seen casual and relaxed among their peers since cameras of any kind were forbidden and the only reporters allowed to pass the entry were Pulitzer Prize winning senior editors now retired into a life of erudite non-fiction and semi-autobiographical accounts of foreign political affairs. The young women–models, actresses and talk show hosts–were covered with plaids, denims and wools whisked in from Europe's most exclusive shops while the older ones– ex-senator's wives, magazine publishers, philanthropists, and museum docent heads–were more chic in high waisted pleated khaki trousers, long Peruvian woolen capes, scarves and rustic dresses adorned with Navajo concho belts, silver necklaces, earrings and heavy, tooled bracelets that reached half way up their forearms and cost as much as a small car.

A pall of blue smoke settled in the air above. Most of the men chewed on long, dark cigars and many of the women as well. Huge vent fans had been installed hidden in the ceiling of this exclusive residential compound outside of town just for this event, the prestige of it being a much sought after thing. Randall DesVergers did recognize two of three Supreme Court justices as Ashton had predicted and vowed he would maneuver to make their acquaintance before the evening was over. On one long table rows of glass topped humidors were lined up, each one labeled from a premium manufacturer of hand rolled cigars as they had been donated in an advertising gesture by the companies themselves for the Smoker, which was followed closely in the aficionado press throughout the world. They were categorized by region; Cubans most prominently including the Bolivar coronas and El Rey Del Mundo, Ramon Allones and Cohibas; then Hondurans such as the Hoyo De Monterrey Excalibers; Dominicans highlighted by Arturo Fuente Reservas; with showings from Jamaica and Mexico as well. Bottles of fine wine and decanters of brandy and cognac were close at hand. Waiters in black tie snaked through the huddles of guests holding silver trays lofted above their heads laden with hors d'ovres and drinks from the bar. Sumptuous food was laid out buffet style in the long, low formal dining room adjacent and sunken three steps below the front of the house. Rand saw no trace of her, dark haired Teake, and as the light faded from the surrounding white forest he began to wonder if it had been a ruse to deflect his advances. Failure set in.

He found himself surrounded by a group of men that included a famous actor who looked exactly as he did on screen only smaller, a futures broker from Chicago, a CEO of the largest waste management firm in the world, a tennis star, a Republican representative from his district in California and an architect who was cause célèbre of the moment by reason of his radical design for a museum in Portland that had instigated riots. They were discussing real estate and other investments with the sanguine wisdom a cigar and snifter gave a man when an older gentlemen appeared and shook hands with the actor. He was out of character. His conservative, graying demeanor did not blend in. The man was tall and angular and looked fit for what Rand estimated his age to be at mid-sixty-something and was introduced around the circle as Judge Mezzaluna, Dansen Mezzaluna an appellate court judge from Los Angeles. He shook Rand's hand firmly.

"That's right," he said, "I'm with Van Riper, Hazeltine & Brock."

"Of course," he replied still shaking the hand, "I'm very good friends with Jason Brock...'*Sue the bastards!*'"

Rand had to laugh. "How did you know?"

"That's what impelled him through law school."

Murmurs from the crowd shifted through the room, growing loud and boisterous in one corner then another. The discussion went into high gear and the men became animated with alcohol, stressing their meanings with shifted weight, chests thrusting and pointed fingers holding half smoked cigar butts as if their presence gave a more forceful showing to their object. The haze grew to a din.

As the blink of a tigers eye reflected wholly the complexity of the Malaysian rain forest without having to speak one word, without having to move at all so the sight of her impressed itself upon Rand when he was least expecting it. Across the crowded room she circled in and out of view, a glimpse as if a mirage and then gone. Excusing himself he set out after her, but when he reach the place where he thought he had seen her, she wasn't there and he felt he must have imagined it.

A hand grasped his elbow. A body pressed up against him. Warm breath. "Didn't think you'd come."

He turned to her brown eyes. "I thought I'd missed you."

"I saw you talking to my husband?"

"Your husband?"

"Yes. Judge Mezzaluna." He looked over the crowd of heads and spotted the gray hair of the tall angular man whose back was to them now and wondered at his cupidity. "Surprised?"

"Yes."

"I thought you'd seen him last week."

"No."

"Doesn't matter."

"Yes."

"I'm going to get a drink and come right back. Stay there, OK?"

"OK."

He watched her walk away from him making her way through the crowd. She wore a loose, knit wool serape of gray, ivory and deep maroons with tight, ribbed leggings tucked into high boots. Cascades of black hair were braided and tucked up off her neck revealing the graceful slope of her olive skin. When she reached for the wine he saw that the serape was shawl like with an opening for her head and just draped over her held in place by a belt. Bare skin was revealed beneath and the unmistakable round curve of her breast. A breath escaped his lips as she looked back over her shoulder seductively and beamed a smile at him knowing all along the effect she was creating.

Her lips pressed to the glass of clear, white wine and she drank slowly with her mischievous eyes on him all the time, watching for a weakness, smiling, agitated, ravenous.

"Are you hungry?"

"Yes." She answered, and then as they began to walk to the dining room and the lavish spread of food she hesitated, looking back over her shoulder while sipping her wine.

"Shall we eat? he asked wondering if she was uncomfortable with his hidden desire.

"Sure," she said taking a few more steps forward, and then stopped, turned and pressed her hand to his chest. "No."

"Are you hungry?"

"Yes."

His eyes were bewildered as she fluctuated in hesitation before him. "I don't want to waste time," she said looking over her shoulder with the innocent beauty that radiated from her body, the clear whites of the eye and cream complected skin and said, "Lets go upstairs." Without looking at him she headed away. His eyes traced her contours and he felt a knot form in his stomach.

Once she disappeared at the top of the flight he followed inconspicuously clinging to the rail, unobtrusive as his stomach fluttered and his legs grew weak with what he thought was fatigue from the skiing, but was actually fear. As he turned into the hall the house dwindled into darkness with all the lights off making it clear that the owners did not wish their guests to wander unescorted into the wings. The whole compound, inside and out, was constructed of wood finished in a golden oak with full logs, their bark still on them, laid under the roof as ceiling beams. He ran his fingers along the wall as he walked to give him balance and fortitude.

"Here," her voice said urgently and he peered into the unlit doorway. Soft lights played along the corridor casting a dim glow into the chamber. She stood by a huge, four poster bed that hovered three feet off the floor and though he could not see her face he could see the serape lying on the ground and the outline of her shoulders with her arms crossed over her breasts her face turned away as if in shame. Rand entered and closed the door with a click of the latch. "I've never done this before," she said tersely, "I mean...since I've been married. I hate lying." She lay slowly down on the bed in the darkness and pulled off her boots one at a time letting them thump to the floor, then stripped her tight leggings down her legs with only the starlight and that of the crescent moon radiating softly through the window. "I'll let you do anything you want to me." Teake whispered deliciously as she laid back and then as if to make her meaning clear she emphasized from deep in the back of her throat, "Anything."

The fuming rage that lurked beneath the social veneer was truly ominous, all consuming and more ancient that all the collective wisdom in books. It was primal. Searing back down the lifetimes into the reaches where spirits soar impassioned, emblazoned, screaming across the sky in a primordial howling cry of the forsaken that has resonated throughout the ether since before the beginning. Forsaken in a self abnegation. It is true we are born lost and Rand spun into the abyss feeling his hand holds loosening, foot holds giving way slipping endlessly, spinning down and all the while wondering where were the tenets, the structures of everyday life that lay in tangled webs throughout existence to catch him? Where was his resolve, his inner voice now that the seduction was upon him and he desired it out of a dark reason, where was the heart he once knew? All these thoughts collided in profusion dulling his acuity and rendering him incapable of determining consequences and so he slid into the danger of her arms enraptured by her feel, her smell and her taste. Bewitched. Her muscles were tight like a sea creature who having been disturbed from its haunt under the rocks latched on until death its tenaciousness inviolable. Her hands ripped at his clothes until they lay in heaps next to the serape. He sought out her mouth and once seared with a kiss, she broke away. Hands upon him, rough, demanding, obsessive. He stroked the sinewy cords of her legs, thighs, buttocks and pressed both his hands into the curve of her back that was as smooth as glass and pressed her to him grinding his pelvis against hers. Teake jolted in waif like energy, buckling and undulating and jumping over him inciting Rand to a physical aggressiveness he'd never known. It made him spin even more, expecting a pliant young woman whose passions had been neglected by a husband nearly three times her age, but instead he confronted a thrashing, insatiable raw urge embodied in a small, tight, sinewy brown skinned woman who threatened to engulf him body and soul. Her mouth sought him out and bit and absorbed and nibbled yet she would not be satisfied and rolled him over and over gripping and pulling and stroking while he groped, and tugged, explored and probed each touch eliciting further rage from the lithe woman and making him more combative. At last he could not stand it and grasping her waist with one hand, her hair with the other thrust himself into her while she gasped audibly arching up to meet him in fury that matched and easily doubled his. The two naked figures moved frantically together as if in battle, pounding against one another, flailing, fighting for dominance, requiring submission, all the time Rand, feeling numb and driven and caught in his body's racing tide, abandoned himself as never before relentlessly pummeling Teake while she demanded more, blow by blow matching his frenzy with her own cyclone of frustration neither afraid to hurt the other. Sweat poured from their bodies. Skin against flesh, slick, sliding, engulfing each other unquenchably until finally they were spent, exhausted, having butted together, mingled antagonisms and flowed as one seething mass into a dark and fuming conclusion that left them both unsatisfied, confused and racked with unrealized sexual energy.

At that instant the door opened. A tall, gaunt figure of a man stood awkwardly peering in silhouetted by the flare of light from the hall his features indistinguishable. Nobody moved. Breathing ceased. Not Rand, nor Teake or the man in the doorway flickered, but just stared at one another, breathless, in a moment absent of time. Rand remembered his father immediately and all the silent times when he had peered into the room after returning home late from work just as he was going to sleep and then as now the huge figure loomed in silhouette just as this man did. All the time he thought his father was working. He'd been betrayed. The door closed as suddenly as it had been opened, swiftly and with no noise and all was quiet and as it was except that both of them had grown cold, still wet with perspiration clinging naked to one another searchingly in love's grip.

Hot winds bore down on the city. They had fumed up out of the pitiless Mojave desert brushing against its belly and carrying off pieces of it in dust to the far distances. It came from the Panamint Valley where the ring of low lying mountains made a cauldron from which air could swelter out over the huge volcanic stones that lie scattered about from eruptions long forgotten. A colossal, relentless sun whipped it into a blustering frenzy. Locals called them the Santa Anas and they came of their own accord and wicked away all the moisture in the air until leaves were left crisp and brittle yet still green and uncurled because it happened so fast. Locals said they didn't mind, *it's a dry heat*, so they said, *a dry heat*, but it kept people awake, made babies cry and dogs bark and rolled great, tumultuous plumes of black smoke up into the sky from the devastating fire storms that inevitably followed and sometimes the black smoke of riots when the city got so hot it boiled over. Old people died in the heat. Young ones became restless.

Naomi did not sleep all night. She left the windows open to her bedroom, but it did not help and curtains fluttered like flags in the moonlight when gusts would rake them until they slowly became still again in the swelter. Surveillance helicopters and traffic noises echoed across the city. Thin cotton sheets clung to her moist skin as she tossed in pursuit of escape until finally they were flung off onto the floor and she lie naked on the white expanse of the bed as if surrounded by the sea. Naomi pulled the curly hair up off her shoulders and tied it behind her head, but it did not help. Nothing made it cooler, but there was something else in the air that disturbed and unsettled her, something that came with the hot winds and exposed wounds that had not healed and laid raw desires that reached their peak after two AM and tugged at her consciousness denying sleep and yet not allowing wakefulness. Perspiration appeared on the soft skin of her breasts, her arms and across her brow. Her heart beat heavily. Eyes scanned the ceiling imagining landscapes in dark shadows, unable even to dream, unquenched, waiting for no one, wishing for something.

She lived her life as if it were suspended on a wire that was stretched taut across the earth out over a raging black water that feathered in gales and currents and racing tides that she could never touch, but only watch passing. Her fingers hungered for the real, the physical and throbbed with the desire to enter life and there were moments of self inspection when Naomi questioned her own values and came close to giving in to an urge that bellowed in her ears that rose convulsively out of the center of the body making her falter on the wire, lose confidence and look back in regret at opportunities missed.

The complexity of the law had filled her and had camouflaged the void in her personal life. So, she was ferried through the night where spirits of the flesh brushed against the exposed self. Naomi would not allow the images that came in the ultramarine; strong muscular bodies gleaming with sweat moving against one another, bathed in light and shadow, teeth, eyes, a glimpse of faces...she would not allow it and so remained awake as the sexual brew churned ruthlessly undulating beneath the surface. When dawn appeared around her she watched the light slowly turn through its evolutions until everything was clear in the room and the shadows fled back into the darkness from where they had come.

The office was always quiet when she arrived early, as was often the case having neither husband nor children to sidetrack her, and Monday it was even more quiet than usual. She loved the comfort of the place, the walls of law books in the library trimmed in red and gold, the posh offices with their doors ajar offering a glimpse into the private spaces where others spent their working lives, and the great long carpeted hallway leading from the reception area where an architect had created an environment that would reflect the essence of Van Riper, Hazeltine & Brock. Here immense, hand burnished rosewood panels jutted out from curved, brushed aluminum walls and were adorned with original prints of the depression era in the mode of Thomas Hart Benton showing industrial scenes and agrarian landscapes with strong armed men, their sleeves rolled up, man handling sheaves, scythes and wrenches in the service of progress. On one wall was a complete WPA mural that had been salvaged from a demolished post office in the San Fernando Valley. Scattered across the red marble floor were Italian designed couches and chairs whose lines, according to the architect, were a perfect compliment to the jutting rosewood panels that had just the slightest curve to them creating a bowl that caught the light and brought out the redness of the wood. The lighting was low and moody. The air was always cool in the summer because the air conditioning was left on day and night and all through the weekend so that it would still be comfortable Monday mornings.

Naomi had just entered her private office carrying a steaming cup from the coffee room and was about to settle down with some work.

"God dammit!!" Someone yelled, muffled, through closed doors from down the hall. She decided to ignore it and frowned, not having had any sleep at all and desperately looking forward to the first cup of coffee when it happened again accompanied by a crash.

"God dammit!!"

She burst into Rand's office and found books littering the floor and papers scattered all across his desk. He sat dolefully on the couch with his head buried in his hands muttering to himself, driven to distraction by a rage.

"What in God's name...?"

Rand peered up at her through his fingers. "I've got to be in court in ninety minutes."

"I thought that was..."

"It got set forward on the calendar," he uttered miserably. "I forgot."

She breezed into the room and began to straighten up the papers and replace the books. "Somebody should have stayed home this weekend!" It all came as a natural act to her and she took a veiled pride in her ability to look after him without his knowing it.

He looked up sharply and scowled wondering how much she knew, "What do you mean?"

"You're not prepared mister!" She said dropping a pile of papers on the table in front of him and then turned to walk out the door. "It's all in my computer...I'll print it out and be right back." Suddenly she was full. The hollowness of the night before mysteriously vanished and a simple pleasure replaced it.

"Jesus!" Rand mumbled hung over in the extreme from the long weekend in Aspen, rubbing his eyes confused and unable to think clearly at all having had little sleep himself just arriving at five AM that morning.

Naomi hurriedly put together two complete copies of the case's paperwork, pulled all relevant files and dragged a reluctant Randall DesVergers into the small conference room where she plied him with coffee in an effort to make him more manageable. Everything was spread out in categories on the table and she meticulously went through each series of documents in detail refreshing Rand's memory until he almost came up to speed on the issues of the action. Then she drilled him. Ruthlessly, much to his annoyance. She threw every variation she could think of at him and gave him the opportunity to rehearse his responses.

"Van Riper, Hazeltine & Brock is not a collections office!" She nagged. They had not garnered a prestigious name by losing cases and every single action, no matter how insignificant, was treated with the absolute maximum care. Everyone knew that. It was more a matter of economics than pride and Rand knew, as did all the other partners, that the business they were engaged in was ruthless, highly competitive and there was simply no place for runner up. The big accounts were acquired by word of mouth, and that was generated by one thing alone, wins with the court. Rand had seen his share of hack lawyers who had failed to keep up with the race, like Gavin, past his prime and out of luck. He had also known plenty of young men who never made it in the first place, people he had gone to school with who had not progressed past struggling with a local personal bankruptcy practice. It had all been so easy for him. Perhaps if he'd been forced to skirmish out of an intellectual disability or some other handicap his pinnacle would have more value, more meaning. This morning he was dwelling on his mistakes and regretted like the plague he had ever gone to Aspen.

"I'm missing the concept of this!" He pronounced exasperated throwing some papers down on the table, "I had it all worked out, completely worked out! Now, I'm a blank. A fucking blank!"

"You'll get it, just keep going..." she placed her hand on his shoulder and instantly felt the warm surge of life that passed unspoken between them, which she was not certain he felt also. "We've still got some time."

"I dunno..."

"Come on..."

"Jeezee...haven't been in court since...when? January?"

"November."

"That long?" He paused. "Really, that long?"

"Yes."

"Really?" It was as if he emerged from a cave into the light just long enough to get an idea of where he had been and in that instant recalled things he had not thought of for many years, not since he had been a boy in Michigan. "Funny," he said, "Isn't it funny how memories are like packages and when you think of something in the past all of the feelings come to life again?" He remembered when he first wanted to be a lawyer, and when he knew nothing of the law, nothing at all except that phrase he would hear over and over again throughout all his years in school. *The Rule of Law.* How sanctifying it seemed to him then, and for a long time after until the significance of it just dropped out of sight one day no longer having any relevance to his routine. It had been a routine, rote, predictable and repressive, though it never once occurred to him that his life was like that. To him the whole enlightening experience was rolled out before him as some glorious experiment in living that would illuminate the secrets of the breathing civilization that festered and wrestled in fits of rancor and ecstasy, in stages of brilliance and apathy, in epocs of affluence and bust. Rand knew now, but refused to admit that the secret was that there was no secret at all and in that sullen understanding the spark had died, the ebullience, the frivolity, the whole point. In its aftermath, not being able to pinpoint the exact moment only being dimly aware of an antebellum before he had lost his slow struggle with angels and had become consummately human, was only the technology of the law which he applied with some skill as any technician or repair man felt obliged to do. Though he was driven by the pursuit of pleasure now and everything else that his income could provide. In that brief moment he began to question where the driving inquisitiveness had disappeared to, the extraordinary grasp of funda-mentals that gave him, among his peers, a greater ability to reason than they and was why it had come so easily to him. The feeling of joy that used to be his with great competence wisped across him in faint remembrance of what life used to be all about.

"My heart's just not in it I guess."

"Nonsense..." Naomi rebuked him sharply, "your heart'd better be in it at ten o'clock!"

"Right. I did a crazy thing this weekend. A crazy thing."

She wanted to delve into his secrets, but withdrew thinking it was better they were unknown–even though it wasn't.

"Jesus!" He burst out of the chair. "I just don't think we can do any more. Look, why don't you just come with me?"

"No, no I can't."

"You know the case...you're organized."

The court buildings were only a twenty minute drive; fifteen if one hit all the lights. Rand had made it in twelve before. "God! I nearly killed myself on the slopes," he announced energetically as he slumped in the driver's seat of his new automobile. He held up his right hand, in which he grasped the smart phone that was never far away from him, and slanted it towards the road. "It was this steep...can you believe it?" With his other hand on the wheel he was swerving around cars narrowly missing bumpers and cutting off the slow ones while at the same time punching in a telephone number and finally, with some diffi-culty, managed to place a call. A horn sounded fading in the distance. "I didn't fall once...hello, hello...Dale? Is that you? I know, I know...I should have. We'll be in court for about two hours, then I'll call you and we'll meet at the house. OK?" After a moment he cut off the call. "You shoulda seen me, really...I was good!"

Naomi looked straight ahead. "You can get a ticket for not using hands-free...do you know who the judge is?" Her fingers dug into the leather of the cushioned seat as she watched every car on the road half expecting a collision at any moment. She didn't like anyone else in control of her safety.

"No," he replied.

"You want me to look?" She began to rummage through her brief case. "I've got the schedule..."

"No, not necessary...appeals judges are all alike," he answered absently having drifted off again into his own universe relieved that Naomi was accompanying him and assuming she would handle the bulk of the details in court so he didn't have to think about them. "I'm buying a house."

"A house?'

"That's right. In the hills. Its only got three bedrooms, but has a pool...and what a view! I'm right on the edge of a canyon and you can see the whole damn city from my deck. It's expensive, but..." he glanced over at her sheepishly as if he was doing something he knew he shouldn't and wanted approval, "it's pretty nice. Buying it through a friend in real estate...figured it was a good time. Best investment you can make, real estate."

The news made her feel sad without reason. "I like to swim."

They reached the Federal buildings with only minutes to spare and agonized waiting in line for security scans. They loped through the hallways past middle aged men in cheap, shiny suits explaining excru- ciating details to Asian or Mexican or Middle Eastern couples; tattooed and surly teenagers in T-shirts and baggy pants; women in pastel busi- ness suits with tight skirts too short for their heavy legs carrying bulky briefcases–a wake of flowery perfume wafting behind them like crop dusting spray. Groups of men milling around all puffed up with dark suits hanging open with satchels in their hands gossiping in between appearances. Hundreds of long faced jurors on benches outside closed courtrooms waiting their turn. A pall of darkness hung over the whole spectacle dimming the hope that anyone would ever catch up with the backlog and truly bring about swift justice. When they reached the room in which the hearing would occur, after a few words with the bailiff, they took their places at one of the two long, wooden tables. Naomi spread out the paperwork precisely as she had in the conference room.

Rand leaned over and kissed her lightly on the cheek. "Thanks for coming."

The bailiff's voice pealed. "All rise."

Randall DesVergers stood quietly next to Naomi with his fingertips on the table at the front of the courtroom touching the edges of documents as he perused their contents, refreshing his memory and at long last began to breathe with confidence as the conceptual understanding of the case and its issues again enveloped him. He had unique ability and it had propelled him to the forefront of corporate legal representation to the degree that none of the senior partners had the slightest doubt of his acuity, reasoning or ability when it came to an important client. Naomi, however, knew differently. She shadowed his thoughts, filled in the gaps, made up the insufficiencies and tried to shelter him from any implications that would reflect badly on his reputation that had evolved deservedly out of his first decade of legal work. She was his witness and had first become attracted to him when she realized these flaws, his crumbling inner design, and took it upon herself as a surrogate to watch over him. His failings were dear to her yet only because she assumed the power to resurrect him.

"Jesus god!!" He hissed through his teeth without moving his mouth his eyes now upon the judge who was just taking his seat on the bench. Confusion fell on him and swirled above in dark masses.

""What is it?!" Naomi whispered in alarm.

"Nothing!" He grimaced through clenched teeth.

"Don't tell me nothing!" She wheezed back. "What the hell is it?"

"Judge Mezzaluna, Dansen Mezzaluna."

She looked up at the tall, gaunt yet elegant figure of the man on the bench arranging items in front of him before taking the first case. "So?"

SHaking his head pressing his lips together so that they nearly turned blue. "He's tough," he lied.

"Ha..." she said in ignorance, "thought you said they were all alike!"

At that moment Judge Mezzaluna looked down and his gaze landed squarely on the eyes of Randall DesVergers. Immediately the image of the dark haired woman intruded. He wondered what the man knew and if it had been truly been him in the doorway ringed by light, staring down snowblind by the sight of his young wife still locked in love's grip, belly to belly with a strange man. Who did he see that night? Were the shadows enough? Was the shock of lost innocence too much? Was it another lost guest at the wrong door? Did he know or not? There was only one thing that was clear, he hated the man and longed to run out on an open plain of the Mojave with the hot winds and the sky.

"Don't worry," Naomi said, "don't worry. I'll handle it, I'll handle it..."

Considering the fact that Rand contributed nothing to the proceedings it was not a disaster. An appeal against a judgment leveled toward one of their largest clients for industrial pollution. "It went fairly well." Naomi said after they had reached the office again, Rand pulling his sleek, teal automobile up to the curb. "At least we didn't lose a client!" She scolded mockingly. Rand pulled her to him and hugged her impulsively as a boy might do to his mother or an old lover. Naomi was still–he had never done this before. "Don't worry about it," she soothed, "don't worry. You just try to do too much...you've got to make some choices."

"You're just great!"

Naomi smiled, her cheeks flushed and her heart beating rapidly as she swung her legs out of the car gracefully. "You just need someone to look after you." Rand pointed his finger at her, smiled broadly, and then was gone. Before he had reached the corner the cell phone was in his hand and he was arranging to meet the real estate man at his new house for the close already having nearly forgotten the unpleasant courtroom experience.

Rand started drinking at four o'clock. It was highly unusual for him for he rarely drank in the daytime even forgoing mandatory luncheon drinks with new clients that inevitably turned into drunken evenings. But for once, he let it all slip. Perhaps the courtroom experience festered unknowingly beneath his consciousness and his basic goodness was suffering, so he drank unable to form any other way of being responsible. Only two drinks and he felt a sudden wildness, a windblown recklessness as he drove out into the Santa Ana winbds that still bore down on the city in relentless assault with all the car windows open and the radio blaring, up into the hills above the teeming metropolis where millions and millions of lives were woven tightly together in a seamless story that none could escape. He left the truncated city blocks and the swarms of dingy apartment buildings that always needed painting below where the flatlanders scrambled for anything that wasn't nailed down and if one wanted to get rid of something, just place it on the curb and it would be gone within an hour, and where the helicopters hovered noisily over the latest crime scene. The low hills were where the mid-priced older homes lay surrounded by condominiums and tightly fenced land where mere inches were grounds for lawsuits and owner-ship rights were the greatest points of contention– neighbor against neighbor. Until finally he arrived on high where the elite spread out and their villas, not so grand as the red tiled ones he looked down on from his office, but nearly so, hid behind bountiful and elegantly manicured landscaping and gated drives.

There was no better investment and now was the right time to buy. He could retire at fifty-five, if he wished, and be secure the rest of his life. He didn't want to work forever.

His real estate friend Dale met him at the security gate to let him in and then followed him up the private drive. The house was set back off the road that snaked along the top of the ridge overlooking Los Angeles and was hidden by eucalyptus trees and low lying juniper and other evergreens whose tips, he had noticed, were a light sage assuring him they were robustly healthy and shooting out with new growth during the spring season. A manicured bonsai garden surrounded the entryway, which with its windows encircling the frosted glass door, were the only source of light on the side of the house facing the road. Once inside however the whole ambiance changed. Both ends and the entire back side were glass gently encircling a concrete and redwood deck that hung out over the canyon. Below was nothing but chaparral. Dale sat down at the breakfast bar in the kitchen and began filling out papers. Rand walked from room to room sliding back all the glass doors to the deck until the whole place was open to the wind. A huge flagstone fireplace filled an entire corner, as was the style when the house was built in the 1950s, and the ceiling was covered with tongue and groove white pine with narrow, roughly finished fir log beams Southwest style crisscrossing it and dotted with opaque sky lights. The pool was a long, narrow rectangle whose surface shimmered in the late afternoon and its bottom was rendered with a granite texture to match the cascading waterfall constructed at one end. It gave the impression of a setting somewhere remote and natural. In the long distances, out across the heaving megalopolis spread incomprehensibly below in unfathomable richness he could just barely see, through the smog and the coastal mist of late daylight, the outline of Santa Catalina island that lay twenty six miles offshore and sheltered a famous casino that had been a haven for gamblers and smugglers during prohibition.

"You can't move in until escrow closes," Dale said to him as he signed papers, "but you can come and go as you wish. Nobody cares." And he handed over a set of keys.

It was still hot when night fell. The thick, humid scent of jasmine hung heavily, almost oppressively, its sweet perfume wafting through the open doors of the house across the canyon from the home which Randall DesVergers had bought late that afternoon, until the Santa Anas came rushing in and blustered it away. The man lifted a glass to his lips and lingered there letting the cold moisture from the ice cool him before drinking the last watered swallow. Only a brief respite from the heat. There was a wet ring on the wooden table where the glass had rested though it was unnoticed because there were more important things on his mind.

A light shown in the darkness across the canyon, one light that was more important than all the others. It was not the light of truth but neither the light of indifference. Perhaps the light of reason fading. The man kept to the technical disciplines of which he was a devotee. On the table was electronic equipment; monitors, computers, amplifiers, digital modems and other communications peripherals. On the roof a small satellite dish was stationed unobtrusively. A tripod at the window held a high capacity CCD video camera focused at the light across the abyss in Randall DesVergers' new house. It was flickering fire on the sea that night with its stoic glow steadfast and angry, though inside it was fragile. Amidst the simmer of the millions of other lights it helped form a bay of diamonds spread haphazard on the endless deep, the ocean of human lives, the soundings of streetlights, the mysteries of auto-mobiles forever rushing into the haze. From the house in the hills he could bear witness to the pillage below where young warriors roamed and irresolute hearts sought peace. But instead he would transmit the private goings-on in the home across the way to Bangor Maine where his employers at LYNX had a vital interest in what ever deals might be being made behind their backs. They were still impatiently awaiting promised funding and asserted their right to know what was going on feeling out of the loop. Monitors simmered thousands of miles away in a small room with the dim image of Rand's house and the sounds of crickets and owls emanating from the speakers exactly as it was in the hills above Los Angeles. Derian Baxter waited intently for something to happen.

"Am I early, or are you late?" On impulse Rand had invited Vero-nique to dinner. When he arrived to pick her up at the Wilshire Boulevard high rise she emerged from the elevator into the lobby wearing a sheer, black dress that was cut low in the back and took his breath away. She moved like a waif through the hot air directly towards him and met his eyes with a belligerent gaze unsoftened by her femininity.

His head was spinning. After he had left the house he drank some more so that by this time he was certifiably buzzed and it made him bolder than usual thinking it gave him more flair. The teal automobile spun down the boulevard and he gaily engaged in conversation on every topic that happened to enter his head, excluding all forms of business and legal issues that is, and the moment she mentioned anything remotely associated with those categories he would abruptly change the subject. "Tonight," he announced with subtle histrionics, "I'm going to discover who you really are." And he said it with such sincerity and charm that Veronique was intrigued despite herself.

"I like them because they are grown men." Rand commented on the maître d'hôtel, who was a dark, burly man that commanded the floor help as if in the military, "...and they all have the right accent." In the dark restaurant he ordered two separate bottles of wine at the same time, one a Chianti Classico and the other a Tuscany and explained that both were superb, one having the flavor of the earth and the other of wood, and he could not dine at the restaurant without tasting each one because the owner had them imported directly from Italian vinyards and they were not available anywhere else in the city. The delicious meal was delivered one course at a time, each more enticing than the last.

As the car was brought around she asked, "You want me to drive?" Rand was noticeably more intoxicated, but still ebullient and full of conversation. Veronique had consumed far more wine than she wanted to and found herself glowing warmly yet still steady on her feet except when she looked up into the sky mystified that there were so few stars visible.

"Of course not!" Rand barked and slid heavily into the driver's seat. "Come on...I'll take you to see my house!"

"Oh...so you have a house! By all means."

"It's my first." he confessed and told her the entire story of how he happened to find it including the history of his relationship with Dale and other irrelevant details that came to his mind only because he was fairly drunk. Despite that he negotiated the corners sufficiently well. They shot up the canyon road through neighborhoods languishing in the heat with open windows and yellow lights bathing yards through half closed curtains and palm fronds. Every time he came this way he remembered how it was supposed to be with families and children and relatives and occasionally entertained the thought that some day, when he was older of course, he might appreciate a family and children of his own. When that might be, however, was never clear and there were enough bad memories from his own childhood to prevent any rash moves. The thought crossed his mind that maybe he'd never been in love as his eyes passed over Veronique's exposed legs crossed in the seat next to his and he stole a glance as the car passed under a street light smelling the night blooming jasmine from the yards they passed. He'd felt obsession, but had never been comfortable with a woman for any long period. It was a sexual fever, like a gasoline fire that flared brightly and then vanished. As they pulled into the private drive to his new house he was thinking of an obscure Indonesian lizard whose iridescent emerald and vermilion shone most brilliantly just before he expired.

They wandered ghost like through the darkened rooms neither one speaking illuminated only by diffused moonlight. He had left the sliding doors all open and so the wind filled every corner of the house and dashed about the vacant space restlessly in gusts and rivers mussing their hair and tugging at their clothes.

"It feels wild." She said. "It feels like the sea shore."

It was only a flicker on the consul, but was enough to pull the man to it from all the way across the room. He hurriedly picked up the headphones and slipped them on. Nothing–not a sound. Then he looked at the monitor and saw motion, shadow upon shadow. That was when he placed the call to Bangor Maine where in the small room those same shadows appeared. Derian Baxter answered. "Yes."

"It feels haunted." Rand replied. Liquid crystal displays flickered and his voice was recorded in the house across the way. He found the switch to the lights in the pool and suddenly the monitors sprang to life as a glow surfaced from the deck illuminating the two for the sensitive camera trained upon them.

"It's beautiful." Veronique said standing before the deep gray pool with the infinite ocean of lights spreading out across the Los Angeles basin to the sea impossible to imagine for anyone who had never been there and experienced it with their own eyes–enraptured with the behemoth life force that had come to rest creating one of the greatest cities on earth.

"Yes, it is."

"Is it heated?"

"You kidding," he reached over and splashed his fingers in the pool, "in this weather?"

Another dim light flicked on from within the house and across the country another man was monitoring the movements of the images and the voices all transmitted digitally via satellite. "See it." Bax said into the phone, "adjust the timbre on the audio just a bit and we've got it." He followed the movement of the two figures around the deck and shortly another man joined him and then there were three sets of eyes. Three unknown intruders.

Veronique walked around the pool to the edge of the deck where she stared down into the night canyon. "How far down?" she asked.

"A thousand feet."

At which point she leaned precariously over and peered far into the heart of the brush that lay tumbling below untouched by men even in the crowded city. Rand said that deer lived in the hills and they raided the yards looking for tender greens and once he had seen a huge, eight pronged buck in the grass and that when he was spotted it vanished into the canyon with two six foot high leaps over the edge. Raccoons were everywhere he continued, opossums and skunks and three or four kinds of squirrels and he'd seen a huge, white barn owl too.

"Sounds like quite a menagerie." She turned on her toe and sashayed heavily on her hips balancing the symmetry of her body perfectly without any unnecessary motion.

He marveled at the contradiction of her. The physical that seemed to have a life of its own and exuded an energy that was primal and natural contrasting with the linear, business oriented mind whose calculating machinations never ceased and the only way he remembered she was a woman was to keep off the subject of commerce so that her feminine qualities came through unobscured by harsh economic realities.

"You are really lovely," he said quite soberly, and then caught himself remembering she was a client. "...I hope you don't mind me saying so?"

She continued to stroll with a hard, pouting, deliberating look on her face paying no attention to him at all. "We could make a lot of money in this deal you know."

"Well..." He threw up his hands in mock disgust, "there you go...I knew it was too good to last." Rand watched her out of focus against the blur of the city lights. Though the curves of her body were outlined with a razor sharp edge.

The wine had set Veronique's mind in motion. "They're preparing to go public you know?"

"Who?"

"LYNX."

Across the canyon the man behind the camera perked up and zoomed in closer on the two figures riveted by the mention of their company. "You get that?" He whispered into the phone he held tightly to his ear, so tight that sweat rolled down his neck. Tense images watched the screens in Bangor Maine.

"We've got their initial filing with the SEC complete. It's a hundred and forty nine pages," she said intently involved with some mental plan of which her words only sketched.

"You promised me..." he teased and raised his hands skyward, "why waste this on business...god! Makes me think about court," he shook his head miserably, "and I don't want to do that."

She glanced at Rand mischievously out of the corner of her eye and ground down her back teeth determinedly drawing a slight smile to the corners of her mouth. "We know more about them than they know about themselves."

"I'm not listening..."

"Two of them have declared bankruptcy. One of them two times."

Rand stepped out on the deck. "Did you know that there's not one large native tree to Los Angeles. They were all imported. No palm trees, no eucalyptus..."

"The head of the company is making three hundred and fifty thousand a year, the officers not much less."

He walked toward her as she retreated around the pool. "The Spanish built twenty-six missions up the coast and the road that connected them in the sixteenth century is still a major highway..."

"They don't pay their employees much. Few stock options planned, except for the heads of the company...they're tapping into the over capitalized high-tech capital market."

"Stop, will you...look how beautiful!"

Veronique smiled an evil smile at him. "Gordon thinks they're just trying to make the most of it, good capitalism...I think they're taking us for a ride. Once they get our funding and support they'll go public and when the stock initially shoots up they'll sell out leaving all the technology exposed to competition and us committed, unable to pull out."

"I think its time." Rand walked faster towards her while she skirted the edge of the pool. "You're going to get wet if you don't stop talking business."

"We're going to buy. They'll never know what hit them. It's almost all arranged. We've got investmemt banks ready to snap up all their stock the minute it hits the floor."

He rushed at her, "That's it. You need to be dunked." But nearly falling in himself she easily eluded him and laughed breathlessly playing with him.

"That's where you come in." She taunted. "Don't you want to be rich?"

"I almost am already."

"Not this..." She spread her arms in disdain embracing his property. " I mean...rich with a capital 'R'".

"You've had it." And he lunged at her again losing his balance and staggering despite Herculean efforts to suppress the effects of drink.

"Once we have complete control we'll slap an injunction on them so fast their heads'll spin and sue for industrial espionage..." she said standing with her legs firmly apart, watching him closely. He sprang at her again and tried to tear at her dress. She squealed and whirled out of his way placing her right hand firmly on his chest and pushing him down into the pool where he landed, spread eagle, flat on his back with a resounding slap sending sheets of water flying into the air.

He sputtered when he surfaced laughing and trying to unbutton his shirt and remove his shoes at the same time.

Vernonique stood hovering above him glaring down with an aloof and victorious stare. The smile on her face was harsh, thin lipped and cold. Her eyes blazed with hidden conspiracies. Crossing her arms slowly over her breasts she clasped her shoulders as if cold, then ran the fingers lightly up them tantalizingly brushing the skin and slipping them under the thin, string like straps to the sheer black dress. Lifting her arms the dress fell suddenly around her ankles revealing that she wore nothing underneath. Nothing at all. In one deft motion she dove into the pool hardly making a splash.

Rand felt her tugging at his trousers. "What are yo..." And he was pulled under by her strong, wiry arms. He kicked free and surfaced hysterically laughing while she tugged open his belt and ripped the seams.

She surface at the far end of the pool. "We need you." She spit out.

"Fine way to treat a business associate." He struggled towards her, but she dove and through his drunken eyes he could not follow her fast enough until he felt her hands stripping the last remnants of his trousers down across his legs. He sputtered again pulled under, but managed to grab Veronique and his hand slid sickly across her small breast pulling her body to his while she squirmed and struggled free slipping away from him in a flurry of spray.

She burst from the water gasping, and then turned and looked at him like a cat with a mouse. "You're in it aren't you? Come on, don't you want it?"

In an explosion of speed and boiling water he raced towards her while she screamed and futilely tried to bound through the shallow end to the escape of the steps. Half way up onto the deck he caught her by the leg and pulled her down sprawled over the edge of the pool pressing his flesh against hers for the first time and feeling the thrill of the foreign, the alien, the completely different life system that lay squirming beneath him. "What do you think you're doing." He demanded with the good humor intoxication gave burying his face into her neck and clasping hold of her breast with one hand feeling the hard nipple on his palm while reaching around her submerged thigh with the other firmly pressing his fingers against the wet hair of her sex and lifting her slightly with a grunt he could not help but emit.

She pushed him aside. "Give me your support," she breathed roughly, rasping, "I want to be rich, very rich. If you want it...if you want me...I have to know that you're in to the end."

"I can't resist your offer." She pressed against his groin bringing one knee up on the pool step, arching her back to his touch then reaching down under the water, between her legs where his fingers probed and kneaded her mercilessly and grasped him savagely forcing him inside her with a hard, jerking motion. Rand reacted as a machine, completely oblivious to what was happening, his head spinning with alcohol and moved passionately against her as if in a dream pushing harder and straining his muscles against her until the moonlight mixed with the dim light from the house reflected off their wet curves and hollows; splashing in the water noisily, awkwardly and unceremoniously thrashing against the elegant woman who was now reduced to animal like movements as Veronique, completely silent, desperately tried to crawl up over the edge of the pool making it unclear if she was trying to escape the humanness or was climbing the ladder in her own mind and only making it so far, reaching out her arms across the still, warm concrete, breathing heavily, rhythmically, bent over the edge with one leg up accepting the man's basic needs.

Long distance calls were already in progress and the principles of LYNX were being awakened in the pre dawn hours with the news believed to be too startling to keep. The images of the thrashing, naked figures had impressed the volatility of the situation where billions of dollars were at stake and all their words and actions had been recorder for future use.

Rand and Veronique had fallen asleep on the warm deck. She had crawled from him and collapsed three feet away and he followed, laying gently on top of her listening to the sounds of her breathing as if it were an incredibly complex symphony feeling the rhythms of her life. His body was still wracked in the grip of sexual pulses and he looked heavy eyed out over the far distances where the haloes of lights radiated through the hot midnight wind and thought to himself that life couldn't get any better than this. This was the best it could be. Sleep found them exposed to the sky.

He dreamt a strange dream unlike any he had ever known before. In it there were no buildings or streets or any evidence of civilization as he had come to think of it, yet he felt the order of things, the cultural diversities and the codes that bound together all living things that were headed in the same direction. The landscape of his vision was verdant, green and lush with trees and roots and vines; dappled sun drifted through broad, dew covered leaves and the sky was pregnant with huge, cumulus clouds. Although he saw no other living animals, he heard them. Their cries were as plain as if they were right next to him, the rustle of their movements unseen, the scent of their markings lingering in the dawn where the moisture brought out its full bouquet. And he felt like he was being watched. Intensely watched. Followed in a way that humans had lost the ability to do having their natural attention cut short by conveniences and machines that accomplished the working tasks for them leaving weak willed, dependent creatures in their after-math. Rand became so uncomfortable that suddenly he opened his eye wide, without moving a muscle, his cheek pressed against the bare skin of Veronique's back.

Across the deck, at the other end of the pool on the periphery of the light in the penumbra of the shadow seven sets of glowing, irides-cent eyes stared back at him. Motionless. Glimmering. He sucked in his breath with terror and desperately tried to focus keeping absolutely still. Then he saw them. Coyotes. Their long ragged fur edged against the pitch black of the canyon dark. A hunting pack. Immediately he could smell them; musky, sweet, pungent, bitter. There was movement. One broke the frozen pose and paced sideways carefully watching Rand. Then another did the same behind the first, the dominant male. Then still another and others until all seven of them wove in and out and restlessly paced the end of the deck all eyes upon him, riveted, fixated as if trying to determine the lay of providence. Rand felt vulnerable, but could not move. He had never heard of a man being attacked by coyotes, but they were large animals and he could see their strength, their teeth, their pride that was hidden in the daylight, the time of men. He saw their muscles moving beneath the brown gray, yellow, cream and white fur that had flecks of black. He felt their impatience as they decided their course of action. Pondered the consequences. Divined whether this was an offering. Their eyes locked on his, unwavering and Rand was seared to their lives in a surging flash of energy that transversed across the space between he and them, between man and animal so far yet near, intimate, both species doing what they must to survive. He saw in that one glimpse lives more pure than his, purposes more defined, more in step with universal law, more in tune with God. Shame swept across him and moisture welled up in his eye as he silently witnessed the magnificence of life shimmering before him like an apparition in the dark.

Rand felt humbled and blinked away the tears. When he opened his eyes they were gone.

BETWEEN THE LABYRINTH AND THE SKY

X

"Are you sure?"

"Yes! Yes!" The proprietor insisted.

"Are you sure?" He demanded as if the fat man whose full beard was cut close to his ruddy face and completely white and whose hair was long and curled over his ears had not answered properly.

"I checked it myself!" The man expelled red faced in exasperation spewing little drops of spittle as he did so leaving one dribble on his beard, which he wiped off with the back of his left hand. Then, after a moment's reflection to regain the certainty that he really was sure, added, "I am quite certain."

"Then this must be..." he held the small volume up to the light.

"Yes. Yes."

To think that he held it in his hand. The big man looked at it in wonder, his shoulders rolled and powerful concealed under a mackintosh still glistening with rain. A puddle had formed on the dark, oak slats of the floor and soaked into the wood where the finish had been worn away in front of the counter leaving a dark blot. He opened the flyleaf and looked again at the cover plate. *Las Contes Drolatiques,* it read, by Honore de Balzac, published in March, 1832 by Gosselin of Paris. "When I was a boy," he said in a resonant, distant voice that issued of memories, "I would walk the streets in autumn full of leaves–yellow and orange, sienna brown and pale green–slushed up against the side of the curb…abandoned…I used to dream of Touraine. To think that now…"

"Yes. Yes. Look," he rushed from around the counter in a flurry of celestial realization and gently pointed to the short preface written in the name of the publisher, but in fact penned by Balzac himself, "look," he pointed to the signature gone dull with age and in his mind translated from the French, "he claimed for his book the protection of all those to whom literature was dear. Don't you see?" he beseeched, "The signature. It's authentic, beyond a doubt. I checked it myself. That proves it!"

The blessing of the little man was like the burning of rubine sealing wax with an emblem of state heated to a dull amber, it had the same finality because he was the most prestigious antiquarian book dealer in Atlanta and was recognized all over the world as an expert. People paid huge sums to have his opinion. The shop was on the street level of an antebellum building that in turn was located in an elegant old quarter which had escaped fires and tumultuous events of rushing armies, riots, strikes, depressions and other more private human calamities to assume its present incarnation somewhere around the changing of the 18th century. Walls that housed a fabulous collection of first editions, especially of American writers and specifically Southern ones, loomed in archaic yet orderly oak shelves built connecting the floor to the ceiling adding strength to the structure at ground level and perhaps aiding its survival for so many long years. From the door landing that was faced with French windows like the front of the shop, there were three steps down to the interior. Here the atmosphere quickly changed from one of airy delight occasioned by the white lace curtains and light that beamed through during the morning hours to austere judiciousness at the interior where the weight of men's minds grappling with the universe took over. Here the caprice of life took an ominous turn. Dr. Morgan Jagger was aware of the consequences when a man decided to consider life's deeper meanings and to shun ideological complacency. Perhaps this was why an irascible sensation of deliciousness swept over him as he felt the weight of the volume in his hand, a feeling he could not resist.

"Can you tell me how you came by it?"

"Just like the others."

"How then…"

"It was delivered by messenger. I called you as soon as I could authenticate it."

"Yes." He wistfully replied to no one leafing through the volume.

The coolness of the shop contrasted with the warm, humid spring rain that had not chilled even as the sun went down. Through the years he had grown accustomed to the climate and now felt cold and shivered in the air conditioning where the humidity was maintained at the perfect level to preserve the rare books. Many of the volumes were made of paper corrupt with acid and their yellowing folios were easily crumbled and just as easily damaged from the slightest fluctuation in moisture and the heroic effort to cling to these deteriorating icons when good solid reproductions, even facsimiles of first printings for many of the more popular works, could be had seemed to most unnecessary. For others, however, it transcended the mortal bounds as they grasped for the endlessness of original beings who left behind their footprints for others to marvel at and decipher in their absence. There were men of grit whose indomitable fury and spark brought about a landscape in the mind where once there had been only barren fields forsaken and sallow ringed by ignorance and intolerance and the other terrors of civilized men. How brief and precious their lives seemed in retrospect. Fleeting. A moment bathed in moonglow. The hope was to preserve the living age by maintaining the touch, the final human gesture, if not with the person then at least with pages impregnated by the tears of their wisdom. If one could sit down and hear from the mouth of Julius Caesar first hand the glorious intoxication of conquering the known Western world before the name Jesus Christ was ever heard, how sweet would that experience be? Here, cordoned off from the street under the hooded, flowing night was the first translation of *The Civil War* written with Caesar's own hand when he was 52 years old just prior to the Alexandrian war and only four years before he was to be brutally assassinated. Hands reach across the eons, human touch to human touch. Mortals can do no more.

He paid the man by check, which was fingered humbly and never looked at once to see if the amount was correct. The book, as all the others had been, was wrapped unceremoniously in brown paper and tied loosely with white string, the kind which is becoming more and more scarce and only the older generation still use it at all. He thanked the man abruptly and walked up the three stairs and out the door leaving the slight ringing sound in the air of the bells that hung and were jostled each time someone came or went and had done so for nearly a century. The older man felt a little sadness with the passing of the volume as he always did having the feeling he had been in the presence of the great writer himself and not just a facsimile, but had become resigned to the fact that his role was as a bridge from that world to this and must necessarily be wrenching to the soul by reason of the great art that passed briefly through his hands. He deposited the check into the cash box he kept foolishly under the counter and gazed up at the door forgiving the abruptness of the man and the brief yet polite acknowledgment knowing that he was truly a worthy recipient of the messages from the past and they would not be lost on him. He would sleep well tonight.

Rain streamed across his windshield in colliding rivulets. The car was moist on the inside, the windows partially fogged over and he suddenly felt clammy after spending so long in the cool shop so turned on the air conditioning to breath its freshness. Large powerful hands gripped the wheel, hands meant for some other work than the business he was embroiled in. It had consumed him. As he left the old section of the city with its few low wood and brick buildings resplendent in history the refracted glows from the street lights and oncoming automobiles created a multilayered mirage through which he could not see clearly; a veil of rain, one of luminance and rushing motion against the city's landscape that he knew so well, but appeared foreign and half remembered.

He had moved the main sales offices to Chicago and commuted between there and Atlanta where his own private office was located and his primary residence, the house he loved so well. There was the summer home on Bois Blanc Island near the Straights of Mackinaw on Lake Huron, which was a short flight from Chicago by seaplane where he found respite from the heat that was constant in both cities during the late summer and early autumn. For some reason he felt at home in Chicago and Detroit as well, both cities being as detached and culturally unlike Atlanta as could be imagined. Something about the ubiquitous presence of industry got into his blood, the ash and smoke and ancient factories and warehouses mingled with his life essence in a rush of spiritual energy that inevitably culminated in long winded tirades on the great American vision. Ponderous stratospheric social concepts came to him and overwhelmed him with significance that would never have occurred at his home, in his library surrounded by the books and the generations of wisdom. Morgan Jagger considered himself an evangelist for Americanism, and late in life had returned to school to gain his doctorate in political science. Sometimes he would drive all the way to his lodge on the island from out of Chicago carrying the wrath of its business with him; its teeming crossroads of trucks and trains, loading and unloading cargo endlessly as the transfer point and clearing house of the nation; through Detroit with its gray soot pall and derelict sections of the city festering in fits and starts as it futilely tried to recapture the glory days when the automobile industry fueled hope. Following the route north through Ypsilanti, Pontiac and Flint he would break free into the true landscape that he could glimpse between small towns, farms and forests exactly as the French and English had seen it in their contest of wills to control the new world. In the end industry won out. Arms engaged in work was an argument that nobody could disagree with. Food on the table, clothing on the back, men who bit the bullet and sweated until the end for a living wage. Life was tied up in that bargain. Dr. Morgan Jagger was an ardent believer in those values.

He was built for labor. A thick black man endowed with a powerful muscularity that made the menial tasks of living effortless. Once he had the makings of a champion athlete, but it never appealed to him and he preferred to spend his time in libraries and academic pursuits hounded by his obscure purposes. He ignored his color and hated the term Afro-American and if pressed referred to himself simply as a black man, or a negro, but neither had much meaning for him. It was the handicap he relished as if running a hundred yards with weights strapped to his back to test others' ability to keep up with him. Life was a test of will, of strength, of courage and ingenuity. Although he had a firm sense of justice, he did not support the NAACP, the Urban League or the contemporary civil rights movement at all feeling that they had served their purpose. It was up to individuals. They were just an excuse for the indolent. This was a fact that caused him a great deal of trouble with the American Civil Liberties Union and labor organizations not to mention the enmity it brought down upon him by colored people. None of it mattered, he didn't consider himself tied to anyone by reason of race–his friends were those who worked hard and made it go right. Morgan Jagger challenged the world to throw up obstacles to which he replied, *is that the best you can do?,* and then continued on as before.

A whoosh of water fled from beneath the tires of his automobile. It was an austere taupe color and a sturdy yet expensive car that he felt had the solid construction he always associated with quality. The sound of one ferocious slam of the door in the showroom, to the consternation of the sales manager who dropped his glasses on the floor cracking one of the lenses, sold him. Driving with a firm, solid base gave him pleasure. He had grown up in Atlanta and stayed out of a determination not to be defeated. His family had been poor, not destitute as some yet never having the reserves that allowed for mobility or the satisfying of basic human needs let alone private, personal ones. They worked extremely hard to stay in the same place. Here his values took shape, gained form and from nebulous ideas were revealed to him in a manner that had religious significance. When he was fourteen years old his father was severely beaten by white union picketers for attempting to cross the line. They lived week-to-week, hand to mouth unlike the Teamsters who were paid out of the national strike fund, some of whom had been shipped in from other towns to make a showing in the waning years of union influence. The issues were trivial revolving around part time workers, vacations and benefits, none of which affected his father in any way except that he had to work every day or starve. Everyone insisted it was not racially motivated and the same would have happened to a white, which had not even entered into Morgan's head being, even at that young age, a firm believer that evil had no color. His father was laid up for a month in the hospital leaving him with an insurmountable debt that consumed whatever ambition he may have had left, bleeding it out of him month after month with payments and interest. But Morgan Jagger was determined to take charge of life and the lesson proved to be a pivotal one. The Teamsters won their strike, but not before causing irrevocable losses to the business so severe that when it finally did reopen it had to lay off sixty percent of its work force due to lost acounts and a firm that had taken four decades to grow had been broken in ninety days. His father was one who lost his job. The union celebrated the win and newspapers heralded the resurfacing collective power.

The automobile raced past a tavern on the interstate as he headed out of Atlanta towards the exclusive community where his home was. The image of its half working neon beer signs from the windows flashed against the speeding car and projected the image into his memory where he still harbored ill feelings from that time. He remembered the other bar of so many years past and the hot night he had gone there looking for trouble. It had not been hard to find out who had beaten his father, apparently the strikers were well known and were hell raisers proud of the confusion they disseminated and from their own bragging he had found them. In his neighborhood strength was a virtue, its exercise was an inalienable right and one that was entirely separate from the indenturing of men to the fact of rote work, slaves to the living wage that neither gave them a better life nor promised one. Just enough for the next week, for as long as there was physical ability there was food. The old simply died if there was no one to look after them, or became wards of the state welfare system winnowing down through the final years. The youthful work force resented them for their helplessness. Morgan was at home as a young man in those neighborhoods with the raw energy peeling off his muscled arms that radiated with health and rippled each time he moved. That night, he remembered, that hot night he wore a skin tight T-shirt and was ready for anything.

"You Ellison?"

The man looked over his shoulder from the bar where he was perched on a high stool covered in glossy, red vinyl on chrome legs. A Tammy Wynett song played indistinctly in the background. The shoulder was big, in fact he was a massively solid man who was twenty pounds overweight and as he turned his head on the stump like neck it made a double chin that gave him an almost friendly look. He looked at the thick, black boy and narrowed his eyes. "I am."

"I'd like to talk to you."

"What about?" The man said and looked up at the bar tender who was cleaning a class and observing everything that happened in front of him with a uniformity, nothing having any greater importance than anything else and in that way avoided slighting anyone or knowing anything that would get him into trouble.

"Business."

The man turned on the stool and revealed his massive chest through the sweat stained, old pale green T-shirt that was almost white. "Business?"

"Business."

They sat at a booth with high wooden backs along the wall with four other booths all empty. There was a chrome napkin holder on the table, salt and pepper shakers and a coin operated juke box machine at the end with metal framed pages to flip through by the tabs that poked out of the slat on the top listing tunes one could choose, and red and ivory plastic buttons on the bottom front. There were twenty lettered keys and twenty with numbers. Morgan had found Ellison through some acquaintances who were always in trouble. He had phrased the question put to them very delicately so as not to give away his meaning, but it was a futile gesture because those of many crimes could recognize motives a mile away. And it was with knowing glances that Ellison's name finally came up and was left with the proviso that... *I'm not responsible, take your own chances.*

Ellison was hired muscle. He had worked sporadically as a long-shoreman, in the repossessions department of a loan company and as a freelance troubleshooter on the streets whenever someone needed something done that hovered between where the law ended and crime began. He did not consider himself a criminal nor did he associate with any, but a businessman. This was where he made his mark, mostly because he enjoyed hurting people and in his leisure hours that topic monopolized much of his limited conversation as he recounted the scrapes he'd been in and the fights relishing the manly details. But this was business and from the first instant the black boy had asked his name he was professional down to his shoelaces. Morgan had never had any experience with such a person and was not violent or even physical himself despite his strong physic. He told the man about his father and the job that had been lost and the hospital bills and the fact that they could not afford a lawyer and justice, along with medical care, was for the well to do. The police, he added, sided with the union. But Morgan could not leave it at that and from what he had heard was hoping the man understood. Ellison stared back sipping at his beer with glazed over eyes neither showing understanding or ignorance.

Morgan got to the point in the brief, concise manner that would later become his trademark in business. "I want those men that did that to my father punished." He said matter of factly as if Ellison were already in his employ hoping that he could bluff his way through the awkward interview. He gave the burly man across from him all the information he had managed to gather on those who had done the beating and then handed over a wad of money all folded and rolled up so tight that it sprang open at once soon as it touched the table. "I got three hundred dollars here. That's one hundred for each man." And then he added in a funny tone for a boy so young, but in such a way that even Ellison felt a shiver. "It took me a long time to get that money."

Ellison looked at him forever without saying a word like a dull, carnivore deciding whether he would eat Morgan or not. He had not spoken since he had been sitting at the bar. Finally he reached over and slowly scooped up the bills into the palm of his hand and shoved them with effort into the front pocket of his jeans, which took a few moments because when sitting his belly hung over and made them too tight. Then he picked up the envelope with all the information that Morgan had gathered and stood up, looking down menacingly for a moment, and walked away.

Morgan never heard from him again and he now wondered whatever became of Ellison as he fled through the rain in the darkness throwing up shoots and plumes of water behind. Some bad end no doubt, though he always pictured him retiring to Costa Rica with a small Spanish speaking woman who dotted over him as his hair fell out. He remembered how he had expected to see two line newspaper headings with a photo caption under the picture of a man in a hospital bed whose head was completely wrapped in bandages stating, "He jus' came up outta' nowhere, whupped me wit a board and then whin I was down stomped all ova ma face." But nothing ever happened. Nothing. He was furious for a while at the idea of someone ripping him off, especially a white man, of being a black man and a fool. As his fury subsided he realized that it wasn't that at all, it wasn't anyone else causing him to feel the way he did. Morgan could confront his father again however, and when he saw him that night thought the man looked just a little bit brighter, for some reason a little more hopeful.

The car veered from the interstate and planed down the off ramp coming to a hesitant stop at the intersection before turning left into the night. It was raining harder now and the sound of it drumming on the roof accompanied the sloshing of the wheels restlessly pushing toward home. It all fit together for him after the incident with Ellison. The scheme made sense. He no longer felt effect of a rapacious economic structure that did not include him and had never admitted his father into its chaste community either.

He had been born without a voice and had grown to a young man within a community of men without voices and when he hired Ellison he was forming a covenant to regain his voice from those who had kept it from him. Morgan never once felt like a victim and lived with a demand that others would have to acquiesce to or get out of the way. The incident with his father was a great lesson; it was a pivotal point in the vector of his life that was tumbling forward on its own momentum toward some destination he was not yet aware of.

Men without voices have few options.

He first met the Koreans when he was only twenty-five as a result of a spontaneous impulse. He was working for a company manufacturing components, part of an old electronics empire that had pioneered many of the appliances and home electronic devices taken for granted in the modern age. It had been the place of choice for any young engineer with an eye to the future before the Japanese cut them off at the knees. Working for them was stable, moderately profitable and prestigious because they spent more money than anyone else on research and development and out of that came work a man could base a reputation on. He was a section manager in the assembly facility and because of his aggressiveness management adopted him as one of their own, which gave him a head start. But they overlooked the fact he was voraciously opportunistic. When he got word that a group of South Korean businessmen were in Washington for trade talks he flew to the Capitol and, pretending to represent a Senator's office, managed an appointment with a minor player. A representative for the South Korean electronics industry that was just on the verge of a world wide boom. Morgan made a deal. A deal to be the exclusive American sales and distribution arm for the Koreans. A deal on the basis of his connections with U.S. electronics companies, which he had exaggerated grievously leaving the Korean with an impression he had just jumped in bed with the old guard. Morgan knew the government was reluctant to have the Koreans flood the market with inexpensive components thus capturing the business– still in shock from the Japanese coup of the home electronics industry from which they never recovered–and he knew the Koreans knew. He promptly quit his job, ran his credit cards up to the limit to finance an office and spent all his time promoting the Korean components to American manufacturers. At one point he was over a hundred and fifty thousand dollars in debt. He was a millionaire before he was thirty-five. Morgan attributed his remarkable success to the blessing of being in exactly the right place at the right time and having the balls to take what he wanted without asking anyone, just as he had with Ellison.

All the unpredictable things of life became clear to him. The mysteries of justice, economics, success, all condensed down crystallizing into a ruthless will that transcended the cries of victims and the pandering voices of the special interests and the rule of law itself, which he lamented as a reflection of the political and economic powers that be at any given time. Business had its own velocity. The free market made its own rules, evened out its own inequities and demand dictated the right to rule. It all seemed very spiritual to him and his business dealings began to take on holy overtones and soon enough he found his niche with the religious right whom he indebted with his funding and support. Morgan Jagger had finally found his voice and it was on the evangelical pulpits around the country where he was invited to expound on his version of Americanism and the free market to a willing audience.

The idea of rule as a divine right of the intellectually superior came to him as an axiom so obvious that if ever it had to be explained to someone, then it was beyond that person's grasp. His new perspective divided the world into those who would make and carry out policy–not elected of the people whereby the process itself would nullify any exceptional human beings and would inevitably deliver candidates in the category of base common denominators–and those who would follow it for the greatest good. Dissent would not be tolerated. Democracy was an anachronism. It was a new order. Around the time when these theories fully crystallized and Morgan began to have periodic euphoric flights which sent him on a medical tour to try to solve before he realized they were divine moments, he formed connections with paramilitary groups in the South and far West whom he saw as his ethical arms. The sword with which he could carry out policies such as he had with Ellison as a boy that taught him the first valuable lesson. This was his best kept secret. No one knew about his secret liaisons, no one until now.

The grand, taupe, touring sedan pulled up into the circular drive of the stately, majestic home throwing water out in all directions until it stopped. The house was built on a hill, covered with lush grass and deciduous trees of many varieties, in the federal style with tall, impressive square columns holding up the triangulated gable above the double entry doors of black lacquer with brass fittings. Headlamps sliced through the drizzle, yellow knives dissolving in the distance that was obscured by the precipitation and darkness. A cool wind blew on the rise and the sally of air and water disguised the sweltering humidity that was only abated temporarily to let the showers pass. He slammed the door securely and with his briefcase covering his head and the brown paper wrapped book tucked neatly under his mackintosh he jogged for the door trying to miss the puddles whose surface rippled in the breeze. The porch light cast moving shadows; frolicking, tripping, shuffling, prancing shadows all choreographed to the vast movements of air that swept the hill and made the huge trees rustle in their beds. Out of the corner of his eye he thought he saw a movement, but in the same instant guessed it to be a shadow and so kept for the door. His hand touched the smooth, cool knob and he slipped the heavy, metal key into the latch and turned it.

"Did you like the book?"

Morgan froze. Without taking his hand off the doorknob he peered back over his left shoulder into the darkness. He realized instantly he was at a disadvantage being in the light while any intruder would be in the cover of darkness. "I'm afraid I didn't see you when I pulled up."

"We were waiting for you."

"Here?"

"Yes."

"How?"

"In the car."

He turned to face the intruder ready for whatever may come flexing all his muscles as he did so. "What do you want?"

A tall, thin, angular man stood directly in front of him wearing a navy blue cashmere overcoat under which were a navy blue, two button suit, white shirt and a striped neck tie that was predominantly red. His dark hair was short and tossed in the wind and appeared very black against his unusually white skin. Morgan immediately identified him as an office dweller who rarely went outdoors. He was flanked by two, nondescript round faced men, both with short, brown hair in an athletic cut, meaning that it had no particular style and contoured the curve of the head without any stray hairs visible even in the storm, and wearing khaki trench coats. All of their faces were covered with raindrops. "I'm sorry." He said finally realizing that Morgan was startled and defensive. The fact that they had been sitting in the car up the drive for two and a half hours, so long that their legs had gone to sleep had made them insensitive. "My name is Kirkland Bosch. U.S. Assistant Secretary of State for Int..."

"...International Narcotics Matters," Morgan completed the sentence. "Yes..." at a loss, "I've heard the name."

Kirkland gestured to the right and then to the left and then shrugged. "Secret service. Can't leave home without them." He smiled disarmingly as he had learned to do in awkward, diplomatic situations that could not be avoided.

Dr. Morgan Jagger showed them inside and the men were visibly relieved to be out of the storm. "I've got to go to the library," he told them, "to get this book out of the humidity."

"Ahh..." Kirkland Bosh responded, "Yes, the book."

He tossed the wet mackintosh into a chair and headed for the broad, carpeted flight of stairs that curled lazily up around a corner to the exposed hallway of the second story that was enclosed by a polished walnut railing on white, carved dowels. "We can meet up there if you like," he announced suddenly comfortable with the protocol, "please be quiet, my wife's probably sleeping."

Morgan unlocked a massive door and allowed the three men to enter first, then carefully closed it behind him. He raised the lights revealing a huge library with rows of finely crafted bookshelves, many with glass doors, creating sixteen foot isles capped by an ornamental molding where walls met the ceiling in pale green and cream colors. Everything else was made out of wood. "Custom made." He told them. "Used cedar for the most part. Little known fact that it not only deters moths and their larva, but book worms too." He looked quietly from the side of his eyes at the three men, none of whom realized he had just made a joke and were wandering around the foyer which was replete with large salon chairs of 1940s vintage placed there for one reason only, to read books. "I've got over fifty thousand volumes here..." he stopped himself, "but then, you know that."

"Well," Kirkland confided, "not really. I mean," looking rather amazed, "not so many."

He walked down one long isle and placed the latest book in his new arrivals shelf where others sat awaiting a spare Saturday or an evening when he would log them in to his computerized card catalog, attach a bar coded chip to the glassine jackets he had specially made for each of his fifty thousand books at a shop in Paris. "Plastic is terrible for books," he told them. "It promotes mildew and attracts dust between the jacket and the cover, which when left for long periods makes a smudge. With some of these books a smudge can mean tens of thousands of dollars."

"I am impressed."

Returning to the foyer and giving them his full attention, which noticeably made the two quiet men uncomfortable. "Please," Morgan said graciously to the men, "feel free to look around while Mr. Bosch and I have our talk. I have some marvelous first editions, original Arabic astronomy texts from the first century, illuminated manuscripts hand written as well as many popular novels." Kirkland nodded to them as he removed his cashmere coat and sat deeply into one of the huge chairs.

"It's cold."

"Climate control." Morgan replied calmly then narrowed his eyes. "I have to thank you."

"Me?"

"The books."

"Yes. The books."

"The Balzak is a rare find."

"Rare?"

"Yes. You know of course that in writing it he created a triumph in literary archeology...?"

"Really."

"A literary triumph. He anticipated harsh criticism, you see, because he wrote all the stories in the archaic language of sixteenth century France, Touraine to be exact. But the signature you see, the signature...that's the real treasure. It is the author's signature to the prologue that defends it as an artistic work written in the name of the publisher, though it had always been thought that Balzak himself penned it. Now there is proof. My bookseller authenticated it."

"Fortunate."

Then he asked quietly, "Is he working for you as well?"

"Who?"

"The bookseller."

"No. No. He's as eager to lay his hands on these volumes as you, maybe more so."

"He's the best you know." Relieved.

"So I've heard."

"I'm almost sad the mystery is complete. You have no idea how exciting it is to make a discovery like this one, a call in the night...how many is it now? I wonder, which have come from you?"

"I really don't know."

"You understand I could never give them up."

"We're counting on that."

There was no offense taken. Morgan Jagger appreciated a shrewd business deal even if he was on the losing end. It was his blood. He was surprisingly comfortable with the clandestine meeting in his house and engaged the State Department Official in relaxed conversation about current world affairs and U.S. policy. The time had to come, he knew it, but had not once guessed that the mysterious arrival of antique books had anything political connected with it other than the fact that he assumed, wrongly, that they had come from the televangelical ministry to whom he had lent his financial support. Ministers were reluctant to put gifts on the books for fear of audits, so they often came unannounced and disguised. There were so many, at least thirty over a two year period and a few really important finds such as the one tonight. It had to happen eventually, he was in the public eye too much, was indeed a political figure himself and the whole scenario just confirmed what he had always known, that politics was a financially based institution and, with law, reflected that economic power. He did not view this with disdain in any way, but to the contrary believed that the truths of the free market were inevitable and incontrovertible so that no matter who was in power or by what means he governed the fact of money would inevitably course its way through ideology. The levees hastily constructed by hungry people more eager to thrill to their own rhetoric and multiply the laws on the books, contributing to the staggering, unwieldy complexity, than to allow the market to surge ahead freely and cleanly into the future were doomed from the start. He, Morgan Jagger, was the voice of that future. A blind certainty lingered inside him that was unshakable. It came in clear, lucid words that soothed congregations across the country to whom he had spoken and gave them an alternative to the old, outmoded democratic institutions of which the man seated before him now was a representative.

The evening grew on the two men. It enveloped them in its shelter. Neither found he was in much of a hurry to get to the point of the visit. A bottle was broken out of a cupboard in the wall and a couple of plain, tall glasses set on the table between the chairs. They liked one another. Shared common attributes that made them good company consisting mainly of a knack for expanding an oratory from a few sketchy facts and pulling it off with polished precision so that they sounded consummately informed on whichever subject became the topic of conversation. They wandered into the early morning hours neither growing tired. The men who had accompanied Kirkland Bosch were both reading books, one asleep in a chair with his mouth open and a volume spread haphazardly across his knees. Soon conversation turned to *The Drug War*, a term the man from the State Department bandied about with a familiar, cavalier attitude, as a general who tired and inured to the horrors around him no longer flinched at atrocities.

The U.S. Assistant Secretary of State cradled his forehead with his fingers, a thumb placed on the cheekbone. His addled eyes were squinted squarely up drawing lines at their corners betraying his age, which up until that point had been androgynously hidden behind the mask of protocol. "Greatest power on earth," he fumed, "... never been anything remotely like our position in the world since the fall of the Soviets...never for Christ's sake, and still it flows through hidden veins like some god dammed virus!"

Morgan, clasping his two big, rough hands together with elbows on the armchair, chin resting on his entwined fingers, grunted, "The big money."

"That's it! It's the third largest business in the world." Kirkland responded candidly, utterly mystified, exasperated. "Little doses of death. Makes me wonder why people want out so badly...what the hell's so bad about living?"

"Seems to me," the black man sat back in the overstuffed chair, tilted his head and looked down his pudgy nose, "we ought to put some of that military budget to use."

"It is a tempting thought, isn't it."

"Prosperity comes out of order."

"Believe me we've approached the problem through every avenue. We've funded their military units, assigned Peace Corps workers to work with rural farmers and develop replacement crops for coca, we've sent in assassins..."

"Mobilize."

"Yes, gunboat diplomacy," he nodded eyes wide in frustration, "it is a new world. Money, votes...they follow the politically correct and it's not our call anymore. Special interests. We can't defoliate rural fields of coca because the farmers have no other economy! Victim culture. Not one sovereign government that will accept troops, yet they clamor for help, we sign agreements, give them aid..." he raised his hand slicing through the air in front of him with emphasis on each word as if trying to chop away at binding ropes, "if it can't be changed dammit, it's agreed with. If there's no solution, then...hell, it just becomes part of the society." Kirkland's head was spinning from the drink and he felt confined and reckless. "Might as well legalize fucking marijuana, they already have medical use...!"

"The big money." Morgan reiterated quietly secure in his grasp of relationships.

"Shit," he pursed his lips and sighed deeply with frustration knowing that he had violated his language code during negotiations, but the alcohol loosened him up and besides the man across from him was straight ahead. "People haven't the slightest idea how much money."

"I would never have the patience. My attitude is fuck it, if you want something done...just do it. Consequences be dammed."

"Diplomacy calls for a more subtle approach. You have to realize in my line of work there's more of them than there are of us. Law is all we have as an arbiter, it's impersonal, there's no one to shoot. My job is to negotiate agreements...bring people to the table." He smiled

"Trouble is, they just want money, everybody just wants money...and the missing data is that there's a limit, for Christ's sake, minimum wage is only around seven bucks, the fact is Dr. Jagger..."

"...Morgan, please."

"...fact is Morgan, we don't have any more money to give. The bulk of the appropriations are going into border patrols, DEA personnel and hardware, rehab centers, legal fees and clean needle programs. Foreign aid follows economic, not moral priorities."

Absorbing the frustration before him Morgan faced the man stoically knowing in his heart that it must be a personal shortcoming that led to such inaction and that he would never be so constrained by public opinion. "What can I do?"

As if waiting for that one instant, as if the whole conversation had been an intricately scripted monologue crafted to incite his involvement voluntarily, Kirkland's frustration and apparent confusion resolved into a cold, hard professional demeanor that cut through the social veneer like a surgical blade. His gun metal gray eyes revealed a hard boiled career diplomat who was but a soldier in the larger war of ideology and whose weapons consisted of an unflagging belief in the American way and its ever changing values. "Something we can't." He answered directly.

Three days later Dr. Morgan Jagger was infused with a new sense of purpose that made him swagger and take long moments looking people in the eye before he spoke. Not only were his ideas, some of which had been attacked as radically conservative, vindicated, but now the value of his paramilitary connections had been acknowledged by someone that mattered. It all fed his conviction that no matter what he may do he would be right, which was somehow reasoned out of the completely illogical idea that in order to function well with a group, one had to act alone. It was in this spirit that he flew to New Orleans and secretly met with a man who had gone to great lengths to obscure his identity. They sat across from each other in a four star French restaurant over a wide, round table covered with a crisp, white cloth. There was a chilled bottle of La Doucette Pouilly Fumé resting in a silver ice bucket and the large men each delicately pressed long stemmed crystal glasses to their lips as they lightly sipped the wine savoring each golden drop.

Neither engaged in small talk, the kind that comes naturally to friends and materializes out of similar potentials as if the physics of the spiritual universe accounted for creation, but regarded each other with a respect that came out of their differences. One could not exist without the other. The relationship had been formed somewhere in Paleolithic history where the separation of management and labor first occurred with the realization that men were not equal.

His name was Raiko Barba. For the last decade he had been employed by the Drug Enforcement Agency under another name belonging to an identity that he had meticulously crafted over a period of twenty-five years and was the finest point on his resume proving his expertise with the fact that he had never been uncovered or even suspected of being anyone other than who he presented himself as. The truth was that no one knew him. Morgan was fully aware that he may not even be Raiko Barba, though the consequences of that fact made little impact on him for he judged men by their ideals and had the uncanny ability to ascertain character from the first meeting, infallibly. Raiko believed in the work he was doing with the DEA where he was a senior operative having devised and run many operations in Mexico and South America. He was the kind of man that needed leeway, room to take actions that, though obvious, could not be accomplished from within any organized system. Flexibility, he called it. In his mind swirled compartmented and highly structured thoughts concerning his craft and a myriad of contacts and he was currently involved in the process of comparing the features and benefits of different handguns that he had been looking at obsessively for the past two weeks. He carried weapons made of advanced polymers which, when disassembled, could pass through airport security undetected. It was not something he wished to discuss and so he sat silently eating his chicken breast covered by a thick, creamy sauce with grapes.

Morgan described the meeting with the Assistant Secretary of State for International Narcotics Matters. He omitted the books, he could not bring himself to discuss anything personal with Raiko Barba and concluded it would be detrimental to discipline. He went on to outline a mission that he had spent the past three days detailing, "... generated at the highest levels", which was the purpose of this meeting they were now having. Of course, he confided, the man's name came immediately to mind, "as if you were ordained for it," because, and here he stretched the truth for the sake of success, "no one else can handle this assignment."

"How specific was he?" The man asked bluntly unimpressed having had much experience with bureaucrats and their inclination to use nebulous innuendo in an effort to avoid taking responsibility for anything.

Morgan Jagger was overflowing with confidence, it engulfed him. "He left no doubt in my mind. This affair is an extension of U.S. foreign policy." Then he went on to detail exactly what was to be accomplished. "You are to orchestrate an abduction. There will be no interference from the Brazilian authorities, assuming you exhibit your usual discretion. The man will be brought to California where he will be tried for drug trafficking."

Raiko Barba suddenly felt the rush of life. His arms tingled with excitement and he clenched his hands open and closed twice. He reached over and grasped the long stemmed crystal glass and placing it to his lips gulped down its precious contents in one long swallow. Between jobs he did not exist. He was nowhere. The occasional activity at the DEA acted as a shot in the arm that only kept him from atrophy mired down as he was with administrative and legal paperwork, research and dogged investigations that went on for years building cases for the courts, of which over seventy percent were lost. He had learned computers, was a master at compiling detailed evidence and documenting its recovery in anticipation of some obscure ruling that would disqualify its use in a court of law. It was tedious and overbearing and as he saw it a symptom of a government that had become petrified, archaic and detached from the actual lives of its citizens pandering to victims where the squeaky wheel got the grease. He perceived drugs as a coming out of a mysterious, concerted effort to sublimate the last gasp of human vitality and turn it into a controllable, effectual conglomerate of people too enmired in enjoying the destructive qualities that caused their addictions to extricate themselves and the gigantic system devised to handle their fall. Between jobs he did not exist.

There had been times, plenty of them, when he felt absolutely worthless, useless and without any intrinsic value at all with which to give something that other men might support him for. Out of that bleak hole in his life he had found others who felt equally misutilized and with them had formed a paramilitary unit through which each of their potentials might be approached. The simplicity with which they viewed life as a cauldron of justice, the fact of being able to act for the greater good with impunity and the lack of bureaucratic and political restraints gave them a heady, euphoric buoyancy that kept them all above the law. What else was a man meant for if not to control life with his own hands?

"One more thing," Morgan added, "you're on your own." At which point Raiko Barba felt the full force of life thrust against him and imperceptibly frowned with grim determination as he thrilled with the secret knowledge of the self sufficient.

BETWEEN THE LABYRINTH AND THE SKY

XI

Upon the river's back a deep water freighter could travel for over a thousand miles inland. It could carry sailors who have seen nothing but blue horizons for months far into a flourishing, tropical ecosystem that still eludes the covetous hands of North Americans and Europeans after five hundred years. Ships of lesser tonnage could go further still until they became lost, absorbed by nature. It has always been that way. Always.

Thunder pealed out of the angry dome of heaven. Great cathedrals of cloud towered into the stratosphere and ranged inland for twelve hundred miles. It was heard almost every day somewhere in the vast, impossibly diverse landscape. The empire of life consumed over three million square miles, nearly half of all South America. It stretched lazily from the semiarid northeast plagued by intermittent draughts to the damp, fertile forests and expansive plateaus of the central frontiers and south–the mythical Amazon whose waters flow nearly thirty nine hundred miles from the Atlantic coast to the mist laden jungles where only filtered light seeps down into its secretive heart. The land over-flowed with natural resources–minerals, oil, timber; and is so imbued with living spirit that even the rocks seem to move, give admiration to the passing parade and lend credibility to the saying that *God is Brazilian.*

Tarisco boarded the hovercraft that would carry him across the bay to Niterói where he would meet Andrade. He had been consumed with doubt for nearly two months and was glad that the time had finally arrived for once the business was completed he could move on with his life.

The ship he rode on was English, imported, as were many of the things in his country. It had been shaped by foreign hungers for hundreds of years. First for Brazilwood from whose meat a red dye was extracted and was the only reason the Portuguese stayed at all. From this came the land's name. The Dutch had cleared swamplands and processed sugar cane shipping it to Europe where foreigners were obsessed with the white powder that dissolved in a sweet burn on the tongue. When they were defeated, it became the work of the Indian slaves of the Portuguese, who fled like birds to the interior to escape forced labor and en masse chose death to confinement. Black slaves were the solution–as they were in the Caribbean for the French and English–and fueled the industry until nearly nineteen hundred. Africa was raped of fifty million souls to satisfy the sweet tooth of Europe. Some say they were more afraid than the Indian so they stayed and worked like dogs, but perhaps they just had more of a will to live. Ore, too, was gouged from the earth by hungry foreigners, along with timber, nitrates and other raw materials destined to support the industrialization and wars of the white race. Great seaports still are dedicated to these primary industries: Recafe, whose sugar loading terminal is capable of handling 100 tons an hour around the clock: Vitória, the capital of Espírito Santo, the embarkation point for most of the iron ore and consequently leader of the country in tonnage. But what wages will a mineworker ever make? A sugar cane worker? A slave?

Tarisco thought of none of this, he only knew his final destination was to be Vitória where both he and Andrade could be easily anonymous, their cargo was less subject to inspection than in Rio where forty percent of the country's goods passed through, but more importantly Valdemiro Veloso was less likely to discover his subterfuge.

He had gone to great pains in order to keep the plan from his *patrão* and that distressed Tarisco because of the respect he held for

Miro, after all he was Tarisco's *pistolão* and could not be given a bald faced lie. It was only because of Miro that he had been able to be godfather to a hundred and fifty children, *pivetes* such as he had been; and could begin to measure the roads he had funded in the *favelas* by miles rather than meters; and the water and sewers and even the land donated where cinder block houses now stood, never mind that they had no glass in the windows yet, on sites that once were jumbles of scrap metal and corrugated paper. But most of all he was truly thankful to the *orixás* for the *Sambadromo,* the place where Carnival begins. That was where his glory shown in profuse splendor reflecting money spent on his *escola de samba*. He paid no attention to dissent from middle class fops who complained that the popular spirit of the samba parades was being perverted by the flood of wealth from *Jogo De Bicho* bosses who wanted nothing more that adulation and notoriety like some narcissistic small time hoods. Tarisco was deeply insulted by the implication, nevertheless always wore his best white linen suit on the day of the parade.

He could feel now the sounds of hundreds of drums in the wind flushing off the gray water between the bay and the towering sky. It gave him a point in time to look forward to, which propelled him through difficult periods where he was forced by circumstance to do things he did not necessarily agree with. It was the culmination of the year and all his accounts revolved around that one day because he had instructed his accountant to create his fiscal year starting and ending at that moment, always keeping detailed fictional books in the event that some official or another might get hold of them and try to assess him for back taxes or freeze his accounts as had been done in 1964 by the government to combat excessive liquidity.

The Carnival parade. Out of the air it came fleetingly at first like the flapping of wings, then insistent, aggressive, overpowering until the mind was numbed, mesmerized and could not think of anything else. A hundred, then three hundred drums, all starting with the first one; drummers milling around at the entrance to the *Sambadromo* all chasing down the elusive rhythm until it reverberated beneath the whole city causing its foundations to tremble and threatening to shake the mountains down. Conceived by the same architect who sculpted

Brasilia, a city still foreign to the central plains over a half century later, in oddly flared angles and modernesque design the *Sambadromo* is an elongated stadium that ran for blocks in downtown Rio. A huge tarmac lined by spectator stands. The humming of the drums erased all other sounds as the dancers assembled, flocks of them, hundreds, thousands of them, feathered, adorned, bejeweled in taffeta, satin and tulle with sequins, rhinestones and glitter sparkling with the confusion and tumult of a great human sea of color and splendor.

A hundred thousand spectators began to stamp their feet. Their hips swayed with the movement of the samba. It seemed as if the whole southern continent moved with them, its jarring causing tsunamis in the Atlantic and Pacific both, vibrating carnally, sensually. Industry closed down. Shops folded up. Banks took a holiday. Then the dancers came. More than three thousand of them in outlandish, tribal head dresses, capes and fantastic coordinated colors that swept down the street in waves–for hours, hundreds of one hue then of another cascading with beautiful, laughing faces. In their center were the enormous floats meticulously constructed through sweltering months of labor adorned with bare breasted women shimming their shoulders and rocking their hips shining with perspiration and glitter. Some rise over three stories high and are the creative efforts of committees who decide on the themes in contest with each other in the annual competition. They dwarf the throng of undulating bodies that seem the flesh of one gigantic living organism whose resident spirit is of the *favelas*. Whole neighborhoods jam the stands. Strangers embrace in the streets. It is the one intrusion of the *favelados*, the poor, the *descamisados*–those without shirts–into the mainstream. Television cameras tirelessly focus on them for three days, their lewd carousing and their bare backsides.

Outside the *Sambadromo*, in the streets, the people of the favelas unable to afford a ticket cling desperately to metal scaffolding and rails to catch a glimpse of the splendor, the costumes, the performers of who they were brother, father, lover...in the darkness they too were overcome by the swelter of the drums, the swell of emotion generated by a whole city dancing as one in the bacchanal of love and harmony.

The music was loud and black and poor. When first the samba appeared in Parisian nightclubs, Brazilian newspapers denounced it as a national disgrace though they praised famous composer Villa-Lobos for his haunting airs based on the same sources. Brazil is a white country even though up until the nineteenth century slaves were arriving at the rate well in excess of twenty five thousand a year. Tarisco was inured to the insolvable dichotomies of life. He had stood outside the *Sambadromo* nearly all his life and now that he was inside he could not allow his position to be jeopardized. It was pride that drove him, pride in his own strength, his own tenacity and ability that had resulted in raising himself by his own bootstraps from out of the favelas, and then returning to improve the lives of his brothers in meagerness. Poverty was a social disease, it was the byproduct of wealth and establishment that had been paid for by the free labor and exploitation of millions so that a few may eke out an artificial existence untroubled by such banalities as lack of health care, the daily struggle for food and fresh water, and most of all the hopelessness brought on by a complete absence of future. For the *favelados*, there was no *panelinha*, no little saucepan of friends and family that together nurtured and sustained careers thereby ensuring a system of upward mobility.

Tarisco could not afford to violate his unspoken blood pact with Miro yet he saw in the face of Andrade the look of his own people. The stories were true, the man was a mestiço, of many breeds such as himself, even though Miro was white cariocan his son had the calm, coffee colored skin, had inherited the high, wide cheekbones and the broad, flat nose with a gentle look in the eye Tarisco himself saw each day in the mirror. He could not refuse to help him even though there wasn't any logic to it at all and if he were found out, it could mean disaster. More than life was at stake.

Andrade was on the dock waiting in the late afternoon light diffused by the threat of rain.

"So, you decided to show up?" Valdemiro Veloso's son grinned and ambled loosely down to the edge of the quay where he slapped his father's *homem de confiança*–right hand man–on the arm.

"Shit." Up in the lot on the hill Tarisco saw Andrade's gull winged Mercedes. "We can't take that thing."

"Why not?"

"We'll have to rent one."

"What for?"

Tarisco did not answer. The two men walked up to the vintage silver sports car with the red leather upholstery that was smooth and without any major flaws and listened as the motor fired up in that hollow, perfectly tuned roar that sounded like an alto saxophone. It was the only one like it in Rio and Andrade could remember seeing a photograph of the old movie star Clark Gable standing next to one just like it with two toned shoes and an argyle vest sweater. Tarisco rented a nondescript, metallic blue, Japanese sedan and made Andrade park two blocks away from the rent-a-car office in a restaurant lot where he slipped the attendant the equivalent of two weeks salary to watch it for them until they returned. The young man gave him a thumbs up, the national gesture of Brazil.

Rain was falling in huge, buoyant drops that hung suspended in the muggy air as if sacks of water and not the innocuous dribbles from heaven North Americans always expected, exploding upon impact, half dissolving back into the atmosphere instantly absorbed and half flooding everything within reach to the core. Much of the landscape was completely sated with water anyway for if there was one thing that Brazil was blessed with, it was moisture. It ran in rivers and streams and under the earth in subterranean caverns and deeper still through the lush turgid leaves of tropical vegetation that flourished in every available space except on the dry plains of the *sertão*. The *Nordestinos* were not the poorest people for lack of money, it was for lack of water that was abundant elsewhere in the juggernaut named for the red trees. Fortunately the car, which lacked other amenities, had at least six speeds for the windshield wipers so that the view was clear from the moment the downpour began.

"Why are we driving to Vitória?"

"I explained that already."

"It's nearly five hours in the rain."

"Can't be helped."

"Tell me again why we couldn't do this in Rio?" Andrade moaned willfully. "I'm missing a dinner party."

Tarisco glared at him sharply and was about to take the back of his hand to him as he would have to his own son, if he'd had one, but then restrained the sudden blaze of irritation. "Have you forgotten what we're doing?" He said sternly. "Don't be stupid."

The boy, he always would think of him as a boy, was like his own and they had been close all the years he had worked for Valdemiro. Andrade had been entrusted into his care often when Miro was out of the city or in danger and the boy was not at Father Javier Abraho's school. He had tried to give him direction that suited an honorable man regardless of his station in life. Vertical advancement was difficult if not impossible in Brazil for the social strata had crystallized long before the emancipation of the slaves and though racial bigotry had never achieved the cultural popularity as in the United States, it had been sublimated by a person's station in life. It was a miracle what he had accomplished finding success and death was preferable to life again in the favelas, so he had devised a plan of extraordinary complexity in order to preserve the safety of his young scion and that of his own social position.

"Vitório is an industrial port. It is very busy and is not under the bright lights like Rio," he glanced over at Andrade, "where any fool would drop his package and run at the first hint of trouble."

"Ahh...well I'm not scared if that's what you think!"

Tarisco smiled severely. "You're a kid. They are flying in tonight from Manaus. We will meet them at the harbor. If everything is in order it shouldn't take more than three hours."

"I wish we were flying in!" Andrade complained in bemusement. "Even in the rain, I'd rather be flying." The automobile sped up he coast highway heading north out of Rio De Janero where the Atlantic ocean was in view much of the time yet now slowly turning invisible awash in clouds and rain and the descending night. An urgency traveled with them. One man harbored a hope for the future and the other a fear.

Off the coast a small seaplane was negotiating a landing in a gray choppy sea. Its beacons flickering out as tiny insignificant dots over the great ocean, the Mare Atlanticum, which yawned at this tiny flurry along its coast men called a storm. Lights from the shore were only intermittently visible through the driving tropical rain and the mist that rose at eventide. Two grim men sat rigid, nervously strapped in their seats, one gripping the armrests and the other the controls. Neither was afraid to die, it was the suspense, the waiting. Wind pummeled the craft and slapped against the bulkheads like hammers violently tilting one wing up and then the other. The aircraft dropped free fall hundreds of feet at a time as it hit pockets of low pressure and then rose back up shaking with violence. As they drew closer to the water wild salt spray shattered against the windscreen and was swept away by the powerful wipers designed to de-ice at high altitudes. The whole plane shuddered from the straining engine.

Suddenly a pontoon bounced off the crest of a wave showering plumes of white water into the wind and jolting their brains. "Christ!" said the pilot and sucked in his breath baring his teeth drawing his lips taut.

Once again they bounced, this time with more force and the passenger, a stocky, good looking man with a thick neck, folded forward and grunted through his own gritted teeth, "C'mon buddy, you can do it!!" Again they hit and water covered the windshield. At last the plane began plowing through the chop, which was just beginning to feather in the wind, cutting the crests, slamming the pontoons across the jagged, watery landscape making the aircraft tremble with the strain, and shake and rattle as if it were going to fly into a thousand pieces. It went on forever, suspended in time between heaven and purgatory. Then suddenly it all just stopped. The craft slid down the back of a swell and the men inside could hear the rain beating on the fuselage. Sweat covered their faces. The air acrid with fear.

"Jesus god dammed fucking mother of Christ I thought I was gonna buy the farm!!" The pilot expelled.

"You were alright." The passenger said stoically.

"Ahhh...Christ! What a god dammed night to fly!!"

"Don't hold back now."

"I sure hope this trip is as important as you say."

The passenger didn't look again at the pilot, but kept his eyes on the lights of the harbor they were just beginning to enter. "Always important buddy."

Raiko Barba picked up his gear, three large, heavy duffel bags of black ballistic nylon, and one watertight, bright metal briefcase, as soon as they were unloaded from the plane onto the slick wooden dock. The pilot was in the small sheltered office wiping his face off with a white handkerchief and recklessly smoking a cigarette.

Raiko stuck his head in the door. "Those things'll kill ya buddy. Thanks for the lift."

"Shit." Said the man in disgust.

"If we're not back by three, get't hell outta here." He walked to the parking lot carrying all the baggage with straps crisscrossed over his torso and, producing a set of keys from his khaki pants, unlocked the rear door of a late model black station wagon. Tires squealed on the wet asphalt as he drove away.

The small warehouse had been rented for a month. It was empty, save the trash, papers and other detritus of the former tenant, an exporter of Taurus handguns, one of the only Brazilian small arms sold on the consumer market around the world. The building was of cinder blocks with a double layer corrugated roof that roared with the raucous tattoos of rain pouring down. All the doors were heavy metal with double locks and a state-of-the-art alarm system a ruminant of the last tenant. One man sat on a couch and another on a chair in the office that was separated from the warehouse space by a wall with a large safety glass window. The one on the couch was *côr do carvão*–the color of coal–and the other a light skinned *mestiço*. Neither spoke. There was one metal desk that had been left behind with a dirty, beige, multiple-line telephone on it. Lights were off, except in the one room.

Raiko Barba drove through the unfamiliar streets knowing exactly where he was going. Every turn and landmark had been drawn in his mind during his preparation weeks ago. He followed the long road down into the wharves where huge storage buildings lined both sides forming miles of unlit corridors in the darkness and past great mountains of iron ore that were straddled by the mammoth shoots and conveyer loaders sticking out into the night over the quay where no freighter sat. He concentrated on the last conversation between himself and Dr. Morgan Jagger and in his mind tried to piece together a visual image of the enigmatic Valdemiro Veloso, of whom he had heard so much. He was a very private man. Without reason, Raiko Barba was compelled to understand this person lacking a face who lived in the grand colonial *fazenda* as had been done in earlier centuries, perhaps because he had never developed any roots himself. The urge to know Veloso's inner workings grew stronger as he became part of the man's landscape and also out of a longing to comprehend his own alienation.

Raiko Barba was a man who felt at his best in transit, whose home lay between destinations, in a suitcase, and the story of his life could best be told in departures and arrivals, of comings and goings, of the places he would be and those where he'd been. There was no great crushing incident to be found in his history that had brought about this quality, in fact he had grown to be a young man on a prosperous farm in Tillamook Oregon, home of the famous cheeses, where time moved especially slow among the rushes that grew in sluices around tall leafy trees and across the broad fields of long grass that seemed perpetually green. Unlike many rural communities, the farms of that county had remained virtually unbroken by reason of the equity in the cheese, which could be had in any major city in the United States, and that gave them a secure source of income seemingly immune to the fluctuations of other market segments. If a farm was sold, it went in the whole, fully equipped and operable and only a few times over the past century had a good working spread been subdivided and even then the circumstances were held suspect by local landowners, as if subterfuge had muddled the thoughts of their former neighbor making him do the unforgivable. Real estate agents were unwelcome there as the bond with the land was still, even in the present era where things that mattered were volatile, ingrained with the life that it engendered. The symbiotic relationship could be felt traveling down narrow roads whose edges were over-grown with ragged grasses and thistles beneath trees whose boughs formed a canopy through which the sky blinked in yellow sparkles.

He had never been a part of the spiritual interchange inherent in the community and was cursed with the constant feeling that he belonged somewhere else and that whatever he was doing, he should be doing something else. This did not inhibit his concentration in any way, but enhanced it. Because he had to struggle so hard to focus it made him a competent individual, meticulous and thorough, but it also gave him a discontented streak causing others to be put off and gave him few friends. As a boy he would range all alone the lands that spread out in the rich, coastal valleys that edged the Pacific Ocean and the rolling hills thick with undergrowth and conifers lush with the constant moisture of the Northwest. He learned to ride a horse by himself at just seven years by jumping on the animal's back from off the corral fence. After he had fallen enough to know that he didn't like it, managed to stay on even the most skittish animal. He would leave the breakfast table when not in school and often not be seen again all day. His father, a slow talking, solid man whose only delight in life was hard physical labor, could not understand the boy at all and though he attempted to talk with him, the sessions usually ended up in silence. Their farm, however, was exceptionally prosperous, even by Tillamook standards, and so it was with great dismay and surprise that the news of Raiko's disappear-ance entered the town's gossip at coffee shops, feed stores and the local bowling alley where many of the men hung out. He was the prodigal son, truly, they said in envy of the productive farm and secure in the conviction that he would return beaten with the realization that nothing could replace the bountiful lands that worked for you and provided food and shelter and even a grave in the end. But he never did return. Raiko Barba cared nothing for these things.

The seventeen-year-old hitchhiked to Portland because he was dying to see the city and break away from the claustrophobic, rural life. He worked there for two years at odd jobs, mostly construction so he could be outdoors, finally landing a position with United Trailways Bus Company as a trainee; a situation he had always coveted since a small boy when he'd see the drivers of eighteen wheelers on the highway and would go to sleep dreaming he was one of them, rolling down endless roads never having to stop even for food because of a small ice box he kept in the cab filled with cherry cokes and potato chips. At first he was only allowed to drive the local runs, but as he grew more experienced he was placed on longer and longer routes until finally he was assigned to the intestates, and that was fine with him, just fine. Four years later though, he was in Houston working as a oil rigger.

Many men travel their entire lives and never gain the insight necessary to connect with their true promise. It was on the flaming dirt plains outside Houston where Raiko, now growing barrel chested and muscular, lanky arms corded from the labor and dark from the sun, discovered the first mystery of himself. While working with the Mexicans he learned to speak Spanish, fluently, like a native so that it was nearly impossible to distinguish his American accent. It only took him six weeks. He had never once considered that it was difficult knowing things and so approached new experiences with an innocence tempered by a willingness and an unrestrained ability to apply force.

The result was astonishing. He began to understand the engineering behind the pump mechanisms, and then the geometry of piping and the principles of the refining process. He initiated complex repairs and improvements that the company had hired experts to design and implement before. When the chief engineers came by on their rounds, he learned their language, spoke with them in the theoretical nomenclature of one who was initiated into their mysteries. Soon he was a foreman, and then an assistant to the chief engineer. When the company contracted for drilling and refining in the Middle East, Raiko went with them and spent the next ten years in Amman, Jordan, the United Arab Emirate, Saudi Arabia, Iraq and Kuwait. In return the company invested in him and he took his degree in civil engineering at the University of Cairo where he also studied Islam under the Mullahs whose duty it was to determine what the orthodox manner was in which a Muslim should live in the modern world.

When he returned to the United States he was a different species than the young man from Tillamook Oregon whose driving ambition was only to escape the farm. He had acquired a worldview, and as a result of his religious education had developed a strong moral sense that translated into a social consciousness and prevented him from doing many things he would have done otherwise. He became very selective of the projects he got involved with.

It was out of this moral sense that he first contacted the Drug Enforcement Agency, who, after initially shunting him off because he had no legal or law enforcement training, suddenly realized that his experience in the Middle East and his uncanny ability with languages, which now included classical Arabic, Farsi, Swahili, Portuguese and Spanish, would be uniquely valuable to them. He embarked on intensive training, which he absorbed in his usual voracious manner and after only a few years was one of the top operative directors for Mexico and South America. Raiko traveled constantly, he enjoyed the work, it satisfied the moral principles he had constructed for himself and everything went along fine for many years.

It wasn't clear at which point the discontent began. Later he decided it was a consequence of the incredible bureaucratic slush at the DEA and the overbearing command chain in which every person involved wanted to be the author and nothing was approved except by those who held power and whose ideas were pushed to the forefront. It was an internal battle of wills fomenting stagnation, funding deficits and ill conceived and executed activities. Somewhere in the confusion Raiko Barba decided to go outside as an independent. His agile mind and voracious appetite for practical knowledge gave him a feeling of aloofness, of separateness and alienation that he did not recognize as a characteristic of his entire life and so attributed it to the effort to hold him back from achieving his full capacity.

And as he grew older he was finding the one thing he could not get enough of was danger. He used it as a sort of aphrodisiac to help combat the lack of spice, the dullness he felt encroaching upon him whenever he was in one place for too long. Dr. Morgan Jagger was perhaps his only friend, though not socially. Only he came to Raiko with the true recognition of who he was dealing with and never told him what to do, but hired him for his unique abilities. Competency that exceeded what was asked for left him bitter, disillusioned, overqualified and approaching middle age.

Inside the small warehouse the black station wagon was parked dripping water onto the dusty cement floor. Muted ticks sounded in the half light as the engine cooled off. Raiko sat in the office behind the glass window and was talking with the two men while they waited for the others to arrive. Both were Brazilian, both members of the anti-narcotics unit of Brazil's Federal Police. He had worked with them before. Nothing was left to chance. Eyes were dark and intense.

"I understand," he began enunciating each word carefully, singularly imparting its full meaning, "that after Valdemiro Veloso lost his wife he never remarried." Raiko paused thinking, considering as if trying to comprehend the unfathomable nature of something. "Tell me, what was she like?"

"She was a woman of inconsolable beauty." The dark man replied frankly in the hollow of the warehouse with the rattling of the rain incessant upon the corrugated roof. "By that I mean she was unearthly, translucent..."

"She was a whore." The other man spit out while picking his teeth, slouched back on the couch with one foot up and then added with inordinate emphasis as if to drive his point home, "A slut for God's sake, why do you romanticize?"

Raiko, shocked by the sudden intrusive language looked at the mestiço in surprise, the vaporous image of Valdemiro Veloso forming all the while, and asked, "Is this true?"

"The orixás favor such women." The dark man answered. "Their spirit is more sensitive."

"Tell me." He said, "Tell me about it."

"She was an initiate I understand, but that is only what I have heard and rumors, as you know, are the source of trouble...but it is said she lived with a babalorixá–a mother of saints–in the Rio das Pedras favela. It is only rumor now, but what I am telling you is what I was told, and it all began with thieves..."

"A drug smuggler's *puta*, that's all...!" The dark man injected viciously." Nothing more. There are dozens on Barra Beach with their backsides hanging out if you want them."

"...four men went on a spree." The mestiço continued unperturbed, as if he were used to the dark man's behavior and only glanced slightly at him revealing with his sad expression that he felt pity. "They broke into the apartment where the two sons of the President lived with his estranged wife and his mother. Nobody was home, so they stole money and jewels, naturally, and the car of the President's mother. Later, they stormed the old Military Club, an organization of gray haired, retired army officers once the citadel of the elite, and made them lie in the dust with the employees on the floor while they rifled cash registers and emptied pockets and put a bullet through the head of one old gentleman for no reason at all. A Greek ship owner was found dead that afternoon three miles from the airport where he had just arrived with fifty thousand dollars to meet his payroll. The money was, of course, not with him. Two Federal Police officers, who had been keeping track of the Greek, gave chase and the four men escaped to the slums of Rio das Pedras where they held up given sanctuary by the *favelados*. The federal Anti-Terrorist Police were called in and soon the helicopters swept down on the ghetto and the resulting battle lasted all night, destroying a dozen or more shanties and in addition to killing the four men, caused the deaths of six *favelados* including two children." He stopped talking as if to see if he held Raiko's interest. "That's what started the invasion."

There was a condominium complex that had been vacant, in receivership for two years...down the mud hill, in sight of the Rio das Pedras shacks, and in fact most could see it from their windows. At first a few people ran fleeing the shoot-out and took refuge there, then others followed. Soon nine hundred and eighty two apartments were occupied. But that was just the start. It caught on, a good idea everyone thought, and soon there were ten more occupations with over five thousand families in vacant buildings, half finished housing complexes and vacant lots. To make it worse, the new socialist governor of the Democratic Labor Party rode through the streets on the back of a flat bed truck with a *pivete* by his side and vowed he would support the invaders with the cry that he would do everything possible to put the slum dwellers in the properties and the owners in the slums. It was an invitation to the thousands of families living in mud holes to take the initiative and the movement spread to the state of Rio Grande do Sul who also had a liberal governor."

The dark man sat forward and placed his elbows on his knees and was suddenly impassioned. "You have to realize that the propertied middle and upper classes are small compared to the landless majority of people who constitute the true social power in Brazil. Nearly fifty percent of the population is under twenty-four. So, you can imagine how this went over with the banks, who ultimately held the paper on the unfinished properties and vacant land and even with the military—they were a slender force compared to the human wall they confronted. This is when they called in Valdemiro Veloso who was well known to be a protector of the *favelados* and famous among all the slums of Rio for his graciousness and generosity. There was a private agreement, even though everyone knew that his import export business was a drug smuggling cartel, he was the savior of the banks who by this time were loosing millions of dollars a day in held up construction and damages."

The mestiço lit a cigarette and everything was silent except the constant drum of the rain. "The woman?" Raiko asked.

"That was how he met Ryxa. It is said that he was so taken with the girl that he could not eat nor sleep for three days after he had first beheld her and finally sent his car all the way up into the favela so that he could see her again. He brought her to his house where she lived with him and soon they were married in the church."

"What happened?"

"They had a son the following year and she died in childbirth. He showed no emotion publicly, no emotion at all but simply withdrew from the world of the living and spent all his time building his empire and amassing huge sums of wealth that even the Federal Police have not been able to trace. He refused to speak to anyone about her, would never mention her name. His whole life revolved around his son, Andrade, whom he has sheltered from the streets, given the best education and completely lives for caring nothing about his own life seeing in him, I suppose, a part of the lost Ryxa. She was an inconsolable beauty."

"She was a whore." The dark man could not help but enforce once more as if to justify the act that the men had gathered to do by denying any human traits to the victim.

Raiko fell silent and turned his head as the wavering mirage of the man, Valdemiro Veloso, began to breathe on its own accord without his bias or prejudice and the idea of the drug lord as an individual began to live in his mind. The rawness of the image made him shrink from the cruel irony of life because he could relate at once to the bitterness the man must feel. But he did not feel regret for the act he had come to Brazil to commit. In the final analysis a drug dealer and his whore deserved little sympathy.

BETWEEN THE LABYRINTH AND THE SKY

XII

In another place, far to the north, across the Amazonas-Venezuelan border; past the straits of Panama and the jungles of Belize, Honduras, El Salvador; beyond Chiapas, where rebel descendants of the ancient Mayans, decimated by the Conquistadors in the fifteenth century, held out still for their land; over the great Sonoran desert filled with the giant Saguaro and up the gold coast in the land that once was New Spain, a huge house sat just north of Los Angels on the hills surrounded by oaks and sweet smelling chaparral overlooking the grand sweep of the Pacific coast and the endless, pristine expanse of blue water. Freshening winds sailed up off the sea and white fleecy clouds slowly crossed the horizon.

Randall DesVergers nervously held the gilded invitation in his sweaty hand as the men scanned his body with metal detectors. He walked through an x-ray booth like those at airports and to his embarrassment the alarm went off with a shrill buzz. Sheepishly he withdrew all the remaining items from his pockets. Once more the alarm sounded and this time a huge man in a dark suit and mirrored sunglasses approached and deftly removed Rand's belt. "Try again." He said. The alarm was silent.

Gleaming automobiles lined the private road that wound up the hill from the Coast Highway like a string of jewels. He looked down at his own shining sedan singularly glad that he had bought it and laughed now at his original misgivings over the price. "Randall...!" The wheezing, guttural salutation came wafting over the lawn in front of the house where a few people were lingering in their formal suits and long dresses and were beginning to perspire in the heat of the sun. He looked over to see the stocky fiftyish man, who appeared much older by reason of his lugubrious, asthmatic speech and slow deliberate movements, waving both arms at him in an open embrace inhibited by the chewed on cigar he held in one hand. For him smoking was not an effete social event, but an addiction acquired when his doctor demanded he give up cigarettes to stave off his chronic bronchitis and signs of emphysema or he would have to find someone else to watch him die. There was always a wet butt in his mouth, lit or not. His whole being reeked of smoke and ash.

Jerzy Klimas was a Polish immigrant who had come to the United States as a young teenager, but never lost his thick accent. In the 1970s he made a fortune producing pornographic films. When the videocassette craze hit in the 1980s it catapulted his modest fortune into the big leagues further magnified by wise investment advice. Consequently he had become a cohort of the wealthy media, entertainment and industrial elite of the West whose prerequisite for the social calendar was simply satisfied by a certain dollar amount in net worth. Jerzy was regularly listed by numerous magazines in their insightful features on the highest grossing individuals in the country. In the game room of his home was a life size blow up of a photograph taken in the late 1970s showing Jerzy, in his curled afro haircut, standing arm in arm with two plump, pasty white, dark haired, red lipped, semi nude girls dressed in miniature cowboy outfits with their breasts and their buttocks spilling out. He kept it there to remember his roots and also as an obscene gesture to the moneyed and the powerful whom he had venerated all his life. He had awarded his whole account to Van Riper, Hazeltine & Brock and considered himself Rand's mentor and had even gone to the length of sponsoring him at an elite country club.

He slapped his arm across Rand's shoulder knocking him off balance and hoarsely chortled in his ear. "Not every day the President visits your house!"

"That's right." Rand said affecting a smile though he felt nothing for the man, absolutely no feeling whatsoever.

"Come here," he grabbed his arm and pulled him aside on the lawn with his face a mere eight inches from Rand's ear subjecting him to the fallout of his breath. "This is opportunity for you."

"What do you mean."

"Very important people here." Jerzy nodded patronizingly and patted him on the shoulder. "This campaign fund raiser was...guess whose idea?"

"Who else?"

"Of course..." he pulled Rand even closer, "the President's got a fat assed wife."

"Not everyone has your taste."

"He makes a fool of himself, but he'll get lots of money for reelection and won't forget where it came from either. I'm tellin' ya'..."

"So...?"

"Politics. We were talking about you running for office... very seriously."

Randall was suddenly alert. "You're kidding."

"Just yesterday. You're starting to get noticed, making your name. Go on, go on inside there and see if you can do yourself some good." And then the man turned away to greet some of the arriving guests.

The threshold to the palace was an intricate maze of glass and wood built around an elevated walkway that hung suspended over a natural spring, which was stocked with giant koi languidly swimming in and out of the shadows, oblivious to the passing of the illuminati overhead, masquerading their common carp origins with bright orange, pale whites and spotted scales. Inside he was hit with a rush of cool wind from the air conditioning that blustered out of the huge atrium leading to the center of the building and the living area where people congregated. The whole side of the house was one great glass wall. It rose up nearly three stories and Rand was astonished that there was the capability to manufacture a series of plates to cover so broad an area. Outside the window was an unobstructed view of the Pacific Ocean that spun out onto the roiling mists of the horizon farther than anyone could ever see with the naked eye unaided by mechanical lenses. There was not another house in sight and the whole coast appeared as a primitive landscape distant from any turmoil and reminding anyone who viewed it of their own eternal longings for the illusive inner peace.

Rand stood self consciously near the center of the room. He recognized some well known entertainment executives, media personalities and other older, more subdued public figures of local politics from where the bulk of the money actually came. There was no sign of the President or any of his retinue. A sudden lightness overtook him and he felt dizzy at the nearness to the reins of power and in order to get a grip started drinking and soon was engaged in robust discussion with a small clique of other lawyers who were debating the finer attributes of golf clubs.

"I haven't actually played that much." Rand commented, "Seems like an impossible game. How can you get any better?"

"Got to have the strength of a gorilla and the intellect of Einstein."

"Most people don't."

"Angles, it's all angles," another rejoined, "intellectual skill, strategy."

A graying man spoke up, the oldest one in the group yet tanned and fit, "if golf's the price for one meal in that fabulous restaurant at Pebble Beach, I'll play."

"Jesus...that's right. What a view, incredible!"

Rand injected. "What the hell's a 'sweet spot'?"

"Easy...even I know what that is."

"He reads all the magazines and that's how he knows."

"Well now just because you base your arguments around articles in the *American Law Review* doesn't mean that enthusiasts' magazines are responsible for my golf game."

"Yea," quipped another man obviously getting high, "what there is of it."

The realization hit that he was touching the edges of power. If he could just get a hand full, just grasp enough stardust he too would be propelled mysteriously into the light where men, such as these he was talking with, hungered to be. Power was the only intoxicant he had not

226

tried so he began to seriously consider the comment that Jerzy had let slip as he was arriving. *Congressman DesVergers*, he liked the sound of it.

"The sweet spot?" One said, "isn't that where you hit the balls?"

"I always thought it was where you put your balls," the older man cracked accompanied by derisive laughter and more than one elbow in the ribs.

"You're a member of the country club now aren't you?"

"Yes," Rand answered hesitantly, "I suppose."

"Whadya mean? Either you are or you...aren't."

"Well, I've been sponsored, but I haven't paid."

"That's the way to do it!" The older man cut it, " Perfect. You can go on like that for years."

"Might as well," said someone else, "get invited to three of four clubs.

"Hell, records are so bad you could spend your whole life there without having to pay."

The older man gave Rand a playful tap in the stomach. "Keep it up buddy, you're doing great."

"We gotta play sometime."

"Sure." Rand replied not looking forward to it.

"Can't do business without golf!"

"Yep," a couple of them replied. "That's right," said some others and it was a bonding point. "I get more Japanese clients that way." They all laughed secure in each other's company now that they knew they understood one another. A waiter breezed by and the men quickly whisked the canapés and drinks off the trays.

"Seen the President?" One asked excitedly.

"Not yet." Another replied stuffing a ball of smoked salmon and Beluga caviar into his mouth.

Across the room Naomi stood holding a chilled glass of white wine. She had come with Ashford Van Riper, but he had gotten sidetracked by some cronies and so she stood alone watching Rand and the small group of men. She had known she was in love with him for a long time, even longer counting the months she denied it and tried to force him, unsuccessfully, from her thoughts. For many years in her life she had been man and woman both, until she found him. Though she knew there was an essential element missing in his make up that she could not define or name, she was equally certain it was within her to fulfill him and that she alone could complete the man. This conviction was so strong that despite the night journeys into sleeplessness and the erotic dreams that denied her satisfaction she maintained a constant vigil over him monitoring his moods and tastes and most of his current women without any jealousy. Secretly waiting for him, being a harbor for his life when he needed to reach dry land. She watched after him. Naomi took no other lovers. It wasn't at all that way with her, it was a lonely winding; it was being windblown and restless; it was being snowblind, lost and then resurrected; it was the howl that screamed above the earth, out into the ether where spirits came and went and lingered with unattainable visions. "I have seen you," she recited to herself, "and you have spoken deeply into my silent heart."

The car came to a stop on the road beneath the looming hulk of a huge freighter. Its shadow brushed quietly over them falling into deeper shadows, but which compared to the shadows in men's hearts were faint and insignificant. The air was slightly cooler now that it was late and well into the night and no one could go back, even if they desired it, for the day had closed, wrapped up and gone the way of all the previous days to dust and gentle voices reminiscing over the past.

"We are early." Tarisco said looking at his wristwatch. "Good. That will give us time." Rain was still falling and angled through the pale yellow lights that shot ahead before them into the harbor's heart illuminating their way as they lurched foreword again, but never far enough ahead to be able to know the full outcome of an action. For in the world all things are linked to all things and when one player in the game shifts, so must another. Though an act may come without motive, as many do contradicting the pundits that say everything must have a reason, there is rarely an act that comes without consequences.

"What is the name of the boat?" Andrade asked, tired from the long drive and itching to stretch his legs.

"The Aurora. Panama registry."

"Where will she go?"

"French Guyana, Surinam...they fly it somewhere from there... Amsterdam, Paris, it does not matter. We are paid on delivery."

"Why do they fly it in?"

"Junk boats used to go up and down the Amazon without stopping. It's more difficult now. The U.S. gave almost four million this year, some of that went into river patrol boats. It's more difficult now. Besides, the Rondônia connection has the protection of certain politicians in the state, and it costs a lot more to extend their radar than it does to buy a boat. The border is 5,450 miles long and only a fraction of it is covered. The airstrips are protected by the lumber companies too," He glanced at Andrade, "they partly pay the Surui chiefs in cocaine for their timber rights."

They were both silent and the repetition of the rain blended with the slush of the wheels on wet streets into a white noise. "You have to be careful with your money." Tarisco said suddenly as if reminding himself of all the little incidental things he had never mentioned to Andrade and that the boy would not know for himself. "It can't be obvious. Like the taxi drivers that suddenly own car dealerships. Tax authorities investigate them. Twenty three now they got."

"Where does it come from?"

He shrugged. "Many places." A few years ago a Mayor built a 40-mile dirt road from a little town called Costa Marques through the jungle and across the Guaporé River to the Bolivian town of San Joaquin, which was only reachable before that by air or boat. It was a major center of laboratories for a while. Now, I don't know."

"Have you ever lost a shipment?"

"Yes. Planes crash sometimes. Once a pilot missed a connection and dropped eight hundred and eighty pounds of cocaine on an Indian village.

"I hope our plane doesn't crash."

"Yes." Tarisco was silent once again listening to the rhythms of the automobile. "I will call you Helio, as we agreed, to the others. Do you remember that?"

"Yes."

"That is very important. They will not question me because they think I am acting for your father, Valdemiro...but if word gets back to him, we are finished. That is very important. Do you remember that?" He asked now that the apprehension was beginning to become real to him as they drew closer to the rendezvous.

"Yes."

"That is good."

The small, blue sedan turned down a quay with the numbers forty-nine painted clearly on a sign that was posted high on a piling as it was on all the quays, rusted and old, but lucid. The windshield wipers seemed suddenly loud. One bare light bulb hung over it. The car slowed and turned moving steadily down the wharves splashing through puddles past a row of shadowy vessels, most of them dark and some with only a few lights visible, from out of some obscure cabin, over the metal stairs that served as a gangway hanging off the stern reaching all the way down the to the low lying dock. Tarisco drove past them all. At the far end there were lights. A ship that lie awash in a hive of activity gleamed in the mist with the rain making its wet sides appear freshly painted. Men scurried under huge rope nets filled with crates being hoisted up over the deck and lowered down into the hold where other men, black men in soiled and torn T-shirts whose faces were slick with a sheen of perspiration and whose arms rippled with muscle drawn taut to the maximum, worked to their limit and driven past the point of exhaustion to where the labor was carried out purely on spiritual energy their will being so strong. In their minds and hearts was a burning terror that failure imposed upon a grown man who could not keep pace with the rest of humanity and gain the purchasing power that invested its specter of respectability and righteousness in the person who could earn a decent living. Most here supported whole families, sometimes more than one family, for under a hundred and sixty dollars a week. When they went home, after twelve or more hours of labor, if they could get it, it was to a makeshift shelter that had been carefully crafted from industrial scrap with a dirt floor, or perhaps a floor covered by a few boards, or tarpaper. Sleep came to them only as a result of exhaustion. It was God's gift, for in a room, which housed maybe seven people, help was needed in order to attain rest.

The sedan pulled up in the cover of the warehouse adjacent to the towering steamer whose rust streaks were now visible coming from out the high ports in the bulkheads meant to let water escape from the decks, and down from where the huge anchor chain and ropes had worn away paint and primer through years of abuse. Her name, Aurora, was faintly visible on the top side of the bow and abaft above the word Panama written smaller. Tarisco killed the engine and suddenly the rain, after having heard it for over five hours on the drive up the coast, seemed omnipresent, as if it were a medium through which they traveled, plasma that ferried them to their destiny. The squealing hoist could be heard outside and the surly and fearful voices of men shouting orders, acknowledgments, curses. Andrade peered out the window at the ship, nobody looked back as if they were not there and he thought for a moment that they hadn't really even arrived, but somewhere had gone off the road way back there and met disaster. "Let's go find the Captain, shall we?" Tarisco said and as Andrade turned he heard the sharp, metallic clicks that were unmistakable and saw the dull, black hulk of a nine millimeter, automatic pistol in the man's brown hands as he slapped the ammunition clip into the butt and pulled expertly and absently back on the sliding breech to chamber a round. Then he replaced it in the holster under his coat that the boy hadn't even noticed and looked at Andrade as he climbed out of the car. There was no expression on his face. Terror bit into the boy's stomach like acid.

"It is good to stretch the legs." Andrade said tenuously. Neither one of them had gotten out of the car since they had started off in Niterói and now that they were walking the distance across the quay on wet, tar covered wood that extended out past the concrete they felt strong and instantly refreshed. Rain pelted their faces, but neither paid any attention to it for it had been that way all their lives and was as natural to them as breathing. The odors of sodden wood and the sea greeted them mixed with the harsh smells of sweat and the acrid stench of refuse floating as flotsam and jetsam in the still waters of the harbor. Warm and cool air slapped their cheeks in puffs of wind, eddies and boiling mists from out of the darkness beyond the massive freighter where the open ocean lie and the mysterious life of the Sargasso.

"Tudo bem my friend?" Came a crackling voice barreling down the thick, cascading ropes slick with moisture and sediment from the salt air, which was viscous, humid and filled with overpowering perfumes like no other place on earth.

Tarisco looked up to the third deck at the spectacle of a large, burly man wrapped in an old army jacket with the collar turned up against his neck over the full beard with light streaming from behind him out an open door. He waved his arm and spoke through his teeth. "Gorka Panopoulos. Captain Gorka will ask you a lot of questions. Be discreet. He will test your weakness." They climbed the metal stairs hanging at the stern by corroded chains that clanked against the metal plates of the vessel in dull thuds.

Once on deck, Andrade followed Tarisco who, in his eyes, seemed to grow in stature and bearing assuming command of the space and exuding an aura of strength and machismo. He had never seen this before in the man throughout all the years they had been so close and then he realized he had never once been witness to Tarisco's professional life, only in the shelter of their filial relationship where he, knowing now the truth of it, had been sheltered from the brutality of making a living. Andrade felt humbled and self conscious vowing to act like a man no matter what happened. They climbed the metal ladders up the outside of the decks until suddenly, looming above them as a bear might rise up on his hind legs to intimidate an opponent stood the great bulk of the man he had seen from down below. He extended his massive maw and helped pull them up the final few steps to where he stood.

"My friend!" He guffawed cuffing Tarisco on the shoulder and knocking him a bit sideways secretly observing whether the little criminal was carrying a gun or not. *Of course,* he thought, what did he expect?

"Captain Gorka." Tarisco said.

Andrade shook the large man's hand. "Helio," he replied remembering the warning.

The three of them went inside the cabin that was organized as a makeshift sitting room, was relatively clean and very comfortable filled with old stuffed couches and chairs that had been worn down and sagged in the centers of the cushions where tired men had slouched across them for a decade or more. It was warm and humid in the confined space where not a breath of air came and the sounds of the loading drifted by the open doorway enshrouded by the constant shake of the rain.

"Have you seen them?" Tarisco asked standing close to the door.

"Sit down. Sit down. No, no... no!" The big man intoned slapping down three chipped, porcelain mugs whose clear glaze had yellowed and fragmented into thousands of tiny cracks. "They haven't shown their faces yet, and I did not expect them to. Weather like this, bound to have delays, unexpected circumstances." He poured the black, steaming coffee into the three cups and the aroma instantly filled the stagnant air with its bitter bouquet. Gorka Panopoulos turned his attention to Andrade and beamed a grizzled smile at him. "From Rio?"

"No." He replied stoically keeping in mind Tarisco's advice, "Taubate." And took a sip of the hot liquid burning his lips and tasting the strong, dark brew that slid down his throat fortifying the weakness that lie there waiting to be ferreted out.

"Tell me," Captain Gorka continued, "how are the roads tonight?"

"Wet. How's the ocean?"

"Wet you sonofabitch." They laughed easing some of the tension, as the electricity of danger was present even though none of them might have admitted it. It was, perhaps more than the money, the draw, the paymaster that that winnowed in men stranded whose circumstance had pushed them to the extremity, against the fringe and for them there was no other choice as if they'd been intended from their origin to this moment and others like it where the crisp thrill of running the edge seeped into their blood. It kept them from the lethargy the tropics demanded of anyone who had been there too long. Andrade fiddled with the cellular phone he kept in his pocket, which his father had insisted he carry at all times. It was linked to a satellite service so he could make calls from anywhere to anywhere in the world. Right now he wished he could call his girlfriend and just listen to the honey drip of her voice, for even Tarisco had taken on alien qualities as he watched the man's face become hard entering the nether world of which Andrade knew little.

Close by in the small warehouse the rain still pelted the double corrugated roof and sounded in an unrelenting tin-pan symphony. Raiko Barba had spread out the contents of his three black bags on the dusty cement floor and was assembling equipment. Three other men had arrived earlier and all five of them now stood in a semi circle around the kneeling figure strapping on Kevlar vests, shoulder holsters and radio transmitters looping the earpieces and microphone contraptions over their heads. They all sweated profusely under the dark, heavy clothing and close fitting ordinance protection. The three recent arrivals were Americans, all DEA agents who, like Raiko, were not opposed to a freelance job now and then to enhance their incomes, which none felt were adequate for their experience and what they contributed to the whole. They had come in on a commercial flight under assumed names from Montevideo Uruguay using a local carrier, Viação Aérea Rio Grandense a cooperative whose record keeping was notoriously bad ensuring there would be no links to the United States. The large, aluminum metal case had been cracked open and lie exposed on the floor while inside hundreds of rounds of ammunition ominously sat in gleaming brass with hollow lead points.

The men were silent. They were pumping themselves up. The adrenaline rushes came and went in waves as each one thought of what could go wrong and the Americans recoiled from the idea of lying dead and bleeding in the oil slick puddles so far from home.

Raiko Barba spoke intently as he worked, having the ability to detach his mind from the mechanical details he had to deal with keeping both universes precise and studied. "It is very simple, very simple." He said. "I don't want anyone losing their head. We have one target and nothing else matters...leave everything for another time, that is how we will make out. Keep very focused and do exactly as we have planned. That is how we will make out."

When the men were ready they filed quietly outside the door, leaving it unlocked trusting the anonymity of their arrivals to keep it safe from thieves for the few hours they would be gone. A sign with the numbers forty-nine hung high on a piling above where they walked. In Raiko's mind Valdemiro Veloso breathed life and his face was now partially visible, his eyes averted to the side as if hearing a noise in a quiet house that he could not distinguish the source of. The men were absorbed into the hush, embraced by the velvet darkness as they fled into the moist womb of the harbor.

The hulk of the Aurora trembled under the thundering assault of the massive, churning engines that had been started a half an hour earlier by order of Captain Gorka in event the need for a sudden casting off arose. Men were stationed at the fore and aft lines, fire axes lay at their feet. No one knew what cargo they were taking on, none ever did, but since they all lived by their own laws and wits on the peripheries of sovereign powers each man was ready to do whatever it took to preserve the only group he had allegiance to. The ship, its crew and the burly master on its bridge. Those who hung on the cargo nets and crane lines like monkeys, and those deep in the vessel's belly who may be innocent victims were inconsequential. The three had heard the truck arrive, but did not move at first just falling silent and looking at one another knowing that soon it would be over and they could go their separate ways where each felt more comfortable in control of his own destiny. Andrade was the first to go to the door and peer down unobtrusively at the dark olive green flatbed, whose dull paint was shining with rain, with a canvas canopy stretched across ribs completely covering the cargo area. Three men were climbing down from the cab all wearing T-shirts and light jackets, except for the driver who had on a quilted hunting vest and a baseball cap. They shook their legs out and then, with the easy movements of predators, walked around the front of the military type vehicle that had the emblem of an oil company emblazoned on its door. Four other men clambered out of the back and jumped heavily down to the ground their feet landing squarely on the wet dock. These men all held automatic pistols with long ammunition clips by both hands and spread out strategically around the truck.

The longshoremen, stevedores, rope and crate wranglers looked once at the spectacle of the new arrivals and then turned back to their work unruffled not fearing the guns in the least. Midway between loads they finished unpacking the crates from the net and then hauled it high up into the air again and waited, as if en masse a signal had been given them that keyed in a vital genetic code common to all.

Tarisco shook the man's hand. He was an extremely handsome, cocky, straight up young fellow who smiled confidently, though his eyes were sleepy and dull.

"Como vai? We were held up in the rain. One of the engines went out in the fuckin' plane and we almost ate it, then there was trouble loading the goods into the container and I haven't eaten anything all day except for a candy bar and coffee. I get jittery with too much sugar."

"It is always best to eat a good breakfast." Tarisco replied.

"Who's this?" The man jerked a thumb at Andrade, who was standing nearby.

"My friend, Helio."

"Como vai?"

"Como vai?"

The driver nervously paced up to them his vest turning dark at the shoulders getting soaked from the rain. "I'm gonna pull it."

The man looked at Tarisco, and with a nod agreed. He barked orders to the men by the rear of the truck and they leapt up inside and slid out two worn, metal wheel ramps that extended twenty feet beyond the tailgate and secured them in position. The driver walked up one and soon the sound of an automobile starting up wafted from out of the back of the truck and a puff of blue smoke appeared.

"It's burning oil." The man said absently to Tarisco. All of a sudden a late model English car slid cautiously down the ramp, reaching the concrete and then was driven around in front of the truck under the hanging net. Soon it was securely strapped with cradles under each of its tires. The man turned again to Tarisco. "Same account?"

The clank of the hoist lever being engaged resonated across the docks with an ear splitting shock and the squealing gears engaged yanking the car from the ground. But it masked another sound as well.

"I sent through an electronic deposit before we left. See how I trust you?" But the man did not answer and stood stock still facing the truck. "You see?" He inquired again.

The man fell face foreword onto the tar covered wood and landed directly on his face, smashing his nose. He lie absolutely still and did not move. Tarisco leapt down and turned him over. Above the right temple was a small, round purple hole through which blood ran in a river down into the puddle where it covered his shoe. He veered back with his lips drawn like a feral dog at Andrade who, like everyone else was oblivious to any danger and thought the man had fainted from illness or fatigue.

"Run!!" He screamed at the boy in a hoarse, raspy voice frantic with intention. Andrade just looked at him dumbfounded. He jumped up and kicked the boy in his butt as hard as he could and screamed again holding up his hand covered in blood. "Run amigo!! Run!! Don't look back. Don't look back whatever you do!!"

At that instant the explosion of gunfire burned the air with its caustic bite and bullets danced off the concrete in a tattooed pattern sending up little puffs of dust despite the rain. They tore into the wood planks of the quay ripping up great splinters that flew off. Tarisco dove under the truck and landed on his belly with his nine millimeter already pulled and pointed forward having emptied half the clip before he hit the ground. The four men at the rear dropped dead weight to their knees and let loose a barrage in the direction of the initial fire that screamed into the low hanging sky echoing back off the buildings. Single shots came from the bridge of the Aurora in rapid succession while all the time the hoist kept lifting the car to its zenith, raising it slowly, laboriously. Tarisco could see no one, could hear nothing except the deafening roar of the rapid firing automatic pistols that were consuming, non-stop, their entire magazine loads. He slammed another clip into the nine millimeter and fired it off rapidly in the direction of the perceived assailants holding the pistol with two hands, not taking one breath, not having one thought. In just moments all their clips were empty and the air was filled with the mechanical clicking and sliding of magazines being ejected to frantic motions and new ones being inserted. White gunpowder smoke and the smell of ozone lingered, but there was no other sound except for the winch, which by now had taken the automobile to the apex and was lowering it into the gaping hold undisturbed. The *descamisado* longshoremen just kept working, some ducked slightly knowing that they had little to fear because their worth was so little that no one would bother to kill them unless they stood deliberately in the line of fire. Such was the fate of the eternally in debt.

There was not another shot fired. It was silent. All the men remained motionless for the longest time while blood ran from the one casualty who had never known what hit him. Suddenly, Tarisco thought about Andrade and jerked sideways to look for him, but there was no one in sight. The long line of the wharf was empty and stared back at him in hollow disbelief. His heart leapt into his throat beating wildly.

Andrade ran until the muscles in his legs burned. He ran from the eruption of shots that bore down on his ears shutting out all sounds completely except those of bullets singing by in the air, which he heard individually with a brilliant clarity, and of his own breathing. The rush of oxygen to his lungs, the crushing expulsion as he slammed his feet down on the wet surface of the quay, helter-skelter splashing the brackish water from puddles, sending up rainbow sheens of oil coated wetness into the night, soaking the pale, cream linen of his pant legs and filling his shoes until they squeaked and squished with each horri-fied step. He had seen the man go down, what did it mean? Breathless he ran though he heard no further shooting, he ran because Tarisco had told him to run. He did not look back once, until he reached the edge of the dock and heard footsteps ringing behind him.

It was then he turned. Sweat burned his eyes with salt. He squinted in the rain against the glare of the far off lights from the Aurora still loading the cargo. It was then he saw fleeting figures, apparitions, mirages against the panoply of flared light, shadow and darkness all mixed in a crazy jumble lacking any composition, any reason. Terror absolutely filled him, he had never experienced emotion so strong, it shrieked in his ears and gripped him arms and legs and shook him violently until he felt senseless, exhausted and about to explode. He dropped to his knees unable to bear the strain. Fumbling, he pulled out his cellular telephone and in the darkness punched in the numbers that his father had made him memorize, made him promise that he would call if ever he was in trouble with the police and needed help. His vision blurred through the sweat and rain and tears.

"Hello." A man's voice answered after what seemed an eternity.

"I need your help right now!" Andrade whispered in Portuguese, trembling as the figures approached in the night. "Pier forty-nine, I'm at pier forty-nine!!"

"What's that? I can't understand you..." Came the reply in English. And then there was silence on the line.

Thousands of miles away Randall DesVergers inspected the screen of his smart phone and not recognizing the number and seeing the line disconnected replaced it in the left breast pocket of his Italian suit, which he had specially altered by a Chinese tailor who had relocated from Hong Kong until it approached a custom fit.

"Who was that?" Smiled a blonde woman who stood next to Rand in the palatial wood and glass house of the ex-pornographer.

"I don't know." Replied Rand staring out into the now crowded room where everybody stood around in anticipation of the President's appearance as he had promised to say a few words and greet people before the perfunctory fund raising speech that was to come later. "A Spanish speaking gentleman, I couldn't understand him. Anyway," he turned to her and smiled charmingly, "I never take business calls on the weekend. There's plenty of time Monday morning for that."

Tarisco fled rapaciously into the rain streaked darkness after Andrade. He ran with all his heart as soon as the realization had hit.

Panic gripped him and waves of illness bathed him bringing weakness, desperation and a crazed longing suddenly to be close to God, fearing that no man now could help him and he was doomed to complete and utter annihilation. In hopeless, uncontrollable lunges he raced down the docks in the direction the boy, his entrusted duty, had disappeared flinging himself into the nihilism of the moment quite certain that there was no further depths for him to plunge and that no matter what punishment were to be meted out to his body he was far below death and it would be pointless. Footsteps echoed off the line of warehouses. *How could he have been so stupid?* He beat himself, how mindless and pointless it all seemed right now, in the abyss where the fisher's net could not reach and he would languish for eternity. When he arrived at the end of the quay he found Andrade's cellular phone lying on the dock. He picked it up. The numbers of the last call were still visible. "Here is where they got you my boy," he spoke to himself, "I would gladly give my life for yours." All was lost. He peered over the edge half expecting to see a corpse bobbing in the swell, but knowing no one would be that foolish. It's either ransom or extortion, one or the other, the price of doing business in the underground. Tarisco could not bear to think of facing Valdemiro Veloso and tell him his beloved son was kidnapped, especially under these circumstances. He could not face anything.

His honor, his life and everything he had ever attained in his wretched existence was gone and so Tarisco slunk back into the wharves hidden from even the night, into the darker shadows where his black deed could be buried in alcohol and anonymity and the misery which he had brought upon himself.

XIII

"We have come up with," Ashford began once everyone was settled, "a financial and tax program that we believe will take you into the next century. In addition," he smiled broadly feeling that this bit of information was a direct result of his business acumen, even though it had really nothing to do with him, "we have some ideas to generate income before the system is even online."

The long central table was custom made in a Vermont workshop of solid Brazilian rosewood, its patina was the result of weeks of hand rubbing and buffing until the luster and magnificence of it radiated. Strewn down its center were baskets of fresh baked pastries and brioche, plates of paté, foie gras and select cheeses and bowls of fresh fruit. Coffees from Sumatra, Guatemala and Kenya steamed in the corner. The large conference room was reserved for formal client meetings and was never used for routine, daily business. For this reason it always looked new. Ashford paced impatiently at the head of the table. Gordon Dahlquest and Veronique picked at the food. Rand was seated next to Naomi and three other members of the Team.

Ashford Van Riper loved to be right and would go to any lengths to prove himself so. The law, he had said, was on a plain higher than that of the Bible because it gave real solutions to troubled existences clergymen had always tried to cure with faith alone. When he was like this nobody could really talk to him because everything emanating

241

from him was out of his own inner visions alone. He became agitated if others pressed their ideas too hard. *How do you know?* was his famous phrase, as if the act of having complete conviction in oneself violated his right to exist predominantly in the enterprise that had evolved around him and in which others' contributions, though laudable, were minor compared to his own. He wasn't always that way. Many people considered him quite sociable and a level headed person even if he was a lawyer and prone to self-aggrandizement and overblown opinions on the social worth of his profession.

He had visited a spiritual healer in southeast Texas to cure his back pains once, flew into a small dusty town with his mind set on a miracle. He found a Mexican Indian Brujo who told him that first he would have to die, so that nobody would remember who he was and would stop contributing to his pain, that of the *old* Ashford Van Riper, then he could give it to some object such as a rock or a fence post. He took a Mesca-line preparation and during the subsequent hallucinogenic experience symbolically died. He returned unable to withhold his enthusiasm for the power of the spirit–although he still had his back pain. But it did not shake his faith in the deeper precept that law, in its theoretical state, could supplant the human thought process and provide more logical solutions for almost any given situation. He had no doubt that by the mid twenty-first century the entire human condition would be codified under law and that it would engender a worldwide government and a standard of behavior throughout. He told few people this belief, but made sure his closest associates knew his opinions in case the scenario came to pass and he could then be remembered as a visionary–if only by a few. Today, Ashford Van Riper was holding court.

Aware of this, Rand had prepared a report that couched the whole program for ISC within Ash's initial brief headings and so made all the work done by the team on the new account appear as if an offshoot of his direction. That was what set him off this morning and Rand was pleased at his cunning having slipped factual information past his superior for once without even a discussion let alone a battle.

He launched into a detailed accounting of the multitiered financing program from private sources so that when the company went online with its compressed, satellite interactive TV signal it would still be a privately held corporation. Once the patents for the LYNX technology were secure, the company would launch a media drive and go public. This would ensure an initial inflated stock price driving up their net worth and providing greater collateral for further expansion and repaying investors. "It is conceivable," he visualized, "that you may want to divest the media companies of the cable stations since once they understand that they are rapidly becoming obsolete they'll want to sell cheap to minimize their losses–you'll sell before that becomes common knowledge, take over their call letters and the bandwidth equity that comes with them. Most of their staffs you won't need because of automated technology so right there you cut overhead. No people. In this way you capitalize on the existing brand image of the stations, cut operating costs by eliminating staffs, avoid excessive start up corporate fees, taxes and capital gains fees for the first few years by having the acquisitions to balance your tax liabilities. It's a dodge in other words, perfectly legal."

"But where," Gordon Dahlquest injected, "will the initial implementation capital come from exactly."

"As you know, and as we discussed from the start, we handle the Veloso foreign investments and acquisitions funds. The net worth of the fund is somewhere around eighteen billion dollars U.S. right now with a liquidity factor of twelve billion. We are authorized to divest his holdings up to two thirds of the full amount for into ISC. That's a four billion dollar, tax free initial start-up fund. More than adequate I think. If it pans out, he wishes to buy into the company."

"Has he been involved in the media?"

"Import-export."

"Then..."

"It's for his son, a very bright young man."

"I see." Gordon replied.

"Which brings me to the next issue, Rand? Would you like to take over?"

Rand leaned forward at the table and felt Veronique's eyes upon him. There had been no sense of recognition since she had arrived, the cold calculation of her mind drew a shade between any private feelings she may have had the other night and her business acumen, which was direct and insensitive to a fault. Rand resolved that he knew nothing of her inner workings.

"Brazil is the home to the world's fourth largest TV network. Tele Globo." He began. "Of well over 160 million people more than two thirds tune into that network daily. It is also a land of staggering illiteracy; its population is mainly "teleliterate", what they have learned is from the TV. I don't have to tell you the implications of this. The network is a political agent. Whoever they back wins elections. It is still primarily broadcast, although cable is making inroads and of course they can pick up traditional satellite. The country has just sold the first foreign cellular phone service rights, they are trying to lower the national debt, which is one of the largest in the world. Our plan is simply this, provide ISC interactive satellite service free of charge by contract with the Brazilian government, who will see it as a political organ, and support it by funding the initial start-up capital in South America while we are pre-selling package deals." And he continued to discuss the possi-bilities of exploiting the sixth largest economy on earth by putting their internal broadcast networks out of business and utilizing the new ISC technology as a selling tool. "It's a whole new market."

Rand spoke with pride. The Team had done magnificent work, and he invested all of his energy into selling their ideas, consequently adding to the illusion that he had guided the research and planning when in actual fact he knew little about it until the night before when he got the final draft and spent several hours rehearsing with Ashford in his smoke filled office. They were all going to be very rich, and although Ashford honestly didn't care, Rand was excited and he knew the ISC people would be too.

"Exactly who is this inscrutable Valdemiro Veloso?" Asked Gordon, still the cynic even though it was clear the planning laid before him could magnify their monopoly by many times.

"He is a rare and intelligent gentleman." Ashford replied, "Let me say," and he leaned back in his chair pressing his finger tips together pausing to savor some memory, "that I believe he is one of the most gracious men I have ever met. His wonderful home was built by the Portuguese during the Imperial reign of Dom Pedro II, around 1841, and I understand his family was very politically active in the modernizing of the country and had tremendous land holdings in Matto Grosso where they engaged in cattle ranching and mining. I haven't inquired whether he still possess the lands, but his fortune speaks for itself." Ashford sighed in an unconscious longing for a simpler time when all the issues of the world were not so complex and immediate, when people had time to think things through. "I know him the best, I believe, from the many nights I have spent with him at his ancestral residence, a walled colonial compound on the Avenida Vieira Souto at Ipanema in Rio de Janero. An old world gentleman. It was always cool in that house. It is elegant yet still embodies a colonial quality, a rural and pioneering quality in the plastered brick walls and broad framed windows where louvered shutters still hang. Most nights the high doors remain open to the Atlantic that reaches out from Ipanema Beach, and is especially beautiful when it is clear, and late after the city has died down and the waves can be heard washing up on the shore and the smells of the Sargasso Sea waft inland."

The scent of the Jacaranda trees mingled with the flavors of the sea air. They filled the courtyard and provided a gentle, filtered equatorial light during the hot afternoons when the humidity is the highest and kept the brick patio cooler. Clouds of freshness reached into the house after dark slipping along the old mahogany plank floor, which had grooves and hollows in it from the footprints of a hundred and fifty years. Beautiful flowered curtains hung to the ground pulled back at every large window, but never closed. Valdemiro liked the light and in the evenings he liked the air and the smells and the noises of the city that spoke to him of his history. He reached down and clasped the cognac glass with his fingers bringing it to his lips and swirling it beneath his noise to release its bouquet. The heady scent intoxicated him and he drank, slowly, letting it burn its way down inside him so he could feel the life. Tonight he needed it, the bracing punch of the spirits, the solidarity with his home where he had grown to become a man and where his son Andrade had grown. An image of Ryxa passed his spirit eyes. She was a woman of inconsolable beauty, too ethereal for this earth, too precious.

Now they were both gone and he couldn't let it rest. It was as if his beating heart had been ripped from him and he no longer felt anything, nothing at all. Not the bond with the people of the city he had always lived in nor the reminiscences of joy or those of sorrow. Nothing. A stranger had come, not even someone he knew, while he was having a late supper alone after a long day talking with the representatives of a politician looking for campaign financing. He had taken the opportunity to negotiate for contracts of his own in the event the man got elected, which arguably was slim, but with enough money...Valdemiro had always negotiated in the same way for the same elemental things and so was considered a political figure and one of the most outspoken citizens on the matter of the landless poor, for whom he felt great empathy. Just why this was so was an enigma that many had tried to explain and there had even been newspaper editorials plumbing the subject to no avail. It defied comprehension. He was not what anyone would call a social denizen like the buffoons who pranced in front of the paparazzis with their bosoms peeking out behind three thousand dollar dresses or arm in arm with telenovela stars so popular that whole cities took hours off each day to follow their fictional exploits or international weapons dealers who had become rich during the Middle East wafrs by supplying all sides with arms, which were wholly manufactured in Brazil from the raw ore to the parts to the munitions. These people all adopted causes as penance for their wealth; Amazonian Indians were invited into their homes, they marched in front of the television cameras with the *descamisados* protesting floodplain cattle ranching that overran their squatter's farms, but they were never present when the men came late at night with shotguns and the roster of the disappeared grew ignominiously. He was more pragmatic. It was simple exchange. Valdemiro looked out for the *favelados'* welfare and they, in turn, looked out for his. He could not have hired more loyal soldiers, and the politicians knew this and so all parties courted him for donations and support. The fact that his import-export business was rumored to be a drug smuggling cartel was pushed aside, he was after all pioneer stock, one of them, a Cariocan.

The man who had come to his door was not. He was a Nordestino, a man with strong arms and filthy clothes who had driven all the way from Vitória with a letter. Miro's maid had let him in the front door knowing that while he often did not want to see ordinary visitors, and especially official ones, he never turned away one of the *tabaréus*, the *jacas* or *caboloclos*–the peasantry–with whom he felt a mysterious bond. The letter began:

My Dearest Friend Miro:

It is with a heart of blackest stone that I sit down to write you this letter and to my great and everlasting shame that I am not able to face you myself and bring you this news. But I could not. Tonight I have committed a grievous wrong for which I am heartily sorry and have already been to the cathedral and there is no priest who can ever bring comfort nor penance that can wash away the blackness. So then I must tell you the depth of my betrayal to ease the defeat I feel.

Andrade, your son, has been kidnapped. I do not know who has taken him or why or where he is. I am sure someone will contact you. It is either for ransom or revenge. The way in which this happened is the point of my letter because if not for me he would be safe right now and I would be still your friend. I will relate to you now all that happened...

And he told of the whole misadventure from the start, before the samba school and how the boy had wanted the money on his own to

247

have a life apart from his father and with his indian love whom, he was sure, Valdemiro would not approve of because she was a *caboclo* and not from the city. Tarisco related their drive up the coast, the storm and the wharf and the first bullet that no one heard, which had taken the life out of the man from Rondônia. At the end he vowed he would not rest until the men who had done this were tracked down and Andrade returned home, and would not insult Valdemiro with his presence until then. However, he added in a postscript, "…if there is anything I can do for you to redeem myself in your eyes…" and he gave a post office box in the small town of Itabuna, where he had a friend who would forward any mail to his place of hiding.

After his initial full day and a night in a drunken stupor Tarisco walked out on the sand in the cool dawn and stripped all his clothing off. The fishermen, who were just sliding their small dories out into the misty water and those that were already afloat and raising the single mast and rigging the one sail, laughed and pointed their fingers at his swarthy, fleshy body many also having had bad nights full of demons of which alcohol was the least. Tarisco ran at full speed and plunged into the sea furiously swimming with all the strength he could muster sending up a huge, churning wake as if an outboard motor propelled him. When he had reached his limit and had absolutely not one ounce of energy left and began to float like an old rag he swiveled in the water and looked back at the shore shocked to see how far he'd come and how small the men with their boats were on the sand. He was breathing heavily and the blood raced to his head and though he had originally intended to swim until he was exhausted and then slip quietly beneath the waves hiding all traces of his existence, now he suddenly felt differently.

It took a few days to put things in order, but he had always been a resourceful man. First all his money was transferred to accounts that he knew could not be traced. Then he arranged a stand-in for the *escola de samba*, which he felt should not be made to suffer for his mistake and spread the rumor that Tarisco, himself, was on vacation in Buenos Aires and did not know when he would return. Then he flew to Manaus a thousand miles up the Amazon where he could lose himself among the tourists, the *mestiços*, the *mamelucos*, and the *garimperios*, gold miners, who wove an impenetrable tapestry of high rises overlooking the virgin rain forest canopy; a colonial opera house built by nineteenth century rubber barons, high tech electronics factories and riverboat squatters who made up a floating favela all blending in a tremendous collision of man and nature.

Valdemiro crumpled the letter his fist. The Nordestino was visibly shaken and began to sweat with fear standing with awkward unfamiliarity in the immense *fazenda* which of itself was enough to give him second thoughts. "Pay the man." He said, and the maid pulled out a few bills from the roll in her apron which she always kept for small household items and to purchase fruit from the sidewalk vendors on her afternoon walks and slipped them to the man who she knew had already been paid once. "Thank you." Said the man in shock backing out the door and although a strong, rough character he felt empathy for the elegant, older man who had not even looked at him.

"There is always someone with the big eye." He told his most trusted colleagues knowing that someone would talk eventually because everyone wanted something. But he spoke without faith because Tarisco had sullied his confidence and he struggled with the conflict wishing he could rely on someone yet without finding reason, which was not needed before. He could not sleep and stayed up in his office-library and paced into the night unable to concentrate. Fortunately, Valdemiro did not drink heavily, only an evening cognac, because it did not agree with his constitution and the fact that he did not like to have his acuity impaired. He had always prided himself on his quick perception and brightness. Even as he grew older and found that the print in books became blurred and that sometimes, when he was very tired, the room seemed to go in and out of focus, he never connected the fact with his perception which remained, in his mind, crystal clear.

Perhaps it was because of Ryxa who, in her brief passing through his life, had acquainted him with the pantheon of *orixás* and he found that he could not deny them as his love for the ephemeral girl was too complete, too absolute. He learned from her the art of summoning and how to open the gate and gain help and power from their strength. It was clear to him, being a highly educated man and one of considerable experience, that there were instances in life where one could just do no more. On the last January she had been with him they had gone to the sea where the celebration of Imanjá was taking place and he watched new initiates wading out into the water at dusk and filled a little boat with the statue of a saint and relics and lighted candles then pushed it off into the surf and watched it go down as the water goddess listened. Sometimes the boat comes back to shore because she is a vain, capricious spirit and so the ritual has gone since the black men came to Brazil from Guinea and Angola lying chained in rows pressed against each other in layered racks covered with filth and excrement. Those men prayed to her also.

Ten days passed. There was not a single word. Valdemiro was beside himself with apprehension and grief for his only son whom he had carefully educated at Father Javier Abraho's Jesuit school and kept insulated from anything illegal. Until now. He cursed Tarisco bitterly and the fact that they had been so close made it all the worse. No one of his government connections could tell him anything, or wouldn't, they offered condolences, and afterwards would not return his calls afraid to get mixed up in something truly dangerous having all heard the rumors surrounding Valdemiro Veloso. The police were thorough, but reticent knowing that there were strata where they could not go and that greater forces were at work in the country than local law enforcement, plus the fact that if they ever wanted to advance in their careers it would be with the Federal Police so they proceeded with caution. There was only one avenue left.

At twilight the maid entered the room as she usually did with Valdemiro's cognac and set it down on the end table by the chair where he liked to sit and look out the window at the ocean. She could get him to eat little, but he always took his cognac. He was not there. The window was open and the curtains rustled with the breeze from outside where the Jacarandas hung heavily wet with drops from the late afternoon shower and the clouds glowed in the darkening sky. He had gone out hours earlier and driven himself in his small German car across rain slick streets to the far end of the city and parked, left his jacket and valuables locked in the trunk and began the long hike up into the favela to see the *babalorixá* with his crisis for he had remembered, suddenly, without any reason while sitting in his library looking out over the sea, that tonight was a sacred night. It was a woman's voice that had whispered from behind his head into his ear and he was certain now that it was Ryxa. She wanted her son back.

It was dark by the time he arrived and the smells of the night greeted him. Palm oil from cooking pans and refuse, wet soil and the sweet smell humans and animals made congregated together closely in the heat. The rhythm throbbed from between the corrugated and cinder block shanties long before he was close. It wove through the narrow, lightless corridors. People were all around, cooking out on upside down oil drums, sitting in chairs talking, children playing and squealing and staring out windows with dulled expression longing for something though they didn't know what. Valdemiro passed them all. Then he saw the fire, blazing as high as a man in the distance with figures flitting by in front, near a shack that sat alone under cover of a bluff near the top of the hill, down the other side of which the whole decadent extravagance of Rio came to life in glittering, shimmering lights beckoning the *favelados* into its heart to seek out its fortunes. It was the home of the Father of Saints, the *babalorixá*. The drums lacked the joyous vibrancy that the *batuques* of the samba elicited and were more primal, more tribal and reached the deeper places and even in he, jaded with the emerald city running through his blood for well over half a century it caused an apprehension to rise up despite his resolve and he had second thoughts just as he arrived, but then the old man recognized him and motioned him to come near, to join the *bembé*–the ceremony.

The Father of Saints embraced him and patted his back with gnarled, brown hands. "You've come for your son, haven't you?"

"What!" Miro straightened suddenly shocked. "Do you know something?"

"Exú told me you would come last week," the old man said weakly being frail and thin.

"How did…"

"He is only a messenger, unimportant," he brushed his hand aside in the air, "only relays what he is told."

"But how…"

The old man grasped both of Miro's shoulders and held him firmly, the fire of his eyes burned. "Everyone knows you are a friend of the favelados–the *orixás* know. Probably Yansan told him, she is the only one who isn't afraid of death. See that girl?" He pointed to a dark, muscular girl with long, loose hair starting to move to the drum. "She is a daughter of Yansan." And then he turned back and imparted with complete confidence. "You will find your son."

"I must!" He said breathlessly from the climb. "I must." And looked into the swirling flames out of which sparks flew on the wind like witches out over the city below.

Valdemiro sat behind the locals who formed a circle around the fire. The pelting drums were constant; they had not wavered in their summons. A fat black woman with a stubby cigar and a huge, flowered dress draped across her landscape rose and started moving in time to the rhythm, her wide hips shaking the fabric violently joining the daughter of Yansan. Pretty soon others got up and joined them, many drunk from the cheap liquor they had been swilling, stumbling and brazen. It all seemed to go together; the drink, the smoking, the dance made it easier for the *orixás* to enter, easier for the gate to open. Particularly the putas–the whores…they were favored, the ones used by sailors and dock workers and cabbies, the ones that hung around the dives… they were easy, they were favored; everyone is somebody's daughter, somebody's son, there is no money in the spirit world. Fire whipped up the blackness showering sparks into the night air that lapped them up deliciously, rapaciously, and they floated high down the hill over the clapboard shanties and into the city of millions where people of all classes listened to the Saints. Soon the ground reverberated with the thunder of the beat and Miro sat all alone as did each person there come to ask the *orixás* for aid, come to ease the trial of living they were going through in which they saw no light, the burden being too heavy the task too overwhelming and he thought, *I am just like them, the same.*

Here now came the old man, the *babalorixá*. He stepped jerking in time too frail and light it seemed to gyrate and shimmy in the small train that was forming outside the ramshackle hut sitting separated off all alone on the hill under the bluff. Still he joined in. Wind showered sparks. Drums beat. The Father of Saints rarely danced, he was a helper, usually sat it out and concentrated his strength on summoning *Elgba*, owner of the roads, master of the doors...nothing can be done in either world without his permission and a good *babalorixá* has a very close relationship with this one. But the old man came. The firelight shone off his leathery skin and his wide eyes no longer were the clear white of youth but were yellowed with the sign of someone who has decided to leave the body, who has grown tired of this life. Suddenly, without warning he screamed and fell to the ground stark still and cold. Some-body whispered next to Miro, "Must be important, must be Oshosi." Valdemiro knew the name, he was the hunter. But then the old man cried out, "Oyá! Oyá!" and shook on the ground until even the drums stopped. "Oyá! Oyá!" Then he rose and the pounding continued and the frail old body leapt and twirled and danced lifting the legs high and shaking to the driving rhythm so that those watching were afraid he would hurt himself. Miro knew this name as well, Oyá, known as Yansan, patroness of strong women, "Mother of Nine", as Ryxa had told him once, "ruler of the winds, whirlwind at the gate, goddess of the dead."

He felt the breath being knocked from his body just as if a hand had clapped him on the back and he gasped for air. A wave of fear and grief crushed him and he struggled to keep from being overwhelmed. "He is dead." Miro spoke loudly, "He must be dead!" But then he thought it wasn't so, perhaps Oyá would find him, would bring him back from the deceased...nobody can cross over past her, she is the ruler of the underworld, was she not? *The whirlwind will find him*, he told himself, *the whirlwind will find him*. And he stayed long into the night breathing the wafts of smoke from the wood fire until his throat was soar and let the rhythm and the dance bind his spirit to the Saints and let the wind carry him.

The very next day while he was sitting in his library one of the men he had beseeched to help find his son came forward and handed him a few sheets of paper. "We have traced the last cell phone call that Andrade made," he said, "It was to the United States...Los Angeles, California."

Miro was dumbfounded holding the papers in his right hand alternately looking down at them and then up at the man's face concentrating to ascertain if there was any deception, even the slightest hint.

"The number belongs to a Randall DesVergers."

"Who is he!?" Valdemiro demanded.

" A lawyer. The unit is a company phone belonging to Van Riper, Hazeltine & Brock. I believe you know them."

"The law firm..."

"Yes, your firm for investments. We have found Andrade."

Valdemiro jumped up from the chair knocking it backwards and grabbed the man by the shoulders, "Where!"

"Florida, Miami. In custody of Federal Marshals...under indictment for drug trafficking."

"Oh my God!" He gasped falling back into the chair numb with disbelief. The weight of his crimes came to bear full force upon him in that one instant, a weight for which he had always been willing to be completely responsible allowing the moral turpitude of his actions to roll off him with clenched fist determinism believing that a man's path is predestined and therefore sacred and inviolable. He believed all things balance in the world, the good and the evil canceled each other out and were part of the makeup of the universe. Now the scales had been tipped by a truly malicious force and he spun with the implications of his dearest son being brought to task for the sins of his father. "No," he said calmly, "They want me, not him. This will not do." Feeling the cosmos quake with the heinousness of the incident. "We must speak with this Randall DesVergers, we must talk in depth with this malignance that dares to violate the unspoken code!"

It happened so suddenly that Rand had no chance to think it through, but then many of his thoughts had become confused and blended with each other causing him to loose much of the clarity that had been his hallmark and had made him the exceptional legal thinker people always thought of him as. So, it was with relief that he accepted the request of Valdemiro Veloso to fly down to Rio for in depth discussions, as he succinctly described it and as Ash had relayed with the invitation, on the ISC financing program his Team had just finished outlining. The prospect excited him.

Rand was certain that it would meet with the man's approval, though he had not the slightest idea of the billionaire's temperament and had to judge him solely from Van Riper's glowing account. He leaned back in the seat of the *VAIRG* flight and closed his eyes tired without reason, though he had been sleeping too much recently he enjoyed the rest and the flight over the cities and jungles below. In his dreams were tumultuous, migratory images of unrest and impermanence inspired by the landscape over which he passed. He felt strangely pulled at, hearkened to, summonsed by animals who lurked in the shadows of his fantasies unseen yet omnipresent about to leap into view. Below the world was being torn apart by contrasts. The old and the new collided, the primal and the sophisticated, refined beyond human recognition, vied for the limited attention men had to spare as they struggled to meet the daily needs of survival.

One could not possibly know the land, Brazil, many could not know her. Too vast, too complex, too unfathomable. It is the collision of the past and the future where the drama of the next millennium is being played out amidst million year old forests; the largest groups of indigenous peoples on earth being forced into extinction; a fantastic gathering of rivers replenished by daily rains; multitudinous species of animals and plants known and unknown; the infinite sweep of grasslands the human eye can not find the end of; frontier wilderness in need of settlers; apocalyptic, industrial behemoths like the *Valley of Death* between São Paulo and the Atlantic coast where one of the largest industrial complexes on earth lies paling even those on Germany's Rhine or in the big shouldered cities of the Great Lakes-Milwaukee, Chicago, Detroit, Cleveland, Toledo–and where acid rain and industrial fallout cause birth defects, defoliation and slavery to subsistence wages. The *casas de cômodos*–slums of Rio de Janero and the south–and the seven million homeless children all seeking a future along with the other fifty percent of the entire 198 million population that are under twenty-four years. The old world has been here a long time. The Portuguese, Spanish, Dutch, English, Americans and even the Chinese all forcing the beast, the uncontrollable wild, natural monster to be a primary producer of elemental resources needed for the burgeoning industry and sophistication elsewhere leaving them the internal economy of laborers, miners and lumberjacks. Inflation since 1980 has averaged 400 percent–foreign debt looms over 400 billion. Gold, rubber, tin, iron, timber…they have been up for grabs as the conflux of humanity's blind thrust into the future meets head on in wild collision. The wheels are in ineluctable motion. Confusion lay in their aftermath, a roiling turmoil of values and ideals and Gods all mixed with life and death and survival where many things are right and many viewpoints are valid. Who is to be the final voice in this perfect metaphor for man's tenure on planet earth?

The huge door carved from a single tree swung open and Rand was greeted by a small, dark *curiboca* woman–of African and Indian blood–who spoke good yet halting English. "Welcome Mr. DesVergers." She said politely and ushered he and the driver carrying his luggage into the heart of the walled compound that, though right off the modern streets of Rio, seemed to be a time chamber reflecting the gentle, aristo-cratic life of a hundred years ago. "Please, wait here." She said.

He was a tall man, taller than Rand had imagined and carried himself with the bearing of someone much younger and though he appeared to be well into his sixties, looked strong as if the aging body were supported by a vibrant spirit raging with an inner power. "I am Valdemiro Veloso," said the elegant man in a melodious voice who was dressed in a well draped, cream linen suit with a starched white shirt and no neck tie. "Welcome to Rio de Janero and my home." Rand detected no warmth though brushed it off assuming it was the unfamiliarity of the circumstances and the fact that it was purely a business meeting he had come for.

"Thank you," he replied, "I am very pleased to meet you." And for some reason thought he saw a flare in the man's eye though dismissed it as an illusion brought on by light or jet lag.

He did not see Miro again until dinner. The suite of rooms he was to stay in was situated over the front of the house on the second story overlooking a huge, brick patio enclosed by an adobe like wall easily twelve feet tall and three thick. There was a thin line of coiled razor wire hidden from below along its top held in place by ceramic couplings leading Rand to believe it was electrified. It was plainly visible from the balcony on which he stood taking in the overwhelming aroma of the densely, filigreed branches of Jacaranda trees that flooded down over the whole front of the house and kept it in shade all day long. Through their boughs he could see the Atlantic Ocean and glimpses of Ipanema beach, which was not crowded that afternoon. The sounds of traffic strangely drifted up from the street in the warm, moist air across the centurial gap, which the house had created and reminded Rand he was in the heart of a massive, teeming modern metropolis that was one of the greatest urban centers in South America.

Rand had been told not to take the buses, particularly those that were not air conditioned because the poor rode them to and from the favelas and other low income areas and they were crowded, hot and unsafe for a tourist. The air conditioned ones were slightly better, but it was best to take a cab, or so he'd been told. It had been unnecessary to rent a car because Veloso had sent his driver, who was also available for transportation, but Rand felt better on his own. So, with a whole afternoon before he would meet with Valdemiro, he rode off in a taxi determined to get a glimpse of the famed shanty towns that in his mind, even after having seen pictures of them, he could not believe really existed.

The whole sweep of South America seemed ethereal, unreal and completely out of reach to him, a *Norte Americano*, whose frame of reference did not include millions of impoverished nor the stratospheric richness and diversity of the region. He rode past the Cap Ferrat apartments, which the driver, assuming he had a sightseer in the back seat, told him was the most expensive in all Rio and that many of the smaller units went for well over a million dollars. Rand smiled politely and watched small children playing near its front doors. They had torn T-shirts and wore no shoes on their dirty feet.

The map clearly marked the neighborhoods and the company travel agent had quickly circled in red the areas of town to stay out of in her hurried indoctrination to the intricacies of Rio's etiquette. With a pencil he drew a line on the streets that he hoped would take him on the periphery of the hillside favelas and afford him a glimpse into their world without having to embarrass himself by asking the driver to take him there. He tossed the map into the front seat. "There." He said, "That's where I want to go." The driver picked it up and looked at it, then laid it down backwards beside him without the slightest reaction being used to tourists who wished to see the favelas, but were too shy to ask. The taxi sped off into the areas on the other side of the red line the travel agent had circled.

The sight was as foreign to Rand as anything could have been. The houses literally hung off the hillsides staring in the windows of the high rise condominiums and offices below. "My God," he said "The view."

"They have the best in the City. No one can afford a view like that, you have to give up everything." Said the taxi driver in thickly accented English. "For people like me who work hard and are so lucked that we don't live there, we are caught between the favela and the Cap Ferrat, can't go forward, won't go back. Not like the *Estados Unidos*, hey? Where anybody can make it. Hey?"

"Yea." Said Rand drolly. "Anybody. Pull over."

Rand got out and walked a few steps away staring up the side street to the hillside. "I'll wait." Said the cabby shutting off the engine punching a button making sure the meter was still engaged.

He had only to go a half a block to where the sounds of Portu-guese flooded his ears and the foreign sights and smells caused him to completely detach from his own culture and simply be an infatuated observer. He felt unreasonably secure. The hot sun beat down on his shoulders and the top of his head making him sweat and his clothing wilt in humid exasperation. He had left all his valuables at the house except a photocopy of his passport, which he had been told to carry at all times because Brazilian law requires some form of identification. Rand was oblivious watching the people in the shops and on the sidewalks and after about a half a block up the street while he was staring through the buildings at the hill beyond a voice called out.

"Hey mister." A child's voice. He turned to see a ragged, eight or ten year old boy standing at the corner of a building by a shadowed entryway. "Gotta cigarette?"

"No," he said shaking his head in case the boy didn't understand English and waving his hands in front of him as if to stop traffic, " Don't smoke."

"That's OK." The kid said. "Gotta dollar?"

Rand looked at him, his T-shirt was stained and the shorts had water marks and frayed edges. His shoes were leather oxfords that had been wet and had dried many times and he could not say no. "Yea. Yea, sure." He said walking across the street to where the boy stood leaning against the bricks with no expression at all on his face wondering why he wasn't running over to make his mark. "Here you go." He held a fold of about twenty-five dollars and quickly peeled off a single." Still the boy didn't move. He kept walking until he was right next to him and then it happened.

Someone grabbed his shirt and pulled him backward into the dark shadow of the doorway and all of a sudden he was sprawled on his back in the stoop. "Hey!" Rand started to get up but a foot crashed down upon his chest and thrust him back.

"Stay there!" Commanded another boy standing over him who looked about fifteen and wore a sleeveless shirt with baggy khaki colored pants and running shoes. "Whatchu got?" He snarled nervously looking sideways to make sure no one was watching.

"Nothing! I got nothing! Here..." he tossed the wad of bills to the boy's feet and the younger one swooped it up and started running not looking back once.

The older boy didn't move and now the glint of sunlight revealed a knife in his hand. In a flash he reached down and took two rapid swipes at Rand and then yanked his slit pockets inside out. Satisfied, he barked, "Gimme the watch."

"Aw shit." Rand whined noticing that the boy was scared and stepped back a step. Then he handed him the wristwatch. Suddenly he heard heavy footsteps and without even looking the boy disappeared like a shot.

"Hey you little *pivete* sonofabitch!" The taxi driver yelled as he came running. "You OK?"

Rand was shaken. When he returned to the Veloso house he had to ask the maid for a drink to calm himself. At dinner Valdemiro sat expressionless across from him and when he related his adventure could not help but feet the man was smiling.

"It is a big problem with tourists," he said. "Some of the larger hotels and more prestigious stores even hire assassins to kill the most persistent children, otherwise, they say, it will ruin their business."

"Jesus!" Rand exclaimed having heard rumors, but never thinking it still went on, "How can they afford to hire killers?"

"Seventy-three dollars is not much."

"I'm sorry," he replied not knowing what else to say and feeling that in some way it was his fault that the children got murdered.

"Why?"

The next few days were filled with meetings and Rand had little time to venture out into the streets of Rio. All the meals were with Valdemiro who questioned him mercilessly about the financial plan, except one dinner where he had accompanied the most senior of Valdemiro's accountants to a very fine, expensive restaurant in which he had the spiciest and most delicious beef he'd ever eaten accompanied by a rich, Peruvian red wine. Miro wanted to know everything. He wanted it all explained in plain detail. But what was most curious to Rand was that he wanted to know who else had the full knowledge of the plan and what would happen in case he were busy or called off to work on some other business as if he expected a change of personnel. The whole experience was extremely stressful and all the time he was under the Veloso roof he felt an ominous, powerful force was drawing his life out of him as if the great forests of Brazil were claiming his élan vital as their own. So, he was more exhausted when the time came to leave than when he had arrived and what he had expected to be a respite had instead turned out to be a rigorous tour de force of endless details.

Valdemiro had arranged one of his private jets to fly him to Manaus, which he had wanted to see and perhaps take a trip up the Amazon in a tourist boat since this was his first visit to Brazil and spend a few days vacationing before he caught a direct flight home. "You will enjoy the flight." Valdemiro said shaking his hand as he left, "If it is clear, you can see the whole rainforest." There was still no expression on his face.

The morning was clear and beautiful as they took off in the small jet aircraft and Rand looked back out the tinted window at the *Corcovado* and the outstretched arms of Jesus raised in benediction for the dispossessed. As they rose into the sky he could plainly see the great rift that was the *Mata Atlantica* that covered the coastal region with rainforest and resolved to return someday when he could take the time to investigate the lush territory thoroughly. The Atlantic stretched far into the distance reflecting the aurora of the sun steadily climbing into the sky. The high whine of the engines blended with the hiss of the air conditioning shooting through the vents. He felt the warmth of the light streaming in the window against his face and saw the towering, white clouds forming, which undoubtedly would produce rain by the afternoon. Rand let out a sigh. He had no thoughts. The past few days had been intense and he had felt a mysterious wall between himself and the enigmatic Veloso that failed to soften even with all their discussions. The hard edge of business remained and so he concluded that it was just the man's nature and was as well the nature of business when it involved dollar amounts that high. When fortunes ranged into the billions men ceased, he believed, to be connected to the human condition, and further he thought that men of power were detached to a fault and that the whole of the democratic process was devised as a resolution to the self aggrandizement and tendencies of leaders to become inebriated with the scope of their power. But now he let it go, and looked out across the vast, transcendent landscape mesmerized by its magic.

For three hours they cut a diagonal across the states of Minas Gerais, Goiás, Mato Grosso and finally into Amazonas while Rand watched the terrain out the window it being unusually clear for most of the trip. Now, however, the sky had grayed and though he had been looking at the extensive green carpet of the indefinable forest for some time, with the clouds he felt for the first time they were over the legendary Amazon. He shivered, reached up and turned down the air conditioning. He shivered again and pulled his jacket up close turning the collar against his neck, then he drifted off drowsily feeling lost in the clouds and alone but for one other person and insignificant in the face of God and of men who were swarming over the earth in the billions each desperately seeking to survive.

It was sudden and unexpected. He awoke to a tremendous jolt followed by a noise, a shattering, ear splitting boom and to the smell of toxic fumes. Chaos loomed. Rand jumped straight up in his seat restrained only by the belt and looked around the small cabin frantically yelling, "What? What is it!?" He prayed it was just an air pocket like before and was so disoriented he could not tell the angle of the plane. Air roared outside. The pilot said nothing and when he looked up to see him panicked, pulling levers, pushing buttons and flipping switches in a frenzy he yelled again. "What the hell's going on!?" The only response from the man was, *Oh God! Oh God!* ...and nothing more. Now he could see that they were angled downward sharply and could feel the pull of gravity. His heart sank, he gasped for breath and felt the cold pool of fear solidify in his stomach as he pressed back against the seat, but could not believe it. With his hands he gripped his seatbelt until they burned, until blood flowed and he clenched his teeth chipping their back edges where they came together darting his eyes around desperately trying to grasp the situation and looking for a way out as fumes filled the space. He had not even looked for an exit when he first boarded being so lulled by the luxury of a private plane ride, but now...he saw it but didn't know what good it would do. The pilot kept repeating *Oh God!* as if he had lost his senses and Rand lashed out and punched him on the shoulder, twice he hit him. The man looked back with terror struck on his face, but said nothing and again returned to struggling with the controls. Impulsively Rand looked for parachutes, as if he knew how to use them and suddenly felt completely, utterly hopelessly vanquished with the wind shrieking outside and the pilot muttering *Oh God! Oh God!*

Unexpectedly flames licked from the rear bulkhead. He could feel their heat. He nearly passed out with the fear and then there was a white flash, as if he had overloaded and snapped and he felt instantly calm yet completely numb.

Rand saw fire now blazing out of the cracks and then at the delirious pilot and then with complete command reached over and pulled the red handle on the emergency door watching it shoot away in horror as if torn by explosion. The blast of wind was deafening and slapped his face nearly knocking him unconscious. He struggled with the latch of his belt and when it broke free he floated up in the plane toward the back of the cabin where he flames burned and smashed against the roof. Fingers numb he pulled himself over to the door until his head was slightly out pummeled by the force of air. He looked to the aft and saw mangled, torn metal where once the tail had been and black smoke streaming off in piercing ribbons into the sky. With a tremendous burst of energy he catapulted himself free of the cockpit and into the open air. The velocity caught him and he tumbled helplessly, like a rag doll buffeted and tumbled and bounced. And then, from some sense of preservation that he never knew he had, forced his arms and legs out spread eagle in all directions and held them as rigid as he could.

The tumbling stopped. Though he could barely hold open his eyes against the blast of moist air he could make out the plane falling below him, diving almost vertically increasing speed at a geometric rate headlong into the forest mists. Rand saw all this as if from above himself. Exterior. He knew was going to die and wondered if he was already dead for he was certainly out of the body and viewing it all impassionately, with resignation and apathy though numb with terror and fear. Then he thought quite rationally, *fear of what?* He pondered this falling to earth as a wingless bird. Pain, he thought, it was pain that he was

263

afraid of most. If not for pain he could face anything. And with that he felt better for some reason and resigned himself to keep his arms and legs spread for as long as he could and perhaps...the landscape below was green, thousands of square miles of green. There were no clearings, no openings, no respites from the solid green. From higher up it had looked like grass, but now he could see the trees, almost individually, their subtle shades of green rushing up at him, the different textures and densities and volumes. It all made sense to him now, everything. It was all extremely simple and he wondered what he had spent so many years figuring, trying to understand life in all its disguises.

Rand went unconscious moments before he touched the top of the canopy. His legs hit first racing along sideways at an angle and his body spun propelled into another branch, lush with life and vigor and an over abundance of leaves. It bent under the power of the blow and Rand skidded off it into another bough whose tip slowed his fall ever so slightly, and then to another high in the forest, skimming across the top of the canopy twelve hundred feet above the earth. He skipped across the canopy for eight hundred feet and then he entered it. Branches clutched at him, boughs laden with leafy hands grasped for him and vines cradled him rocking him from one tree to the next, in nature's heart, caring for its own, slowly dampening his tumult to earth, spinning and twirling out of control until at last he appeared from the ceiling of the forest amidst a great shriek of monkeys and a flurry of bird's wings and a scurrying in the bushes and finally collapsed onto the ground, the thick, compost of the forest, hundred of years of rot and decay and bark and fallen leaves and there he landed bouncing like a ball into the rich, humid air and then coming to rest beneath a giant, low, spread out plant whose leaves were twice as long as a man is high. Then Randall DesVergers lay still in the forest. His eyes were closed. His face was peaceful. The gigantic leaf sheltered him from the rain that now began to trickle down through the branches from high above.

BOOKIII

A Spirit Obscured By Clouds

A Spirit Obscured By Clouds

XIV

The hush passed through the forest as a wave of green fingers. For miles and miles in all directions the timbre of the moment was felt. The shudder of life energy. A line of tiny leafcutter ants paused in their industry. Above their heads they waved the severed pieces of plant life looking like an armada voyaging up the tree limbs ten-million strong, the miniature sheets of leaf fluttering like sails out over the sea as they all seemed to take a moment and seek benediction from their maker before the final assault. The great tree itself receiving word from the underground network of limbs touching limbs, brushing, caressing, of root gardens so ancient that within their labyrinth of ecosystems and communities and long distance lines was the memory of the forest without men from a time before humans walked. It reached out beneath the fallen leaves and branches and decaying boughs upon which mush-rooms, fungi and all sorts of mysterious growth blossomed iridescently and on until again it stretched farther than imagination can travel. No man knew how far. It was a secret even to the denizens who were in syncopated breath and step and swarmed as one in ebb and flow as if the tide washed over them all alike when danger was present.

Perhaps it stopped when the roads began, or when the cities sprang up and covered every living thing in lifeless concrete and asphalt hoping to smother the vitality out, to forget, to simply forget the lost heritage of which the empty street is evidence. Although they say that in the heart of São Paulo, a long way to the south, the lots buckle from beneath with the pressure of the roots and vines trying to escape and in many places they have taken back their hold crushing like paper the erudite architecture and thousand foot stacks belching black smoke and industrial waste into the azure skies below the Southern Cross. On the wing it came as it always had in a flush of color and excitement that the figure on the river in the small dugout canoe witnessed as nearly a thousand toucans roaring through the canopy completely silent except for the cyclone their turbulent feathers made. The stream of bright yellow orange beaks flickered like fireworks against the muted, dappled, infinitely faceted green tapestry of the leaves. A capybara rushed from the water to the dark shadow of the brush and was quiet. A wall of flying insects passed immovable, the forest simply fleeting through their porous net as if an illusion. Even in the few clear patches of sky he could see them graying out the light. He closed his mouth to keep from catching one. Held his breath. Hundreds fell in the water around him as he waited for their migration to be through. Piranha boiled up out of the brackish liquid of the alcoves, from the hidden inlets and shaded creeks to eat the fallen bugs helplessly struggling on the surface. Soon, they too were gone. It was silent. He realized he had not paddled for a long time having been overwhelmed by the movement of nature around him that scintillated in the aftermath of some significant event of which he had no knowledge yet. He dipped the paddle into the black water. The canoe moved ahead.

In a short time Utitiaja came upon the two whirlpools in the river that were the demarcation between the lands traditionally hunted by his people and those of another who, though many were relatives and some of each clan had married into the tribe of the other, were really not friendly. They were not on good terms at all, his people and theirs, not at the present time at any rate, because of a feud that had been in progress intermittently since before he had been born. A man who was now the *wishinu*–the shaman–reported that his father's brother had been killed in a jealous fight over someone's wife. Who's wife was of no importance whatsoever since women had no souls and that part of the story had failed to come down in time, but the events leading up to

267

the taking of the woman as a wife were questioned because it was that quest which shaped the society. How else was one to obtain comrades in war as committed as brothers-in-law? The important element of the tale was that jealousy had flared and in anger and rage a man had been killed. The man's spirit then, since it was deprived of life in such an ignominious manner, refused to leave the village. It had been the cause of many sleepless nights for various individuals and, although the spirit had caused no illness and was a well liked man in life, it was time for him to go. The dead have no place among the living. Their possessions must be burned and the name must never be spoken again. It then fell upon the *wishinu's* father to avenge the death and take the head of the victim, fill it with stones and boil it properly until it became a *tsantsa*, of course with fiber through its eyelids and lips, and hang it upon a pole by the dead man's place at the hearth, whose name can never be spoken, in hopes that he would then leave feeling vindicated.

A raid was carried out and it was done. A *hantsemata* was held with the full celebration taking three days until the head had been properly cooked. They had eaten smoked meat and drank the fermented beverage made of saliva and chewed yucca root until they were intoxicated and sick from the rich food. Then the whole village slept for a full day. Everyone was fairly satisfied that the man's spirit had moved on and all was as it should be. However, as soon as it was settled and people began to forget some of the men from the enemy village claimed that the spirit had taken up residence there and, feeling enormous rancor, was causing illness and discomfort. A hunter of the tribe had begun having trouble with his left leg and limped badly, which obviously affected his ability to obtain and provide food. Another was having trouble with his vision, things going in and out of focus and those close up being muddled without the exact details he had been used to seeing. He had poked himself in the finger while preparing his darts for hunting and had gotten *curare* in his system forcing him to take salt, which as everyone knew was the antidote. It was dangerous just the same, he had insisted, as he could have poked himself without realizing it and become sick and possibly died of the poison without realizing what was happening. A woman expired shortly after giving childbirth and the child, even though carefully looked after by the head man's wife, followed shortly thereafter. As a consequence there was retaliation, neither group finding equity somewhere in the balance of strikes. And so it went.

Every now and then there was a reprieve. Some homesick wife or lost sister or forlorn brother or tired father would get it into his head that enough was enough and cause adequate agitation that one tribe or another would sue for peace. Especially if one or the other had become involved in subsequent hostilities that would severely tax not only their manpower, but their armaments as well since the men were the providers in addition to being the warriors and armorers and tacticians and defenders. There was only so much time in the day.

As Utitiaja passed the two whirlpools, the large one being called Thou Shalt Weep Greatly, and the small one Thou Shalt Weep Bitterly, he remembered that he had taken no meat yet this trip and he became seriously concerned that someone might know by reason of a far walking trip or worse still, a far seeing trip. When he returned things would look differently because the hunting up ahead was rewarding and well worth the extra day's journey. He had fled violence, someone had even taken a *tsantsa*, a fact that if anyone, such as Rene Boas, from FUNAI, the Brazilian Government's Indian services, found out Federal troops would be sent in as they had been in the upper Xingu region last year where they decided too many murders were taking place. A very old warrior was captured, manacled in chains and taken to Pará and tried before a court, convicted and sentenced and is now languishing in prison somewhere with the street punks of the industrial south and drug traffickers.

Rubber tappers, loggers and gold miners had been killed before without reprisal from the government. The Indian lands were supposed to be sovereign, but policies and boundaries changed reflecting the social and economic powers of the moment. Utitiaja understood the concept of retaliation since it was an integral part of life, it was the fiber and he could see it in every leaf and moving thing. He thought of it as the flow, a balance, where any action left a hole in the universe that demanded to be filled lest the entirety of the illusion collapse. This is why he never took too many of one species, and why he had come this far to hunt because he was reciprocating, exchanging with the forest that supported everything. He had once told a *garimpeiro*–a gold prospector–"I don't rape your mother!", and held him down so that he could cut off his hair and teach him a lesson. The man, who only spoke Portuguese and didn't understand, tried to stab Utitiaja in the back and so was killed and left unceremoniously half submerged in the river. He heard nothing about that and had danced with some other warriors when he returned to the village at night reenacting the thrust of his lance that had been the death blow. Women and children and dogs joined him at the end. He purged himself of the man's spirit in that way.

Hostilities had escalated. The *garimperios* inched their way closer to his territory up river and there had been raids by the Indians and the miners both. It was not the same kind of fighting that had traditionally distinguished his people, the human beings, but was perverse and dirty as if sullied by ideological differences that left the dead on both sides lingering between the two worlds unresolved, unable to move on. This was why the *tsantsa* had been taken, in the old way, as an effort to bring order to a chaotic spiritual realm where the anarchy of greed nullified common sense. And this was why he hunted alone, an unusual circumstance for practical reasons such as carrying the heavy bundled of game back to the village and watching the brush for danger such as the eight foot *jararaca* whose bite would kill within minutes.

The canoe plowed into the muddy bank of the sheltered inlet on the river, which was a tributary of the clear waters that ran close to his home at their confluence, and he leapt out careful not to land his foot in the shallows where brackish water hid electric eels, which infested the region. He was not afraid of them and had spent many hours standing thigh deep in the unclouded river upstream from the women, who held reed fish traps to enclose racing schools, lancing the eels and laboriously tossing them, some longer than a man, on the banks before they reached the net of fishers. Though he had never been severely hurt he had welts on his legs from shocks received, but had watched in horror as a child was stunned unconscious by an eel that had slipped through the break of warriors and brushed his leg with it's five hundred volt charge. Utitiaja pulled the canoe into the dense bushes. Chances are it would remain undiscovered, yet he had learned never to take chances and was renowned among his tribe for his attention to detail consequently giving him the reputation of being completely reliable and therefore valuable by reason of what he could give others. Exchange, he knew, was the key to relationships.

Then he ran. Utitiaja unleashed the coiled energy that had built up by crouching in the damp canoe for so long and stretched his legs as far as they would go carrying him quickly across the forest floor fleeting into its bosom where he would find animal people waiting to sacrifice themselves to him. That was their gift. He flitted through shadowed and dappled light, the red, black and white paint on his body disguising his true form in careful, abstract patterns, giving him, a human being, an identity among the dwellers between the earth below and the canopy above.

Rain had come and then moved on in the late afternoon as it always did, sometimes earlier and sometimes later, but consistently each day without fail in the inevitable cycle he had come to rely on as part of the ritual that gave form to his life. The odors of the jungle were released by the fresh moisture. All things were part of the weave, each having its purpose and none capable of existing autonomously. Utitiaja grasped from an early age the symbiotic existence he was a part of and he dared not flaunt the elements as his thread was just as slender as all others. When the light began to fade he climbed the buttresses up a huge tree, whose trunk was many times the width of his own body, and strung his hammock high in the branches where he was further out of harms way than below frightening away two scarlet macaws. With others he had been known to chase off naked and unafraid into the night forest in search of a jaguar whose voice awakened them in the hours after the stars fell. He never thought to show fear then, even though he may have stepped on a snake doing its night hunting or even become prey of the jaguar himself, but none of these things crossed his mind. The skills of a warrior were acquired at a young age. He had learned to endure pain without complaint and had developed extreme physical endurance. From the earliest moments he had been taught that every injury must be repaid, that above everything else, and he could remember his first lessons still, lying in his mother's grip and playfully batting at her with his uncontrolled arms while she batted him back. One for one. Strike for strike. Reciprocity was the basis of life and vengeance was part of that exchange.

He had still taken no meat, and had not even shot at the macaws, which would have made a tasty breakfast, but relied on the hours surrounding dawn. That was the time of conflux, when the creatures of the night and those of the day crossed paths and was the most abundant moment for an alert hunter. Darkness fell. A hush of wintergreen silence descended. Time passed. For a while there was nothing and he rode its void knowing that as the illusion dissipated and another formed to take its place he would be safe as long as he did not move. Then he heard it, animal voices, the first sounds of nightfall. Others came traipsing on the still, humid air and he heard them too; the rustlings in the brush, the flapping of wings and the thumps as creatures landed on the trees. He imagined the spider monkey swinging by its tail, the kinkajou racing up the bark, and the two-toed sloth being stalked by the boa or the agouti trotting down to the river all quietly moving in the drama around him as he slept. All through the darkness he heard every sound in his vicinity as he lay waiting for sleep looking up through the canopy of trees a thousand feet above and beyond to the canopy of the world whose flickering lights could be glimpsed intermittently through breaks in the leaves. Utitiaja even heard the dream noises as he slept, close to the surface as he always did in the forest, alone, at night.

With a rush of coolness it came and stirred the leaves where he had slept, but he was not there. Utitiaja was waiting on the forest floor far away from his night roost where he knew his scent might give him away. The day before he had taken all his darts and lined them up in the sand points up. There he had carefully spread the dark, chocolate like mixture over the ends for about an inch and carefully let them dry before placing them in his monkey skin bag. Cajke, the *wishinu*, had prepared the mixture as he always did adding fire ants and spice, peppers and snake and the one real vital ingredient the root from which *curare* came. He placed the gun to his lips and blew, hard. A white lipped peccary scurried a few feet being hit in the buttocks, then after a moment stag-gered and collapsed. He also bagged a few monkeys, several toucans and a caotimundi. Forced to kill a bushmaster snake, which he did not plan to eat, he stripped the skin from it for use later and cut the head off careful that its post mortem snapping did not catch his fingers. After the prime morning hours had fled he drug all the game back to where he had hidden his canoe, tied them up in palm bundles and loaded them up to the gunwales.

The breathing was what made him turn. It was muted and low yet unmistakable. There was nothing. He waited. One attribute he possessed that was distinctly human and which had been honed to perfection by a life on the river with its unvarying patterns that were the predominant rules of life, and where everything that moved against one was often mistaken for something else. Strangers thought it was laziness, or boredom. But it was patience, the secret element of genius. And so when it moved he saw it. The golden yellow with black spots, the almond eyes staring directly at him, the heavy sounds the paws made padding from its perch. He took out after the jaguar with only his lance and the monkey skin bag flopping at his side. The animal shot away like the wind. He tracked it by smell and by sound and by prints. For an hour he tore through the undergrowth running as fast as he could until at last he exploded into a small clearing whose ground was spongy with detritus and where shafts of light struck far down into the murky heart of the forest catching their edges on the mist ever present in the air.

Huge, broad leafed plants ringed the slight meadow in the penumbra of the tree shadows. Under one of the leaves he saw it, yet did not move for it was a sight as unexpected as he could have imagined and never in his whole life had he seen anything like it nor heard of anything similar, never. Beneath an enormous leaf lay a man, a white man, with clothing ripped and shredded, the body bruised and bloodied and lying at a bizarre angle that even he could tell was because of the fact that some of his limbs were broken. In fact he could see the bone protruding from his forearm in red and white jagged edges. Silently with his spear at his side he moved forward and stood directly over the man for a long moment deciding what to do. Then he knelt down and put his ear within an inch of the man's nose and held his breath. There was a whisper of air, not much, but a whisper of air. Utitiaja placed his hand over the man's heart and could feel its weak beating. The skin was cool and damp.

The man was soft and white and smooth like the mushrooms that grew out of the rotting logs and he knew instantly that he was not a *garimpeiro* or a lumber man or a tapper or oil man or even one of the experienced *sertanistas*–frontiersmen–from the pharmaceutical companies that tried to get them to explain about plants or anything else for that matter. He was an enigma. He did not belong. He was perhaps a messenger, a servant of change that for so long now he and others of his people knew must come, but had little idea exactly how to make the transition. Perhaps he grew from the ground, from the thin soil that supported the tremendous ecosystem with twelve hundred foot trees yet could not hold up a small field of corn, nor of tobacco or any other domestic crop. Perhaps he grew like fungus without roots. He turned the man over and saw that he was bleeding there too, and then he groaned. A slight, very weak moan, and then was silent. Utitiaja was shocked.

It did not take him long to decide his course of action. He had completely forgotten about the jaguar and set to work cutting down several of the giant leaves and braiding strips into strong strap like cords. Then he looped the ends behind the white man on the ground slipping them under and between his legs, around his arms and across his back until he was trussed up like a bird ready for the spit. He coiled the straps in front of the strange man and twisting them over his shoulder as he turned his back on the reclining figure pulled them taut across his own back and hoisted the body up off the ground like he would a bundle of freshly butchered meat. Hoisting him closer, Utitiaja lit out for the canoe he had left loaded with game.

It took him longer to return than it had for him to get to the clearing, but he made good time even carrying the heavy load which although a strain was a burden he lifted without inner complaint and did not set it down once for a rest. When he reached his canoe he dumped the white man on the ground and shoved off holding the boat close to the edge of the inlet. Then the body was tossed across the game so that it's cheek lay flush on the bloodied haunch of a tapir, which he had butchered and bundled up in palm fronds much as had had the man. When in position, he carefully pushed the boat into the open flow of the river. Water came up to one inch below the edge of the gunwales from the heavy load, but he did not have to get rid of any game a fact that made him believe all the more that fate had acted in his behalf. Two days later they reached the village.

At first everyone thought Utitiaja had killed a man and there was great excitement, but when they found out he was alive no one could understand jeopardizing the entire catch of game for a white man– one that would probably, from the looks of him, not live anyway. He was upbraided by the elders who accused him of becoming soft and suggested he might want to endure the pain rituals of the coming of age ceremony once more, it not being uncommon that a man undergo them two or three times in his life anyway. Utitiaja paid no attention to them and knowing the white man was the catalyst for what will be in the future sought the advice of the *wishinu*, Cajke, on exactly how to proceed. As it turns out he was experienced in just such matters and had plenty to say on the subject, which Utitiaja dutifully listened to and finally they decided to place the frail and battered white man in the care of Shuara who had lost her complete family in a raid a year ago and her baby just two months ago to a fever. She was living by the graces of Cajke anyway, who had taken her in unable to bear her grief, and would be happy to have some responsibility.

As soon as Randall DesVergers was placed at her hearth she knelt down with the gentle forest look that came naturally to Indians who have remained uncrushed by encroaching civilization and took up his hand. She held it very close to her breast for a long time while she looked lovingly into the closed eyes of the mysterious crumpled stranger and then brushed it over the whole top of her body. After that she began to strip away the tattered clothing which was completely useless in any case and scrubbed his body with the chewed off end of a yucca root flushing with water from the river. Utitiaja was right he was pale and smooth. She didn't know what to do about the bone sticking out, lesser breaks had been fixed by the men easily and was not outside their skills, but this one, torn flesh and all was beyond her. So, she laid medicinal leaves across it, which she knew would keep it from festering and becoming red and swollen. In this way she treated all his wounds front and back, but he still did not regain consciousness. She poured water on his lips so he would not die of thirst. Many people came to her hearth and looked at the man lying in a hammock now his face painted with red dye in a sacred manner. They had not seen a white man like this and were curious, especially the children, to see if he was like them. After the first night Shuara went to Cajke and told him that he must help the white man even if he did not want to because she had done everything she knew and he had still not awaken. If he should die here, she said, how would they get his spirit to go since he is lost and not familiar with the surrounding area. It could cause complications, she said hopefully. At first he was very angry and yelled and threw up his arms and scowled telling her that she knew there was trouble with their neighbors and that now, right now, at this very moment he was in the final negotiations for a feast that would bring the two tribes together and cement a peace and a cooperation which was long needed for both their benefits. But then he could not stand to see her grief, plus the fact that her warning about the white man's spirit, which he had no experience with dying in their midst, had made him think and so consented to tend to him that evening.

Cajke sat with some other men since before dusk. They had taken turns placing the long, hollowed out pipe to each other's noses and puffed up their cheeks blowing the drug into the other with a forceful exhalation of air. When Cajke received his he fell back off his haunches, slapped the top of his head with his hands and grunted loudly several times. Then he got up and jumped around in a grand, bellicose manner as he contacted the spirits he would need to perform a cure and so it went for hours as others arrived to watch the healing. The shaman finally stumbled over to where Rand was lying unconscious in the hammock followed by three other initiates who, all hallucinating madly, assisted him gratefully in hopes they too would learn enough to help others some day on their own. The urge to help is stronger in some that way. He strutted around the white man arching his back and sticking out his chest and launching into a diatribe about evil spirits and possession and how everyone in the village should be on the alert for tracks in the dust of shamen from other villages who would sneak in the night bringing demons. "Look!" He shouted, "There are tracks!" And he pointed down to the ground leading up to Rand's hammock and all eyes followed. Smoke from the fires, three of which surrounded them, swirled up and hung in the breathless air under the eves of the thatched roof of the one long house, which had no walls and under the cover of which all families lived each by their own hearth. "Barmio!" He shouted, "Barmio!", which was the name of a well know *wishinu* of another tribe whom they had always suspected of poisoning their food, making their women sterile and causing illness. Everyone gasped. He reached out with ferocious intention and, with one leg bent and the other straight, ran his hands forcefully up Rand's sides, brushing across the ribs in the direction of their flair and up the neck and the sides of the head and off the top. He immediately clapped his hands loudly right next to Rand's ear and leaned down and shouted something unintelligible. He followed this procedure for about a half an hour, loudly repeating it on the white man's back as well. Then suddenly announced, "That's it, I'm finished."

Early the next morning Rand opened his eyes. They fell upon the gentle face of Shuara who had remained awake all night watching him. He looked about the mysterious surroundings without any thoughts and only knew that he was thirsty, so thirsty that he could not form any word in his mouth. He could not move one of his arms, but managed to point to his mouth with the other and for some reason she guessed he was thirsty and dribbled water from a gourd. Rand drank and drank until he desired it less and then slipped back into unconsciousness without having the slightest idea where he was or what was happening. Shuara was so excited she flew across the large open courtyard in the middle of the village to tell Cajke, who was speaking to some of the other elders about preparations for the upcoming feast. "He's alive!" She said, "Alive! Like I told you. What about that?"

"Of course." Said Cajke unruffled and barely able to pull himself away from the discussion long enough to acknowledge her presence. "Now go away, we are busy."

Over the next few days he regained consciousness several times, once long enough to eat some smoked game, which he wolfed down making Shuara more convinced than ever he would recover. But then he would lapse back into a sort of unconscious sleep and so was fitful all during the time preparations for the feast were being made. No one could know the intense pain he was in. Rand could not distinguish it at first. When he awoke again he remembered who he was, but had no idea where he was or how he had gotten there and the people he saw he could identify as Brazilian Indians from pictures he had seen, and he could remember the start of the flight from Rio, but little more. *There must have been a plane crash,* he thought, but remembered none. He was voraciously hungry and managed to eat some of the tasteless meat he was given, some manioc and water but it had made him feel ill on top of the excruciating pain that did not seem to be localized. There was not enough courage in his weak state to lift the leaves and survey the damage to his arm, which he only perceived as a dull throbbing. He drifted off to sleep as an escape. A fever rose as well, which went unnoticed, from infection that was setting in despite the medicinal leaves.

Cajke had Utitiaja coming and going. They were going to host two hundred and fifty people and they all had to be fed. "I can't do it all myself!" The old shaman complained to Utitiaja, "When will you bring more meat?" Utitiaja knew that there was plenty of meat. In addition to all the forest game of the past week brought in by the hunters a huge pirarucú and a twelve foot caiman had been caught in the river along with the forty pound cachama fish and others. All the game had been bled on open grass mats and then initially smoked to preserve it and to ensure there was no blood visible at all–meetings such as the one planned were tense affairs, former antagonists facing each other and not even the slightest insult could be allowed. Then it had all been boiled in shifts, the fires going all day and night, then smoked again, this time for three days. Fruit of every variety hung up along the line of the roof of the long house and the men had taken their special ladders and climbed the spiked trunk of the peach palm trees, which were individually owned but harvested communally for this important feast. The women chewed yucca root continually creating the fermented saliva drink that was so popular and that adults drank a quart a day of. Drugs were prepared, seeds roasted, bark stripped, leaves shredded. Everyone worked. It was important to the whole village. Each man collected everything he could imagine would be useful as gifts. Hours were spent, days pondering the significance of the giving and the items as each man tried to assume the viewpoint of the recipient and ascertain how it would be received and if it would increase his esteem. Men argued over who would host the important figures of the other tribe and it had gone like that for several weeks. Then the emissaries arrived. Three splendid warriors appeared at the end of the village with beautifully feathered headdresses walking briskly and purposefully past the long house and all the people sitting on their haunches making frantic preparations. Cajke met them. He was nude, but painted well in black and red. There were white feathers in his hair signifying peace. The men greeted each other tersely and then sat on their haunches. The visitor, a wiry, gaunt faced middle aged headman of the other village, began to speak. The words came out staccato, barked and exaggerated, punctuated with facetious looking head gestures. Hands flew in emphasis. It was a ritual discussion. All the right things had to be said, after all these men were enemies and these kinds of meetings often erupted into violence. They barked, postured and threatened in the best tradition of western politicians until finally the first to arrive, Barmio, the famous shaman, stood and complained that he still had sickness from the spirit of Cajke's relative, whose name was not mentioned, and wanted it cured. Cajke stood and prepared. He applied himself much as he had to Rand and after a while simply said, "I'm finished." Barmio in turn exorcised recent demons from Cajke and it was agreed that in two days the tribes would meet. As the emissaries were leaving Cajke yelled happily after them, "We will sleep with your women!"

Rand grew worse. He had more energy, but was becoming delirious and could not make anyone understand. He was afraid that he would die, and felt cold from the fear even though it was very warm and humid all the time. A few days earlier he had watched the men, in one of his wakeful states, carry the body of a woman who had just died from a fever out into the plaza fronting the long house and lay her on a funeral pyre. The whole village was wailing in grief and mourning incited by Cajke who yelled, "If she can't hear you, she will come back to haunt you! How does she know you care for her if you are not crying loud enough?" The fire was ignited in the darkness and Rand fell asleep once more to the laments wishing he were dreaming and wondering where he was and what his chances of getting out were.

Then, the night after the emissaries had left he awoke again with a start, wide awake. His mind seemed clearer even though he was burning up and weak and dizzy and he knew he was out of the body, viewing things from the ceiling and it made him wonder if he were actually dying. There were six warriors in the center of the house, by the main fire that was communal and that everyone shared in keeping burning. All were very young, smooth skinned and strong with gleaming white eyes. Each wore elaborate headdresses of feathers and quills and hair and were painted from head to foot in wild, electrifying patterns. They had arrows and bows and knives stuck in the belts looping over their shoulders and around their waists and were all moving incessantly. Cajke was with them, speaking in the same ritualistic way as he had with the emissary, but they did not speak back only grunting responses. Soon, they trotted off into the night disappearing as the darkness swallowed them. Trickery was afoot. Anxious women were awake too and they looked at each other with faces that transcended cultures.

When Randall DesVergers awoke the following morning Shuara was gone. He weakly searched the village, what he could see from the hammock at least, but could not find her. Rand felt suddenly grim and hopeless. Her constant presence was the one thing that had given him sanity. Now it was gone.

Desperation has driven people to remarkable feats. Necessity has given inspiration beyond any religious fervor and has been the catalyst behind the scenes for a change resisted yet welcomed, feared and longed for. Now the river carried her, she with no soul, whose greatest value in life was to provide brothers-in-law to her husband to tip the scales on raiding parties. She paddled fiercely against the current. Her family had been young, she had not even had enough time to learn the secret things about her husband, which nobody but she would know and that would have given her an altitude when it came to him. In her mind a thousand times she imagined them together and sharing these secrets passing them between each other in the silent firelight when the world was cloaked and animals could be heard restlessly scrambling somewhere in the night and the owls hooting and the whoosh of their wings and the giant storks that waded in the shallows. Private things would have passed between them that nobody would have known. Swept away. War vanquished dreams. It is the more powerful of the two, she thought irresolute in her dedication to it. The tribe lived in a constant state of vigilance. The threat of warfare overshadowed their lives. Once only their neighbors, which they would fight furiously and then pacify with feasts like the upcoming one when everyone grew weary of its aftermath. Now the *garimperios*–the gold miners–too. She could not imagine inviting them to a feast and how they would arrive smelling of dung and alcohol with their puffy, white bodies filled with hair. No, it was not possible. The world was different. She knew that from the moment she received news that her husband was dead, that her father and brothers as well were gone. It was as if her breath was stolen from her mouth and since that time she had been without enough, always in need of breath. The illness that her baby suffered did not seem like much at first, but he did not recover. Cajke's magic did not help. He would not eat and became almost hot to the touch until one day she awoke to find him cold. From that day on it was as if her heart had ceased. She lived breathless and heartless from moment to moment.

It was not as if the white man meant anything to her, not anything at all. It was something else. She could not fail again. This was why she battled her way up river against the current to the FUNAI encampment, which she knew from the far walking trip she had been on where she met Pilar Escandinha, a tall mestiço who, though could not speak their own language, could not speak as a human being, knew other languages that were similar enough to bring about an understanding. She had spent a whole day with her and afterwards felt her breath return, that was why she headed there, so she would not lose again. Perhaps Pilar Escandinha knew the answer to the fever that burned hot to the touch and then cold as death. Perhaps this time her heart would start beating again.

The day of the feast had finally come. The people from the other tribe had arrived late the preceding day and were encamped outside the village down close to the river. They were preparing also, painting their bodies in the most perfect way, wrapping children's knees and elbows with colored fiber twine and adorning themselves to make a show of fierceness so that their guests would know it was better to have them as friends than as enemies. Feathers were luxuriantly arrayed in headdresses and along war lances. Men were naked, but women wore a modest garment consisting of a thin fiber that encircled the waist and another connected that passed down between the legs on the end of which was a one half inch square that was tucked neatly into the crotch. They were laden with gifts for exchange that was the basis of all social life and starting with the ants, from whom they learned communal living, they knew the ideal person was hospitable, except to his enemies, and gave gifts graciously including prized tobacco wads and food.

In the village all the people were ready. Rand lay awake yet delirious and fevered. No one paid any attention to him. He knew something was happening, but had no way of knowing what and almost wished he would die, yet even that act of faith was beyond him and so he struggled out of some misplaced sense of loyalty to the body. Suddenly there was a great *Whee-Dee* and the visiting people came rushing into the plaza leaping and shouting and shaking their feathers and animal hair and quills in terrifying outbursts displaying their ferocity. Even the women leapt and yelled and hoisted feathered war lances above their heads in euphoric chants enticing the men of the home village with their inflammatory dance. The entire visiting village had its chance, and then it was the turn of the locals. They roared and stomped and danced and chanted and yelled war cries that sent birds rushing from the trees in all directions. The young men ran beneath a burning log which a shaman held high in the air and was striking sending showers of sparks down upon their bare backs and faces, which they endured without a sound.

The visitors were impressed by their bravery and let out a cheer of affirmation and solidarity. That was when Shuara led Pilar Escandinha into the long house from the far side, away from the festivities and to her hearth where the white man lie in the hammock. He looked up and saw her face.

"Where...where you been?" Rand uttered weakly.

"Pilar." Shuara replied, the only word she knew in any other language," Pilar."

"What the hell happened to you?" Pilar said bluntly as she hovered over him and he looked up suddenly to see her there. She lifted the leaves from his arm. "Mother of god...!"

"Where...where...?" Rand tried to ask.

A crescendo of voices rose up from the village plaza as each community rushed at each other in mock battle to signify the self mastery they had gained, though intricate precautions had been taken against the poisoning of food by the visitors. They leapt as if to strike and then at the final moment pulled away landing lightly on their feet with terrible, grimacing faces. The commotion shook the land and Pilar looked at Shuara with sudden concern. The Indian did not waver in her gaze knowing that the people were only blustering like little storms out over the plaza and were as afraid as anyone else of illness and decay that crept invisibly toward them at all times, striking without warning, cutting down the strongest mid-stride, taking the little ones from their arms and fragmenting hearths and social order. This was why, she knew, they were so loud, to hide their fear for it was not the visible men were terrified of, but the unseen, She placed her hand on Pilar's arm.

An olive metal case sat at Pilar's feet that had once served the army as an ammunition container so was airtight and waterproof had made the perfect transport for medical supplies. "I'm going to give you some quinine," she said matter-of-factly, "unless you're ready for jungle baptism..." stuffing some capsules into his mouth, "drink this..." pouring water from a gourd. "The arm we can fix, malaria you've got for life."

"No..." Rand struggled to speak, "American..."

"Yes..." Pilar replied rummaging through her bag in a brisk, businesslike manner paying little attention concerned only that he might die before her, a circumstance she could not allow for it would not be good for her image–weak magic the first visit to the village. They had been encamped for three months trying to make full contact and gain trust and all their gifts and manufactured goods had run out three weeks ago. She had always been told that once the Indian got a taste for steel he could never again do without it, but she knew that sorcery was the stronger of the two devotions. "Ahhh..." She exclaimed loudly and pulled out an aluminum splint that was about two feet long and had a grip at one end where the hand could be laid, each finger in its own place, to keep it immobile. She barked at Shuara and the girl rushed off shortly to return with a large, hardened leather sack filled with water, which she placed directly upon the fire. Pilar began the survey of Rand's body while he faded in and out of consciousness and, with Shuara's help, stripped the final remnants of clothing from it to make sure there were no hidden injuries. He was covered with bruises and abrasions, lacerations large and small and a few insignificant puncture wounds. Her hands ran along his bone structure checking for breaks, poked at the vital organs to see if there were ruptures in the surrounding walls, listened to his weak heart beat, which she had to gauge from the feeling unable to hear because of the commotion surrounding them. She was inured to this after tending to Indians, miners who had fallen to accidents and fights, tappers and oil workers and so her kit was complete and she replenished supplies every time they were near a hospital or clinic. Pilar had been force fed first aid, learned it on the run where it was either buck up or watch people die. Now there was no back off, she had seen worse, much worse

The two tribes had congregated and were talking, laughing and jostling gregariously among themselves. Soon, they sat where they were facing each other and the stream of the ritual rose up high into the forest, to the tips of the thousand foot canopy where a myriad of birds fluttered, attracted and repelled by the noise. Gray clouds formed together and then broke apart in the endless churning of the rain forest's heaven waiting for the moment when the daily deluge would begin. The bittersweet aroma of perspiration mixed with vegetable dye was overpowering and wafted in and out of the long house between the scents of the forest.

When the water boiled it was placed into gourds and set aside for a moment to cool enough so that it wouldn't burn. Pilar washed the white man, cleaned his wounds each one thoroughly and individually hoping she could scrub away some of the infections that were setting in, though none badly yet. The arm must be set she knew and so that was cleaned the most thoroughly and covered with antibiotic ointment since it would be wrapped. A throng of children gathered around her and leaned close over her shoulders with rapt attention to see. None of them smiled and she thought it was as if small adults were there and imagined each one gathering what bits of knowledge they could for the time when they might have to repair a broken, injured body. They learned and she was glad.

Rand came and went on waves of unconsciousness knowing that he was being tended to, but unable to muster the strength to speak or remain awake for long. When he struggled to the surface he saw Pilar's face looking down at his arm sweetly and in his delirious state imagined her to have a glow, to be encircled by an aura and carefully tracked the contours and plains of her. The brown eyes, that gentle look of the Indians yet with a brittle, hard edge beyond the boundary of which was unknown territory, as if it was not to be crossed. Coffee colored skin, flawless across the wide cheekbones of natives, flat nosed yet small and straight as a European. Coal black hair tied up behind her head. He smelled her breath and it was like perfume. He could not feel the arm, just a dull, throbbing pain and a tingling with intermittent pressure from where she touched him. He was burning. At last she looked up, eyes full of concern and endless depth. Rand was about to speak, to thank her for being there, to mention that he was lost and was an American and that he couldn't quite remember how he happened to be there, though it was probably from a plane crash, which he couldn't remember, but did recall the start of the flight, and the pilot, turning back and repeating *Oh God! Oh God*...then Pilar yanked on his arm with both her feet tucked under his armpit and in addition Shuara holding his shoulder. "Oh

God!! Oh God!!" Rand screamed at the top of his lungs startling the wits out of the children and causing most of them to scatter, except for the older few. And then he was unconscious. Shuara looked frighteningly at Pilar, but at a confident nod relaxed.

The bone had set perfectly, it had been a clean break and she could see where it knit past the muscle, which was still exposed. After bracing the arm, Pilar sewed him up, a skill she had acquired from being handed the aftermath of knife fights in the *garimpos*–the gold towns that dotted the rivers of the Amazon basin. She sewed expertly, layers of skin patching perfectly. And then bandaged it tight so that it would heal with a minimum of scarring. The arm was bound tightly as well, not having cast making material, and reinforced with some straight sticks in addition to the aluminum splint. Then she bathed his face, and brushed the hair out of his eyes and was saddened by the dark bruises under them and the swelling and the scrapes wondering what catastrophe had befallen this poor white man who obviously did not belong in the jungle. She wondered if he might have been in a plane crash. There were many small strips in the forest where the *garimperios* flew in their supplies, sometimes a hundred flights a day, and not all of them were good pilots. She hoped he would live, and gave Shuara antibiotic capsules and quinine and explained how and when to administer them, several times she explained this and made her repeat it. The she left carrying her olive case without even meeting any of the important people of the tribe who were still preoccupied with their guests. She hoped he would not die, because he was her calling card and the Indians respected strong magic.

The giving of gifts had begun. The men were seated facing each other, resplendent in their finest feathers and armlets and painted with such careful precision that each appeared as a living work of art. They gave arrowheads and bows and manufactured goods they had acquired from trading along with tobacco, sugar and coffee. One man stood and called out, "I could use an arrowhead. Nobody's offered me an arrowhead. I would really like an arrowhead." With each gift more lavish the esteem grew between the groups until at last there were no more items to bestow. Cajke distributed the food. He directed everyone to their places, pointing at vacant spots beneath the roof of the long house, hearths that still had room ensuring all had enough to eat and that none of the hunters received any of their catch, which was taboo yet unlikely since it had all been communally smoked. Men vied for the important visitors pulling at their arms so they might have the honor of hosting them. Smoked meat was handed out, fish and game and then fruit, manioc and the fermented beverage the women had been furiously creating for weeks. The human beings feasted in peace and plenty and everyone thought well of their neighbor for the time being. This was as it should be, thought Cajke, euphoric that his plan had worked out so well.

Randall DesVergers lay hopelessly adrift oblivious to the festivities ignored by all present except Shuara who sat on her haunches by his side and Pilar who kept him in her mind on her journey back to the encampment. A sudden breeze passed. Rain fell. Everyone smiled. Exchange was the key to all relationships.

A Spirit Obscured By Clouds

XV

Rand awoke in a sudden fury. Utitiaja stood over him. Cajke and Barmio stood close by. They gave the white man the once over, up and down and made comments to themselves. The morning light flared through the trees. He squinted up his swollen eyes and realized he hurt everywhere. His left arm throbbed with excruciating pain that nearly caused him to black out again. Shuara bounded to her feet the moment he had awaken and snatched up three of the capsules Pilar had left, which she had carefully strung out in a line along the full length of a piece of wood showing the entire ten day regimen. Under each were scratched notations in pictograms. She quickly stuffed them in his mouth and placed the gourd of water to his lips. Rand drank it dry. Then he let out a long, deep sigh, deeper than any he could ever remember or had ever heard from another and looked cautiously around. Rand spoke. "Where is this?" But he could not understand their reply.

Certain things Cajke knew. There were specific areas of knowledge he had specialized in since a small boy when he had decided to become a *wishinu*. He looked over the work of the *mestiço* who Shuara had called Pilar and reached out his fingers and touched the bandages that were very white and unsoiled against the pale man's perspiring skin. This was strange work.

"He looks better than he did." Utitiaja commented.

288

"Perhaps," replied Cajke, "I used magic on him the other day just to help him along, but he was badly hurt and you can't overstep your authority. The spirits will get mad. If he is so close to death I must ask myself if I am interfering with the way of things to make him live. It could be that he doesn't want to live."

"Still...he looks better than he did. At least I didn't drag him here for nothing." The last part of the comment leaving Cajke a little miffed, though he was careful to conceal it, implying, or so he thought, that the *mestiço's* magic was stronger than his, a human being.

"He needs different kinds of magic." Shuara interjected wiping Rand's face with an aloe leaf not forgetting that Cajke's conjuring had little effect on her poor dying baby.

His nostrils flared and eyes sparked and he turned quickly to the young woman. Then he saw the gentle look, the gladness that was in her from the wiping on the white man's face and a grand and elegant idea came to him. "Yes," he said wistfully to her surprise, "you may be right." And abruptly walked away. This was an opportunity surely divined by the same spirits who had made possible the reconciliation between the two neighboring groups. Hadn't he seen Barmio's footprints in the dust next to the white man? Hadn't he pointed them out to everyone while he exorcised the spirits? Now he would solicit Barmio's help while he was still gloating from the feast and gifts and terminally handle the one last element of the alliance that fixed his attention. The fact that he may use trickery to send demons. If Barmio thought they needed his help, that would cement their relationship, and Cajke would prove his own magic by making the shaman whose footprints he had found complete the magic started and remove what he had done. When he returned he carried the long pipe and small pouches full of hallucinogenic drugs. "Barmio," he said, "we must talk to the spirits."

They took turns blowing the powdered substances into each other's noses with the pipe. Soon Barmio was busily exorcising the spirits from Rand, who understanding none of it and still being half delirious with fever, pain and now the potent antibiotics swooned with the rapture of the dying unsure whether he would ever see his teal green automobile again. Halfway through the ceremony however, he felt a tremendous weight lift off him and a flood of emotion overcame him and he cried. He cried rivers like a child until Barmio, who was used to this kind of reaction, had finished and then he felt better. Later, when they had all left except for Shuara he remembered everything that had happened. The few days with Valdemiro Veloso in his cold inhospitable house, the airplane ride and the explosion, which had taken the tail off and the subsequent crash. He remembered the last moment just before he went unconscious as he plummeted towards the trees and how sublimely calm he had felt and how he could see his own body as if far away. After that there was no memory except that common sense told him he must have somehow miraculously survived the fall.

In a few days Pilar returned. This time Cajke jumped up and intercepted her as she cautiously entered the village alone and spoke gruffly, yet with a slight respect for he had accepted armloads of manufactured goods from the FUNAI people and now he could see for himself that she had certain powers. All shamen had specific areas of knowledge and the *mestiço* was no exception.

"You may enter the village because you helped with the spirits. Here," her handed her the head of the bushmaster snake that Uititiaja had killed, which had been dried and strung through a necklace of fiber, "take this. It will help you."

"Thank you," she said slipping the loop over her head elated that she had the opportunity to meet the head shaman under good circumstances and now knowing the white man had not died, "I will always use this in my magic." That made Cajke extremely happy and he strutted away confident in the knowledge that while she, a *mestiço* and not a human being, had some knowledge, had some magic, it could not compare with his which was of the forest, which was of the generations, which was of the eons and had been passed down word of mouth for forty, fifty, seventy thousand years or more much of which he could recall while talking to the spirits and hear his ancestors' voices, the nameless ones, in the night whispering among the trees.

"I am a lawyer." Rand explained.

"Thirty percent of all the professionals in Brazil are lawyers."

"I am an American," he said grimacing from the pain his head swirling with delirium. "I fell out of an airplane."

Pilar paused in a hesitant, gentle beauty that was as if a wild creature had come upon a meadow filled with streaming sunlight and was stunned by its magnificence. "I guessed an airplane crash, but never falling out of one."

"There was an explosion, fire, I jumped."

She wiped his forehead. "You are braver than I would have been. And damned lucky." He looked at her a long time after that, just watched her soft eyes and languished in the pain and delirium and the idea of being brave, which had not once ever crossed his mind in his entire life. He had always felt rather cowardly, and attributed it to being an intellectual. Now he basked in the idea and it made him realize that courage had other guises. So it was that as he slipped from consciousness again he feeling better about himself for the first time in a long while.

He lay in the hammock for two weeks without once touching the ground. When the antibiotics finally bit breaking the fever and the pain started to subside into aches that did not force his back teeth to clench until his jaw was sore he swung his legs down to the ground. There, for a while, he sat feeling the earth beneath his bare feet yet still dizzy and disoriented. It wasn't for a few more days that he was actually able to rise up out of the hammock and walk around, which caused delight among the human beings, especially Shuara. Many attributed her with the cure and consequently started bringing their afflictions and difficulties to her if they were too minor to bother Cajke with. No one in the village liked the sick. There had been too many losses. They could not face the invisible against which no one could fight and so tended to ignore the very ill leaving it up to them to die or recover exhibiting a primal instinct that told them no one could walk for another, and though one can carry them, not for long.

Pilar Escandinha. Rand discovered her name during one of the many visits she made to the village. She told him they were located about two hundred and fifty miles from Manaus down a tributary of the Rio Madeira in the state of Amazonas. Pilar, herself, had been there almost eight months trying to make contact with the tribes in the area since that was the mandate of FUNAI, the government organization she worked for, to help protect indigenous peoples from the encroachment of civilization. She was the daughter of a wealthy rancher, a *fazendario*, who sent her off to the university where she took her degree in engineering and he was heartbroken when she had become a cultural anthropologist.

"He is a very conservative man and has many friends in the military. I didn't like wearing hard hats." She said, "I preferred the life of a *sertanista*, sort of a frontier person."

"How can I get out of here?" Rand asked almost automatically as a matter of course not even imagining that anybody would actually want to stay there.

"Don't know my friend," she replied looking at him with soft eyes. "Right now you haven't healed well enough to travel, not in the jungle anyway. And I can't leave."

"Don't you have a radio?"

"No. Stopped working."

"Isn't there someone that can take me out?"

"Not from our encampment. A boat isn't expected for three months or more. We are what you might call a garrison mission, stationed here. It takes months, sometimes years to gain the confidence of tribes like this one...and you see, thanks to you, we have that now and cannot jeopardize it for anything. Even you I'm afraid."

"I can't stay..." he struggled for words gesturing around him in futility, "here! I don't even like the woods!" And he collapsed back into his hammock, which had become the center of his world in the village.

"Yes," she said sadly. "You can't stay here, but you must." Pilar left once again and promised to return soon. She had been busy, she explained, trying to negotiate with a small group of *garimperios* who had been prospecting for gold down river and making too far an incursion into the Indian lands. So far unsuccessfully. There had always been trouble between gold seekers and Indians starting with the Spanish, for four hundred and fifty years there had been trouble. In 1559, towards the headwaters of the Amazon, the Spanish had invaded Jivaro country and established three sizable towns lured by gold. The feuding Jivaro clans combined forces and revolted, led by a *wishinu* named Quiruba they massacred almost all whites, between twenty and thirty thousand men, women and children, except for a few of the younger women who they took as captives. The greedy governor they abducted and poured molten gold down his throat to make sure, they said, he was satisfied for once with the riches. The men down river were hungry *Nordestinos* and, since there were no official demarcations of the boundaries, were fortified by the fact that they believe the law is on their side. "Partially true." She continued. The President and legislature had failed up to that point to order the surveys needed and were continually calling for more studies even when the funding for the surveys came from outside sources such as environmental groups. They had taken action before against encroachments. The largest tin mine in the world was virtually shut down when the road that illegally cut through Indian lands was closed, and at times federal troops were sent into vast areas of native country and had evacuated all the miners, sometimes as many as thirty or forty thousand. There had been skirmishes in the area, but nothing major yet. And so she was traveling a lot, up and down the river while trying to hold the fragile thread of respect between herself and the Indians.

Rand became desperate. He screamed for civilization and felt adrift, completely abandoned without any of his possessions or his office with the familiar faces of his coworkers that accepted his flaws and weaknesses as part of the human experience and allowed for them with company benefits such as medical and dental and retirement plans. Randall DesVergers felt like nothing. He looked at an old Indian across the plaza who was making some type of trap with bent wood and fiber and lance points dipped in *curare* and, estimating his age to be mid-sixties, saw his sagging flesh and withered face move under the power of strong, developed muscles forced by circumstance to keep him running full speed until he dropped. The old would just die. The infirm would drop away. There were no counselors here, no backsliding, no excuses, no finger pointing, no passing the buck–everybody was in motion and no one was idle for very long. Rand was not prepared for this and had no doubt that without the Indians he would die in short order. He was terrified. He formed in his mind an absolute determination to escape by whatever means he could. Nothing was more important.

Shuara, however, was constant, never leaving his side. She had adopted him knowing full well she was destined to lose this piece of her life as she had the rest of her family so found pleasure in the things she could do for this white man who looked so desperately unhappy. Rand learned a few words of the native language such as that for food, water, forest and for certain common animals and birds that were plentiful enough to make their appearance nearby. There was nothing for him to do in the village and much of the time he was left with the women and children while the men went hunting. He developed a great respect for the hardship of their lives for which they had developed tremendous resource and skills, but as he grew stronger, he grew more anxious.

For a long time he watched the old man, the most elderly person in the encampment. He rarely left the village and spent most of his time making traps of various kinds and weapons such as lances, bows and arrows, blowguns up to ten feet long that he patiently hollowed out and darts by the hundreds carved from dried and hardened yucca. The ubiquitous yucca. They ate boiled yucca nearly every day and used its fibers for everything from necklaces to binding rafters and canoes. Its hardened leaves were used to fashion knives and darts for hunting, and the women spent much of their time making the fermented beverage called *nijimanche*, for which they chewed boiled yucca for long periods mixing it thoroughly with saliva and then spat it out in a long, white stream into jars, which when full were covered with leaves and set aside to ferment. Jugs lined the ground and the beams of the long house in various stages of fermentation.

Two events happened that changed his outlook. One day while the men of the village were hunting and most of the women were either busy with their *nijimanche* or other tasks he was exploring the corners of the long house avoiding only the women's space at the far end. It was here he saw it hanging against a post behind some pots and gourds. He only managed to glimpse it because of the hair, which was unusually long and lustrous. His heart faltered. He cautiously pushed aside the vessels and then saw its grisly face.

A *tsantsa*–the severed and shrunken head of an enemy. It was the size of his fist, and all the features were recognizable and in good condition, though deteriorating with age. The chin and forehead, however, receded more than any Indian he had yet seen. Chjonta pins ran through the lips and chambria fibers hung from them. Pilar later explained that this was to keep the hot stones and sand from spilling out when the head was shrunk by boiling. "It's probably very old," she said, "no one that I know of has taken a *tsantsa* for many years and with the last instance the government sent in federal troops and arrested the guilty Indian. They don't usually interfere, but white men can't get used to the practice. Perhaps it is the one taken by Cajke's relative that had started the trouble with their neighbors." This didn't make him feel better especially after she told him that if the Indians knew their history with the white men they would most likely kill them all on sight, but fortunately little is remembered of the enslavement and mass murders committed for resources either on their lands or for which free labor was needed. Only certain stories in each tribe are passed down word of mouth and those too are forgotten with time. "They are people like us. They just have different relationships, different preferences and outsiders cannot hope to fully understand them."

A second incident caused his fears to intensify. It was a morning where the night mist had not yet dissipated and lie still in the trees. The forest radiated magic. He awoke early. Most of the others were sleeping except for a few women at their fires boiling pots and some small dogs wandering around. He had never walked far from the village before always keeping it within easy distance, but he felt none of the fear that usually choked him and for some reason was drawn into the brush. Though there were no large predators in the Amazon, aside from the jaguar of course that was mainly nocturnal, he was repulsed by the millions of varieties of insects that thrived there and were constantly turning up when he least desired a confrontation. And then there were the snakes, twenty five hundred kinds, Pilar had said, of which only some were poisonous, but those were fearful. Rattlesnakes, coral snakes, pit vipers. The unseen up until that point had made him a captive of the village whose relatively dry, hard packed earth offered security. At least he could see something slithering after him. This morning, however, he wandered out into the mystical forest enthralled by its beauty.

It was shimmering with life. Undulating. He tread cautiously feeling the moss and fungus beneath his feet. Ferns sprouted up twice as tall as he and broad, leafy plants dwarfed his presence. He moved in a hushed reverence. Rand was stunned by the beauty. He was spellbound by the sheer amount of life surrounding him. Gigantic hardwood trees soared into the mist their tops out of his sight. A howler monkey screamed from somewhere up ahead, wings fluttered in the invisible canopy, leaves rustled. There were mushrooms blossoming from rotted logs twice the size of his out stretched hand, mahogany trees enveloped in vines hanging from their hidden tops and many others held up by huge buttresses that spread out at their base for fifty or more feet. A muted symphony of earth and living things resonated with a sweet murmur in his ears.

Suddenly he heard a rush in the leaves, a scurrying and rapid, frantic movements. He looked back just in time to see a small wild boar racing down on him and then he buckled as its tusk tore across his leg bringing him down crashing to the soft, sponge like compost of the forest floor. The enraged animal kept running straight off into the bushes until he could no longer hear it. He grabbed his calf and looked down to see blood on his shredded trousers. The wound was minor, but it had awakened his sense of vulnerability.

He resolved to arm himself. With the help of Shuara he was able to communicate to the old man that he wanted a lance. A long, sharp spear, strong enough to kill an animal, or a man if necessary. Days passed. The man quietly appeared at Rand's hammock with a long, unusually beautiful carved spear. Its point was sharp and hard and its length was true. He gave the gift across the gulf of worlds. Rand was humbled, his hands running up and down the shaft approvingly, testing the point with his thumb and nodding all the while with a huge grin on his face. The old man watched him gratified at the acknowledgment of his skill. Rand thanked him in the only way he knew how by presenting the man with his leather belt, the only possession he had left.

Pilar visited frequently. She brought him clothes gathered from the men who had come and gone at the FUNAI encampment including a pair of old heavy boots, which Rand was grateful for lacing up tightly as protection, he hoped, against snakes and all the crawling things he detested about the rain forest. He anxiously awaited her visits, not just because she was the only one who spoke his language, but because of a quality he perceived in her that he had never before encountered. She was a stunning figure. Exceptionally tall for a *mestiço,* Pilar was an enigmatic blend of Indian and European with huge cinnamon almond eyes and thick black hair, which she usually wore up on her head and lay hidden under a broad brimmed khaki hat. But the element he admired most in her was indefinable. It was a kind of strength, a resolve and an earthiness that transcended cultural backgrounds and race. Rand discovered a primal feeling that was fuller and more elemental than any he had ever experienced for a woman before. It filled him when he was lost.

After three months he had full use of his arm. He had made some friends among the Indians, Utitiaja included, about whom Pilar had told the full story of his remarkable rescue from far up river in the hostile tribe's territory. It was difficult for him to grasp that he owed his life to the Indian and to Pilar who had tended his injuries. Being lost in the jungle was still unreal to him and each day he expected to see a boat or a party of white men march into the clearing and whisk him back to the city where he could catch a direct flight home. He had few other thoughts and in his mind he was living the life he'd left behind failing to recognize that it was equally as hollow in memory as it had been for real.

Utitiaja saw the distance in him and knew it was unhealthy. He began coaxing Rand out into the forest, now always carrying his spear even around the village much to the amusement of the warriors, for longer and longer walks as he went gathering things the village needed. Soon Rand was helping, and also carried a monkey skin pouch and a basket slung over his shoulder into which he piled the forest products he had discovered the value of from Utitiaja. Many things he learned to eat right from the source, a fact which gave him a small sense of security knowing he may be able to feed himself with fruit and roots though he doubted he could ever kill an animal, except for the boar who had cut his leg who he was dying to run into again now that he had his spear. After a while Utitiaja began to carry his blow gun and Rand witnessed the Indian bring down toucans, macaws and spider monkeys with one dart from great distances. He was also shown how to coat the end of his lance with *curare*, which looked to Rand like chocolate, and because he was not certain how toxic the poison really was began carrying a small bag of salt with him learning from Pilar that it was the antidote. He became more confidant and the forest less threatening to him and finally one night as he lay in his hammock falling asleep he even felt joy for a brief moment, ecstasy at being a part of the great flow of life that was the rain forest.

He saw Pilar one last time before the hunting trip. She had spent the whole afternoon with him and he was certain that she felt the unmistakable energy between them. She was laughing and the smooth, moist, coffee colored skin of her face was vibrant and lustrous. But it could have been the *nijimanche*, which she drank and persuaded him to try and which tasted rich and malt like and produced a mild buzz. Many of the Indians drank four or more quarts a day, but Rand was disgusted by it.

The following morning Utitiaja fetched him as he usually did when they were going into the forest, only this time he had more pouches strung across him, was beautifully painted and wore the bright feather of a toucan. He also carried a lance and had a bow draped across his back as well as his long blow gun. Soon they were on the river in a narrow, dugout canoe paddling upstream. After several hours they had passed through a landscape that all appeared the same to Rand. Though a white man couldn't tell one point from the next the Indian knew it all individually as well as three hundred and fifty or so species of plants that he could identify and use. They passed many large alligators lying halfway up the banks some of which reached well over twenty feet and a capybara who was drinking quietly. Rand remembered that Pilar told him why the Indians didn't kill them when they were near the water. She explained that because it was such a large animal the *curare* would take a while to effect it and by the time its respiratory system was paralyzed it would have jumped into the water and been far away, likely sinking to the bottom and would never be found. When Utitiaja had reached the place he was looking for they landed and hid the canoe in the bushes as was his custom. Rand followed him grinning with exhilaration running briskly through the trees searching out game.

They ran for a long time. He watched while Uititiaja built a blind out of huge elephant plant leaves, which they hid behind. For a half an hour they sat motionless and then the Indian stuck his head out and made a perfect bird call, the kind which Rand had heard many times on the trails around the village. He did this several times and soon, whisked out a dart, notched it with the sharp teeth of the piranha jaw he had hanging at his waist, stuffed it in the hollow tube buttressed with a wad of cotton and taking a moment to draw a bead puffed his cheeks and let it fly. Rand saw a distant slice of color fall through the trees as a toucan fell.

After an hour they gathered up the fallen birds stuffing them into their pouches and once again were on the move. For most of the day Rand exhaustedly followed Uititiaja as he collected small game such as monkeys, a curassow, a margay and two small peccary. On their return they were coming into a glade shrouded by ferns when suddenly Utitiaja froze. Rand stood motionless behind. In the rippling light that bathed the forest with shadow and sun were the unmistakable golden yellow and black markings of the jaguar. It had been surprised and arched its back drawing its lips over the long white canine teeth. Both men laden with game knew if they moved the large cat would spring. They waited tensely hoping the cat would lose interest. But it jumped like lightening and reached them with one bound. Rand dropped to the ground in terror covering his neck with his hands and heard the crash of bushes and the terrible thrashing sound of someone hurt, dying and enraged. He could not look and soon it was quiet. Then peering through the grass he saw Utitiaja standing. The cat lay at his feet with a lance sticking straight out of it. The Indian had brought it up as the cat leapt and braced its butt in the ground impaling the animal on the sharp, curare covered tip and with one hair raising snarl it was dead. Rand's heart was trumpeting in his chest so loudly he was afraid Utitiaja would hear and know he was a coward.

The Indian was triumphant. Their boat ride back to the village was a voyage of victory because not only had he returned with plenty of meat, but he had killed a jaguar. It was a sacred animal, though Rand could not know this, and great warriors' spirits were said to become jaguars two years after they died and return to the territory of their enemies to cause trouble. Utitiaja had killed an enemy today, he felt the honor and would tell of it around the fire in the twilight when all the other men and the women and children surrounded him and could share in his glory. He would wear the jaguar tooth necklace, the most prized possession a man could have next to good weapons. He gloated to himself as they walked the trail from the river to the village looking forward to the festivities of the evening.

At that moment it happened. It was then that the scream shattered the forest's magic and sent birds fluttering high into the canopy and monkeys screeching and scrambling for their lives. A human scream. A sound that made all the animal noise pale before it. More primal. More terrifying. A cry not unknown to the rain forests of Brazil where the Portuguese led slaving parties looking for free labor and the Spanish too seeking gold and led by their dogs that chased the Indians into their shelters and gnawed on their bones while they watched in horror, and the Dutch and English and others. It was as if an echo now rang mirroring the long inhuman history of the Americas where the theater of life repeats itself among the illiterate masses with inevitable cycles until at last there will be no one left to witness the carnage.

Utitiaja froze for the second time in the day. He let fall the game and the prized jaguar, which he had carried tucked around his neck. Then without looking back he ran forward, but after about fifty yards as if in premonition turned and dropped to his knees, raised his hands up against Rand, who was struggling along after him, as if to stop him, to ward him off, to hold him back. His face was strange and dark, Rand could not recognize him and had no way of knowing that the warrior always chose to die. There was no other way. Rand stopped still and another scream pierced the air more blood curdling and terrifying than the first. Other voices could be heard. Indians shouting and above that Portuguese voices. Gruff, guttural, rasping. Utitiaja ran off again, and then when he was far away turned back again to make sure Rand would not follow and once more motioned him back. This struck horror in Rand suddenly alone in the forest and he turned and fled so afraid he even forgot to drop the birds and small game that he carried. On one last impulse he looked back and a long way off, through the trees beneath the cool dappled light saw Utitiaja struggling with a white man. He saw the arm raised and then fall. He saw the Indian collapse and the glint off the machete as a beam of sun caught it in its lethal duty caring nothing for the worth of a man cutting down the elevated as well as the base, the good as well as the evil. He convulsed and his knees buckled, crying out silently and tears flooded his eyes, he gasped and sobbed and ran desperately into the forest while his spirit screamed for his friends Utitiaja, the constant Shuara, Cajke the healer and the old one who had helped him be a man.

Down to the river he raced where the boat had been hidden and he was certain he heard footsteps chasing him. He pushed off from the bank and hurled himself into its narrow cavity nearly capsizing and making it sink to the tips of the gunwales under his sudden weight. Fumbling for the paddle he struck at the water frantically, missing the deep thrusts and catching the oar sending out spray and waves in the commotion yet moving slowly, sluggishly. Finally, he dug in and with a few solid strokes sent the canoe out into the strong current and then turned down river toward where he knew the FUNAI encampment was and where he hoped he could find Pilar and help. Tears streamed down his eyes so that he could hardly see and the small white figure floated out on the ancient black waters beneath the violent looming beauty of the forest that cut through his heart like fire.

Randall DesVergers paddled breathlessly. He strained until his arms burned and then pushed some more. The jungle slid by, immursive, mysterious and foreboding. Its dank shores now seemed gloomy and austere in their lush overgrown fortresses. Caimans slid off the banks into the water, but he paid no attention to them paddling strong and straight in the center of the current that carried him with its full power past the frozen leaves of the late afternoon. A capybara swam along next to him for a while. His mind was staggering with disbelief and denial, recklessly trying to fabricate a reality different than the one he was in, other than the thing he'd seen, which he could not banish the image of. Try as he might to push away the thought of Utitiaja falling under the blows of the machete, he could not and the more he tried to push it away the stronger it became until it propelled him forward doggedly, though growing weary, into the eventide of the rain forest. Soon he searched the banks frantically even slowing so he would be certain not to miss anything. The FUNAI encampment must be near the river, he thought, it must be for he could not leave this road and began to search on land because he knew he would quickly lose his way where everything looked like everything else. Besides, he justified, darkness was coming, he had no way to make a fire and the snakes would be hunting. He cringed at the thought of the snakes and crawling things and resolved to stay on the river until he found the camp. *It must be here*, he thought in desperation, *it must be!*

If it was, Rand could not find it though he searched the banks slowly creeping down river until the light faded away so that he could not distinguish one shape from another and began imagining figures off in the distance flitting through the brush. He slipped under the cover of darkness a captive to the stream. There was no light in the jungle that night. The moon was still in other skies. The stars hid behind clouds and the whole world was transformed into darkness upon darkness, shadow upon darker shadow. Fireflies wove by knitting their way across the river and it made him think of the children of the village and how they would catch them and place them in each other's hair. He cried once more less for his own fate than theirs. He cried and drifted. For hours he drifted paddling lightly keeping as straight a path as he could without seeing anything knowing only by the sounds when he got too close to one bank or the other, the gurgling of a submerged tree, the chirps and croaking of frogs, the heavy splashes that he imagined to be crocodiles or some huge aquatic rodent of which he had seen several varieties. The consequences of his capsizing did not occur to him, he felt safer in the boat than he ever would on land. So he kept the oar in motion as the symphony of the million frogs resounded accompanied by the untold myriad of insects, bats and other nocturnal creatures he dared not think of.

He was the interloper, the foreigner. His arms burned from the strain of paddling for twelve or thirteen hours and as agitated and frightened as he was his eyes began to droop. He grew dull and tired with the shock that swept over him in waves forcing his eyes closed, while he made them stay open by will alone. A man's will. But he was a prisoner in the heart of nature. The forest won out in the end and he sank into a dreamless sleep.

A Spirit Obscured By Clouds

XVI

A city of greed, of noise, of lights floated in the surreal ecstasy of constant expectation surrounded by the emerald forest. It was a world that used nicknames only, no questions asked. *Boca de Lobo* it was called, The Wolf's Mouth.

Rootless men were drawn here, it was a magnet for the dispossessed, men without voices. They traveled from the south up *Transamazônica*, the fantastic highway that transverses the rain forest from Caracas to Buenos Aires, though still a red dotted line in many places, dirt roads with no traffic. Out of the industrial Valley of Death near São Paulo, from the drought plagued *Nordeste*, the frontier of the central interior where landless peasants died at the hands of big ranchers to settle on the *várzea*–flood plain forest–that had been drained for cattle grazing and out of the favelas of Rio. Here they assembled to experience the anarchy of living on the edge. Scholars that followed such grand migrations called it the greatest gold rush on record with maybe a million people involved, but nobody really knew how many there were, or how many sites were being mined only that here was the final crucible on earth where dreams in shambles met the virgin forests in the quest for wealth, where a man went when all else in his life had failed to make one final heroic effort.

The *Garimpos* were a way of life. The word meant more than just "mining camp", it had no corresponding English translation. It was a state of mind, a wild, lawless, intoxicating boom-or-bust arena where thousands and thousands of men clambered over the river, the earth and themselves for that one chance, that single moment of redemption. It was refuge for fallen hopes where even the dead could be resurrected if their luck held, if they managed to strike it right. The *garimpos* were where the independents operated, often outside any law, often illegally on Indian lands, often running on fumes, machismo and courage until it ran out somewhere around forty-five years old. For the river, the jungle and life were relentless not letting up for one moment and in these places men came to settle all accounts once and for all. As the politicians were fond of saying, in the Amazon, the government has lost control.

From the air they appeared as orderly bright blue and yellow rectangles. They were tarps, the roofs on the mining barges, the *dragas*; double decked wooden shacks on steel pontoons, rafts cluttered with pumps, long ramps and hoses, home to the miners and drilling platforms for suction pipes. But on the surface they were a frantic hive of activity and rattled, rumbled, shook and shivered twenty four hours a day, seven days a week and nobody ever knew what day it was except for the ones just returned from depositing gold with the owners. It was flown out every two days, because gold was just too much a temptation on the boats, by *cowboys*, bush pilots with dubious credentials who were the only ones foolhardy enough to fly in and out of the rough makeshift landing strips hacked out of the jungle. It was easy to spot an air strip just by the presence of wrecked planes.

A miner fell into the river and an alligator took his leg. One night three miners went to sleep on their *draga* and the mooring gave way, they drifted downstream and were never seen again. Now many lashed their boats together for safety, to avoid breaking loose in the strong current of the river and running into someone else where at best a fight would start and somebody could get killed. There were sixty thousand miners spread out over the Rio Madeira and its tributaries and ten thousand *dragas*, competition was ferocious. Men killed each other over claims, for stealing gold under their fingernails, over disputes weighing it in, divers knifed other divers in brawls about who had rights to a section of river bottom or cut the other's air hose. Nobody took their eyes off the flakes for even a fraction of a second. Humanity was left at the last highway community before the jungle became impenetrable, at way stops and frontier towns that had sprung up as logistic headquarters for the teeming hoards that rushed headlong into the wilderness often with little more than the shirt on their backs. Here was a dusty main street three hundred feet wide lined with clapboard storefronts advertising hardware for the *dragas* and digging, provisions, restaurants and whorehouses, along with makeshift signs offering to buy gold. Everyone bought gold. From the barber shop to the mechanic's garage it was universal. Gold was the reason. The source.

Close to shore, over a section generally agreed that had been mined out, four *dragas* were lashed together and securely moored. They were owned by Pixote de Lima a big, broad chested, rambunctious man with a heavy beard and a full, long mustache who had come to the river ten years before fleeing the poverty and nihilism of Rio Grande do Sul where his girlfriend had mocked his distress. He came like the others in oxidized and dented economy cars filled with men like himself sweltering down BR-364, the *Transamazônica*, trousers rolled up past the knees against the heat and chain smoking cigarettes. In frontier boomtowns he crowded into the camps along the river and spent a month trying to hitch a ride on one of the steel outboard *flying boats* that ferried crewmen to and from the *dragas* doing whatever he could to earn food. After many fits and starts he arrived at Boca de Lobo five years earlier when there were only three boats and nearly starved as he learned to eat roots, fallen fruit and leaves from the forest and pan for gold with a piece of hollowed out bark that provided him enough to live on while he searched for work from the absentee owners, who came and went only to collect their bounty.

Finally his break came. One of the *dragas* broke down and the owner, purple with unrealized greed and desperation, was forced to wait for a *flying boat* to come from the settlement fifty miles away as there was no airstrip yet. Pixote had learned about motors when he had worked as a fisherman on the *Nordeste* coast off the windswept beaches of dunes where wealthy vacationers from Rio far to the south would sit in the sun and watch him toil for a few fish in the sea. He worked three weeks without pay, just for food and for once lodging bringing his hammock in out of the trees. When the *draga* was relaunched he was hired on as operator and in the first day made more that he did in three months in his home where his girlfriend had mocked him. He spent nothing determined never to be destitute again and let his share of the gold mount up in the ledger book that he, like all other *garimpeiros*, kept to tally their take. He could cash in at any time simply by asking the owner and be paid in cash or bullion. But after a few years had learned to follow the price of gold because he had seen some of his fellow *garimpeiros* loose up to eighty percent of their savings by impulsively cashing in when the price was deflated. So, when the moment was right and the fever pitch of speculation had inflated the price beyond wild imaginings he sold out and, instead of returning home and buying a small house as many others dreamed of doing, bought a *draga* for himself. He did not, however, began dredging but anchored the boat in a muddy depleted shallow and headed for the settlement. When he returned he had two girls with him who had wild black hair and wore skintight pants. Pixote had bribed them out of the makeshift jail where they sat after allegedly killing a man who cheated them, so their claim went, by using rubber bands, pieces of wood and his thumb while weighing their gold. He bought them from the magistrate, who was himself nothing more than a business man looking to cash in on the gold rush, and told them each that on his *draga* men would offer them money a hundred times a day to sleep with them. So, like many other established men held in esteem by their community, a great enterprise came from humble beginnings.

Pixote de Lima had hit upon the one thing, aside from gold, which he had no control over, that the miners just couldn't get enough of. Soon, he brought in more girls and had purchased three other *dragas*, which he lashed together and made one a hardware and general merchandise store and the other a restaurant with a hotel of a few beds out of the third, when it was not occupied by the clients of his girls, which was almost never, but he did have a sign made that said *Hotel Flutuante*, the Floating Hotel, which was a bar-brothel and the center of Boca de Lobo's cultural life.

Shacks appeared along the shore and soon rudimentary businesses appeared, dominated by gold buyers and provision suppliers but almost anything could be found there and the town was now over a mile long. Pixote invested and owned a guesthouse and several general merchandise stores. The airstrip came last, after the phenomenally big hauls were finally made when the first layers of silt on the river bottom had been dredged up and the rich placer deposits uncovered. Air and boat were the only access. Then came the mining companies and other wealthy business people investing in automated dragas where men no longer needed to dive, they just sucked it up from the decks. Dredges clogged the river. They bought licensees from the government and tried to drive the independents away. Death was common and many times the bodies of previous night's victims were left to swell in the heat of the sun. Ten tons of gold a year were brought out by the mining companies, but over seventy tons by the independents mostly untaxed and uncontrolled. Much of it left the country to Bolivia or Columbia where a black market flourished and it went to buy guns or drugs. *Dragas* were often used for money laundering. Even the Minister of the Interior owned a boat on the river and was prone to pulling out clumps of gold in his plush, antique laden office in Brasilia and telling visitors proudly, "From my draga." He exclaimed to the press the need for demarcation of Indian lands and regulatory control over the Amazon's resources while secretly lobbying for the rights of miners and particularly the large investors who did not extract the ore in such a slipshod manner as the *garimpeiros* loosing forty percent of the find. No one was immune to the drug.

The city shimmered on the water. It hummed and vibrated and bustled in the mists rising off the primeval soup that drifted by slowly in the shallows where the *Hotel Flutuante* sat and swiftly toward the center of the channel where moorings and anchors secured the lashed together dragas that still slipped away on occasion despite the precautions. First light peeked over the tree tops of the canopy and monkeys chattered, birds chirped and capybaras rustled in the bush having their breakfasts all greeting the coming day. On the *dragas* there was no sense of time and the symphony was missed altogether as the lights of the night blended seamlessly with the light of day as little rushes of air rose with the first breath. Men worked wearily. Three hours on, three hours off. Diesel smoked blew into their faces, but they didn't notice it.

Rand was awakened by strange sounds. He lie on his back in the dugout canoe and through squinted eyes saw that the sky had cleared in the predawn hours and would be blue today, a fact that had no impingement on him at all. He had surfaced from a realm of dreams more frightening and sobering than anything he had ever experienced and in the aftermath was disturbed to the core. His great fear of the river at night had been numbed and overshadowed by the specter of what he was running from. No predator could be more terrifying, no animal more savage than men without moral sense, driven to the edge by inner psychosis that had no reasoning power. He drifted in the current still frozen with disbelief. The river was wider here and he could view the whole of heaven without looking through the filter of branches, a sight he hadn't been able to see for a long time. His mouth was cottony and his body ached. The diesel engines of the dredges whined away in the distance and at first he did not connect them with anything real and imagined the sound to be the humming of his mind still half dreaming, but then he was suddenly startled by the jabber of voices and bolted upright fully awake. There it sat like El Dorado shining brilliantly in the morning reflecting its floodlamps off the glassine water and flaring out of the haze as a fabled mirage come to life. It looked to Rand as a city in the clouds, unreal and ephemeral, a figment of desperate imaginations looking for a day of reckoning.

In disbelief he paddled towards the *draga* closest him not knowing what to make of it with its churning noise and black diesel smoke and as he drew near he could see the figures at work on deck, a man holding a big hose, another squatting in front of a box like machine and there were others inside the wood enclosure. No one saw him until he was ten yards from the deck, they were too tired and involved, and besides not one of the *garimpeiros* expected a man to come out of the forest, especially a white man. Rand placed the paddle across his knees and drifted nearer.

"Hey there!" He shouted to the man on the deck. "Hey there." The scowl caught him off guard. A black look startled and miserly. The muscular young man stood and placed his hands on his hips saying nothing, just frowning. He then turned his back on Rand and continued to work at the machine in front of him. "Hey there!" Rand repeated, "Where am I?" This time the man glared hostilely and brushed him away with his hand. Shooed him off. And Rand stopped the canoe dead in the water not prepared for any sort of confrontation, especially following the ordeal of the day before he was still trying to force from his consciousness. So, he angled around the boat and soon viewed other *dragas* with similar men in similar moods and cursed his misfortune again and again repeating over and over miserably, "Why me?" Then he saw the sign. Hotel Flutuante. Rand made for the edge of the four boats lashed together off in the shallows still cast in the indigo shadows of night with fog drifting up around them and when he had pulled the bow of his canoe up on the deck rushed in the only door, which was facing aft of the largest boat, the one with the sign. As it happened Pixote de Lima was sitting in the small, partitioned off chamber he had appropriated as a combination office and lobby for the hotel where he assigned rooms to the girls or to the occasional legitimate overnight guest. He was drinking strong coffee and had not even combed his hair yet when Rand burst in.

The white man made an impressive sight, like someone wrenched from a dream pale and haggard, hollow eyed and gaunt. His clothes were streaked with sweat and soil, there was blood on his shirt from the monkey skin pouch where the game birds still sat neatly tucked away from the day before. "Where am I?" He beseeched without breath, an agitated panic in his eye.

The big man looked up nearly startled out of his wits despite his bravado and physical prowess and replied in perfectly good English albeit with a thick, regional Portuguese accent. "Whatchamean where am I?"

"I'm lost."

He paused to get control of the situation and looked at the strange apparition and because he had found over the years that was the best way to avoid saying something later regretted. "Boca de Lobo. That's where you am."

"What's that?"

"It's where you are," he said with a slight tinge of disgust tempered by a respect for the crazy stare in the man's eyes, "the *garimpo,* Hotel Flutuante. You looking for a room?"

Rand glanced around the boarded up walls. "I lost all my money." He said absently.

"Too bad my friend." Pixote dismissed him as another *riberirinho*– river dweller, abandoned to the flotsam and jetsam, down on his luck.

"I been in the jungle for months." Rand exclaimed in frustration beginning to shake a bit, feeling the weariness overtake his senses. "I'm an American."

The man looked up paying more attention to Rand now and surveying the look of him and nodding his head. "Plane crash?"

"That's right."

"Figures. Happens a lot around here." He said as if discussing the weather. "Seven people died in one last week just up river."

"Indians found me."

"Lucky you're still alive my friend. There's trouble sometimes. We have trouble sometimes."

"Can I have some water?"

The big man looked suspiciously at him. "I suppose so." And he got up, returned with a bottle half full and handed it to Rand. He watched the American drink greedily and saw the bird feathers sticking out of his monkey skin bag still strapped to his side. "You stink mister."

"Yea." Rand replied his mouth full of water. "Been living with Indians. Had to leave suddenly."

"How come?"

He decided not to tell the story of what had occurred the previous day because he did not have a good feeling and the voices he heard were Portuguese and he was still afraid and the terror gripped him like the feel of cold steel on his insides. Rand would say nothing until he was sure who he was talking to. "I'm hungry." He said.

"Yea. So's everyone comes out here. It's where men come when they're hungry."

"Where can I get some food?"

"Without money? Dunno...*garimpeiros* are not charitable people usually. They roughed it, figure you'll have to as well." But the white man looked so downtrodden and sad and hollow Pixote relented remembering his Catholic upbringing and the sanctity of charity. "I'll give you one meal," he said in admonishment, "just one...but you don't you tell anyone OK? That OK?" And he made Rand promise.

They sat at a table in the restaurant and an Indian girl in a tight, short dress with foam rubber thongs on her feet served them. He gratefully stuffed food in his mouth from the plate of manioc, fish and beans and discovered there was a landing strip close by where planes came and went to fly out the gold ore. "No one's gonna fly you for free." He revealed quite convinced. "The Indians charge them a fortune as landing fees and cowboys don't do favors. They don't live long enough. Besides, if they're flying gold they wouldn't trust you."

He was shaking from the shock of the night. "But I gotta get out!"

"I don't even think you could get out on the flying boats. They only run when they're full, and then they're all paying passengers. Unless you wanna rent the whole boat...then they'd take ya."

"Auggh... shit!" He stuttered, and then let it go relating the full story of how he had ended up at the table that morning, except the part about why he had to leave the village so suddenly. Rand told him about Rio and the few days spent with his enigmatic and wealthy client.

"Valdemiro Veloso?" Pixote exclaimed in surprise.

"Yes." Said Rand. "That's right. You heard of him?"

"Heard of him...? HA!" The man guffawed as if Rand was stupid. "Everybody's heard of him. He's the biggest dope smuggler in Brazil. A legend."

Rand did not believe the man and thought he exaggerated to seem important. "What...?! He's a business man, and...his family owns land."

"Yea, where they bury people...come on! You worked for him? Ehaa...If I was you, know what...I'd lay low." He said through silted eyes, tilted back head and tight lips. "Let him think you're dead. He was trying to kill you my friend."

Spinning in disbelief and denial Rand exclaimed. "Why?"

"Who knows?" Pixote said picking his teeth. "It's big business." He gestured out the door. "Half the *dragas* on the river are laundering drug money." He shook his head. "Don't let him know you're alive. Maybe he'll forget. Don't tell anybody else about him, maybe he owns one of these boats...you never know in the *garimpo*, you never know."

Randall DesVergers didn't believe him. Couldn't believe him. It didn't fit in with his mental image of himself and how he conducted life. He thanked the man and promised to send him some money for the meal when he got back home and soon was pulling the canoe up into the brush exactly the way he remembered seeing Utitiaja do it. Exactly, though he had no feeling left and the memory was cold and mechanical and detached and he dared not think of his friends or Pilar, the one he could not find.

After he had first recovered he had spent weeks expecting a rescue party every day, and even as time passed could not grasp the fact that they would not come. It seemed a simple matter to Rand; plane goes down, search party goes in, rescue is made. He could not have known and in his naive way would not have guessed that Valdemiro Veloso saw to it that the flight plan of his plane gave a false destination and paths, nothing unusual in the illicit trades, and he had altered the time and place events enough to throw off any suspicion or guesses at accurate location. Consequently, there was a search party, an enormous effort backed by the firm Van Riper, Hazeltine & Brock and enjoined by the army at the request of Valdemiro himself, but all centered in the wrong jungle. The rescue effort was nearly a thousand miles off and they had never once come near the isolated tributary of the Rio Madeira where the *garimpos* and the Indians coexisted in tension and despair.

He walked the full length of the aggregation of buildings that was called a town from one end to the other and at every store front went in and told his brief story, he was an American, had gone down in a small plane and needed to get out. Then he looked at them plainly, expectantly. "Sure," they all said good naturtedly, the ones that could speak English, "wait a while, someone will give you a ride. Maybe the flying boats." But he began to think about what Pixote had said. What if Veloso had targeted him and then he resurfaced? Rand couldn't get used to the idea that someone had tried to kill him. Him of all people, why would anyone want to do him harm? But it made sense in some inscrutable way for the tail of the plane had been blown off and though he didn't know much about aviation, he knew that was something that couldn't occur by its own devices. There was nothing combustible back there, he figured, it wasn't jet fuel or the whole plane would have gone up in a blast, and it was a certain way to bring a plane down.

Rand sat on the board sidewalk that had been built over the mud and dirt of the bank and surveyed the place. He was still numb with a suppressed nausea. Heat was rising as the sun drew higher and there was a humid stench in the air from all the people and refuse. *A lot of boats in the river,* he observed for the first time, *an astonishing number, maybe two or three hundred.* They stretched magnificently for several miles, though most were congregated where the river was widest fronting the town and Pixote de Lima's Hotel Flutuante. The noise from all of them made a sort of blinding hum that hung in the air like the sounds of the freeways at home in Los Angeles, a white noise that couldn't be located. It was an amazing spectacle. People were everywhere rushing about with a strong determination in their eye he couldn't quite place. They were so different than the Indians, and the whole place was flush with activity. Suddenly, he became aware of himself in their midst as if he hadn't even been present before and looked down at the soiled, frayed clothing that Pilar had given him and the thought struck him that he hadn't shaved properly or had a haircut for months. *How I must look,* he thought. And he did stink, the game in his bag was ripe and he wasn't much better. "I have no money." He said to himself, and repeated as if it hadn't sunk in..."No...money." Rand shook his head unconsciously like he'd seen derelicts do back in the city. What good would the next outpost do, couldn't eat, couldn't even make it to the nearest telephone, which he imagined being thousands of miles away. And then he started shaking. Violently. He fought back tears because he was so ashamed.

Rand went a short ways up stream and stripped all his clothes off and washed them in the river, rubbing the folds of fabric together and beating them on rocks partly to wring them, but mostly to let out the grief and frustration he felt. He beat the hell out of his clothes. Although he was afraid of alligators, which he knew were in these waters, he was more afraid of the piranhas that Pilar had warned him of that liked to congregate in the murky back streams and inlets like where he was at that moment. So it was an act of complete faith when he jumped off the bank into the silty river that was so churned up and muddy from the *dragas* he couldn't see for three inches beneath its surface. The warm water rushed over him and as he plunged under he had the idea that he might never come up, that he might just stay down there and when it got too bad take a deep breath of river and let the body drift down stream for the caimans to feed upon or for the vultures to pick at. He had never had a thought like that before and he reflected upon how desolate he felt. Shock, he supposed, shock did that to a man and he braced himself against it having spotted that much and so thrust up out of the water refreshed and, he was sure much cleaner than he'd been in months. After he'd scrubbed himself he stretched his clothing out on nearby bushes and sat there naked watching the *dragas* and smelling the churned up mud from below.

Across the surface of the river he could see the divers going over the sides of the poorer looking boats with big hoses in their hands. Suction dredges he guessed. They had no scuba gear or diving helmets, just face masks and a garden hose which they breathed out of and they took the end of down with them. The thought of it made him shiver. The young men went down and he lost track of when they came up it was so long.

About midday his clothes were finally dry enough to put on and he smoothed them out as best he could and shaking each piece, slipped them on. They felt good against his skin even though it was hot and muggy. He had washed and cleaned his game conscious of the need for food and had gutted them using sharp rocks the way he recalled seeing the women prepare them in the village. He wrapped each in leaves and placed them back in his monkey skin pouch to cook later over a fire. Nothing else occurred that first day and the whole time he walked around as if in a daze trying to get through to people and even trying to trade his game for a haircut and a shave...nobody wanted his story or his birds. That evening he had made a place for himself in the forest not far from where the town sat, close enough to see the buildings and the lights that gave him comfort. He had carved out a niche for himself from the leaves and the undergrowth as he had seen other men do around the *garimpo*, newly arrived such as himself, busted and destitute as he, but they had come of their own accord to find a new life, and he was hunted trying to return to his old one. Tomorrow, he resolved, he would go down to the repair yards where the *dragas* were pulled up on the banks to be worked on, and where he had seen many men congregating, idle men, desperate faces like his, looking for work on the barges, or even in the town. He had to get enough money to feed himself, though he supposed he could eat fallen fruit, as he had done tonight, and cook small game on a shared fire, as he had also done, and so would not starve. Randall DesVergers felt more secure as he drifted off to sleep next to the wide, silt filled river that raced by under the pontoons of three hundred *dragas* each one working feverishly at full capacity lit up like roman candles in the forest night.

Randall DesVergers, Harvard lawyer, partner in the firm Van Riper, Hazeltine & Brock, recipient of numerous awards, esteemed member of the California Bar and the Bel Air Country Club who had driven his grand, teal automobile with disdain by the army of swarthy, illegal Latinos on Sawtelle Avenue in Los Angeles longing for work from passers by now stood in the boat yard and vied for jobs with the rest of the rootless men. He had never before experienced anything like it and after the first day he felt energized as if a cleansing process had begun that somewhere, far beneath his surface, brought happiness. He returned every day for a week, occasionally getting some small job in the town somewhere cleaning up or doing some unskilled labor on the boats, enough to buy a couple days food. He was unprepared for anything else, his erudite education had not given him anything to exchange with the dispossessed. And then he was back with the others and surprised that he could never quite make anything over the price of a plate of fish, manioc and beans and what he thought was going to be a simple process of putting some money away for the trip to a major town became a battle that he rose to at dawn each day just to survive. He had to get work on one of the *dragas*. Those men were paid with a percent of the take and so there was incentive, some had become *draga* bosses, some owners themselves and richer than the rich, though that was rare. But they just made more than enough to get by. He began to make friends, men he saw every day who were remarkably like him, only more savvy, more in tune with nature's breath and step. One *garimpeiro* had hit it after months of struggle and spent the equivalent of three months pay for a night with four of Pixote's prostitutes. Another made it big and rented an entire hotel on the town's street where he lived drinking every day with women and gambling until his money ran out. He too returned to the yard where they all were equal.

There were children in the *garimpo*; Indian, mestiço, mulatto...it reminded him of Rio and the *pivetes*, but the children he saw by the river were working hard. They were ragged and tired and none of them smiled. He had learned from one of the other men that they were not paid close to what a man earned, they were paid hardly anything, "...they gotta eat, no one feeds 'em for notin!" They cleaned the sluice boxes and reclaimed mercury from the crevasses with their bare hands, untangled lines and carted equipment all over the *garimpo* until little legs staggered and little faces grew black with gloom. They were on the shore panning for some nearby *draga* where the operator could keep an eye on them, standing in the water ten to twelve hours a day making the equivalent of two dollars and fifty cents. The kid looked about ten, skinny and tough. His arms were drawn and sinewy and black hair spilled over his ears in a flood. The man was big and tried his best to ignore the pleading and badgering as the kid followed him around and pulled at his shirt, hit at his leg and was pushed away, swatted, and yelled at. It didn't deter the boy at all. Not one bit.

A man elbowed Rand, "Won't pay him."

"He what...?"

"Owes the kid money..." The man snickered, "won't pay."

All of a sudden Randall DesVerges was between the burley *garim-peiro* and the boy both of whom stopped bickering and looked at him strangely. Rand reached over and touched the boy's chest with the back of his finger. "Owes you money, right?"

"Yea." Said the boy unhappily after a moment.

"You do good work?"

"Yea."

"Did you do everything expected?"

"Yea."

"Any complaints?"

"No."

Then he turned to the big dumbfounded man who was watching in confusion. "Did he fulfill the obligation you had asked of him?":

The man wheezed. "Fuck you!"

"No," said Rand in an extremely cordial, businesslike manner yet with a quiver in his voice betraying a suppressed fury. "The question was did he fulfill the obligation you had asked of him?" His face turning crimson.

"Awww...does what I tell him. So the fuck what?"

"No complaints then?"

"Naww...go away!" He said and started to walk.

"Did you know that you have a contract with him and that verbal contracts are binding?"

"What...?"

"Did you know that you are committing an illegal act and that by fulfilling his duties satisfactorily the boy has legally burdened you with an obligation that you must now, under penalty of law, discharge?"

"Shee...fuck you!" The man grumbled and again started to walk away.

But Rand grabbed his shirt and spoke even louder. "...furthermore by your incurring this obligation and then refusing to discharge it in a lawful manner you have obtained his services, on credit, fraudulently and with the intention to defraud, for which you could not only be sued but could face civil charges as well! And furthermore could incur damages, legal and court costs to boot which would stand up in any

318

court or hearing before a magistrate, judge or...possibly you'd want a jury trial?"

The man shoved Rand's hand away. "Who the hell're you?" He snickered.

Rand looked at the boy who was just as dumbfounded as the man, and then back at the surly *garimpeiro* and replied, "I'm his lawyer."

The man hit him with one powerful blow to the face that lifted him up off the ground and laid him out cold, flat on his back. When he awoke both the man and the boy were gone and the men around him, who were shaking his shoulders to bring him around, were laughing riotously.

"A lawyer? Nobody likes lawyers!"

"Is it true?" One said with a huge grin, "What you told him, is it true?"

Rand was feeling worse now than he had when he'd first come down to the water's edge seeing that many of the day's jobs had already been doled out. The sweltering heat oppressed him. The feeling was that something unfathomable in the well out of which his life swelled in subtle waves had been disturbed, something primitive, essential to who he was that long ago had been pushed aside in the rush, the madness, the obsession. Its sleep had been interrupted by recent events in his life leaving him restless. The blindness was a question of value, was it worth it? How much intrinsic usefulness did his services have to people? What were they willing to exchange for it? What was his merit?

He found no work that day languishing in the heat that was uninterrupted by the usual afternoon rain that gave him an ominous feeling as if the balance of nature had been disordered. Rand was about to give up on the yard when he saw a small, inflatable boat coming down the river. He watched as it slid across the mirror surface cutting a wake. He listened to the high whine of the outboard motor above the throaty, chugging diesels of the dredges and saw it go all the way to the Hotel Flutuante where it docked and three men awkwardly got out. They stamped and shook the cramps from their bodies. He hadn't noticed at first, but looking closely Rand could make out the letters FUNAI on the boat.

In an instant he raced across the mud flats of the river beneath tall, stately trees, his heart beating wildly in his throat knowing they were from Pilar's encampment and when he reached the ramp where the lashed together *dragas* were moored he crossed it in two leaping steps. When he arrived the men were already surrounded by others and he pushed his way into the circle. Everyone was talking. Jabbering excitedly. Shock covered their faces. Dismay and fear. Heavy saddened eyes.

"...thirty-five, thirty-six...we couldn't tell so many had fled to the forest."

"When was this?" Pixote was asking in alarm.

"Two weeks ago, ten days."

"Machete you say?"

"Some shot, but most were killed by machete."

"Saints bless them! Jesus Christ...machetes...?"

Rand grabbed the nearest one by the shoulder and yanked on him. "FUNAI? You FUNAI?"

"That's right."

"Pilar?"

The man shook his head with features set as stone. "There's been a terrible event."

Feeling wild, his world dissolving he repeated frantically, "Pilar!?"

"Murdered. We think...couldn't find her. We spent the last week looking."

Rand stopped breathing. The birds ceased in their tracks. The river froze in its bed. Everything was silent as he watched the men describing the massacre, the Indians, their bodies hacked apart with machetes, some of them decapitated, blood smeared on the long house, children shot in the back as they fled, women cut down, skewered on the blade, all lying where they had fallen, taken unawares, a surprise raid by men with knives and guns, butchers, thirty five, thirty six dead; those that escaped into the forest wouldn't even come out to talk to them, they were running, running to the other villages, to warn them, to hide, to seek revenge.

Once again Rand asked wistfully, "Pilar?"

"She was traveling to the village to see someone. Must have come across them. They didn't want any witnesses. She just disappeared."

Rand suddenly gathered a fistful of shirt. "Who did this!!?" He pulled the FUNAI man from the crowd that had gathered around him. "Who!?"

"You're the American, aren't you? You're the one."

"Tell me who did this?"

"Nobody knows." But it was clear everyone did.

Rand was quiet. Resigned. Death was the final arbiter, it could not be argued with, there were no second chances, no negotiating, it was black and white. Later that night the three men and he sat circling a round table in the bar at the Hotel Flutuante. They were all drinking. Even men that didn't drink were learning now. Some things were worth forgetting. Pixote drank with them, and then went off about his business when he could no longer remember why they were drunk, when the images had been drowned. "I'm just an accident," Rand explained, "I don't belong." He related his story to them of what had happened and how he had come to be in the jungle–omitting the details of Veloso out of caution. He told them about Pilar, how she had probably saved his life and set his arm and been a friend when he had been utterly lost. While he talked he remembered her scent and how it had come to him amidst all the other fragrances of the forest. He told them how he had seen Utitiaja cut down and how he had escaped and recklessly floated down river in the night. The FUNAI men had been involved in negotiations with the other tribe, the one that came to visit while Rand was in the village, and that was why they could not leave. "They're safe," a man said as if in consolation. "No one attacked them, but they won't talk to us now. They think we are evil spirits and blame us for bringing the disaster to their neighbors who they had just made peace with for the first time in many years. They see us as terribly bad spirits. We were partly the reason the two clans met when they did. Now what?"

When the men had drunk all that they could hold and found that there was nothing left to say they went upstairs to the room that Pixote had let them use, free of charge, just for one night. They were traveling to Brasilia as fast as they could to set an investigation in motion and would return with the military who had jurisdiction over remote outposts in the Amazon. Randall DesVergers was to travel with them, it was all arranged and the men were happy they could help him and all of them wondered if they had of come to his aid sooner, if they had left when Pilar first told them about him, if things would have been different. They all cursed the inequities of life. Cursed the darkness and the doubt. Cursed their own helplessness to turn back time. Daybreak, they said, they would leave with the sunrise and fly out in the plane that was parked on the landing strip and travel to the town where civilization ended, and from there to the capital. Rand would travel with them. They were thankful they could help. It was the least they could do. So it was all arranged and Rand stumbled back to the room he shared with the mulatto named Ailton who worked on one of the *dragas* and who he had hoped would get him employment there as well. He lay on his back wide awake fully clothed dreaming of the flight out and how much he had missed his life and what the first thing he would do would be once he returned. Finally, a chance to leave, but its promise was muted. The hollowness in his chest crushed him. Absolutely crushed him. His thoughts swam in darkness. Rand could not sleep the entire night.

He had fallen into the cauldron and it had swallowed him alive. The raw and rapacious fingers of it tore at the barriers he had constructed around himself during his entire existence in an effort to separate from things that mattered, from the elements of life that by reason of their essential nature carried with them great liability. There was pain connected with responsibility that he never wanted to confront. There was discomfort and ignominy and it threatened the security of the partitioned off corner where he and all those like him lived in oblivious ritual that all the dispossessed aspired to. The falseness of his life swept across him in the womb the forest with waves so bleak that he would never have believed a myriad of living things surrounded him. And by morning Randall DesVergers was reduced to his primal state and looked out across the river in the dawn seeing the space for the first time as the light filled it, the objects that lived in that space and the energy that enveloped it all. A decision was forming in him, a postulated existence far closer to what he had always imagined for himself, a rebirth.

Perhaps it is the nature of a man's thoughts that his real life is reflected from them, as if reality were but a mirror. For as the metamorphosis occurred within Rand an event took place he did not know about. A small, insignificant occurrence like the one grain of sand that announces an avalanche. The operator who had refused to pay the boy was walking alone at dusk toward the end of the town with heavy steps. He was satisfied with his day's work and secure in the belief that he had a mastery over the events around him and was the maker of his own destiny and his own rules. He mulled over these things many times in the day in an effort to relieve his conscience, to try to negotiate a way out of any feelings of guilt that may intrude on his happiness. He had looked one last time out over the forest and gloated.

"Hey senhor!" The man said who stepped out from behind the building. He was a *garimpeiro* and still dirty from the day on the *draga*, sand from the river in his hair and grease on his cheek.

The operator stopped, casually scanning the figure up and down and exuded an air of confidence and unconcerned indifference. "What do you want."

Another figure stepped out of the half light. "We have come to collect the boy's wages."

"The what...?"

The man in front of him with grease on his face looked around behind him nervously.

"Wages." The boy cautiously stepped forward.

At this the operator laughed heartily. "I owe him no wages, he is mistaken."

"We are his legal representatives." Said the one in front of him and the other nodded in agreement. "That's right."

The man screwed up his face in disgust and annoyance and brutishly tried to push his way through the two men muttering something about another fucking lawyer, one or the other swung a punch and when the melee was over the operator lie face down on the ground breathing heavily. The boy reached into his pocket and pulled out a thin, weathered wallet, which he opened, removed the money owed him and then replaced. Then the three walked away.

When the men from FUNAI came to get Rand he was waiting for them sitting on the wooden sidewalk that lined the street in front of the guesthouse where his room was. He had been there for some time and had watched the light silently paint the mysterious wall of forest across the river revealing the splash of deep green at its peak where the sun just now was beginning to brush across it. He had listened through the constant drone of the dredges on the swiftly moving current, that gave off a damp coolness in the night despite the heat and raised a fog mist in the first light, and heard movements of the living mantle which made up the jungle around him as it yawned and stretched and prepared for the coming day. He had heard since an hour before dawn the community of flying things in the canopy high above the world of land as their voices heralded the coming of the sun. He had felt the stir of wind, the breath of the day as it sighed and gasped all at once awakening from a restless slumber and saw the leaves rustle in waves of motion. He himself was a part of the tide. The men were carrying all their luggage in backpacks and large duffel bags hanging from straps over their shoulders.

"Come on! We've got to hurry!" One barked as they approached.

"I'm not going." Rand replied calmly.

"What?! What do you mean?"

"I'm going to try my hand at gold mining. Get rich maybe."

"Ahh...you're crazy! You won't get another chance to leave for a long time. Better come. Cummon..."

"I can't. Thanks. Thanks for the offer...but I just can't." The men finally gave up trying to convince him and with shrugs all around walked off into the distance where the plane would carry them far away. Rand felt released from some great burden, a lightness that he had not felt since before his father had gone away and he had lain by a forest pool beside a young girl a long time ago.

A Spirit Obscured By Clouds

XVII

Ailton had ridden a bus over a thousand miles before he managed to hitch a ride on one of the steel flying boats to Boca de Lobo. He had spent months in the crowded camps along the Rio Madeira with thousands of others looking for work lured by the promise, but most of all by the escape it offered. Even that was better than the industrial inferno of São Paulo where he had come from that offered not even the slightest glimmer of a better life. Before that he had worked his father's fishing boat and when he had died was left alone to fend for himself. Even if he never earned anything on the *draga*, the hope was enough. But he did earn something, from the first day and so kept on as a diver and then later on one of the automated boats owned by a large mining company based in Vancouver. It was the first time in his life he had steady money coming in and although he promised himself he would quit every year, it had been five now and he was still at it. The feeling of holding the small, crinkled patty of gold in his hand that was the day's take for twenty four hours of dredging after it had been sluiced, and melted down in a frying pan to burn off the excess mercury was still exciting.

People looked at Rand differently that morning, or perhaps it was just a misperception brought on by lack of sleep and too much alcohol the night before. They seemed to have more regard for him, notice his existence and stand aside to allow him to pass more readily than they had done before. Ailton introduced him to the other men working on the *draga*, and only one of them had dirty looks for the white man, the North American who he assumed did not really need the job. It was

325

luck, or fate or a mysterious part of the postulated existence, which Rand had determined for himself that landed him on the *draga*. It had come out of a powerful decision that it was where he wanted to be, and then it happened. The significance of this coincidence did not pass by him unnoticed, but made him watch even more carefully the thoughts and considerations he made during the day which he was certain now affected his future.

The *draga* had become short handed the day before when a man who was swimming and fooling in the water after he had untangled the mooring cable from a clump of brush and logs–shooters they called them, logs that ran loose down the river ramming into anything in their path–and had been grabbed by an alligator, pulled under and he never came up. Nobody saw any part of him again. "He shouldn't have played around," Ailton said, "splashing arms and legs attract alligators." Randall resolved to remember that bit of wisdom.

He was not given any serious responsibility at first, but was expected to do all the jobs that nobody else wanted to do or were too busy to do. He learned all about the cables and moorings and the anchor line and how to keep the boat secure and prevent it busting loose while the dredging machine churned and sputtered and spewed out black smoke or even worse at night when several crew men slept aboard and a night shift worked under the glare of gas phosphorus lights. Rand watched everything for the first few days and began to understand how it all fit together. The fat pipes brought the silt up from the bottom. On his boat they were automated and unlike the poorer *dragas* needed no divers. Ailton's first job had been as a diver because he was an experienced fisherman, the fact that the two disciplines were entirely separate and had no bearing on each other made little difference to the man making the decision, since to him a man familiar with the water was a man familiar with the water. He had donned his face mask and sunk to the bottom with stones wrapped around him and a garden hose clenched between his teeth where he put in a ten hour shift of dredging the silt by hand. "You can't see your hands down there." He had told Rand. There were fights on the river bottom between divers over whose territory was whose. Often a man was killed in a mistaken argument over claim jumping when it had become so muddy that neither one knew where they had drifted to and in fact most of the time were both far away from the original location in dispute. Ailton had a scar that ran all the way up his back from his kidney to his shoulder blade from a knife wound he had almost died from. It was the same silt that had been washed from the Andes near the source of the Amazon and carried down stream by the powerful current past the rain forest metropolis of Manaus where the river was over a mile wide and into the tributaries such as the Rio Madiera and ultimately its branches. The slushing silt roared down two-story wooden ramps that served as sluice boxes covered with a thick, synthetic carpet like mesh that trapped the heavy particles and allowed the water to run back into the river. Every twenty-four hours the men would shake the carpet into metal buckets and then sit down to separate out the find. Only the trusted ones did that, which Rand understood when the take for the whole day could fit in the palm of one man's hand.

Ailton showed him how to pour the silver mercury into the silt filled buckets and then stir it with the long handled electronic mixer that made him shake and shimmy and stutter when he spoke. Then he stuck a hose into the bucket and washed the excess sand and water back into the river. The remainder was a mixture of gold and mercury, but just looked to Rand like a jar of silver liquid. Ailton poured the mixture through a cloth and squeezed it until the mercury oozed out from between his fingers and then dropped a grainy, putty colored marble into a small steel compartment with a spigot on top that was supported by delicate legs. He lit a fire under the compartment and after twenty minutes the excess mercury had evaporated out the spigot and he pulled out an irregular chunk of gold pitted and cracked. "You get three percent!" He beamed, "When you become an operator, you get six." Rand also received a small ledger book in which he recorded, as every *garimpeiro* did, the date and amount of his share making sure his book coincided with the main book for the *draga* so there would be no disputes.

It took nearly one and a half times the amount of mercury as the amount of gold it recovered, much of which was allowed to run back into the river. An estimated fourteen tons of mercury went into the Rio Madiera system in a year. No one, not the *garimperios* or the Indians thought about the fact until some foreign biologists informed them that they were rapidly poisoning the river down stream and that fish and other aquatic species were dying at an alarming rate, the banks were becoming defoliated and barren and people were slowly succumbing to mercury poisoning. This was evidenced by the fact that most *garimperios* tested were found to have minimum contamination of twenty six parts per million, poisoning started at only six parts per million. As a reaction to pressure from the government, caught between the urge for gold revenues and the demands of the international community and the ecologists most *dragas* had a mercury removal machine on the boat. Rand looked at one on the deck wondering what it was and why it wasn't being used.

His *draga* was owned by AMSI, American Mining Systems Incorporated, an international mining consortium based in Vancouver. It operated as a franchise to circumvent any tax liability the Brazilian government might impose on foreign owners if it ever caught up with the wildcat mining operations and to give its franchisees initiative for expansion. There was a tight knit group of corporate boat owners in the region who had formed an unofficial alliance to watch out for each other's interests. It was shortly after this group formed that the real trouble with the Indians started. The tradition of Indian against intruder had a four hundred and fifty year history and so there had always been hostilities. Rand understood the key element because it was of his world, and he had uncovered it, oddly enough, in the bar of the Hotel Flutuante where he had increasingly sought refuge and had began to drink heavily. He was making many friends among the *garimpeiros* because he was a likable man and it was in talking to these men that he discovered it. A simple story. One that had many parallels. It had all the classic elements of the eighteenth century, Rand thought dizzy with drink; Indians, white intruders and missionaries. During one of these late night drinking sessions Rand heard something else, something that caught his attention even though the others could hold their liquor much better than he could.

Unlike them, he was hunted by a terrible purpose.

"I'm so God dammed tired I don't think I'll ever get up from this table." Pixote said after an extended sigh leaning his squat bulk back wearily in the chair. "Not even my girls could get me up tonight."

"You'll get up when the money runs out." Said a man snubbing his cigarette in a small puddle of spilled beer.

"That's right," another jibbed, "you'll have to move your big ass then!"

"When your gold runs out." Rand added pointing to one of Pixote's prostitutes across the room in a tight, short dress that barely covered her breasts. "No flakes, no shakes."

"If you don't," a broad, muscular man named Caetano exclaimed in a drunken bluster, "the *Baixadas* will move you whether you want to or not."

"What's that…?" Rand asked never having heard the word before.

Dark looks spread around the table and it was suddenly quiet. The man who had spoken averted his eyes. "Hey!" He said. "Isn't that Raoni," he said looking at a man who had just entered the bar, "never thought he'd show his face here again."

"Why not?"

"Had a little trouble."

"A fight?"

"Killed someone. But that was a year ago, nobody will remember."

Rand repeated his question, "What was it you said?" sensing that the man had revealed something they didn't want him to know. All of them had reacted as one.

"About what?"

"You know, a minute ago?"

"You don't want to know my friend," Pixote intervened, "you're just passing, we live here."

"Tell him. He has a right to know. Works the river same as we do."

"*Baixadas*." Pixote said with a shrug.

"What's that?"

"It's a group of men.'

"What men?"

"Nobody knows for sure. Perhaps one of us. Perhaps a rumor. They are like phantoms. They were named after a sector where there are a lot of killings in Rio's *zona norte,* the *Baixada Fluminense.*"

"So..." He laughed and took another drink, "what are these phantoms?"

"You call them death squads in your country." Pixote replied calmly, reverently and with a reserve Rand had not noticed in him before.

Suddenly serious, "I think everybody calls them that."

"You have to understand," Pixote explained waving a half smoked cigarette in the air to indicate the unimportance of the discussion, "there is a civil war in Brazil, and the police are losing. They have no more respect for justice, so vigilantes take over. The violence is within the context of a social war, those that have and those that do not. But we," He grinned around the table, "we don't worry about that. We are not rich or poor anymore. We're in between."

A man muttered. "Indians are not in between!"

"Caetano, be careful what you are saying!"

"Everybody knows. We've been trying to move up river for a year."

"Who?" Rand asked.

"AMSI. The other owners. All of us. We know the gold's running out. Some days two *dragas* right next to each other and one pulls up two kilos, the other nothing. It's getting mined out. There's been killings on both sides for years," his eyes glazed over and he took a drink, "just never like this."

Pixote interjected again, "You don't know nothin'. Listen my friend, " he said turning to Rand, "you don't want to know this stuff, this is the *garimpo,* no police here, we look out for ourselves."

"You agree with it!?"

"Of course we don't agree with it. But, what do we do? We want to keep our jobs, some of us done well here...don't wanna wake up dead. It's the owners, it's politics."

"That's right." Caetano said, "Indians have millions of square miles, more than you or I can imagine ever owning...where I come from seven people share a room, three, four families in one apartment. Justice is

330

justice. In Brazil millions of people are hungry. We need *Baixadas* to look out for business interests."

Rand was drunk, too drunk to debate the point and his head swirled, but he stuck out his hand and placed it in the center of the table with a smack. "You only need one thing here," he said, "and that's the rule of law."

"Tell that to Nestor Salinas Machado!" One of the men threw out good naturedly.

"Who?" Rand asked.

"You don't know? He's the man with the big eye! Owns four boat franchises, the one you work on included. Head of the owner's association."

"Ahhh..." said Rand.

"That's right," he nodded importantly, "the man with the big eye!"

The next day two military helicopters landed at the airstrip. He heard them first as the loud deep whooping of their engines echoed down making ripples form on the water. Then Rand saw them from the boat and was puzzled because he didn't think the men from FUNAI would have been able to reach the authorities and start an investigation yet. As it turns out it was something even more improbable. Fernando Lacombe, a well known conservative politician who was campaigning for the presidency accompanied by his entourage and a complete film crew from Tele Globo, one of the largest television networks in the world and arguably the most powerful. Based in Rio de Janero it held captive close to hundred million viewers who depended upon its network programming for their education. Tele Globo gave them the master plan for a modern Brazilian society. They were the teleliterate and on average viewed television more than seven hours a day. It was a medium of tremendous power in Brazil and every politician courted TV because those Tele Globo backed were elected, those they didn't were doomed to a life of obscurity as a minister of some backward powerless bureau. The television signal owned Brazil. *Miçanga* is television, an Indian word for anything that shines. It is jewelry for the mind; sparkling seduction that like the placer deposits of gold is sought after by every segment of society. The controllers and the controlled. The great network was a benefit of the military rule whose hand gripped power in the mid nineteen sixties and funneled public funds into the communication sciences to the detriment of other disciplines because they saw the potential for social control. The junta rode the force, but in the end they too became victims as the signal turned against them and they fell from favor.

Fernando Lacombe landed at the air strip twice. Once with the original helicopter and then again at the request of the film crew for the drama of the visit to the remote Amazon gold fields filled with colorful *garimpeiros* who had assumed the status of folk heroes in the cloistered urban centers. The military did what they were told under orders to extend every courtesy to Lacombe and the film crews, both of whom may be useful in the future and so they landed as many times as necessary to get the shot even to the extent of going up and down long after the presidential candidate had departed just for the perfect light and the perfect angle for the evening news. Suddenly Boca de Lobo was in the spotlight and it was as if Carnival and the World Cup soccer match had both landed there on the very same day. He had brought two vivacious and shapely girls with him who wore tight fitting Lacombe T-shirts and little else. They handed these out and posed with *garimpeiros* and *draga* owners for pictures. The girls kissed everyone. It was a goodwill gesture the politician felt was exactly right for the demographics of the *garimpo* and resulted in crowds of men who had not seen a women in months that followed his every move and thus looked great on TV. The excitement was too much for some and they retreated into their storefronts hopping for the windfall to bring them customers and for others, such as many of the *draga* owners who had advanced notice and chose that day to fly in and collect their gold deposits and hopefully get a moment to speak with the conservative politician with whom most shared views, it was a prodigious occasion. He was pro business, pro industry and pro development, which brought broad smiles to many of their faces after a decade of fighting international interests and liberal administrations that prohibited much of the industrial expansion into the Amazon region and thus condemned their country to the status of a server nation supplying raw materials for products that would be manufactured elsewhere. The country needed power, industry and expanded economic zones in order to develop a true consumer base and so when these men got together there was not the slightest disagreement between them. They were on the same team. Even the dispossessed rallied to his cause and Fernando Lacombe rubbed shoulders with them in the yard where dozens stood awaiting the chance at a job and in fact he picked the spot for an impromptu speech outlining his ten point program to economic revitalization for the country, the largest in South America and the sixth largest economy in the world, he added for the benefit of international viewers. The *garimpeiros* cheered and threw up their hats in a spirited response inspired by the promise that señor Lacombe would be buying cold beer all around as soon as he had concluded his business.

The film crew was having a field day and they shot everything and everybody from every angle imaginable. No stone was left unturned. Fernando Lacombe strutted up and down the wooden sidewalk and met with every store proprietor and praised their entrepreneurial spirit calling it the "...heart of every Brazilian dream." From the boats men watched and some even shut down their relentless diesels stopping the dredges in the hopes that the candidate may chose to board their *draga* and give fame to those who already had riches. And he did board many boats accompanied by their owners grinning broadly to the press to be filmed and shot at every turn and circumstance rifling through his repertoire of short speeches on pertinent subjects in a not quite off the cuff manner.

All of a sudden Rand looked up from the sluice box he was cleaning and saw the politician riding toward his *draga* in a flying boat accompanied by an older, heavyset gray haired man with dark skin and chiseled features. "It's Nestor Salinas Machado," said Ailton, "the big eye with that damn *fascista* Lacombe!" The two men, obviously old friends, clambered aboard followed by a small army of cameramen and sound technicians with equipment.

Rand stood by the sluice box and tried to become innocuous and trembled at the nearness of the *draga* owner, the big eye, whom he suspected was the head of the *Baixadas* from his conversations with other *garimpeiros,* and if so had blood on his hands that Rand waited in reckoning for. There was no other reason for him to stay in Boca de Lobo except to satisfy the purpose that was surging inside him stronger than it ever had before, so much so that he wondered if it was visible. The rule of law. It sparked his life and drove him through the muck and the heat and the despair around him to accomplish his sole purpose, which he was still confused over as to whether it was justice or vengeance. The two were somehow fused in his mind and catalyzed to form an explosive mixture that propelled him foreword with a single minded dedication he was not familiar with. Randall DesVergers was a man hunted by a terrible purpose.

Nestor Salinas Machado showed Fernando Lacombe around the two story *draga* in the way that Rand had shown guests his beautiful sailboat the Sojourner, the one he had purchased in Hong Kong and had paid to have sailed all across the Pacific to his waiting slip. He almost felt ashamed now viewing the spectacle as the men patronized everyone they met talking to them as if they were illiterate puppy dogs. Most of the workingmen on the boat were surly. Their disgust for the rich was hard to kill even though now many of them were amassing sizable amounts of gold dust in the bank themselves. They were of a different nature, and Rand for the first time in his life understood.

Waiting cameramen circled the dredge in their boats getting the long shots, while another set up a tripod on the end of the aft deck and between him and Rand stood the politician and the *draga* owner. He leaned up against the cabin, the deck being too crowded to escape, and settled in for what appeared would be a long, droll speech where Lacombe would define his promises to the working classes, who ultimately controlled elections no matter how much television tried to sell them. The man spoke incessantly while his friend Machado stood patiently next to him basking in the limelight. Every few minutes the blustering man would pull one of the reluctant *garimpeiros* into camera range and try to elicit a smile to emphasize an important political point. It began to appear that the man was slowing down and that the strain of the hot sun was getting to him because he was sweating profusely and wiping his face with a soiled handkerchief. "The problems in the rain forest are the problems of the whole world, but I will never allow foreign intervention, never stop development. Each country must find solutions for their own environmental problems. We have to sit and discuss this with foreign leaders. Contributions and not interference."

Suddenly, he looked around behind him directly at Rand, took three steps back and threw his arm around his shoulder as if they were brothers. "In Brazil," he said, "we have the power to become an economic force. There is room for everybody to succeed and this kind of initiative and expansion is exactly what is going to do it." He concluded with a sincere and confident grin to the camera while Rand was looking at the man's hand dangling over his shoulder that was adorned with a three thousand dollar, bright gold Rolex watch.

Far to the north in Bangor Maine the young executives of LYNX had entrenched themselves in the absolute latest, state-of-the-art technology in an effort to lead their market and fend off competition and takeover threats real or imagined. Every computer and communications device known to be sold was available in their media lab and what software they were not beta testers for they bootlegged from crackers or if need be even bought. Automation was still the object, possibly the elimination of the human being completely from the work force leaving a ghost like planet inhabited by time and labor saving devices while men winnowed away their years as slaves to their own memories of productive lives. There were laptops and tablets and desktops and every other sort of computer all networked and linked with networks and interactive programming secured by dozens of encryption technologies and firewalls at every juncture. The whole place was a bastion of technological paranoia.

Every major television network on earth was received via satellite and automatically recorded digitally and stored for a period of forty-eight hours. Voice recognition and facial feature recognition software was employed to track known personalities as electronic bloodhounds.

Samples of their actual voice prints and facial features were fed into a digital audio visual database which was scanned through constantly at thirty thousand passes per minute to find matches for any of the list of people that LYNX officials deemed it necessary to track. Each of the principles was convinced that they needed to know nearly everything and paid no attention to the wisdom divined by Lao Tzu four thousand years ago who noted that between earth and sky is an inexhaustible source of information and the more it produces the more it generates, it was best, he thought, to be in the middle, to prevent exhaustion. Data overload was not new, but perhaps that was the reason these men began acting so strangely

All of them, including Derian Baxter, were under thirty and with the help of an investment banker had managed to fund their small company through free spending, high-tech investors seeking to capitalize on the continued success of tech companies. They had yet to turn a profit however, and were beginning to feel the burden of their indebtedness because the funding promised by ISC and being organized by Van Riper, Hazeltine & Brock had still not materialized. The moves by Veronique to circumvent them completely and undermine their public offering buying them out and eliminating their personal stakes in the potentially multi-billion dollar technology, of which their contribution was an integral part, had caused Bax to take matters into his own hands out of desperation. He would not allow their dream to be stolen. So it was that the news broadcast from Tele Globo was dutifully scanned and accurate voice and image recognition was made and logged of the backcountry campaign swing of Fernando Lacombe into an obscure Amazonian gold rush town named Boca de Lobo.

When the technician arrived for work that morning the first thing he checked was the electronic log and when he saw the name Randall DesVergers, traced it to its source, pulled up the digital footage and saved it to disk making hard copy of some good likenesses in the process. When he had everything he needed he walked, gloating over his technical prowess, to the executive offices at LYNX.

Bax and two other young executives shared one office. They prided themselves on a paperless office and proudly advertised the fact that they were doing their part to save the rain forest. On the wall was an eight-foot liquid plasma television display, which was only three quarters of an inch thick.

"Have you ever heard of Boca de Lobo?" The young technician asked. None of the three had any idea what he was talking about and were impatient with the interruption. "The Wolf's Mouth." He said. "A gold rush camp in Brazil. Let me show you what I found there." And he proceeded to run the digital video and the huge wall display lit up with the image of the draga from the end of the aft deck and the politician Fernando Lacombe speaking in Portuguese about the economic future of Brazil under his astute leadership.

"So what?" One said.

"Do you recognize anyone?"

They all looked carefully thinking at first that he was referring to the politician or the gray haired man next to him, but then, after a moment, it dawned on all three at the same instant, being so electronically connected they often thought the same thoughts at the same time a circumstance they called creativity.

"Jesus Christ!" Derian Baxter exclaimed, "I thought he was dead!"

"Look at that, he's got his arm around him. What are they saying? Is it a rescue?"

"No...no...doesn't look that way. See...he's leaving, the gray haired man too. DesVergers is still there! He's working!?"

"I'll be dammed!"

"He's still alive!"

"Where is this place?"

The technician smiled having anticipated their questions and had pulled up maps and topographic charts from the internet to show. "It's about two hundred and fifty miles from Manaus in the Amazon on a branch of a tributary called the Rio Madiera. It's accessible only by air or boat."

They watched the segment over and over and soon an idea was forming in all three minds at exactly the same time. "Thank you," Bax said to the technician, "We'll let you know if we need anything else." After the man had left the room the three principles of LYNX conferred about the recent development and how it would affect the upstart take-over plan revolving around their initial stock offering that they thought was a dead issue with the apparent demise of Randall DesVergers.

"This changes everything."

"It doesn't have to." Bax replied after an appropriate pause.

"Meaning...?"

"Nobody else knows he's alive."

"So...?"

"So...he doesn't have to be alive."

"You don't mean?"

"Exactly."

"But how...I'm not going down there."

"Don't be stupid. We'll find a freelancer."

"Oh right...how? Employment agency?"

"Mercenary Magazine."

"What's that?"

"Yea! Yea! I remember that! Didn't somebody go to prison last year for hiring a guy from the classifieds to kill his wife?"

"That's it."

"Pretty out there."

"No one's going to prison for a killing in the backwoods of the Amazon."

"Look!" Baxter was losing his composure, "There's one thing I'm telling you both, we have a lot to loose. Either we become billionaires or are in debt the rest of our lives. Not much of a choice to me."

"Well...if that's the way you put it..."

"How do we start something like this"

"I suggest a purchase order."

And so a funding request was duly submitted to accounting, all expenditures had to be accurately logged and tracked so their books would be in perfect order at the time they went public. It listed promotional expenses as the nature of the purchase and put down the amount of the figure at forty five thousand dollars plus another ten for incidentals. The accountant asked them to please keep all receipts and turn them in to him before the end of the quarter. They said they would.

It took them less than a week to find their man. He had taken out an obscure ad in the magazine's classified that was small and inconspicuous and because of this the LYNX executives decided he was the most professional. They met at a restaurant in Mobile Alabama where Derian Baxter had flown taking the precaution of dying his hair a deep red with a wash-out coloring he had found at a drug store and of wearing thick rimmed, dark sports glasses. He bought special clothing for the occasion and dressed in a way in which he wouldn't be caught dead normally hoping that if worse came to worse he would be recalled by witnesses as a nurdy, eccentric who looked younger than he was.

The man who came walking up to him looked nothing like what was expected, he didn't even look dangerous. He was just slightly under six feet, well built and had a very wide, big boned face that sat unexpressively under closely cropped bleach blonde hair the color of slightly pink straw. He had powerful hands one of which had a swastika tattooed on the flap of skin that connected his thumb to his forefinger. He would not give his real name of course and insisted he be called Dirk and opened the proceedings by asking if Bax was a cop, or FBI or in any way represented a law enforcement agency to avoid entrapment if he was being taped through a wire. The man from LYNX said no and agreed to call him Dirk. The man outlined his credentials in an uninspired, lugubrious and methodical way stating that he had a military background and had spent many years in the police services. In addition he said that he had followed his current line of work for ten years and had never had a complaint. "I'm a crack shot." He said causing Bax to shiver and wish he were back in his office staring at the computer screen. Derian briefed him on the assignment and had brought pictures, maps, charts and airline schedules, private transportation information for the Amazon and a list of inoculations the State Department recommended anyone traveling to the area have first. But could not bring himself to say the word kill and so kept avoiding the direct expression of what he wanted done and only alluded to it, which frustrated Dirk no end being an impatient type to begin with.

"So, you want me to snuff this guy? Is that what I'm hearing here? Is that what you're saying?"

He handed over the complete information packet he had compiled with maps and everything sliding it across the table as if it were infected. "In a word, yes."

"Well, I'm glatt that's settled." He said with a slight German accent.

"We're prepared to pay fifty percent up front."

"Two thirds is standard."

"The standard?"

"Of course, plus expenses."

Bax agreed and arranged to deliver a cashier's check to a post office box in the morning and to deliver the balance on receipt of evidence that Randall DesVergers was dead. The man said he would know how to find him if the balance was not forthcoming, a fact Derian took with a grain of salt, but none the less began worrying about what would happen if the mail got delayed or in some other way the payment got misplaced. He flew home to Bangor Maine that very afternoon and never saw the blonde man again. He was sick on his arrival and spent the next few days secluded in his house trying to wash the red dye out of his hair.

Somebody else had seen the broadcast of Randall DesVergers also. Behind thick, cool walls of his ancestral *fazenda* on the shores of Ipanema beach in Rio de Janero. He remembered the strip of sand forty-five years ago when it was paradise, a desert with fish so big he was afraid to go into the water. Now there were a million people on the beach sometimes. Valdemiro Veloso sat pondering the consequences of his discovery. He had tuned to the evening news just at the tail end of the story, just in time to see the unmistakable image of Randall DesVergers and Fernando Lacombe standing side by side and to hear the location of the report from the campaign swing through Amazonas. *Boca de Lobo,* he repeated to himself sipping from a glass of Argentine merlot. It had shocked him. Later that evening by the open window of his study on the second floor as the pale moonlight flooded the room and the sounds of the small waves came wafting in over the occasional traffic noises he wrote a short, conciliatory note.

"My Dear Friend Tarisco," it began: "Having had much time to consider the gravity of the situation in which my only son, Andrade, has been placed, I find that I cannot entirely blame you. In an effort to rekindle our friendship, which was always one based on mutual trust, I have something you may choose to do for me in order to redeem yourself in my eyes. Please respond directly. With regard, Miro."

The letter was messengered to the post office box number that Tarisco had given in his letter and in three days there was a reply. The once right hand man of Valdemiro Veloso had been hiding out in the *favela* Rocinha, where of course he knew he would be looked for, but relied on his influence with the *favelados* to keep him safe from harm. He was more important here than even Miro himself because of his charity and so he told people he was in hiding, not saying who from leaving it to them to imagine the police. Twenty-three residents had been killed in a massacre carried out by clandestine officers in revenge for the shooting deaths of four of their own by drug traffickers a year or so earlier, so the *favelados* would go to any lengths to foil them and to undermine any efforts they made. Besides, they were his own kind, Bahian, and in Rocinha practically a whole village from Bahia had been transplanted and still showed its roots and were fond of saying "…if we are not yet prosperous, we are at least free." From the hillside, Tarisco could almost run his business as usual. The *pivetes* were thrilled and to them it was like having the Pope in their midst assaying the situation as a prime opportunity to get close to the source of cash and cement their relationship. There was a network that extended out over the whole community and if any stranger ventured past the perimeters everyone would know in minutes from the children at the bottom who would fly kites as signals. Tarisco knew how much risk these people took and so spent lavishly making them all feel worthy and ensuring his welcome. He used his *aviõezinhos* to run numbers for the *Jogo de Bicho* and was almost able to keep up with the volume he had done before, and was even able to peek in on his *escola de samba* on occasion and watch the dance rehearsals, which made him very happy indeed.

When he received the note from Valdemiro Veloso he experienced a tremendous relief as he did not relish the fact of having to hide out his entire life and had not relished making sure that someone went into his apartment every day and watered the plants and fed his cat. When he entered the *fazenda* on Ipanema beach he felt uneasy and though Miro had appeared alone, and was very cordial to him explaining that he wished to settle accounts and to make things right as they had always been between them, Tarisco was glad that he had carried the old .45 caliber Taurus automatic and from time to time during the uncomfortable conversation he fingered it under his coat. He perceived once again Brazil's rigid, unspoken caste system that despite any personal friendships that may develop between employer and employee always put the brown face at the bottom. Few Brazilians could prove they don't have negro blood, it's in the face. If it is white enough, it is white. If it is black...in the *favela* one could forget the suffering. Even the Portuguese were thought of sometimes as a swarthy, lower class European.

"This new governor," Valdemiro complained, "he's ruined the city. Everywhere holes in the streets. Beggars, assaults, everything's decaying. He appeals to young boys who steal watches!" Then he added insultingly, "He's not even Cariocan."

"It's true he is liberal," Tarisco replied politely, "but it is the first time in history the government is not against the people."

"Yes." Miro stated without agreeing. "My maid Fantas, who has been with me for thirty-five years, was riding the bus yesterday and a man came up to her and said, *Give me your ring or I will kill you!* The ring I gave her! Nobody helped. Nobody moved. So she gave him the ring and when he was gone the other passengers got mad at her saying, *Why should we be responsible for you? Everybody knows you can't wear jewelry on buses!* He is ruining the city."

"There is always hope."

"Perhaps."

"I, for instance, have hopes that I can do something for you that will restore me in your eyes, and that is why I have come. In good faith."

Miro got right to the point. "I have called you here because I have something for a man who I trust implicitly. I have always trusted you

Tarisco and that is why I want you to kill someone for me." It was not an unusual request and one that Tarisco had heard before, but this time it seemed unclean as if there was an underlying current of deceit. "He is the man who set up Andrade and I believe him to be responsible." Then he explained it all, excluding the facts surrounding the plane crash making it seem like an accident that the man had miraculously survived, and told how he had seen Randall DesVergers on the television news clip reporting on the politician's campaigning in *Boca de Lobo*. He handed Tarisco an envelope with some cash, a plane ticket and a picture of Rand he had received before his initial visit from the law office as a courtesy so he would recognize the lawyer. "Take this," he said, "There is a direct flight to Manaus tomorrow morning. From there you can take a small plane to the river head, and then it should be an easy run into *Boca de Lobo*."

The voices of the insects at night sometimes rose more fevered than the drone of the diesel pumps dredging for gold. Men were the interlopers here and the forest and the river showed great restraint allowing for their presence, but on occasion, as if wishing to stretch and flex, the natural rhythms ascended to an overwhelming pitch hinting at the power of the wild, which if disturbed enough would strike back with disaster. The earth was a system of checks and balances, it seemed in its symbiosis to regulate itself and not let anything get too out of control. Men were different. They were regulated by conscience and ability, the two not always going together. The Indians knew all of these things, but would never tell an outsider giving them only the non-sacred tales, the ones they could not harm. All great truths were simple and self evident and they felt if one could not see them by himself it did no good to try to point them out.

Rand worked with the others. He got to know them well and observed that some were disturbed by the news of the massacre so close by, but no one did anything. They were afraid for their livelihoods. The current of their lives was dictated by the scarce economies of survival. It became clear to Rand that Nestor Salinas Machado was almost certainly responsible for the atrocities in the forest and the death of Pilar and it was common knowledge, he discovered to his chagrin, that the man literally ran the *Baixadas*, the clandestine death squad that carried out strategic terrorist acts against anyone hampering the forward progress of the mining operations. Even squatters who congregated alongside the roads that developed around the mining community taking the opportunity to clear some land and try to grow something were run off if the land was needed for something else—or killed. All of it was tacitly supported by corrupt officials or outright by laws or lack of them allowing for the control of the area to be usurped by the large mining concerns edging out the independents and the Indians alike. It was business, nothing more.

He circled the table at the bar in the Hotel Flutuante and had been discussing serious issues all night. Rand was subtly trying to incite them to something that he was not even sure of himself as his purpose fumed inside him.

"When I was a boy," Ailton related, "which was not so very long ago, in São Paulo, the police would sweep through the streets every night and collect up homeless children, drag us down to the stations and beat us to make us confess to crimes we didn't commit. Then they would release us because they couldn't afford to keep us locked up. They say the police kill one child a day in São Paulo. So, there I was a *cativo*—a slave, here I am free."

Rand nodded his head earnestly trying to duplicate the viewpoints of these men, which he knew he could never fully do not being of the same world. "What about the military? The men from FUNAI said they would bring them back and start an investigation." He asked. "What about that?"

"Cheee...you gotta be kidding!" Pixote howled pounding on the table a couple of times as if to symbolize the utter futility of the situation, "they're just marginals!" He said looking straight at Rand, "Criminals run by *marajás*—bureaucrats. They won't do nothin' but cause trouble for us. Military is not a good thing here my friend. Officers change clothes quickly when they are off duty so no one will know, they are no longer proud."

He took a drink of the beer that was now luke warm. "There're courts, lawyers..." he fumbled for a handhold so he himself wouldn't sink into the morass of despair that kept everyone so self centered. "I thought there was a miner's union. What about that?"

"That's right." A man named Pelé pulled out a faded yellow laminated card from his pocket that was bent and frayed. "I'm a member, not everybody is. There are about one thousand members up and down the river."

"Can't they do something?" Rand asked in frustration, "People have been murdered."

"They have a lawyer," the man explained, "He lives in Manaus. Every time they want to send him to Brasilia someone comes around for a collection to cover expenses." And then he shrugged indifferently. "I never hear anything after that."

Caetano pushed his chair back antagonistically. "You want to know who has the lawyers?" He spat on the wood floor. "Landowners. The law is for landowners. You know in Brazil," he said fiercely, "fifty percent of the income is made by ten percent of the people. And they own the land. Ten percent!"

Days passed. From the numbers in Rand's ledger he began to get a feeling for what most of the miners were probably earning and had to tell himself that the cost of living was so much lower that it amounted to something. The truth was he was starting to experience the despair and franticness that enveloped the whole countryside, except when the gold came in and the men could add hash marks to their ledgers. They met every night at the bar on the Hotel Flutuante and their drinking sessions began to turn into debating sessions as the massacre ate at everyone. Except Caetano who was right leaning and was strictly in favor of the *Baixadas* believing that they were a necessary force to ensure the future success and look out for their economic interests and he defended punitive actions against the Indians, who he believed were hoarding lands that should be open to all Brazilians. Others, such as Pixote, were morally opposed, but afraid to say much for fear they would loose their hard won positions in life, positions for which there were no alternatives. Rand began to realize that it was all dependent on money, that everything relied on it and that no matter how true the ideals, that didn't buy food and a man could come and pass on so rapidly that he wouldn't even be noticed in the rain forest where nature and men conspired in relentless opposition never letting up for long. He wondered where law fit into it all. He began to ponder what he could really do and if he had made a big mistake by not leaving with the men from FUNAI.

"It's a rich man's game," Pixote exclaimed, "this law you're always talking about. I went to a lawyer once with a small matter of a debt that was in dispute. 'Oh,' he said, 'this is very interesting.' He looked over the matter and discussed it with me amiably. Then he said, 'This could get very expensive you know.' And he gave me a figure one third more that the amount in dispute. I'll never forget the look on his face when he explained to me how much per hour he would charge, a sort of wild glee that rippled over him and made him giddy. It was no use talking after that he was so puffed up and full of himself. He asked more per hour than I could make in a week! The law has nothing to do with people my friend."

"No, no..." Rand insisted the concept violating every illusion, "the law evolved out of the standards of a community. It is people. Common law, it's how people can live together...like...like, you don't steal from the *draga* because it supports you. Common sense."

A small powerful man named Neilson spoke in a measured voice. "You'll have to explain that to us I think. Money changes it all. No common sense in money, no reason...where you get it, how you find it or where it's spent. It doesn't depend on how much you do, or how good what you do is for people, it's who's got the best scam, the best con, can sell it best! Speculators, bankers, land owners...its not people. If you've got it you're legal, if not...?"

"Maybe so..." Rand countered, "Maybe, doesn't have to be...law reflects the tolerance of the community, how much you stand for before you do something? Where the line is drawn."

"Some draw the line, some cross it. We don't need to do nothin'!" Caetano stated sloppily being half drunk. "that's what the *Baixadas* are for, that's the law."

"Some draw the line in the sand."

"Anarchy!" Rand blurted out. "It's arbitrary. Do you think that someone with enough force has the right to do anything?"

"Maybe."

"Sure!" Frustrated and red faced. "Absolutely!"

"You got balls for rich people! *Norte Americanos*! You all drive cars and live in houses up there. Here, food is scarce. In Manaus, a huge city in the middle of the Amazon surrounded by water, malaria runs crazy because only ten percent are connected to the sewer system and drinking from faucets is polluted. Here, the wettest place in the world and people can't get fresh water to drink."

Rand didn't speak to anyone for two whole days. He was certain he'd made a mistake in staying on and cursed himself as a fool, had underestimated the grip with which poverty had strangled any ideals out of these men, if they ever had them to begin with, and perceived himself as a failure in motivating them. They were either scrambling for subsistence, or having established a niche in which they could survive, grappling to keep from sliding back down into oblivion. Shell shocked from a life on the edge. He thought about this while ringing mercury through his fingers watching the chrome like ooze dribble down into the river through the cracks in the floorboards of the *draga*.

He had not thought about sex since Veronique. Women, he mused, drew the line. These men had nothing to loose because the standards were lower than what made life worth living. Perhaps that was where he had arrived starting with the moment he looked back and saw his friend Utitiaja being cut down as if he was not even a man, not a plant or anything living. It was a point beyond which he could not go on living. It haunted his nights and would not give him rest. The scent of Pilar lingered also, her voice, the endless trespass of her eyes.

On a hot night he once again sat at the round table filled with water marks made by unknown glasses with Pixote and the men from the *dragas*. There were more men drawn by the talk, the controversy and the life, which was generated by the questions Rand tossed at everyone that caused uproarious, yet good natured, arguments. They were questions many of them could not answer with their inner voices, though they had plenty to say on the subject. Each was somehow being challenged by something that transcended the physical and it riveted them while frustrating their efforts to remain in control of the situation. Some hated him and were disgusted by his gringo ideas that had no bearing, absolutely no relevance to their lives as *riberirinhos* living in the shadow of the mists. To these men it was a question of numbers, there were more of them than of him. But even they were hooked by the ongoing debate.

"Not here you don't," argued Jorge, a robust man of the age where courage fails in the Amazon. He had the gray streaks in his hair as medals from his many battles. "No rule of law here, that's for somewhere else. You must be mistaken."

"Yea...well...there is 'no somewhere else'! Maybe that's the point! There's only right here, right now! This is it! This is all there is! Men shape their lives by what they're willing to accept! You guys accept mass murder to increase your bank accounts?"

"Aww...come on!" There was a rumble of disapproval as if he had suddenly gotten serious when they were all enjoying themselves so much.

"Christ!"

"Ahhh..."

"Well...now...I wouldn't go that far..." Pixote tried to restore the feeling, "that's a bit unfair my friend."

"Shit! He's a gringo!" Caetano declared with a sneer. "What the hell does he know? *Pistolãos* always been here! There's been close to a thousand deaths connected with land reform in the past five-ten years. Know how many went to trial my soft headed friend...?" he looked around at the large group circling the table shrouded in cigarette and cigar smoke with wide, agitated eyes, "Two."

"That's right, government didn't do nothin' until priests and nuns started getting shot!"

"So..." Rand forced his view, "you gonna wait till then?"

"Hell man... what you want us to do?"

"Yea for saint's sake? You gotta lotta steam, hot under the collar I think! You're just vacationing. Why don't you rub up with one of Pixote's girls?" Neilson gestured to the bar where a *caboclo* girl stood listening. She pulled her T-shirt up half way exposing her breasts and made an obscene gesture. "You don't need this work, what's your problem? We don't have no law here. We don't need your stinkin' law!"

"The law gentlemen," he paused gracefully and rose as if to give stature to his words feeling euphoric, "is in the mind." Randall DesVergers stood and faced the table as if addressing a jury, standing at full height, which was a struggle because he was tired, very tired from the day's labor and light headed from the beer, and placing his finger tips on the tabletop. "My problem is your problem. The rule of law is a man's last stand. When he has nowhere else to go. There's always someone more powerful...someone bigger, tougher... It's not something you have to go and get, it's part of you, a mysterious, ethical essence of each of your personalities whether you want it or not. You know it, I didn't make it up, I never wanted it to be that way... Ever felt a sense of justice? A sense of what's right and what's wrong? No one had to tell you, correct? Just know what's right, what's wrong. Don't need someone to tell you that. Only a fool needs someone to tell him that, a fool and a crazy man."

"Then what are you doing?"

"Just reminding you."

They came later than night on silent practiced feet as Rand lay on his back in the room he shared with Ailton listening to the man breathe heavily with sleep. The rain had let up an hour ago yet he could still hear it falling from the canopy of the forest where it took a half a day sometimes for the water to reach the earth after it ceased falling. It reminded him of being on a ship over some dark sea far out a great distance from land where the fish and the birds met on the horizon at the point the water touched the sky. A low, rumbling tone came over him and he imagined it to be a foghorn. The hover of light from the night operations down on the river drifted through slats in the blinds over the window and reflected dimly off the sheen of perspiration covering his entire body as he lay in the heat and darkness.

Wood shattered with a vicious, reverberating crash as the flimsy door was violently kicked in from the outside sending splinters everywhere. Alarm shrieked in his ears as five black shapes burst into the room and grabbed Rand lifting him like a bag of chaff from the bed. Ailton screamed and jumped straight up only to be grabbed mid flight and flung savagely through the shutters splintering them into thousands of pieces to the sidewalk outside where he landed sprawled on his back. Blood gushed from his head and ran down into the wet mud as he lie unconscious. Two men took hold of Rand's ankles and ran dragging him out the door bouncing along the rough wood floor. They took him down the rustic steps where his head bounded off each one like a cement basketball. He struggled desperately to grab at them, but was being pulled too fast finally being flung into the mud of the street where he slid to a stop. There he was held up by callused, gripping hands on both sides and savagely beaten. His face was pounded by blow after blow until he was absolutely certain it would break from the concussions and this was alternated with a pummeling of the stomach that was so violent it made him vomit and wretch for breath. He tried to scream only to have a dank, smelly hand cover his mouth and nose so that he could not breathe and then they hacked at his kidneys. When he was dropped to the wet, slimy ground they all took turns kicking him as if he was a scapegoat for the frustrations and rage of all the desperate men on the river.

Then it was silent. A man leaned down and put his index finger to Rand's lips and said, "Don't speak."

Both men lay unconscious until morning Ailton coming to first and seeing Rand fetched help. The fact that no bones were broken and apparently no internal damage had been done was attributed to the large amount of alcohol Rand had consumed the night before. He had been simply too drunk to stiffen up and so, while brutally painful, the attack did no permanent damage other than a couple of loose teeth.

"Jesus Christ your nose isn't even broken." Pixote exclaimed as he cleaned Rand up, washed mud and dirt from his cuts and poked and probed for busted parts. He had been taken to the Hotel Flutuante and Pixote brought him to the galley of the restaurant. Soon others heard about the incident and many from the round table debates appeared over Pixote's shoulder inquiring about the health of the gringo, whom they all liked despite being argumentative. After a while Rand came around completely and was given a whiskey to drink. The men continued to gather like the festering conscience of one with a secret crime and sat there, crowding the kitchen saying nothing. None of them left even though the sun was rising and they were expected on the dragas. It was as if the *Norte Americano* had posed another question to them and they were pondering it in their minds, weighing the value of the choices they had made and wondering if it was worth the price.

In the long run the beating was a mistake. It was as if they had all been beaten, and Brazilians did not respond well under too much duress. The military had found that out after they came to power in the nineteen sixties and were eventually toppled by popular sentiment. It was the same blood that flowed through them that flowed through the black slaves of the seventeenth century who, fleeing captivity almost as soon as they were set ashore, founded a clandestine nation called *Palmares* of which they would sing, "*Folga nego, Branco não vem ca*– Rest, black man, the white man doesn't come here. If he does, the devil will take him." Into the Amazon runaways established *quilombos*–secret villages protected by man traps and jaguars that no white man was ever able to find, or if they did was not allowed to live to tell the tale, where they thrived in isolation for hundreds of years. It was the same blood that sent penniless immigrants into the Rondônian wilderness in wave after wave, bus load after busload, over a million people following the one straight road through the trees that an observer likened to a string stretched straight across a field of grass. The *bandeirantes*–pioneers. The same blood as that of the Indian who had lived in a delicate balance for forty or more thousand years before the Europeans arrived. It was the blood of a nation who in one joyful, racially symphonic movement raced toward the future and believed that the remedy for man is man.

After a while Pixote asked, "What do you want us to do?"

"We will establish a rule of law." Rand replied softly without even taking a moment to consider his answer.

"How will we do that my friend?" He responded apathetically.

"We will arrest Nestor Salinas Machado."

A hum of voices filled the kitchen accompanied by the stirring of mens' feet.

"That will do no good," Pixote replied in exasperation, "we have no one to turn him over to."

"We will try him by a jury of *garimpeiros,*" he continued with some difficulty because of the swelling of his mouth ignoring the comment all together, "and if found guilty pass and carry out the sentence. I will preside over the proceeding, but only as a legal guide to keep it within the confines of established rules, only because I am the one who has particular knowledge…I can't trust myself to judge him…but you…you will prosecute and defend the man by the rules of your own lives. You will decide, not me, his guilt or innocence and his punishment. That is, if you are…men enough," he gave them all a fed up look of appeal made stronger by his beaten, swollen face, "and all that sweat is not just for showing off to Pixote's girls."

"You ask a lot my friend."

"I challenge you all to prove you are not accomplices in the eyes of God!"

"Why, why do you?"

"Because law, by its nature, is of people, part of our essence. It has nothing to do with money. It has nothing to do with owning land. If a vested interest is holding the truth out of reach of the majority, then you must take it back! You must! It is your duty. It belongs to those who use it. It has to do with what is right. Your access to law is your access to your own consciences."

A Spirit Obscured By Clouds

XVIII

The silver seaplane appeared in the sky like a brilliant drop of mercury radiating in the sun. Two times it passed over the canyon of the river and each time the sound of its engines echoed from amongst the trees sending birds into the wind. On the third pass it dropped down and lit upon the water showering out graceful filigrees of spray that danced across the polished surface of the swiftly flowing current leaving beads to fall in the heart of perfect concentric circles. The chariot slowed in the backflow of its own wake and with its nose raked somewhat higher than its tail it plowed a way over to the docks beyond the boat yard where men without a history stood in hope.

The *mestiço* was an unassuming and plainly dressed man and took a room in one of the least shabby guesthouses along the street, a room that overlooked the river and had two windows. He paid cash in advance for both his and the pilots quarters, for Tarisco Sivuca could not afford to depend on the vagaries of gold plane flights and would not wait on a steel flying boat so had chartered a cowboy's plane and slipped him enough money so that he could be relied upon to spirit them away at any given instant. He told anyone that inquired that he was a *draga* owner and was scouting prospective mining locations, not wishing to draw attention or inspire enmity by unfriendliness, a story that was completely plausible and did not raise one eye to his comings and goings. In fact it afforded him more courtesy than he would have received otherwise because investors were the lifeblood of the region. Everyone profited from speculation. He looked over the *garimpo* and sighed with the keen confront of someone who had their roots and

353

flourished deep in the culture of the men who wandered the site. He knew what it was like without prospects, had intimate knowledge and saw the landscape not as a dank, torn up shredded sector of jungle waterway as Randall DesVergers had where despair lived along side of affluence, the greedy and the trod upon, but as a foothold in the land in which every native Brazilian held complete faith would eventually be his savior from a life of poverty such as his ancestors had lived. Being in the heart of it made him feel complete, feel a part of the whole evolution of the country.

Tarisco immediately made his routine evident in order to blend in as quickly as possible and fade from view like all the other elements of the environment, which were taken for granted every day without thought by everyone. He rented a small aluminum boat with an outboard motor and made regular runs up the river being steered by his pilot on the pretext of looking for dredge sites, but in actuality was simply enjoying the dense wonder of the rain forest and even landed the boat on several occasions to hike along the shore and so especially get the feel of the majestic jungle. The old Taurus .45 hung heavily at his side in a military style, ballistic nylon black holster with a flap that had a quick release on it and he was reassured by the fact that it was not unusual in the least in the Amazon. He might have looked odd without a gun. He had used it once near Manaus to kill a *jararaca* that he estimated to be at least nine feet long, though he was told they never reached more than eight. One drop of its venom could kill a man in seconds. An Indian had cooked it for him and he found the meat delicious and so had developed a taste for the delicacies not found in any other region. He became a regular at the restaurant in the Hotel Flutuante dining on such fried fish morsels as *tambaqui, pirarucu, tucunaré* and *jaraqui* rarely sampled outside Amazonas. The Indians were the real experts in rain forest management, he mused remembering the video clip where he had seen Fernando Lacombe spout off about wilderness policies, why didn't they consult them? They had been managing it for thousands of years. He thought of the fact that the forest was being destroyed at a rate of something like twenty thousand square kilometers a year, a fact that had been driven home to him one evening when he had seen the thousands of slash and burn fires transmitted by the infrared sensors of satellites on television that lit up the night sky like cities of lights. Brazilians were connected to their land in a strange and undeniable manner that caused them to grieve with pain whenever its promise was blunted, for the landless majority of which he, Tarisco was a proud member, the land was the reason for the country's inexplicable optimism.

The restaurant at the Hotel Flutuante was also where he first saw Randall DesVergers. He recognized the face immediately, even though the man was much more gaunt now, his hair was longer and less well kept and his eyes seemed to blister with a discernible obstinacy not present in the photos and that he could only recall seeing in classical musicians. Conceivably, he thought, it was the little feats in each profession that resulted in the overall triumph that brought on the constant persistence he noticed. But what, he wondered, would a slippery lawyer have to be obstinate about in the Amazon gold fields? He resolved to find out because Tarisco Sivuca possessed two qualities that were intrinsically incongruous with his chosen profession, a sense of social justice and a deep, burning curiosity that caused him to always inspect things before he acted.

Two days following the arrival of Tarisco another plane landed at the airstrip outside of town carrying another passenger. His large head bounced with the rough landing and his teeth chattered as the Cessna bounded over the rough terrain filled with gopher holes, ant hills, roots and undergrowth that couldn't be suppressed no matter how many airplanes came and went. There was an old, yellow oxidized tanker truck at the end of the field with a plow attachment on one end and spray nozzles at the other that had been shipped up river two years earlier. The pilots had futilely hired a down-on-his-luck *garimpeiro* to keep the plant life plowed and bury the animal holes, then to spray oil over the whole field in order to discourage growth. Unfortunately, they regularly had to hire new caretakers discovering that down-on-their-luck men were that way for a reason and consequently the landing field always verged on the edge of impending disaster. The stocky man grasped the door jam of the small plane pulling himself up out of the seat where he had been sitting for five and a half hours. He had close cropped bleach blonde hair the color of slightly pink straw that was not at all out of place in a region where the mulatto population had the corner on unusual hair colors. On the flap of skin that connected the thumb of his left hand with the index finger was a small swastika.

He had decided to change his name again on the slim possibility that his conversation may have been recorded and so assumed the name Berg imagining that it suited his personality. When the pilot had casually, in passing, asked why he wanted to go to such an out of the way place as *Boca de Lobo*, Berg told him that he worked for a pharmaceutical company and he was going to photograph samples of the flora and fauna and to please be careful with the ribbed aluminum case because it contained camera gear. He told the man at the guesthouse that he was a geologist from São Paulo and that the company had sent him there knowing that the German community in the south would lend credibility to his story. Neither man cared or remembered. In *The Wolf's Mouth* there were no questions asked.

Berg was not prepared for what he found even though he had made trips to Mexico and again to Central America during covert military operations of which he was a part, those places were nothing like this. The redolence in the environment was overwhelming and it all had a sickly sweet humus odor of living, breathing and rotting things. It made his skin crawl. The air was moist with decay. He sampled the food with caution careful not to drink any water he had not dropped his disinfectant tablet into or boiled and had tried *cachaça*, sugar cane liquor, and *cupuaçu,* a fruit with the consistency of raw egg both of which made him nauseous. He took quinine out of a dreadful fear of malaria and had a complete battery of shots before he left from yellow fever to specific strains of influenza. On top of that he took vitamins, hands full every day in order to keep his resistance up. But the most disturbing part of the whole experience was all the swarthy people. He was not a racist, did not necessarily feel his European ancestry gave him any superiority and did not consider himself prejudicial towards colored people for one minute, it was just that he felt more comfortable around white people, those more closely associated with his own background. It was a cultural thing he had decided and thought it was ironic that he had come to kill a white man when there was so many of them around. They seemed to infest the earth. One would never be missed, and besides, he considered, they bred like animals and had no respect for the consequences of their lust. Even feeling as he did about the tremendous racial variety that was Brazil and was especially magnified in the Amazon he was compelled toward the girls at Pixote's bar, which he had gone to the first night after surveying the bleak little settlement and realizing that the restaurant at the Hotel Flutuante was the only option for food. He drank sparingly, but when he did it was hard liquor.

On the second night that he began to notice them. Two Indian girls who worked for Pixote and sat at the end of the bar talking between themselves. They were short and had broad, but small stocky bodies with spindly legs and round tummies. Their faces, however, he found beautiful, astonishingly so and he wondered if it was just because of the filth and disorder of the place that he saw them that way. Each possessed the broad, calm look of the Amazon; high, wide cheekbones, a small flat nose and the softest eyes he had ever seen that had a languid, tranquil, exotic look in them. The mirage of the two dissolved all his concerns as if merely smoke and drove him crazy. He caressed their coffee colored skin, which he found flawless and blemish free, with his eyes wondering what they were like in the sack and despite his moral misgivings he finally walked over to them and haltingly tried to start a conversation. Neither one spoke English, and from the sound of their words not much Portuguese either. Each smiled vulnerably with a twinkle and close up he watched their small breasts move beneath the thin, revealing dresses and was driven with a nervous desire to possess them little realizing that they had spent the bulk of their lives completely naked except for a thin string of gut that they tied around their waist. And so he spent the second night in the Amazon in the upstairs room over the bar that Pixote reserved for his girls grunting and sweating like a pig in the dank, humid air over the two, small Indian women that secretly laughed at all the hair on his body and wondered what he was making such a fuss over. After all, it was only sex.

It was when he descended the narrow wooden stairs that morning that he first glimpsed Randall DesVergers sitting at a table eating and taking with Pixote, the proprietor he had met the night before while negotiating for the girls. Berg flushed a bright red that flared all the way up under his blonde roots as if having been caught with his pants down and could not reconcile the fact of his moral depravation and the professionalism with which he carried out his assignments and so slipped from the bar out the side door in infamy to keep from being seen. Even if he was going to kill the man he did not want the embarrassment of his sexual peccadilloes being found out. From that moment on he was obsessed as to whether Rand had seen him or not and whether he knew what had gone on the night before up in the room over the bar with the two Indian girls. He felt suddenly separate from the man and knew that it would be easier to do what he had to do now, so continued to feed the fire making up excuses in his head for his behavior. The following night he went back to the two Indian women and made love to them one after the other and then both at once to prove to himself that it wasn't a wrong thing, that it was perfectly alright and natural. He decided he would need time to scout out the exact moment and location to execute his mission and so settled into a routine.

Berg did not take excessive notice of the environment. It was like a wall of heat and moisture and unimaginable forest to him. It seemed in some obscure way to pose a threat to his perception of himself as the preeminent life form and he dreamt of the region full of cities and express highways with the trees cut back into little abandoned clumps to make way for the coming storm of people.

The men did not meet in the open anymore. They were afraid. None of them wanted dark figures to burst into their rooms late at night and drag them away to become one of the disappeared. Each considered the white man to be extremely fortunate and attributed the fact that he was not killed to his skin color. A *mestiço* would not be so lucky. Most had at least once in their lives an encounter with the mystery, the enigma of vanished men. Jorge, who as a child had lived in the boarder region where the war raged between the ranchers, the landless poor, the drug runners and the military could remember vividly walking along roads and discovering corpses. Once he awoke in the night to the sounds of a grown man screaming. It was the father of the family who lived close by. He peered out the window just in time to see obscure figures dragging him off. The man was never seen again. Jorge had become inured to the occurrence of men disappearing for that was something all too common, but he never forgot the sound of a grown man screaming. Never.

Rand slowly recovered from his beating and every man he passed he tried to see from their eyes if they were the one. Pixote, in between his duties as hotelier and brothel keeper, had become the go between because he had assumed the burden of guilt just as the Fathers had always instructed him was the way of the Church, but this time it had come on its own and he did not have to consciously think about the fact of doing it as he usually did. For this reason he was immeasurably moved and feared above all that in the final reckoning he would be judged an accomplice. On a night when he had not even been drinking he went so far as to consider it was worth giving his life for. Every man has a line, he thought, only with some it had become obscure. He would sit at the round table with Randall DesVergers and talk amiably appearing to the casual eye that he was consoling the gringo and took pity on him for being so ignorant in the ways of the *garimpo*. What no one guessed was that arrangements were being made. Pixote had singled out at least thirty men who, like him, had become stricken with guilt and pledged an allegiance to the Holy Spirit with him resurrecting their Catholic upbringing and bristling with moral fiber. Pixote was proud, suddenly filled with pride that he lived among such men.

One eye was not casual. His was trained for detail and practiced in the art of trickery. By the time he was ten years old he was a past master. No one could fool him for long. He was an orphan of the streets.

Tarisco Sivuca observed with keen interest and followed every stealth like movement the men made. He was piqued to the extreme allowing his curiosity to overpower even his purpose for traveling to *Boca de Lobo* and the desire to redeem himself with Valdemiro Veloso. It was obvious to him that Pixote had taken it upon himself to be the conduit through which the intentions of the slippery lawyer were carried out. What they might be, he had know way of knowing, but was determined to ferret out because he could not imagine a man who had betrayed Miro and himself so openly, so brazenly, with such absence of conscience to be up to anything except another devious plan. Perhaps he would bring about his own end, Tarisco thought suddenly delighted, and he could leave with a clear conscience.

Each day he managed to covertly follow Pixote and eventually decided that there were about thirty men involved in the operation and he began to speculate if they were designing to rob a *draga,* an easy if not rudimentary job for any reasonably adept *pivete* since the gold was kept on board for days at a time before it was taken to the air strip and winged back to civilization and an impenetrable safe. This was the obvious, it could be nothing else...the man was stranded and could not escape without money. He could not contact his associates for help because he knew there would be reprisals for his betrayal, and accomplices among the transient and disenfranchised would be easy. And, on further consideration, he decided they were not going to rob a draga after all, but a gold flight and in order to test his theory he began to stake out the landing field and watch for any of the men he had seen with Pixote.

One evening just at dusk as he was about to give it up and head back to the Hotel Flutuante for a platter of fried fish and manioc he saw them. Five men, Pixote, the lawyer and three others, walking. They skirted the edge of the field as if measuring out steps and then disappeared into the forest. Tarisco followed and only by keeping very quiet and making no extraneous sounds other than his breathing did he catch up to them. The murmur of voices carried through the dense landscape indistinctly and obfuscated the direction from which they had come. It was their carelessness, the snapping of branches as men bent them back to pass and the stumble of their feet through the humus underneath that gave them away. For close to an hour they walked through the darkening forest causing Tarisco to ponder how they would get back, never once thinking of himself, imaging the creatures that came out with the fading light to hunt. He gripped his Taurus automatic. Soon they came to a clearing where there were other men. A fire blazed in its center. Shadows danced. High in the wall of jungle lighted eyes peered down at the interlopers.

Some of the rain forest meadow had been cleared by machete and a shelter had been erected at the end consisting of a lean-to frame of woven vines covered with elephantine leaves some five and six feet long over a log. It was beneath this harborage they sat. Tarisco got as near as he dared, which was not close enough to hear much of what they said because if he tried to circle the clearing and come up behind them he would be betrayed by the noise he would make and so had to content himself with where he was. There he sat on the moist decay beneath foliage and ferns and huge leafy plants. His cheek was pressed against the wet trunk of a tree that he could not see the top of. Through the canopy hovering far above he could witness the twilight sky and the first stars as they twinkled through the boughs. It would not rain tonight. He was lucky.

"I won't!" Exclaimed Caetano, the strong man Tarisco observed sitting between Pixote and the lawyer. But he couldn't make out what was said next.

"You've got to." Replied Rand measuredly out of earshot of the listening man. "More than anyone you represent his point of view."

"That doesn't have shit to do with anything."

Rand felt defeated inside. How could it ever work. It was implausible. "All men have a right to a voice." He replied redoubling his resolve. "It's a debate you see, it's not a judgment, that's for the moon and stars and God. This is a conversation that is required if justice is ever to be approached."

"We know he's guilty."

"There are degrees. Think of the world as a cauldron filled with millions of voices all trying to be heard. In my country democracy demands that each voice be listened to, this is not absolute... ts nego-tiating fairness. You must discuss the principles by which you live in regard to those things people do...you must damn it!"

He was haunted by one flaw in his plan. It raised the specter of a lynching and he remembered how incensed with disbelief he had been when as a law student he had studied the fact that Congress in its seat of moral judgment having been required by the people to represent their wishes would not pass a law condemning lynching as illegal during the years up to and through the second world war because the President and the New Dealers needed the Southern vote to railroad through their social programs. It was nineteen sixty-eight before it was finally outlawed by Federal law. In Brazil slavery flourished until close to the turn of the century and in the major cities carriages were advertised for sale, with their drivers. Perhaps there was no such thing as impartiality, he thought in a flounder at the collision between his ideals and reality, how could a man be truly impartial, he knows what he knows.

"We attempt impartiality." He said to the man. "Like all things in a democracy it is a common denominator of what is believed to be the right thing, and not necessarily exactly the right thing."

"OK." Said Caetano resigned and not seeing any way out of it. "OK. I can tell you what he believes. I can tell you because behind me are millions like me...hungry...without anything and no where to go. If there's nothing to eat, what do you eat? The world has to accommodate us. We are living!"

"Good." Rand answered nodding his head continually. "I under-stand. Good." He said truly pleased that Caetano was in the spirit of it now whether he grasped the subtleties of legal thinking or not.

"I will speak against him." Pixote blurted out bluntly.

"You?"

"Yes." He replied. "I have decided." And no further word was spoken on the subject. It was, after all, not up to Rand to determine these things. He had assumed the role of catalyst and knew he must allow the reactions to run their course autonomously. Perhaps that alone was impartiality. It was crazy and he knew it. Crazy and reckless. Conceiv-ably the *Baixadas* would visit him or any one of them again before the scheme reached its critical point, and certainly they would retaliate afterwards. What had he to lose? He could flee the country and return to the life many here could not even in their most fanciful dreams imagine. But these men would be ruined even if they were denied work let alone pulled from their sleep and killed. There was no cushion. One week, two weeks and then oblivion. It had always been the way that the rule of money had enslaved people. As if it intrinsically made a man weak like a domestic animal who forgets to hunt to forage to find his own food and becomes completely dependent, never leaving the preadolescent state and reaching self reliance. It was a conception of life that he, for the first time, was glimpsing. Here there was no economic juggernaut and he knew that it reflected much of the world outside of the Western block. Even the free wheeling *sertanistas* of Rondônia who homesteaded on land that was free for the price of working it usually sold out within the first year for cash to the large corporate farms and ranches. Like the Amazon the soil was shallow and sandy and though it supported the superficial root system of the trees and other jungle foliage, which was nourished by the thick layer of decaying organic matter that disappeared with the absence of forest, it would not maintain commercial crops. Corn withered and died or did not bear fruit.

The adventurous highways into the rain forests that the military government had inspired were littered with abandoned cabins from those who had come and gone. It forced Rand to think of the whole process as a natural selection where the weak fell aside and the strong usurped everything and set the pace garishly amassing purloined wealth. He thought of nature as a parallel where the food chain comprises the economic building blocks and questioned whether he should just let it go and allow natural selection to work its magic. He imagined bringing a child into the world and christening it with the idea that it was part of the food chain and suddenly the whole concept struck him as completely ludicrous. Of course he couldn't let it go. Why else had it flared up in him and denied him sleep? Men weren't meat, they weren't condemned to any given course. There were many things worth giving one's life for, he now considered, many lines never to be crossed. And as he had these thoughts, which came like little bursts of energy, he could not believe he was living them at last after all the years and he realized that life slips away from one so easily with compromise.

The men beckoned him, telling him they were leaving now and returning to *Boca de Lobo*, and he followed with resolve. Tarisco followed too now more convinced than ever that the men were planning to knock over a gold flight. He tracked with stealth their waving flashlights as quietly as possible through the darkness tripping and stumbling and bumping into all manner of wet, slimy things.

Everyday he watched the airstrip. Haunted its perimeter. He told his pilot to listen for news of incoming flights. To keep his ears open. Being paid whether the flier worked or not, the man took full advantage of the opportunity and spent the majority of his time fishing in the river or just lying on his back in the aluminum boat while he watched the *dragas* feverishly working. However in the unfolding drama before Tarisco a new twist had revealed itself, which he relished and was delighted about because as he had learned long ago from being on the run growing up in Rio nothing goes right that goes too smoothly. Another had caught his attention. A large, bulldog like white man with bleached blonde hair the color of pinkish straw. He didn't belong. There was an incongruity between his story and his demeanor, which was condescending and alien and definitively not Brazilian. So it was impossible for him to have come from São Paulo or to represent a pharmaceutical company for that matter for if he did he would be more at ease in the presence of the locals and would likely not be frequenting Pixote's brothel on an almost daily basis as he was.

The mystery was too much to bear so one night while Berg was visiting the two Indian girls, who had both decided they had discovered a bonanza of their own by charging the foreigner four times as much as any other *garimpeiro* and planning to use the money for a down payment on a house, Tarisco broke into the man's room. It was a simple matter. The locked door opened with one quick turn of the wrist breaking the tumbler and spilling little tiny springs out onto the floor. He entered silently pulling the door closed behind him. It was dank and stifling and he could not understand how someone could sleep in a hovel such as the one in which he stood and was convinced the man was unfamiliar with the region or else he would have taken time to secure a room with two windows such as he himself had where at least one could get the benefit of a crossflow of air. There was nothing in the man's belongings that identified him or indicated his place of origin, other that the fact that everything was made in the United States so he assumed that was where the man had come from. He had trouble getting the large aluminum case open without busting the lock, but, using techniques he had developed as a prodigious child thief finally managed to unlock it with no damage. Inside he found military style hardware. A Glock automatic pistol made with high impact polymers that was x-ray proof, a disassembled sniper rifle, A Kevlar vest of the kind used by police, a pair of infrared night-vision goggles, a large knife and several plastic containers of pills and ammunition. The mystery swirled about him as he left the room exactly as he had found it and he considered whether the person might be working with the DEA or the anti-narcotics unit of Brazil's Federal Police. Either way he determined to watch him, which he did not believe would be hard because the big blonde man did not appear to be excessively bright. He stuffed the little springs into the lock so that when the man came to open his door he would assume he had just broken it. Anyone could walk off with his equipment while he wallowed in debauchery, Tarisco scoffed with disgust.

Three days after he had observed the men in the forest Tarisco appeared at the Hotel Flutuante for breakfast. He ordered the usual *feijoada*, a combination rice and black beans that had been cooked separately, and fish. The blonde man was an enigma to him, he did not seem to fit into any of the scenarios he had devised to explain the observed behaviors. And he was also watching Rand, a fact that made him slightly nervy and more cautious than he would have been otherwise. He ate the fish from the river, some of which he was sure came from his pilot who landing them in abundance either gave or traded most to Pixote in exchange for meals, glasses of whiskey and a drink of which he was particularly fond called a *batida*, which was made from *cachaça*, the crude but powerful light rum, blended with sugar and fruit juices. It occurred to him that there was something different that morning from all the other mornings he had come to eat where he had, in the process of creating a routine himself, become a part of the ritual of others and now something was amiss. The nutty flavor of the rice and beans blended with the flaky freshwater fish, which had been fried with tomatoes and onions and was a specialty this far up the river because whenever fresh tomatoes were delivered they were used in everything until they quickly ran out. Tarisco suddenly noticed it. Silence. That was unusual. Pixote was not there. He was always sitting in the corner going over his account books with a large steaming cup of coffee and often talking with the lawyer or another of the thirty or so men involved in whatever devious scheme they were working on. He had not once been absent. Is it today? He asked himself. Is it today?

The leaves brushed him and he sweated in the early morning heat as tiny bugs landed on his face. Everything was silent except for the hidden movements in the forest around him where the day had been breached hours ago. Then he heard it. The drone, far off, as if a sound of heaven. Tarisco held his breath so he could define it with more certainty. He heard drops of dew dripping to the forest floor from a plant close by and the minutiae of crunching by some large, bright green insect devouring a leaf next to where he crouched. He saw, but could not hear, the army of ants that formed a concourse through the fallen debris of the trees weaving in and out of the obstacle filled path they marched ever on as he imagined they had done since long before men. Other rustlings came across the open landing field, mysterious and subdued. They gave away the unseen. The drone grew louder until it was unmistakable. He trembled. Muscles grew taut and he perspired more. The smell of danger filled his nostrils. Suddenly he could see it, a glint off its wing, the pulsing wave of its engine, the forbidding aura of its presence. It brought back terrible memories, which he had fought all his life to suppress. They came now in the humid brush and caused him to feel a surge of rage, uncontrolled, irrational. Helicopters lurked over the *favela* and he remembered them as clearly as if it were in the present. They shook the walls of the cinder block and corrugated houses with their deep, whooping rumble. It was an abrupt ominous presence as if the *orixás* had risen from the gates and descended all at once upon the homes of the *descamisados* looking for vengeance and trouble. Children scattered in terror as he himself had done the sound riveting through his soul and threatening his sanity with its dynamic portent of death. Running confirmed guilt. Then the chase. The panic. Blood on the dirt streets marked each field of conflict between the ten percent that possessed and the ninety percent that did not and even compelled the rich to dub their country *BrazIndia* as a consequence of the growing disparity between the rich and the poor. Tarisco revolted at the thought of trickle down economics that was supposed by the military government to resolve the poverty and wished the thieves laying in wait success with their gold heist if it would deprive the *fazendeiros* even a little bit.

The single engine plane appeared low over the trees and seemed to Tarisco it would hit the top branches, but miraculously missed as if flying through ghostly boughs. Its motor sputtered as the pilot let up on the throttle and descended for a landing on the makeshift runway. It dropped seemingly vertical into the cleared jungle and as the wheels touched clouds of dust appeared and dirt spewed with grasses and chunks of green yearling foliage that just kept growing back despite the onslaught of plow and oil. It bounced two times and then jumbled viciously over the strip as it decelerated until finally coming to a complete stop next to trees where the paths to *Boca de Lobo* lay. In a moment a door flew open and Nestor Salinas Machado emerged.

Tarisco settled in and prepared to wait the several hours necessary for the man to reach his draga, go over the ledger books, compare them with each of the *garimpeiros'* entries and then return to the plane with his load of gold. It was then they would strike though he was certain that they too lay in wait like him to avoid being seen. But then he was shocked by movement, unexpectedly a dozen men appeared from the surrounding bushes menacingly armed with guns and machetes. After barking orders three immediately lurched up onto the wing of the plane and wrestled Machado down, disarming him and dragging him off forcibly after a sudden crack on the head to silence his shouts and profane insults that echoed from the forest in the still early morning air and made the birds take flight and the monkeys nervous. He watched as the remainder of the men lingered by the plane, then, after a period of negotiation, stepped back and he saw the door was closed. The engine sputtered over and roared to life. It was only minutes before the small craft was airborne again lofting out over the blue green forest heading back from where it had come. Tarisco was completely surprised. Flabbergasted and confused while he crouched without moving he watched the huddle of men, including Rand and Pixote, congregate apparently waiting to ensure the plane did not return. A few stragglers joined them and soon they headed off down the trail that Tarisco had followed them on earlier.

He knew where they were going and so did not hurry but waited instead to see if anyone else might follow, and sure enough some did. They trickled from the trees and set out on the path just as the other men had. Minutes later the blonde man appeared. He too took the trail.

The cathedral of the forest towered above and made them feel humbled. Sunlight spilled off the leaves and cascaded down, tumbling through layers of life, filtering and flickering it washed everything with light and shadow until exact outlines became indistinct and blurred with the onrush of the jungle. Blood throbbed in Rand's temples. He breathed rapidly. His skin was completely dry despite the rising humidity and heat of the day that in the heart of the forest resonated in waves as if a liquid furnace. He had blindly followed the trail to the clearing in the forest with long steps pushing through undergrowth without his usual fear of the creatures that lived there and not even the specter of encountering a fer-de-lance, whose slithering body often grew thicker than a man's arm, or other equally lethal mishap deterred him. His heart raced. He knew he must fight to retain control of his emotions for he was doing something that violated every principle he'd ever learned about law. Extrajudicial proceedings, they called it, vigilantism...all the ideals of jurisprudence that were based on the one fundamental principle of carrying out justice in the public eye were being compromised. But for unknown reasons he was compelled to continue and so sat resolutely on the log underneath the lean-to shelter. The line between himself and the accused man who was before him now became indistinct and blurred.

Unseen the blonde man had spirited himself into a vantage point at the far end of the clearing and, after the surprise diminished, had blackened his face with soil and placed some small branches in his hair and on the front of his shirt hanging out the button holes as he had learned to do in the military and expertly slid down and hid himself in the living wall that surrounded them. He did not have the slightest idea what was occurring and had not even anticipated it. The single intention he had was to keep his quarry in sight for he had never once failed an assignment and though he had received the first two thirds payment plus expenses, the remainder of the money was a big incentive for him as he had recently made some bad stock investments which had depleted his savings. Berg was concerned for his future and as he approached forty felt his body slackening and was terrified of a serious illness or disability striking. The body was all he had. When he died he figured there was nothing, a blackness like extinguishing the lights. God had never really appealed to him. He didn't believe in anything except technology. The Glock automatic pistol rested comfortably in his hand.

This time Tarisco had circled far out around them and come up close behind the lean-to so that he could hear everything and somehow unravel this mystery. The blonde man was an easy mark and he had no respect for him whatsoever because a man that could not tell when his room had been broken into was worthless in the long run. *Government employee,* he mused. If it appeared propitious he would terminate the lawyer right there as it seemed Randall DesVergers was perverse to the end and he could not imagine what reason they might have for kidnapping this man. Ransom perhaps, but that seemed unlikely. It was just degenerate, he decided and watched as men mulled around in a circle. Nestor Salinas Machado kneeled defiantly in their center someone having tied his hands and feet and linked them together with rope. The veins on the side of his neck pulsed. He was incensed. He glared around with his dark strong eyes and flexed the muscles in his arm testing the rope and making them ripple with strength. "You hide like women in the woods, you pussies!" He spat out vehemently, "You scum sucking dogs!" To his right twelve men sat mysteriously on logs that had been recently drug there. Pixote stood next to the kneeling man and the other strong one, Caetano, rose to the left. Tarisco speculated whether the man was a drug runner, certainly more inept than himself, and if so he felt no kinship or desire to help him out of a tough spot. Besides, there were too many men for even him. So, he resolved to watch events as they unfolded as by now his curiosity was burning him.

The stench of fear overshadowed all other smells in the glade. It was as if all the assembled men collectively held their breath. The surrounding forest was suddenly quiet in anticipation. Abruptly, as if incited to get it over with Randall DesVergers spoke. "You are accused of the murder of thirty five Indian men, women and children and a *mestiço* woman named Pilar Escandinha." His voice was clear, strong and resonated as if a bell tone unblemished by timidity or remorse. "How do you plead?"

Nestor Salinas Machado was dumfounded and did not move. His eyes bored into Rand with hatred, contempt and disbelief. "Fuck you fucking gringo! Give me a fucking break!"

Rand gestured to his left. "The men of Boca de Lobo have appointed Caetano Vargas to represent you in your defense." The kneeling man looked up at Caetano, who stared straight ahead his endurance being tested, and like a rabid dog sneered in defiance. "Pixote, whom you know, will prosecute."

At which point the man spat on the ground and uttered, "A shit-house whore keeper." Pixote was unmoved already inured to his course of action and having made his peace with God.

And then as if compelled to speak to purge his own soul Rand concluded. "I am simply a representative of the rule of law. We make no pretense here that we can approach the impartiality of an autho-rized judicial body, but since none is available we have taken this step in an effort to return justice to the hands of the people who live in this community. I will not judge you, for that a jury of twelve men was chosen. I disqualified myself. They were carefully chosen for their grasp of the situation and its consequences. I am simply a representative of the law," he repeated as he had planned the whole speech, but when the moment arrived his plans had crumbled and now he stumbled to make sure nothing was omitted that he considered fair and relevant, "your fate is in the hands of your peers."

The jaw of Tarisco's mouth hung open agape at what had just transpired. He pressed his hand to the ground to ensure he was not asleep and immediately all other thoughts vanished as he became completely aware of his environment. His stomach leapt into his throat and he shook with an effervescent energy that welled up from unknown reservoirs and riveted his attention to the proceedings. Perhaps it was the Indian blood that rushed through his *mestiço* veins that caused such a strong reaction or simply the underlying current of social consciousness that defined who he was, but in either case tears flooded his eyes.

The blonde man watched too, from afar, awaiting his chance at a clear shot where he would still be afforded an easy escape. He was not as agile as he used to be and there was plenty of time, besides he had been enjoying his daily visits to the two Indian girls and their attentions lured him into a sensual reverie that cut across his ability to be at cause over the situation. As a result he demurred to the fact that even if the opportunity to kill the man did not present itself he would take the few extra days needed to find one and in the meantime take advantage of the women for as long as he could. He knew he only lived once.

Throughout the day Randall DesVergers guided the proceedings and worked not to interfere with the context of the men's testimony except to keep it relevant, to the point and as factual as possible under the circumstances. He had engaged in long discussions with the men beforehand and explained to them the rudiments of the action. How they were only interested in fact–time, place, form and events that could be verified–and that opinion, while inseparable from the individual, had no place in what they were doing. The jurors were indoctrinated to consider only facts and as best they could separate all else out. He explained at length the ideas of corpus delicti, reasonable doubt and premeditation. The doctrines of natural law as the 'law of nature and its author', common law and statutory law and gave them a brief overview of how it had become encoded in an effort to create a jurisprudence entirely separate from the politics, economic power and irrationality of men. "Clearly what we are doing is illegal," he said and then added because he knew that most of them had Catholic upbringings, "clearly illegal but not immoral." And then he quoted something he remembered from his early legal studies. "Law is the paramount expression of the moral sense of the community."

At one point Rand nearly lost his nerve. Caetano arose to an impassioned speech that illuminated what they all felt and what he could never really duplicate being of foreign blood. "We are the *descamisados*!" he rallied to the trees. "They have taken our shirts and now they want our pants!" Men yelled and stamped their feet and caused Nestor Salinas Machado to raise his tied hands in a fist and yell with them. Accuser and accused of the same blood. "I told the Indian I was a *garimpeiro*, and that I wanted a better life for myself, my family and my people. He said to me something about the earth and his mother and how could I defile her...? My mother was shot in the *favela*, a bullet came through the wall from an argument outside and killed her! How could they? We are the living! We are all one people! Indians hold back thousands of square miles of land...how can a man need so much land? They are hostile to us! To our survival! I am very macho," he said without any evidence of self mockery, "and I am not afraid of any government. If we want our land we have to arm ourselves! You cannot play with human lives." Caetano struggled to contain his fury as men cheered and stamped their feet and Rand shuddered at what he had unleashed imaging what would happen if the man was found innocent and fumed in a last resolve to face the consequences of his act whatever they may be.

The trial lasted well into the evening as everyone wanted to have their say so fires were lit and cast ominous shadows across everyone's face as people huddled into the light. The relevances were blurred and the whole proceeding became not only a question of the man's guilt or innocence, but a cauldron of voices all desperate to be heard. It was as it should be, Rand thought, the way of democracy, and allowed them all to speak even if they strayed from the question at hand for he knew he was observing the negotiation of justice, not perfect but as close as a group of human beings could come. Finally Pixote urged a man forward that Rand had never seen before. He was visibly shaken and nervous.

"Pixote says..." he began haltingly, looking around at all the men, many more of whom had joined them coming up the trail from *Boca de Lobo* as their shifts ended on the *dragas*, "If I speak we have a bargain."

"Plea bargain." Pixote offered up. "Like you explained."

"Go ahead." Rand told the man.

Pixote turned to the man." Tell them."

"I am a *Baixada*." There was a hush and the sound of movement as men became suddenly restless. "I was there."

"Where?"

"In the village."

Rand flushed with anger and fought to control himself. Pixote continued to impel the man on. "Continue..."

"We killed them all."

"Was Nestor Salinas Machado with you?"

"Not in the village, in the boat. He ordered us. He said we would lose our jobs, the *dragas* would close down operation. He said the riverbed was drying up and that there was no more gold and if we wanted to move up river we would have to fight for the land, like the *bandeirantes*. We know they'd been killing *garimpeiros*, it happened all the time. We fought back. He ordered us. We just followed orders, did what we were told to keep our jobs and keep the river. Where would we go without the river? What have we to go back to?" Nestor Salinas Machado spit on the man's back, but he did not turn around to confront him and after more questions was allowed to leave unmolested.

One after another the men rose to testify tense and sweaty until everything had been said and everyone was exhausted. The air around them was bristling. Rand stood and instructed the jurors in their deliberations reminding them of some of the principles they had gone over and then let them retire to the far end of the clearing, out of ear shot. In their dark eyes was the florid history of the Americas. It did not escape Rand as he oversaw the ragtag effort at justice, but branded him. "We will wait here," he said, "until they have reached a verdict. We will not leave until then." He still hoped he was doing the right thing even though it was too late to turn back. The struggle between the strong and the weak, the rich and the poor, the able and the less able were no longer clichés bandied about by Democrats at fund raising dinners such as the one he had attended on the hills above California's Pacific so long ago. In another country, another world. He would emerge tempered and brittle, stronger yet vulnerable. It was as if his soul were being seared to a cause, seared by hot steel and blue fire.

A SPIRIT OBSCURED BY CLOUDS

XVIII

The spirits of the river vanished before them as quicksilver into fog mists. Muted whispers trickled down through the dense green mansions. A toucan's call. The splash of a caiman slithering from the bank. Monkeys' chattering talk somewhere off in the irrefutable distances. It was an unbelievable collage of nature that constructed towers and high rises, panoramas and landscapes, vistas and grottos, the living earth, the breathing forest, the aria of life. Into the mystic womb sailed three men in an aluminum boat thrust forward against the current by a whining outboard motor spewing little puffs of black smoke. Each day a battle, the men thought in their own individual ways. Shafts of light furrowed down from heaven up ahead turning the darkness into bright lime greens and the muddy slate of the river to scintillating, pearlescent pools of swiftly running water. None of the men spoke. It was a judgment of the moon and stars.

The slowness of rivers have always given men time to think, to reflect on their lives. Perhaps it wasn't the automobile or the airplane or the telephone that brought about the act with no history and no future, that inspired men to desperately grapple with the present embracing the philosophy strike fast, run hard, but their distance from rivers. As the calligrapher's hand moved, the scribe, the chisler of cuneiform so did his thoughts have time to run before the whirling earth and find order within themselves, to coalesce and resolve into what was truly meant to be said. The universe is a chaotic master. All men are guilty of hasty acts. It only takes a moment to discard a lifetime. Nestor Salinas Machado was convinced the men were taking a ride into the jungle to kill him. He would fool them, he thought, because he was not afraid to die. He was strong and did not deny to himself any acts that he had done and in the broad view saw his life as a contribution to the forward progress of Brazil. Someone had to take the initiative, he thought, had to accept the liability for action when others were too concerned with the ill effects on themselves, on others to do anything at all. So they became fat like the politicians such as Fernando Lacombe that he personally knew who had too many years of living the good life and speculated on others' labor raking in fortunes. Or they became shufflers, content with their place and only trying to have security that they may pursue their mundane, quiet lives in peace, as did many of the poor and rising middle classes. The pursuit of pleasure, he thought contemptuously, was the first step toward ruin.

"We are the same." Nestor said defiantly wrestling against the rope around his wrists.

The ripples of the boat's wake spread from it as a fan until they lapped noiselessly upon the shore. "No," came the reply from the man holding the gun on him. "Not the same."

"You dogs!" Sneered Nestor. "You pussies! Can't you even confront me like men?"

The two suffered the indignation and the insults to their manhood because they felt pity on the man because it was as he said, they were the same. The distinctions became blurred in the struggle to survive that was the bond between them where some flourished through a mystery of fate and coincidence and others were condemned to a marginal existence that took them early in their lives, before their time. "It comes and goes," said the man at the outboard motor. "But for fortune you might be here and I in your seat." Then they were silent for a long time.

Nestor Salinas Machado was tense and boiling over with fury, but because of this he had become detached from his body and for the first time noticed the beauty of the environment. When he had first come to Amazonas as a young man it had absorbed his life energy along with all the other living things and now he was as much a part of its make up as any other living creature within it. "I am of the rain forest," he said half to himself, still antagonistic yet wistful, "I have always viewed it as a crucible of life and my role was the corn grinder. I was the one who stirred up the silt in the river to expose the gold. Others took it. I was the corn grinder." And then he was silent again and his words passed into the throbbing living wall that enveloped them.

They traveled for nearly a full day. At a certain point the man at the motor in the stern steered for the bank. They landed. The other man with the rifle stuck the barrel into Nestor's back and urged him out of the boat and soon all three stood about a hundred yards from the rushing water. Its sound could be heard over the restless forest. Everything had a green tint from the light reflected off the leaves and it gave the men an eerie plant like presence as if they too were rooted in the soil.

"So, get it done with. I am not afraid!" Nestor snapped viciously beneath the dappled light flowing down from the canopy far above. "I spit on death." A man moved towards him with a large hunting knife lowered in his hand while the other kept a bead with the rifle. Nestor braced himself and prepared to struggle. "I would rather be shot than gutted like an animal!" He hissed. But the man grabbed hold of the ropes securing his hands and cut them loose. Next the foot shackles were gone. He stared at them in rage and disbelief. "What the hell is this!?" He demanded. "What do you want!?" But neither man answered and they started to back away. When they were about thirty feet one threw the knife and it landed only ten feet in front of the condemned man. He rushed for it diving onto the leaves and humus to grab its carved bone handle and then rose like a pit bull standing squarely with feet spread wide holding the blade ready in his right hand. The men were walking faster, the one with the rifle looking over his shoulder to make sure they weren't being followed and then it struck Nestor, hit him full force. He was banished. Being left in the jungle. "You cowards!!" He screamed. The whine of the motor as the boat left the shore and headed back down river was the most forlorn sound Nestor Salinas Machado had ever heard. He listened for a long time while the hollowness rose in him making him want to scream. But he did not because he was a strong man.

When it was silent he saw it out of the corner of his eye. A bright flash of color. He swung around, but there was nothing. He could sense movement and started toward the river slowly at first. As he walked he began laughing, the pure honest laugh of a sportsman. I am a *boi do piranha*, he thought, and then he yelled, "*Boi do piranha!*" It was the sacrificial cow, the one sent across the river first which the piranha would busy themselves tearing apart so that the remainder of the heard could cross in safety at another point farther on. And then he ran as fast as he could into the forest.

Eyes had followed them for a long time. Invisible eyes. Their faces were painted in red and black and had been since the day of the slaughter. Their bodies were lean and sleek. Bright colored plumage adorned their headdresses as they roamed the forest seeking the spirits that had butchered their people. They had not rested and were inured to the hardness. Bare feet bounded through the undergrowth. Lances held cocked at shoulder height. Their arrows rattled in their quivers, bowstrings cut across their chests. They were hunters, warriors and they knew as every warrior knew that death was the only choice.

Nestor Salinas Machado soared with energy. Reborn. He had transcended fear and was elated with the chase hearing his pursuers course through the forest after him now and then glancing back to see their painted faces and threatening lances racing against the wind, flickering through the shadows. A huge grin broke out on his face as his faith in his fellow men was restored realizing that they had never meant to cut him down like a dog tied and helpless. He ran until his heart was near bursting until his spirit escaped and merged with that of the jaguar.

Another hunter had come to life. He had grown slowly tired of the routine with the two Indian girls, who by now had amassed a small fortune and were already making plans to travel to the city. He awoke one morning and packed everything securely and neatly in his bags, loaded bullets into a couple of new, unused clips for fear the one that had been holding cartridges for so long might have a weak spring that would fail him in a pinch and set out to track his quarry. An airplane sat on the landing field and the blonde man had made arrangements to fly out on it late that night surreptitiously, without telling anyone even the girls. He was brimming with confidence, after all he had never failed an assignment.

He ate at the Hotel Flutuante along with everyone else who could not stomach the food at any of the other eating establishments, but did not make eye contact with anyone. This was not the same Berg who had been there just a few nights before tumbling with the girls in the small, sweltering room up the stairs on the bed with the squeaking springs. He was not the same man at all and had incredibly changed his personality overnight. Even the memory of his debauchery seemed flimsy and indistinct as if he was viewing it through gauze, detached, and therefore it became less real to him and easy for him to deny, in fact, that he had actually done it. Perhaps he may have slipped once or twice, but then he was only a man. But behavior like that was irreconcilable with his high moral fiber. He had gone through similar transformations many times before after each assignment successfully completed until at one point he felt he was becoming fragmented and was filled with so many aliases and nom de plumes that he could not identify himself, could not view things from his own viewpoint. Consequently it was easier for him to terminate people for money, but in between jobs his personality roller coastered like faces in a house of mirrors. He had sought counseling as an attempt to stabilize the swings in mood and temperament, but since he did not come clean and discuss the fact that he was a killer of men it did little good. He often wondered where he was, though he appeared healthy, robust and even athletic, and was in a state of confusion most of the time. The theory he was adhering to was that if he could just do it one more time he would be able to ascertain whether it was really right or wrong, because he knew in the end that moral codes were a personal matter and that he alone was God and autonomous of those around him.

Rand did not sleep for two days. Everyone in the *garimpo* knew what had transpired and the fact that there had been seventy-five men absent from work and missing all through the night had been ignored and the following day when they all mysteriously returned not a word was said about it. The *Baixadas* did not appear as he had predicted and he wondered if they had been present at the proceeding unknown and thought, without really believing it, that possibly they too found some comfort in the rule of law. It was nothing if not an instrument to bring order so that men might get on with their lives. Rand reported to work on the draga as usual, but it was like a ghost ship knowing the fate of its owner and so he could not return again. For the first time since that day in the forest, which seemed like another lifetime, he began to give serious thought to returning home and he could easily have hopped a flying boat. However something strange was occurring within him, a marriage of heart and mind that caused him to have second thoughts about going back to his old life. And so he was besieged with conflict at once not wishing to leave having been forged by action to the fate of the *garimpeiros* yet knowing with certainty he did not belong. He lingered on the periphery avoiding the decision even toying with the idea of studying Brazilian law and coming back to represent them in the crucial issues they faced. They were men without voices.

That night he sat drinking with Pixote at the round table. The big man was garrulously talking and Rand hoped he would not say too much. "Do you think fifty two thousand is enough to put down on a small farm?"

"Sounds like it."

"You see my friend," he leaned over and patted Rand's shoulder, "I no longer have to watch gold prices, but I have to watch their takes... and this I can judge from how much they drink and spend on women...I have to watch their take, because If I go before the gold runs out I can sell my businesses. If there is no gold," He shrugged, "who wants to pay for nothing?"

Rand drank beer that was never quite cold enough. "What do you think will happen?"

Pixote's eyes flared and he grinned. "I dunno. Maybe they'll bring in bulldozers and make a big carnal city like Brasilia! What a ridiculous error!" He paused long enough to take a drink and a deep breath. "Built the whole city and never once thought of where the men who worked on it might live. It was to be the most futuristic capital in the world.

When it was done, fifty thousand people had created *casas de cômodos*, slums, out of scrap building material! Just like Rio! Still nothing there but government buildings and slums. When the ministers get a day off they fly to São Paulo for excitement."

"I have to get back I think. Have to leave."

"Maybe..." Pixote considered it, "maybe not."

"Do you think they'll come after me again?"

"Maybe."

"How about you, the others...safe enough?"

He waited before he answered mulling it over in his mind. "Maybe."

After a while Rand left. He was not so drunk that he couldn't negotiate his footing, but not so sober that he could walk in the dark without paying attention. So as he was halfway down the gangplank to the Hotel Flutuante he stumbled lurching forward. There was a crack in the air. He was silent thinking it must have been a backfire from one of the diesels that whined off in the distance and then continued on.

Tarisco Sivuca cursed under his breath and lifted his Taurus .45 automatic up to eyesight. The barrel was heavier than usual with a silencer screwed on it and so he had to take careful aim. Blonde hair the color of pinkish straw was a dead giveaway in the dark. The man might as well have worn reflective highway stickers or put fireflies in his hair as the Indian children did. Tarisco was furious. He had not decided the fate of the lawyer yet and now this bumbling, pale skinned idiot was trying to shoot him for some obscure reason that he still did not comprehend. He considered the scenario that Valdemiro Veloso may have sent another assassin to kill both the lawyer and himself and the assignment given him was just a ploy and in that way he would be rid of the two men he considered responsible for his son's abduction. Too unlikely, he concluded. The blonde was obviously an American, and Miro would never trust a man such as him. He had no morals. With that he gently yet firmly squeezed the trigger until there was a loud chunk sound and the weapon recoiled badly in his hand despite the custom work he had done on it drilling ports in the barrel to ease its reaction. Conceivably the silencer plugged the holes, he thought, and resolved to have it looked at when he returned to Rio.

Rand descended the walkway and when he reached the bottom he heard a splash close by from out of the murky darkness as if from a heavy object and leapt away from the shore thinking it was an alligator, who he had been told fed at night, and hurried across the dirt flats toward his room on the street with wooden sidewalks. He did not hear the shot.

Lying in the water face down completely still and devoid of life was the large blonde man. His identity had finally been decided, though unfortunately it had broken his string of perfectly accomplished assignments. Caimans, hunting nearby as Rand had guessed, smelling blood came later in the night and drug the body out into the deep current where they feasted on any evidence that the poor man had been there at all. The pilot who had been waiting at the field grew impatient and, thinking the man had changed his mind and been too lazy to tell him, left. The last thing Rand heard as he drifted off into his first fitful sleep since the proceedings was the sound of an airplane lifting off from the runway. He dreamt of the fate of Nestor Salinias Machado.

The sound of boot heels pounding across the wooden slats of the walkway outside his room shocked him awake. Rand slept soundly as a consequence of too much to drink and so missed the shudder that the two enormous dull olive drab helicopters made as they arrived early that morning. They sat like great tropical insects astride the chuck hole filled airstrip surrounded by watchful trees. He jumped up and peered cautiously out the slats in the shutters just in time to see two Brazilian federal soldiers in jungle fatigues disappearing around the corner of the building. His heart skipped and he perspired heavily from the swelter of the chamber. The thought struck him that the men from FUNAI had finally sent a mission from Brasilia to investigate the massacre. Fear unreasonably crept over him.

A long way off in the capital where Fernando Lacombe had taken a suite in anticipation of his victory in the coming elections a military officer simply known as Colonel Magalhães, his first name being lost somewhere in the chaotic days when the army turned the country back over to civilian rule and attachments to certain cliques became undesirable, came to see him. The two men, though neither knew the other, had an immediate rapport. Their politics were in sync, they had similar enturbulated visions of the future and both felt that the rule by the armed forces would have panned out eventually if the ignorant had given it a chance. Success is a long term proposition, both understood, brilliance came with persistence.

"Your friend is dead," the officer had informed him with the solemnity due such an announcement.

The man looked up from his broad desk. "My friend?"

"Nestor Salinas Machado has been abducted and killed by armed *garimpeiros*." Then he corrected himself without the slightest change in facial expression. "At least we believe him to be dead." He had taken it upon himself to approach the politician with the news knowing that his link to power would be strengthened.

"I can't believe it!" Said Fernando Lacombe astonished. "We were just together not one month ago."

"Yes." Colonel Magalhães replied dryly. "I know he was your friend and that is why I am here."

"*Garimpeiros* you say?" His interest suddenly being piqued.

"That is correct."

"Imagine, my old friend...dead." In his estimation there was nothing so good for the country as the complete opening up of the frontier areas for development and had often enough said that. The trouble was with the international community. Brazil owed too much. It's national debt was one of the largest in the world. It made them acquiesce he had always felt, buckled the knees of leaders and made them impotent. He had supported completely each time the country refused to make payments on the debt to foreign banks until the rates and conditions were renegotiated. And then there were the bleeding heart environmentalists who he believed had sold their immortality to keep Brazil an underdeveloped country so that they might take sight seeing excursions up the Amazon. Fernando Lacombe represented potency if nothing else. Implacability. The country demanded a vigorous leader and Fernando Lacombe had proved himself to be just that many times such as on this last trip up the Rio Madeira where he had bagged three alligators with only one shot each. But he was opposed by the new liberal generation where even the governors supported the *pivetes* in the streets and ignored the lions of industry on whom the whole country depended for survival. Where were their priorities?

The propitious opportunity of the moment was grasped immediately by a political mind that was rapier quick and that was how Colonel Magalhães came to be sent to *Boca de Lobo* to ferret out the injustice and criminals responsible for the death of a well known entrepreneur. Not to investigate a massacre of Indians at all, the report of such atrocity still bogged down in red tape and implications. He would display to his opponents that he was quick to condemn the progressive forces in the Amazon when they violated human rights even if they were creating revenue and national wealth. He would show those high waisted liberal sons-of-bitches that he could be as much a leftist as they were, and that should ensure him some votes, secure him some more support.

It wasn't long before Colonel Magalhães ended up at the Hotel Flutuante, the hub of Boca de Lobo, and had cornered Pixote who fended off questions with the sly expertise of those who had been born under the whip and knew instinctively whose hand held it and whose back felt it. He was asked about Nestor Salinas Machado, a very important friend of the politician Fernando Lacombe. "Yes..." he replied, "I remember seeing them right out there," he pointed off in the direction of the *draga* where Rand had been photographed, "that was one of his boats. Maybe they can tell you something." The military men received a similar response when they reached the *draga* and so they spent the day combing the community intimidating everyone they thought might help, their belligerence growing with the heat and the lack of evidence.

Like everyone else Rand was tense. His nerves were strained though he tried not to show it as he stood outside on the planks that made up the sidewalk where the soldiers had first awakened him. He rifled through his options, which only took a matter of seconds because they were slim, and visualized his fate at the hands of the military whom he imagined as archetypal of the banana republic thugs he had always heard about in the United States and so, remembering now Pixote's laughter when he had mentioned an investigation into the massacre, gave himself little chance of lasting. The adage about unfettered speech occurred to him that warned a man can speak as freely as he liked, as long as it didn't get someone too pissed at him. The question as to whether justice had degrees festered. Was truth a matter of conscience or survival?

On impulse Rand headed for the landing field and when out of sight he ran. In a burst of welled up energy he crashed through the foliage overhanging the worn path and as he drew near circled off the trail as to remain unseen. Eyes peered desperately out onto the artificial glade. Two army helicopters sat huge and ominous in the center of the plain casting dark shadows beneath them. They blocked the airport. Nobody would enter or leave until they had finished their business. One plane trapped by events was dwarfed by the dual rotor aircraft and its pilot sat on the wing smoking looking dour and resigned. Slight hope was dashed. He fled to the dockside where he inquired about the steel flying boat praying he could get hidden passage down river and from the headwaters somehow elude the officials but it had already come and gone and was not expected for two days, maybe more. Perhaps, Rand precariously conceived looking over at the aluminum boats, he could make it up river to the village of Uititiaja, but what would he find? They would not even talk to the men from FUNAI whom they knew much better than himself and he remembered that he would be thought of as the spirit who had brought on the disaster. Rand was, after all, the only stranger in their midst at the time, the only change that had occurred prior to the holocaust. He screamed for release and felt things could not get worse. He was wrong.

Even at the far end of town he could recognize the man, the slope of his forehead, the unruly hair, strong back and stance. It was the one who had plea bargained. He was talking to Colonel Magalhães who listened patiently and suddenly waved over a comrade who himself listened intently. Rand felt suddenly ill. Heart thundered.

"They are looking for you my friend." Pixote exclaimed as Rand appeared clinging to his doorway with hollow cheeks, gaunt and sweating.

"Yes," he breathed heavily, "I know. I've got to hide."

"They were just here!"

"You know what they'll do to me!"

It was hot between the two Indian girls and all three of them sweated beneath the sheets. Rand had quickly removed most of his clothing and stuck his feet out the end of the short bed as Pixote had instructed spinning with terror and certain of discovery. The girls giggled knowing something serious was occurring and feeling skittish, but delighted at the appearance of another white man relating all Caucasians to money. They huddled close curious what was next as Rand buried his face in their black hair and smelled the scents of Jacaranda, musk and fish. The door burst open and suddenly a soldier was standing there with a red bandanna tied around his head and an M-16 fully automatic .223 rifle strapped across his chest. Pixote could be heard on the stairway "It's only the blonde man! He's always there. Just the blonde man, leave him alone. They charge him four times the normal price!" After a long incredibly tense moment of silence, the soldier laughed in some way finding the two pale white legs disproportionately hanging off the end of the bed and the sight of the squirming girls taking advantage of the gringo too much, and then he left. "He is making the girls rich!" Pixote called out good naturedly behind him.

Randall DesVergers stayed in the room until late in the afternoon. He knew they would return, everyone winds up at the Hotel Flutuante eventually. So he cautiously inched his way down the stairs careful not to make any extraneous noise and slipped out the door into the river's breath where he walked nonchalantly off into the trees close to the boat docks. Here at least, he reasoned ominously, he might make a run for it, if he had the courage, might make it to the center of the river, or even down past where the *dragas* stirred up the much looked for riches and be carried by the current. Conceivably he might make it to civilization, but it was doubtful. That was a sixty-mile run, some through rough water he'd been told, and only a large fast boat could make it in one day and he had used up his single night on the river alone. Next time would be his end. He stood hugging the smooth trunk of a gigantic tree staring wearily off into Boca de Lobo almost waiting for the soldiers to appear, to see them come toward him, to know there was death if he ran and death if he stayed. Courage was the one element missing.

It seemed so sublimated in his past life that he was unfamiliar with it; his ultra sophisticated existence where everything was so complex and convoluted that nothing was as it seemed and the basic essentials that men had always known about, for thousands of years used as a measure of character became obscure in the techno-speak economics that determined one's station on the ladder. He rested on the bottom. Felt its gravely surface scrape against his soul. There was nowhere else to run. He had demanded retribution and now was ready for his own.

"Why did you let the man who bargained go?" Came the voice drifting into his consciousness.

Rand turned startled out of his wits. He saw the gun first, an old Taurus .45 automatic leveled at his mid section. A steady brown hand held it on him. He looked at the man's face, weathered, calm, a face of Brazil speaking with a thousand voices, a thousand dreams and a mixture of races so spicy and varied they defied classification and description except to say that they are each one uniquely of the great South American continent.

"I myself would have taken the bargain and then executed him." Said Tarisco in response to his own question. "You can't deal with madmen. It's a bad habit to get into." Then he motioned with his pistol for Rand to get into one of the aluminum boats.

They slowly puttered out into the open river barely making any ripples on its surface. I am going to die, Rand kept telling himself over and over trying in some way, not being a religious man in the slightest, to make his peace somehow and prepare himself for the inevitable. Why this stranger would want to kill him was a mystery except that he must be with the *Baixadas* and that he had chosen to meddle with things that were not of his business. On the shore he could see men coming and going about their business and signs of the military men as they still searched for him. On the dragas he could see the *garimpeiros* who paid no attention to them whatsoever and sweated over their dredges pulling up silt as they did day after day, cleaning the sluice, purging it with mercury and noting down their percentages in little black ledger books. Nothing else mattered, they would be gone soon, each thought, after the fortune was made. Every man needed his fortune. He looked at the forest for the last time and was absorbed by its loveliness, its violent beauty, its danger and its throbbing, pulsing life force. Rand had not wanted to leave, and now perhaps as a result of cheating death in the fall from the plane he would not have to. The sky was filled with white fleecy clouds that were just beginning to come together for the first hint of a rain. A rainbow hovered far off.

The drone of flying engines. At first he could not distinguish the sound from that of the diesels on the *dragas,* but then it became louder and he looked up to the sight of a silver plane skimming the glassine surface of the deep running current of river on furrowed pontoons. Its first touch sent up sheets of rain, walls of mist and droplets that each fell one at a time back into the water and formed its own series of perfect concentric circles. Then it plowed toward them and floated to a stop only ten feet away.

The silver door was flung open. Up inside the plane were the impossibly soft eyes of the Amazon. Pilar Escandinha smiled down on him as he gasped and his heart leapt in triumph.

"There's our ride." Tarisco said, and as Rand looked back in disbelief the man had put away his gun. "Your ride home." He thought of the concentric circles and wondered how anything could be so perfect.

Pilar and the two men were lifted from the shimmering tributary of the Rio Madeira that had no name, only one that the Indians had given it. *Atun Huacangui Asua Huacangui,* "Thou Shalt Weep Greatly-Thou Shalt Weep Bitterly", after the two whirlpools far up river. The silver plane swung low up over the hundreds of boats that congregated for three miles dredging the river bottom each man in search of his own personal El Dorado paying little attention to his neighbor. Randall DesVergers stared out the window speechless with wonder. His heart was broken at the loss of his friends, perhaps the only people in his existence he had cared about with honesty, sincerity and valued enough to offer his life to without asking anything in return. He turned to Pilar. The craft soared higher in the sky and as they passed the top of the canopy he was able to see for hundreds of miles in all directions over the endless rain forest that was the womb of earth. Below he saw a million shades of indescribable green that wavered in the shadow and light made by the mix of sun and clouds and breathed with living energy. He was released. "You don't belong here my friend." Tarisco had said as they strapped into the small plane. "Is someone waiting for you... a harbor where you can reach dry land."

Epilogue

It was late in the evening and an unseasonably cool breeze was wafting in off the Sargasso Sea. Flowered curtains fluttered in the open windows. The old man lingered over a desk hand writing correspondence thinking of his life and all the glories he'd had and mistakes he'd made. It all seemed so brief, after the years had fled as white plumed birds disappearing over the horizon. When he was young he thought it would go on forever. Perhaps Father Javier Abraho was right and they were immortal. If so Valdemiro Veloso supposed he had long ago sold his soul and had nothing to look forward to except a future of atoning for his sins.

He came silently in the side door from around the garden where the sweetness of the Night Blooming Jasmine was pinched by the pungent smells of Jacaranda. Tarisco knew how to walk on quiet feet. It had kept him alive. He whispered through the old house embraced by the cool brick walls, over kalim carpets and smooth burgundy tiles. One light shone from the second floor study where he knew the old man must be and as he entered the room he saw him silhouetted by the lamp with moonlight reflecting off the ocean visible through the trees out the open windows. A breeze caressed his face.

"You have made a mistake." Tarisco said.

Valdemiro sat up straight but did not look back. After all the years he did not need to see the man to know who was talking. "How so my friend."

"He was not guilty as you suspected." There was one essential difference between he and Miro, the man who had raised him from the slums and allowed him to know pride. They were not of the same blood. "I remember her," he said quietly and unseen Valdemiro's eyes welled up thinking immediately of his beloved Ryxa, "it is with her spirit that I acted and did not do as you wished." And then he was silent finally seeing that the old man was not going to turn and said, "Never forget my old friend, I am a *favelado,* born without a shirt."

After Tarisco left Valdemiro now knew why he had trusted the man so implicitly throughout all the years. Three weeks later his son, Andrade, was released for lack of evidence, entrapment and illegal transportation across international boundaries. He returned to his father's house in Rio de Janero and Valdemiro became a devout convert of Macumba believing heart and soul that was the reason his son had come back.

Glossary

aviõezinhos
"Little airplanes." children who act as runners for drug dealers in Rio de Janero.

babalorixás (babalorisha)
"Father of Saints". A macumba priest or priestess, in which case it would be "Mother of Saints."

bandeirantes
Brazilian pioneers who opened up the interior in the eighteenth century.

batucada
Samba percussion group. (*batucar*-to drum in a samba rhythm; *batuque*-samba rhythm)

Baixadas
An imaginary group of men who were a death squad in Boca de Lobo terrorizing anyone who got in the way of mining expansion. They were named after a sector where there are a lot of killings in Rio's *zona norte,* the Baixada Fluminense."

bembé
A ceremony where an orixá is met face to face and a priest or initiate is "mounted" in a trance possession

bicherio
A Jogo De Bicho boss. (*See Jogo De Bicho*) Commands the runners, agents, lookouts, tellers and bagmen.

boi do piranha
The sacrificial cow sent first across the river so that the Piranha will busy themselves attacking and eating it leaving the rest of the heard to cross safely.

caboclos
Acculturated Indians, also used in reference to copper-colored mulattos and most peasants of the interior.

cachaça
A liquor made from sugar cane. A crude and powerful light rum that is a popular alcoholic drink.

cafusos / curibocas
People of Indian and African descent

casas de cômodos
Slum tenements of Rio De Janero and São Paulo

cativo
A slave, a captive.

Corcavado
One of the mountains around the city of Rio e Janero upon the top of which rests the huge, famous statue of Jesus with his arms outstretched. It was funded out of donations.

côr do carvão
Literally, *color of coal*. A term used to describe the color of a negro or a very dark mestiço.

cowboys
Bush pilots of the Amazon and other remote areas of Brazil. Often linking mining camps or settlements whose only other approach is by river.

descamisados
The people without shirts. (*Poor workers.*)

draga
A floating dredge used in river mining on the Amazon and its tributaries. A primitive factory, often double decked, wooden shacks on steel pontoons cluttered with pumps and long ramps. Home for miners. Drilling platforms.

Ele não tem educação
Literally, *he has no education*. A standard put-down of a personal or political opponent. A slang expression meaning that the person has manners.

escolas de sambas
Samba schools. A neighborhood organization composed of groups of singers and dancers who create elaborate costumes and compete for the best costumes, dancing and songs during Carnival.

favela
A shantytown. Particularly the slums of Rio which number over 400 neighborhoods and over a million people or 14% of the population. Named for the favela bush, a native plant of Nordeste that produces spice for cooking.

favelados
Inhabitants of the favelas.

fazenda

A large agricultural estate. Almost any agricultural landholding of more than a few acres. Loosely, any large estate.

fazendeiros

Property owners, the landed class. Often used as a derogatory term by the poor.

Funabem

The facilities of the National Foundation for the Well being of Minors. It has 25,000 places for Brazil's 7 million orphans of the streets.

FUNAI

Brazil's Indian protection agency. A government organization formed to contact and protect indigenous peoples from the inevitable encroachment of civilization.

garimpos

Gold prospecting sites. It is more than just a mining area, it is the whole state of mind, the way of life.

garimpeiros

Gold miners, prospectors.

hantsemata

A *tsantsa* feast. A ceremony taking place after an enemy raid has been successful and a warrior has the head, which is made into a *tsnatsa*. (*See tsnatsa*.)

irmandades

Roman catholic lay societies of brotherhoods.

jararaca
A name for the *fer-de-lance* in the Amazon basin. A pit viper that can grow up to eight feet in length, its venom causes rapid and severs internal bleeding.

jeito
A way of getting around the system, finding a way out of an impasse (i.e. *A jeito* [n]): A jeito can involve elements both of bribery and of ingenious maneuvers that are not strictly legal.

Jogo De Bicho
A numbers racket based on animal characters. An animal lottery extremely popular in
Brazil.

macumba
The umbrella term used for two principle forms of African spirit worship first brought to Bahia by slaves; *Candomble* and *Umbanda*. It is the Brazilian equivalent of *Voudon* and *Santeria*. Although macumba is associated with black magic, that is more appropriately called *Quimbanda*.

mameluco
A person of white and Indian descent.

marajá
A bureaucratic fat cat.

mendingança
The van of the anti-truant brigade of the Funabem.

mestiço
A person of mixed race.

miçanga
An Indian word for jewelry, mirrors, anything that shines. Brazilian settlers offered miçanga to seduce the Indians.

mulato
A person whose ancestry in a mixture of negro and Caucasian

nijimanche
A fermented beverage made from masticated boiled yucca mixed with saliva that is spat it out into jars, which when full are covered with leaves and set aside to ferment. The enzymes of the saliva break down the carbohydrates and sugar of the yucca and create an alcoholic drink favored by many Amazonian Indians.

Nordistinos
Inhabitants of the coastal northeast of Brazil. A strip of land that extends from Rio Grande do Norte to Bahia. It was the first point of entry for many black slaves and the state of Bahia remains synonymous with black skin to many Brazilians. The standard of living is lower than the south and southeast.

orixás (orishas)
The pantheon of deities involved in macumba - African orishas. They aid the endeavors of men. They include: Elgba, Ogún, Oshosi, Obatalá, Oyá, Oshún, Imanjá, Shangó and Orunmila.

Palmares
The first independent colony of the new world founded by runaway slaves from Bahia in the sixteenth century. It was located in the Serra da Barriga, inland from the Alagoas coast. Nine thousand men were mobilized by the Portuguese under Domingos Jorge Velho, the biggest army Brazil had ever seen, and crushed the colony in 1695. The head of its leader, chief Zumbi, was brought back to Recife to rot on a pole.

panelinha
Little saucepan. In the social context an informal, primary group that functions to establish and sustain careers among middle and upper classes. Also a system of upward mobility whose culmination is such a group.

patrão
A boss. Employer.

pirarucú
A large red, gold and brown fish of the Amazon and some tributaries prized as food. It is the world's largest fresh water fish and can reach 200 pounds.

pistolão
A person of a higher class and prestige who acts as a lower class member's protector and benefactor in time of need. In some cases he may be an older person or someone of similar status, but more experienced in an urban setting.

pivetes
"Little farts". Homeless street children of Rio De Janero often used to describe the seven million homeless children in Brazil.

pororoca
(*Big roar*) A tidal bore that may reach as high as twelve feet that forces its way inland, up the Amazon, at certain times of the year. It crests with white foam yet moves slowly against the current.

quilombos
Hidden villages in the jungles and groves of Palmeres where runaway slaves lived during the seventeenth century.

radionovelas
Radio soaps exported throughout South America by Cuba in the 1940s.
("A folk art that adapted to modern media without losing the sense of its origins." -Alberto Moravia.)

riberirinhos
The people of the river.

saídas
Casual short wraps of toweling worn by women

sertão
The term is used generally to describe any isolated and little developed hinterland interior. In Brazil it applies specifically to the arid interior of the northeast.

sertanista
The frontiersman of Brazil.

sociedades
Social clubs who create floats for Carnival.

tabaréus
Illiterate peasantry of Bahia: called *caboclos* in the Amazon basin; *jecas* in São Paulo.

Tele Globo
A television network in Rio that owns 2/3rds of the 160 million viewers. Solely owned by one family, a doctor of communications. Globo is the worlds biggest producer of TV programming.

telenovelas
Sultry soap operas of which Globo produces 4 hours a day. They have been known to empty the streets when they are broadcast. Telenovelas have their roots in the radionovelas of the 1940s from Cuba.

Transamazônica
A highway transversing the rain forest, linking Caracas on the Caribbean with Buenos Aires to the south. Built by army engineers the roads were part of a military strategy to link the Amazon which they feared was coveted by international agencies and might one day have to be defended. Still a red dotted line on a map in many places, unpaved dirt roads with virtually no traffic.

tsantsa
The prepared and shrunken head of an enemy. Once a common practice among certain Brazilian Indians.

VAIRG
(Rio Grande Air Transit System)Viação Aérea Rio Grandense, a cooperative foundation with thousands of employees, it is South America's largest airline.

várzea
A floodplain forest.

wishinu
A Jivaro Indian word for shaman. Jivaro country is located toward the headwaters of the Amazon and they are infamous for having been headhunters.

Yanomami
The largest indigenous nation still extant in the Americas. As most of the Amazonian Indians they are in danger of extinction.

About The Author

MICHAEL JEFFERY BLAIR is a writer, designer and media artist. He has created award-winning communications for many of the world's great companies for which he has garnered dozens of national awards. His work has been published extensively in the U.S. and Europe. He has authored stage plays and a collection of poetry, "Fisher In The Abyss." His novels include "Exit Point," "The Architect Of Law" and "Sudden Rivers" and his editorial work has appeared in the New York Times and other publications. His books can be found on all the major online retailers and his website, www.novabook.us.

www.ingramcontent.com/pod-product-compliance
Lightning Source LLC
Chambersburg PA
CBHW051058030726
47504CB00006B/1678